SHOOT

AN F.X. SHEPHERD NOVEL

ALSO AVAILABLE FROM KIERAN CROWLEY AND TITAN BOOKS

Hack

SHOOT

AN F.X. SHEPHERD NOVEL

Kieran Crowley

TITAN BOOKS

Shoot
Print edition ISBN: 9781783296514
E-book edition ISBN: 9781783296521

Published by Titan Books
A division of Titan Publishing Group Ltd
144 Southwark Street, London SE1 0UP

First edition: October 2016
1 3 5 7 9 10 8 6 4 2

A CIP catalogue record for this title is available from the British Library.

Printed and bound in the United States.

Did you enjoy this book? We love to hear from our readers.
Please email us at readerfeedback@titanemail.com or write to us at Reader
Feedback at the above address.

To receive advance information, news, competitions, and exclusive offers online,
please sign up for the Titan newsletter on our website:
www.titanbooks.com

SHOOT

1

It feels like a stranger touching me lightly between my shoulder blades at the base of my neck. My muscles tighten and my head begins to turn, to look behind me and see who's tracking me, but I've learned to stop the thoughtless impulse before my head can swivel visibly.

The trusted feeling of being watched was a gift that came without conscious effort. Magic. The hard part had been training myself to catch my reaction before it could betray me to a watcher. That's why I'm not zipped-in, still alive. Basic Darwin.

You may not believe in occult lore like this but the U.S. government does. They taught me to trust the feeling and act upon it. They also instructed us combat operators not to look too long at our targets—in case they had itchy necks, too.

I was hoping a pet columnist for a New York tabloid newspaper wouldn't need down-range skills. I took a deep breath of New York cab exhaust air. I was surrounded by hundreds of morning commuters, pedestrians, like me. Including one guy who had those Day-Glo orange sneakers you can see from space. It was no biggie that someone might look at me. But the odd thing was, I almost never got the feeling of being watched in Manhattan crowds because people almost never looked into anyone's eyes, or even at anyone else, except to avoid collisions. It wasn't a casual glance. The eye in the back of my neck only blinked when it felt the breath of a predator.

We all moved as one, but alone; a tight mob—a hundred fearful strangers, rushing as if we were being chased, just on the edge of desperation or breaking into a run in the warm June sunshine. Serious, striding close and fast but never touching. Most on their cellphones, some guys checking out girls' asses, but no one spoke or acknowledged anyone else's existence. Everyone distracted, driven, pursued, but I was probably the only one actually being followed by someone.

It occurred to me that I was away from America for ten years and by the time I came back they had all gone crazy. It took me a while to realize I was crazy, too, and for some of the same reasons. Shooting. Killing. Hating. Patriotism. I was so crazy, I promised myself I'd never take another order or fire another gun. So far, so good, considering that, since I returned home, I'd been threatened, attacked, drugged, strapped to a table, shot, locked in a flaming cab and dumped in a lake. And all for just trying to write a pet column and a few news stories for a Manhattan newspaper. I did say crazy.

After ten years in Afghanistan, Iraq, Afghanistan again and lots of other chaotic places I'm not allowed to mention, my body knows when it's being watched. I've always wondered why. Maybe it's a caveman psychic thing. You know, when the saber-toothed tiger is stalking you, you somehow sense that your image is appearing in his brain and you should run like a mother. I slowed down on a crosswalk but the thin, loping shadow also slowed down. I tried looking in store windows but I only caught glimpses of a backwards Yankees baseball cap and red sneakers, dodging through the throng with a rolling gait. Couldn't see a face or hands; could be black, white, Hispanic, anybody.

I'll say one thing for the crowded streets of New York: most of the people smell a hell of a lot better than I did before I came home. In those places, with the same phones but usually without running water, my body stank of the usual unpleasant odors, with the added scent of serious fear. The food helped a bit. We all ate the searing local food, with hot peppers, cumin, onion and garlic to destroy a wide range of intestinal bacteria. We washed it down with lots of arak—a high-octane booze that tasted like licorice-flavored rubbing alcohol. Eventually you sweated it all out your pores and everyone gave off the same subtle stench: a dumpster outside an Indian restaurant. And a licorice stick. In a barnyard.

But on this balmy early summer day Madison Avenue smelled more like a stampede at Bed, Bath & Beyond; a swirling vortex of spring-fresh fabrics, fruity organic shampoos, musky perfumes, soaps, toothpaste, and deodorants. I looked at my reflection in a store window: jeans, blue t-shirt, creased by black shoulder straps of the small black backpack holding my laptop—a gift from Jane—and a few other items. People rushed past behind me, protecting cardboard cylinders of expensive, sugary, hyper-caffeinated coffee milkshakes. My eyes were drawn to the three old parallel white scar lines on my left cheek, fading into my short sandy sideburns. Not my good side. You should see the rest of me.

I took out my new iPhone and held a button until a dinging double xylophone tone answered me and a silver microphone symbol appeared on the screen.

"How may I help you, Shepherd?" my phone asked me, in the familiar female voice.

"Siri, who is following me?" I asked her.

"I don't know who your friend is, Shepherd," Siri replied. "But you can tell me."

Siri was my wingman. Wingwoman. She was great for

finding restaurants, nearby cabs and data on most people. I had gotten into the habit of asking her things a phone shouldn't know because I loved her smoky voice and, sometimes, her funny answers. I got hooked. I know her clever replies are the result of the late Steve Jobs and his computer gremlins programming pre-packaged answers to make her wicked cool. But I was an optimist and I hoped Siri would one day rise to my challenge. Of course, I couldn't tell Siri who was lurking behind me unless I found that out first. I didn't have time for this. I was already late and I didn't want to drag some jerk to my actual destination.

"I thought you knew everything, Siri," I scolded her.

"Let me check on that," she said politely. "Here is some information on that."

Siri displayed a dictionary entry for the word "everything."

Now she was just screwing with me. I once asked my sexy phone voice what her name meant and she answered: "'Siri' has many subtle, metaphorical, and, frankly, contradictory meanings—none of which I am at liberty to discuss, Shepherd. Sorry about that."

I put the phone in my pocket and did a one-eighty on the pavement. I barged against the flowing crowd, right toward the watcher. People complained and cursed me out, as I slightly inconvenienced them by going upstream. Some stepped aside without comment, protecting their scalding Starbucks. Some played chicken with anger on their faces, slowing me down. Ten heads back, the crowd broke and surged, cursed, bumped, and blocked. He was good. And fast. And gone. The flash of blue clothing on the vanishing back made me certain it wasn't Ginny McElhone trying to steal another newspaper exclusive from me. She had followed me before but I'd know her body shape and movements anywhere. I walked around the block and ducked into a Sushi Bagel joint and confirmed I'd shaken my tail. My tri-scar pulsed gently on my temple, usually an indicator of a change in the weather. Next time, I would do a better job of meeting my new admirer.

It wasn't just idle curiosity. The "Hacker" serial killer was behind bars but I still had a vindictive billionaire out there, my former boss Trevor Todd. He was probably the one who ordered his minions to kill me but he left the country before cops could question him. So far, the investigation had not resulted in his arrest and I wasn't holding my breath because he would like nothing better than for me to stop breathing. So, old friends, new friends, I needed to find out.

And then ask Siri.

2

I crossed the huge lobby of the *New York Daily Press*, with its giant, rotating globe, covered with a very outdated map that still showed the Soviet Union in red. Germany was divided in half by the "Iron Curtain."

In the elevator, I thought about the events of the last month. Most of the bad guys I had met were now cavorting in the Happy Hunting Grounds. That would include two of my former editors at the tabloid *New York Mail*, two charming members of the *Mail*'s Human Resources team and four rich victims—reality TV show stars. Even if you won't admit to reading an infamous tabloid like the *Mail*, I'm sure you heard about it. I was pretty famous for a while. Front-page intrepid investigative reporter on the track of the serial killer, whatever. All before my thirtieth birthday. If you didn't hear about it, you should know I only killed one of those four bad guys. He was about to shoot me. Just because I gave up guns doesn't mean I have a death wish. The good news is that moving to New York wasn't all bad news. I met a great woman, Jane. A vet, as in veterinarian. I'm a vet, but not a pet doc, just a former member of the armed forces, keeping America safe. You're welcome. I was also adopted by my best buddy, Skippy, a Siberian Husky and a hell of a pooch, whose master was murdered. Now that the whole mess is over, I just want to write my pet column. I like doing the column, which is from the point of view of the pet, not the owner. The investigative reporter thing was fun but I'm not sure it's for me. I did like working with the cops, especially Detective Lieutenant Izzy Negron, and catching the bad guys. But no one is offering me a detective's job.

I worked first at the *New York Mail* but found the competition with other reporters totally crazy. Like Ginny McElhone—who was at the *Daily Press* then—who would literally do anything for a story and is mad crazy. She also seduced me and sort of saved my life but doesn't play well with others. When I left the *Mail*, I got my current job at the *New York Daily Press*. I write my column but I haven't come up with any front pages on the Hacker case in weeks, which, I assume, is why my editor called me in this morning for a meeting.

My new boss, City Editor Mel Greenbaum, made me wait before summoning me into his office. He was a weird guy and a chat with him was always entertaining. The newspaper business, like my former trade, was filled with gentlemen, and ladies, who wanted to be macho. They cursed a lot. Mel was different, I had been told, because he had lost several lawsuits filed by staffers, mostly women, who said he had sexually harassed them by using filthy language. These tough guys and broads were suddenly freaked out by profanity, which, they claimed, demeaned, humiliated and degraded them. Juries agreed when they heard the recordings and it cost the paper a fortune. Some tough guys. After Mel lost the third lawsuit, he was ordered to attend charm school—sensitivity training. But he was a hard case and still couldn't control his profanity. He was forced to undergo hypno-aversion therapy—with homonyms—or lose his job. He agreed and, technically,

Mel never cursed at an underling again. It made his chats unique and no one could ever prove profanity.

I wondered if he was angry at me for being late but he pumped my hand, slapped me on the back and spent ten minutes praising me for my many exclusives on the Hacker for his enemy—the *New York Mail*. He also lauded me for switching to the good guys, beating the *Mail* and catching the Hacker on the front page of the *Press*.

"That was the best fuggin' job I've ever seen, you breaking that mother-loving Hacker case," Mel told me, beaming with pride, flashing some crooked teeth.

"So I'm getting a raise?" I asked.

Mel's smile vanished. His watery eyes became hard and then softened.

"You just *got* a freaking raise," he said, in a wounded voice.

"So, why am I here, Mel?"

"I just want to shoot the breeze. We should get to know one another."

Mel never shot the breeze. Mel had to be twice my age and I doubted we had anything in common besides the newspaper. I looked around his office, the photos of the wife and kids and pets and vacations. I asked him about them and he told me. He asked about me. No wife, but Mel already knew about Jane, my hot and brilliant girlfriend, because she had also been in his newspaper and many others during the Hacker case. And Mel already knew all about Skippy, because Skippy was, if anything, more famous than me. After ten minutes of pretending to be fascinated with each other, Mel said he would buy me a drink soon. At last, a good idea. It looked like ten minutes was the limit of Mel's social charm.

"It's time to stop fracking around, Shepherd. You haven't filed a cop-socking story in two weeks," Mel said, in a fatherly, curse-free tone.

At last, the real reason for the meeting. Should I tell him I already had a dad?

"I was taking some medical leave. I was wounded in the line of duty, boss."

"Abso-honking-lutely. Sure, you deserved some time off," Mel replied, sounding dubious and using the past tense.

"I was knocked unconscious, shot, basically set on fire and dumped in a lake," I pointed out.

"I'm just saying that you have to get back on the fuggin' horse, buddy—unless you're some kind of deuce-bag goof-off?"

"No, Mel, I'm not a deuce-bag goof-off. I like doing the column but I'm not sure this reporting gig is for me."

He jumped out of his black leather executive chair faster than I thought possible.

"Are you freaking kidding me? You are the best bun-forking investigative reporter I've ever seen."

"Thanks. I didn't say I wasn't good at it, Mel. It's fun but I just don't think I want to do it for the rest of my life. I really liked working with Izzy Negron and the cops, though. I could do that, be a homicide detective."

"You're too old for that, you stupid son on a beach."

"Actually, I'm not. The NYPD cutoff is age thirty-five. I checked. I'll be thirty in July. Besides, with my military credits, I could join up to age forty-one."

"Bull-pit!"

"No. It's true."

"You'll have to qualify, go through the academy, be a uniform for years... You might never make detective, much less a homicide investigator. You just need to drop your cockleshell and get your back to work." Mel settled back into his seat. "You have any ideas about the next story you want to work on?"

"You bet. Dog poop."

It got very quiet in the office. Then Mel laughed loudly,

his pink jowls wattling. When he saw I wasn't laughing too, he stopped. I explained that there had been a study which found that dogs did their business while orienting themselves in a north–south direction. In short, Shar-Peis practiced feng shui.

"I don't believe the study without my own scientific proof, so we'll experiment—me and Skippy. I'll let the chips fall where they may," I assured him.

He glared at me and then, slowly, he smirked.

"Horse-split! This is not how to get another raise, Shepherd."

I told him I wasn't really angling for another bump and was ready to start work on this new column idea.

"Your pet thing is cute as a kumquat but I'm only interested in hard news and you have a father-mucking contract with us."

"Yes, I do," I agreed. "Have you read it?"

Mel blinked. He hadn't. I told him. He didn't believe that his predecessor had signed a contract letter that only required me to write one pet column a week and also to report "any breaking news I uncover."

He called for a copy of my agreement and read it over and over, looking for a way out.

"In our business, everyone gets assigned stories and then they uncover stuff," Mel tried. "That's the way it works, mukluk."

"Not if they have a contract that says what mine says," I countered.

"C'mon, don't be an ace-hole. I have something just up your alley right now. You'll love it!"

"What?"

"Senator Hard-On! What else? You are going to break it wide open!" Mel declared, holding up today's front page:

SEN. HARD-ON SEX PILLS
Viagra in Niagara Falls

Both tabloids and every news outlet in town were hot on the story of our horny Democratic U.S. Senator, Ron Hardstein, now renamed Senator Hard-On for his online monkey business involving dozens of women, his smart phone and his penis. My colleagues were at that moment stalking the honorable gentleman, trying to uncover the names of all the women he had had sex with. Everyone in the country was on the story and it all seemed very predictable. The only thing more boring to me than someone else's sex life was politics.

"You've got to be kidding, Mel."

"Why is the biggest story in town not good enough for you?"

"Because I don't care what Hardstein does with his equipment. His sex life is between him, his wife and the women. It's no one else's business because it had nothing to do with his job. It's not a story."

Mel chuckled. "You're a beginner in this business, Shepherd. I'm the judge of what is and what isn't a story."

To me, his reasoning seemed circular, a self-licking ice-cream cone. If he was the guy who decided what stories went in the newspaper, then all of his choices became news—proving his news judgment was one hundred per cent correct. When I continued to disagree, he threatened me with legal action.

"Okay," I responded.

We sat looking at each other for a while, until Mel thought better of his threat and took a different tack. "Would you at least be open to fugging suggestions?"

"Fine. But I don't have to follow them."

"You've only been working for newspapers for a month or two. You don't know how the news biz works." He started listing ideas for stories, topics for me to dig up scoops on, mostly involving sex and celebrities.

"The next big story will find me," I told him.

"You're really kissing me off. What are you freaking talking about?"

"News happens," I explained, already walking through the door. "You can't go out and create it."

Mel was still laughing uproariously when I left his office, his belly bouncing like a beach ball of Jell-O against his desk.

3

As soon as I hit the street, I took out my phone.

"Is Mel an asshole?" I asked Siri.

"There's no need for profanity, Shepherd," Siri chided me.

Siri is a lady. I apologized. I asked her to FaceTime Jane. As I waited for the call to connect, I got that feeling again, the one that had kept me alive this far. Someone's eyes were on me.

Once the call connected I didn't bother with preamble.

"Mel Greenbaum called me in for a chat."

"What did he want?" Jane asked, her face concerned. She was wearing her pink Dr. Jane lab coat, her stethoscope around her neck, and looked like a blonde movie actress playing a veterinarian. I could see her kitchen in the background.

"Well, he shook my hand, patted me on the back, told me about his family, asked about you and Skippy, and then told me to get back to work."

"Then what?"

"I told him the reporter gig may not be for me. He freaked. He tried to convince me I was wrong. Then he threatened to sue me but backed off when I said let the games begin."

"So?"

"So, we're still friends, I'm working on my dog-poop

scoop and keeping an eye out for the Next Big Thing."

"Which is what?" she asked.

"I have no clue. I think he'll pester me with suggestions. Listen, I think I'll stop by and pick up Skippy for a walk."

I heard a familiar bark. Skippy had heard my voice.

"What's up?" Jane asked.

"Nothing," I lied.

"You're lying," Jane observed.

I should not have done this on FaceTime.

"Only a little," I admitted.

"We agreed about this," Jane pointed out. "No bull."

"Sorry. Someone is following me."

"Ginny Mac again?"

"Not her. Someone else, I think."

"Who?"

"I don't know."

"Then how do you know they're following you?"

"I'm good at that."

"Maybe Ginny Mac has someone else following you?"

"That's possible. I'll see you soon."

I hit the phone camera app and reversed the angle. I held it up above my shoulder so I could see behind me. No Yankees cap, no red sneakers, no visible face. I put the phone away but I still had the warning itch between my shoulder blades, the urgent urge to seek cover, turn, aim and fire. I fought to resist my fight-or-flight instinct. On the other hand, I was on a sunny street in America. What could happen?

Jane's five-story Upper East Side brownstone/townhouse in the fancy Carnegie Hill neighborhood near Central Park is worth major money. When I asked her if she got the cash from her practice, her dead husband, or was she rich, she looked at me like I was a complete jerk.

"All three, if it matters," Jane told me.

I was very new in New York then and didn't know I wasn't supposed to ask people openly about money. Instead, after asking your name—to see if they had ever seen it in bold type in a gossip column—sophisticated Manhattanites just asked where you lived. Their New Yorker Real Estate Radar instantly told them if you were rich, poor or pathetic. If they were still interested in a conversation with you after that, they asked what you did for a living, which was just another disguised money question. I had become used to women asking me the three questions at parties and watching them retreat to the bar after I answered "Shepherd," "Broome Street" and "newspaper reporter." I have my own small apartment downtown, a tiny walk-up sub-let. I couldn't afford to buy it because Manhattan was quickly becoming a millionaires-only spot. Lately, Skippy and I had been spending most of our time with Jane in her fancy townhouse, even though neither one of us had made any actual decision to live together.

I let myself in with my key. The alarm was off, blinking green. I called her and she answered from the kitchen. So did Skippy. I heard his distinctive yip and his trimmed toenails galloping across the expensive hardwood floors toward me, big as a wolf. I went on one knee to avoid being bowled over by the huge blue-eyed husky, who skidded into me and began licking.

"Hey, buddy, I was only gone a couple hours," I told him, scratching his large head where black fur made a symmetrical black cap on his mostly white fur, with two parallel lines descending toward the intelligent bright eyes, the mark of a thoroughbred. I laughed and he leaned into my petting with delight, his tail slamming the floor.

I met Skippy in a bloody kitchen, a murder scene where one of his masters had been butchered, the first victim of the Hacker. It was like we had always been friends, even before we met. We rescued each other. Skippy had helped me investigate that case and protected me. I was sure he liked it when the game was afoot. One of Skippy's fuzzy ears twitched. He turned toward the front door and cocked his head.

Jane was also glad to see me. She gave me a kiss and a hug, her stethoscope and her plastic DOCTOR JANE nameplate scrunched between us.

"I'm beginning to wonder if you like his kisses better than mine," she smirked.

"I would never say that… to your face," I smiled.

"Skippy and I just got back from a second walk," Jane told me. "Don't let him con you."

"That's okay. I need him for something."

"Really?" Jane asked, brushing some blonde hair behind one ear. "What?"

I changed the subject and asked her about her day. She sighed, as if she was going to tell me about the death of someone's pet, then burst into laughter.

"What?" I asked, smiling.

"Today, I saved a dachshund who was choking to death," Jane said, still laughing.

"That's funny?"

"I shouldn't laugh but I can't help it," she giggled. "This married couple brought the dog in because he was… Here, I'll show you."

Jane opened up the EyeBall security program on her laptop and started scrolling around. After Jane and I were almost killed, she sprung for an expensive, wall-to-wall video surveillance system with sound that covered every inch of her office and home 24–7 and was accessible from anywhere, with automatic intruder alerts and security monitoring.

"Here it is. This happened a few hours ago. Wait, it was later… there. Watch."

The camera footage had a slight fish-eye distortion to it and showed a stainless steel examination table, cabinets, and four people moving around a reddish-brown dog on the table; Jane and an assistant as well as a middle-aged man and a younger woman, obviously the owners of the hacking hot dog on the table.

"Did you see what he ate, Mr. Corcoran?" Jane asked the husband. "You have to watch them—they'll gobble up anything off the street."

"My wife was home alone but Timmy only goes out in his dog walk in our back yard," the husband said. "We don't take him onto the street."

"I have no idea what happened," his pretty blonde wife whimpered. "One second he was fine, and the next he was choking. Please help him!"

"I got home and my wife was hysterical," the guy explained. "I put 'em both in the car and rushed over."

"This is where I injected Apomorphine to induce vomiting," Jane explained to me, as I saw her give the dog a shot, while her assistant held the animal still, a basin at the ready.

The dog puked violently. The wife began crying, as her husband held her. Jane used a pair of forceps to remove an object from the basin. It was what New Yorkers called a Coney Island whitefish. A rubber. RIGHT!

"What the hell?" the husband asked.

"A condom," Jane explained. "That was the problem. It was blocking Timmy's airway. He's breathing fine now."

The grateful dachshund tried to lick Jane, who backed off.

"Oh, my God," said the wife, grabbing her husband's elbow and shoving him toward the door. "Michael. I'll take care of this."

"Wait... what?" the husband sputtered, looking at his wife, the dog, the condom.

"Mr. Corcoran, you have to dispose of these... items properly, so Timmy doesn't get hold of them."

"I... I don't use them," he said, vaguely. "I don't need 'em. I got a vasectomy. We..."

"Michael..." his wife pleaded, running out of words.

"*I* don't use 'em." He glared at her. "Somebody else musta left it there! Tell it to the guy who used it! Ask my wife!"

Jane and her assistant looked at each other.

"Who is he? You did this in front of Timmy?" he demanded.

"I'll give you folks a few minutes alone," Jane said diplomatically, beating a hasty retreat.

The video continued, with yelling and tears and the husband storming out. Jane stopped the recording.

"Why am I laughing? This is sad," Jane said. "I'm a terrible person."

"So am I," I told her. "Totally twisted."

We both broke down; two terrible people, laughing.

Me too

4

"I had no idea," Jane insisted, her laughter fading. "I feel terrible. How was I to know?"

"You couldn't," I said. "You were trying to save a dog, not end a marriage. I wonder who'll get custody of Timmy?"

We laughed some more, setting Skippy barking. It took me a few seconds to realize Skippy was barking at the front door. Someone was knocking.

"Be cool, Skippy," I told him, patting his head.

He obeyed, but his snowy seventy-pound body tensed, eyes on the door, his blue eyes cold, ready. I opened the door and found a chubby housewife with stringy brown hair, dressed in a loose yellow sundress and red Crocs, waving some papers and babbling breathlessly in a tearful, semi-hysterical voice about how Dr. Strangelove was missing. Her eyes were red. She lifted a shopping bag and wiped one eye with an elbow.

"I beg your pardon?" Jane said. "Who is missing?"

"My little baby, Dr. Strangelove. There's a reward. Here's his picture," she managed.

She handed us each a Xerox copy of a cute little blonde dog with a wavy coat, some of which was blue, and a pink tongue. One eye was blue, the other white. It looked like a pooch assembled by Dr. Frankenstein. MISSING, $50 REWARD.

"He's a cockapoo-shih-tzu-pug mix?" Jane asked.

"Yes," the woman answered, surprised. "You know dogs?"

Jane told her she was a vet. By this time the woman was inside and Skippy was sniffing her shoes with interest. She began petting Skippy and baby-talking him. Skippy loved it, a new pal.

"You live nearby?" I asked her.

"Yes, we've only been here a month. That's why I'm so worried. Doc doesn't know the neighborhood yet. I'm afraid he'll try to go back to Queens."

"Why Dr. Strangelove?" Jane asked.

"It's a funny character in an old movie." That didn't really answer the question.

"You moved into this block?" I pressed.

"No, around the corner. Have you seen him? I'm terrified he'll get hit by a car." She turned to Jane. "Where's your office?"

Jane told her and was about to continue when I interrupted.

"If we see him, where would we bring him?" I asked. "I don't see your address on the sheet, just your cell number."

"That's the best way to get me. I'm never home," she said. Then she pointed at me, her mouth open. "Wait a second. I know you, your face. You're famous, aren't you? You're that newspaper guy. The one who caught the serial killer!"

"Yes, he is," Jane chuckled.

"I knew you looked familiar," she gushed, shaking my hand with a firm grip. "Wow. That is amazing. I am talking to a celebrity. Oh! Wait!"

She produced a cellphone and hugged me around the shoulders with the other arm in a selfie grip. The flash blinded me. Skippy jumped and yipped. She thanked me and asked me my name.

"Shepherd," Jane told her. "F.X. Shepherd. I'm Jane Arthur."

She thanked us, petted her new friend Skippy, shook our hands and left to knock on other doors down the block. I watched her for a while. After I shut the door, I followed Jane to the kitchen table, inside a semi-greenhouse that overlooked her enclosed garden.

"Did you find anything weird about all that?" I asked Jane.

"All what?"

"I don't know," I shrugged. "I just got strange vibes from her."

"Skippy seemed to like her," Jane pointed out.

I went back to the door, opened it and looked down the block. She was gone.

"What was weird?" Jane asked.

"She gave us no name, no address. Just the name of the dog. She has been in your home, knows our names, what kind of alarm system you have and has my picture."

"There's a phone number on the sheet," Jane pointed out.

I suggested she call it. She dialed and listened, before smiling and hanging up.

"It's the Manhattan Humane Society. You think she's the one following you?"

"That thought occurred to me. What else did she touch?" I asked.

"Just Skippy. And you."

I crouched down and felt Skippy's collar. Then I felt in between his collar and his neck. There was a lump. I scraped it off. It was a small, flat black plastic disc, sticky on one side. I checked my pockets. In my left pants pocket was a thin plastic rectangle. I pulled it out. It was clear, with only one word, AMI, followed by a phone number and an email. I showed it to Jane, and dialed the number. It rang once.

"Hello, AMI. How may I help you?"

It was a different voice.

"Dr. Strangelove, please," I asked, as Jane made a funny face.

"I'm sorry, the doctor is not in. How may we serve you?"

"If you work for the government, I'm hanging up," I told her.

There was a pause.

"We are a private firm. We never work for government."

"You're the one who's been following me? You're a private detective?"

"I prefer the term confidential investigator. May we do this in person, please?"

"Why didn't you do it when you were here? Why all the bullshit of planting an RFID chip inside Skippy's collar and slipping your card into my pocket?"

"You were not alone, so I couldn't talk. I like to stay in practice, so I couldn't resist the plant. I wanted to see if *you* would notice. And you did."

"Just come back and I'll listen, if you promise no more bullshit."

"The proposal is for you alone. This is a highly confidential position."

"Nope. No deal. I tell Jane everything. Also, Skippy."

More silence. I waited.

"I'm hanging up now," I said.

"Ten minutes."

5

I opened the door to a svelte, fifty-ish blonde in a slinky black pants suit, high heels and dark shades, an expensive black leather Coach bag hanging from her shoulder.

"Yeah?" I asked her.

"Sorry I'm late," she said, not sounding sorry at all.

She brushed by me, past Jane—whose mouth was hanging open—straight to the kitchen table. I followed her. I was sure it couldn't be the same person but when she took off the shades and spoke, her eyes and voice settled the issue. As the chubby housewife, she had a higher, fluttery voice, seemed fifty pounds heavier and even walked differently.

"I can't believe it," Jane said. "That was you?"

She looked at Jane like she was kidding. I pretended I wasn't gut-punched by how different she looked. I remembered that this sexy chameleon also looked like a third person, and maybe a fourth, while she was following me on the street.

"People talk to The Housewife, especially if she's looking for her puppy," she said.

"From the top," I said. "Who the hell are you, lady?"

"First, you have to agree to keep anything I say completely confidential."

"Not until you tell me your name and what this is about," I insisted.

"I'm Amy Massi. A.M.I. Amy Massi Investigations. I'm a licensed private detective and I work for well-known people who expect me to keep their secrets."

"Like who?" Jane asked.

"Movie stars, musicians, rich people who can afford me. One thing I can guarantee, if you work for me, you won't be bored," she said.

When I first came to New York, I thought I wanted a good writing job and peace and quiet. But during the Hacker case, I realized a decade of war had twisted me for life. I didn't ever want to be bored. That was enough for me.

"So the missing dog was just a scam?" Jane asked.

"You bet," Amy admitted. "But Dr. Strangelove really is my dog. He's at home with the housekeeper right now."

"What kind of cases do you do?" I asked.

"I work for defense lawyers to prove people didn't kill somebody. I used to do verification and divorce work but not anymore. Right now, I have a priority security investigation, credible death threats."

"Why did you follow me?" I asked her.

"I read about you and the whole Hacker thing and decided you would be perfect for my new case. I have a changing roster of people I use and I like to check people out, test them, kick the tires first. You knew I was on your tail, didn't you?"

"Yes."

"How? I couldn't figure out how I screwed up."

"I don't know," I told her truthfully. "Why do people get that feeling that someone is watching them?"

"But I saw you checking window reflections, backtracking," she protested. "That's not just a feeling."

"So I act on the feeling, what of it?"

"I can follow most people for weeks. They're clueless."

"So am I. Enlighten me. Who is your client?" I asked.

"Not until you agree to keep it secret."

"It's not government?" I asked.

"I told you, we're private, non-governmental."

"Yeah, well, so is Blackwater and hundreds of other scumbags who do bad things," I told her. "All of them hand puppets for Uncle Sam."

"We are a private civilian firm and don't accept government contract work. We're actually quite small, a boutique. A non-traditional P.I. agency licensed in New York. We'd like to make you an offer of employment."

"To do what?"

"Investigate these death threats, what you're good at. As a no-strings freelance investigator. Starting now. At this salary."

She took out a notebook and silver pen and wrote numbers down, sliding it toward me. It was bigger than my reporter salary. A lot bigger. Jane peeked at the number.

"Perhaps it could be fun?" Jane said.

Amy turned to Jane. "And I'm happy for you to help him out, if you keep your mouth shut. It goes without saying I'm not paying you, Doc. One more thing, Shepherd. I always win. I expect the same thing from you."

"Sounds like I'm going to be busy. Can I keep my current boss happy by filing stories?"

"Yes. If we agree that it will help the case," Amy said. "Your press contacts are part of why I want you. 'The pen is mightier than the sword' and all that."

"As if," I laughed.

"You're a reporter and you don't think the pen is mightier than the sword?"

"Nope. I had an instructor who gave a whole lesson on that. He said, 'Even if it's mightier than the sword, it don't do shit against an AK-47.' We had to show him how a pen could beat a gas-powered fully-auto assault rifle. A couple of us came close, but in combat, we would have died. He always said anyone might be a threat, anyone might be a target, and everything is a weapon."

I didn't mention that a few weeks earlier I had successfully used a fax machine as a defensive weapon.

"Okay," I asked. "Who's getting death threats?"

"Are you in?" Amy asked.

"Who is it?"

"Does it matter?"

"Yes. I'm not helping to get any killers, drug dealers or child molesters off."

"Worse. A member of Congress."

"I'm in."

"Wait, that's government," Jane said.

"No. Private," Amy answered. "I've been hired by the Republican National Committee to find out who is threatening to kill Speaker of the House, Congressman Percy Chesterfield, the guy they are about to give their presidential nomination to."

"Isn't that the creep who tried to shut down the government last year and almost destroyed the economy?" Jane asked.

"That's the guy," Amy admitted. "Half the country wants him dead for almost destroying the government and all of the Tea Party people consider him a traitor for *not* destroying the government. He has to appear in public for the Republican National Convention this week to accept their nomination for president."

"Which, for some odd reason, is being held right here in Manhattan, at the new Knickerbocker Convention Center," Jane added.

"Right," Amy agreed. "We... I mean Shepherd and I... have a meeting with Chesterfield and his security team at eight tomorrow morning. We have to keep him alive and find out who is threatening to kill him."

"Shouldn't the FBI or the Secret Service be investigating

this—at taxpayer expense?" Jane asked.

"Chesterfield is protected by an Executive Protection Service team as large as the president's. The FBI is on the case but the client doesn't trust them to do anything in a timely way," Amy said. "He's had experience with the Bureau before and he's afraid he'll be dead a year before they get off their asses."

"Sounds like Chesterfield isn't as dumb as he acts," I observed. "But it also sounds like you'd have a lot of suspects."

"Yeah, that's a problem," Amy admitted. "Forget the liberals. The worst thing they would do is send a strong letter to *The New York Times*. It's the Tea Party psychos we need to worry about. Fifty thousand of them emailed Chesterfield threats—and every single one owns a gun."

6

Skippy and I took a walk west, over to Fifth Avenue, and crossed when the downtown traffic was stopped by a light. We walked uptown, with the road on the right and Central Park to the left. The husky, nose in the air, scoping out every pedestrian, yanked on the leash, pulling me forward. At one point he dragged me into the park for a pit stop. I took careful note of how he positioned himself on a patch of dead grass. I pulled out my iPhone and hit the compass app, which informed me that Skippy was pointing more or less southwest. I produced a plastic bag from my backpack and threw Skippy's leavings into a nearby trashcan. He was not pointing north–south, I noticed. But it was close. Hmm.

We returned to the street and headed back uptown. This was prime RWP territory, as the editors at the newspapers called it. Rich White People. I could see the stakeout in front of Senator Ron Hardstein's home from a block away, a luxury condo building overlooking the park. Cop cars outside, blue wooden barricades on the sidewalk penning in the press reporters and photographers, parked TV news vans, their giraffe microwave masts telescoped vertically, poised to relay to their stations and the world any sudden breaking news about a powerful person's penis. Boring.

"Foof!" Skippy said, as we crossed Fifth Avenue and joined the press corps in their sidewalk pen.

"I know, Skippy. I feel the same way," I told him, as I waved to *Daily Press* cameraman Sparky Starke. He and the other photographers had their cameras up and ready. Next to Sparky was another *Daily Press* reporter. He shot me a dagger glance, obviously afraid I was there to steal his story.

"What's up, Sparky?" I asked him.

"Hard-on should be here soon," Sparky said, without looking away. "You on this one now?"

"No, I just wanted to tell you something but it can wait. I'm going on another job but it might involve pictures or video, if you're interested?"

"Sure, we'll talk later."

Sparky's three black bulky cameras with long telephoto lenses were hung from his neck. One he held up ready. He was dressed for the warm weather, in denim shorts and a black sleeveless Megadeth tank shirt. He worked as many as seven days a week for the *Daily Press*, but he was a freelancer on paper, without sick days, vacations, health insurance, life insurance or pension, because the paper saved a lot of money that way.

In less than a minute, a black limousine pulled up to the curb, as shouts of "Heads up!" rippled through the media mob. The vehicle sat there for several minutes, the occupants invisible behind tinted windows. A uniformed doorman walked out the front door of the residence and stood protectively by the rear door.

The car door opened and senior United States Senator Richard Hardstein, crisply clad in his usual dark Italian suit, emerged calmly from the limo and strode toward his building. The silver-haired politician walked leisurely, as if he had just won an election, the camera flashes sparkling in his blue eyes. The reporters all yelled at once, shouting each other down.

"Senator Hardstein, why do you call your penis 'Fred'?"

"Senator, how many women did you send photos of your junk?"

"Senator Hard-on, did you also send pictures of your dick to your wife?"

"Is your mom proud of you?"

"How many women have you had sex with?"

Skippy barked until I told him to stop. The rest of the smarmy questions, as the dignified target ran the gauntlet, merged into one loud, lewd bellow. For some reason, it made me think of dusty pigeons shitting on a bronze statue of a hero. Every day, the *Daily Press* and the *New York Mail* featured front page, dueling dick puns in bold headlines. Just when I was getting to like the newspaper business, I realized I was working for junior high school dorks.

There was no angry response from the senator, only cool detachment. It was as if the sex scandal, in which he was caught in dozens of affairs with willing women he met online, was about another Senator Richard Hardstein.

Up the block another limo had stopped at the curb while we were all focused on the senator's limo. The sound of a closing door had made me turn. Two young women in bright pastel miniskirts had emerged from that car and were hot-footing it down the sidewalk. It was tough to do quietly in stiletto heels but they were good at it—toward an alley marked SERVICE, like they knew their way around the place.

I smiled and waved. The black girl waved and smiled back but the Latina girl snapped at her and they ducked into the service entrance. I turned back to my colleagues. Not a single one had noticed the ladies' stealthy arrival.

Before the besieged senator could enter his domicile, I saw a bright flash of red curls. I moved closer and, sure enough, Ginny Mac was blocking the politician's path, her large breasts on display in a revealing halter dress she had thrust against Hardstein's chest. It almost worked. The honorable gentleman eyed his constituent's cleavage and genuinely smiled as Ginny gave a spiel I couldn't hear—no doubt a plea for an exclusive.

"Sorry, I have another pressing appointment," Hardstein told Ginny, one eyebrow arching upwards.

He was saved by the doorman, who thrust his gold-braided shoulder between them and hustled Hardstein inside. Everybody got the shot of Ginny and her boobs pressed up against him. Ginny was ecstatic. For her, scamming a story was foreplay, an exclusive better than sex. She was laughing, her job done for the day. Her photographer was showing Ginny his frames on the digital camera screen—Senator Hard-on ogling her goodies. It would be on the *Mail* website within the hour and on the front page in the morning. Ginny would be famous.

"Ginny, these are great!" her camerawoman gushed. "They will fucking love this. Look at his eyes—they're right on your tits."

"I've got a headline," Ginny announced. "How about this? 'MY EYES ARE UP HERE, SENATOR.'"

They started laughing and shouting competing headlines.

"MAKE A CLEAN BREAST OF IT, SENATOR!"

"DON'T BE A BOOB, HARD-ON!"

"YES, TWO SCOOPS, PLEASE!"

But my fellow reporter from the *Daily Press*, rookie Orlando Rodriguez, was not amused. A tabloid newspaper couldn't put a reporter from the competing rag on the front page. Orlando's cellphone rang. He looked at the screen in horror.

"Oh, shit, it's Mel," Orlando whined.

"Dude, the TV people went live with it," Sparky pointed out, scratching Skippy on the head. "The bosses saw the whole thing on the tube."

Orlando had to take the call. Mel was already shouting loudly—so loud, we could hear him without speakerphone. There was a lot of profanity and threats.

"Mel, how was I supposed to stop her? I should have done it first? How could I... I don't have boobs! You're kidding. What? Seriously? Wait, Mel, I..."

The shouting and threats stopped and Orlando was staring at his silent phone.

"Oh, shit. They're sending some new reporter with big boobs. I have to interview Ginny Mac," Orlando moaned, clearly humiliated. "Now. For the online edition."

"For real?" Sparky asked.

"Mel said if I was a good reporter, I would have propositioned Hard-On before Ginny did. Right now, he says The Wood is 'BETWEEN A SLUT AND A HARD-ON.'" The Wood was a newspaper term for the big bold front-page headline. He reached for a notebook and pen and turned toward the jubilant Ginny.

"Mel says I have to ask her why she is an unethical, anti-feminist slut."

"I wouldn't do that, man," Sparky warned. "That will *really* piss her off."

7

While Orlando was interviewing Ginny Mac, I told Sparky about the two pastel ladies. He became very *sparky*.

"Calm down," I warned him. "Don't draw any attention."

"Sorry," Sparky said, gulping a pill and washing it down with Evian water.

As he drank, some new freelance shooter, a young skinny kid with a backwards baseball cap, was backing up without looking and banged into Sparky—who spilled water down his t-shirt.

"Hey! Fuckin' watch where you're going, newbie!" Sparky snapped at the guy.

The inexperienced photographer snarled an automatic "fuck you" at Sparky over his shoulder.

Uh-oh.

Then the skinny kid looked around. He saw Sparky's arm muscles, tattoos and the look in his eyes. Sparky's face began squirming. The twitching spread to his neck, his chest. The new guy froze. He may have guessed from his appearance that Sparky was a bodybuilder and martial arts competitor but maybe not that he suffered from Tourette's syndrome.

"What did you say to me, dick shit-bird motherfucker?" Sparky demanded, his whole scalp and his black, spiky moussed hair now twitching threateningly like a cranky cockatoo. "You wanna fuck with me, mouse balls?"

"Uh… no… sorry, man, I didn't see you," the freelancer mumbled, edging away. "Sorry."

The meds Sparky took to suppress the effects of the condition worked but he tried to keep the dosage low because they came with a cost—bad side effects.

We turned at the sound of Ginny Mac cursing Orlando out. Ginny was aroused by exclusives but her temper was also legendary. She bribed sources, slashed tires, had competitors beaten up, and the rumor was she once rammed a TV truck with her Honda. Orlando retreated. Ginny followed him back to us, shouting so everyone could hear.

"Hey, Orlando, get off your ass and get your own story. Why don't you ask Shepherd there to get one for you? What is he—retired?"

"No, I'm not retired, Ginny," I replied. "But I don't like this story, so I'm not on it."

"Afraid to compete with me?" she taunted. "I don't blame you."

"That's it, Ginny. I'm afraid of you."

"Is this what you're afraid of?"

She pressed up against me, exactly as she had with the senator. He had a hard time ignoring her and so did I. She grabbed my hips and pulled us close. Damn. I fought to keep my eyes away from her chest. She was hard to resist and I wondered if she felt the same way. I tried not to remember our time alone together. At least we weren't being filmed. A flash went off. Ginny's photographer caught us.

"No, Ginny, I'm not afraid of your boobs. Don't you remember? We had sex a few weeks ago—when it was me you wanted information from."

"Oooooo" our colleagues cooed in an ooh-la-la tone from grade school.

They were all watching and listening. More cameras came up.

Ginny's eyes hardened but for some reason she disengaged.

"I think I'll send a copy to your new girlfriend," Ginny threatened. "She might like to see what you do at work."

"Please do," I said. "She thinks I have it easy."

"Oh snap!" Sparky giggled, his mood improving.

Ginny moved away, steam coming off her pink cheeks.

"You're F.X. Shepherd?" the new guy cut in. "The pet columnist at the *New York Mail* who caught the Hacker?"

"Yeah. Right. Now I'm with the *Daily Press*. I also do my pet column there now."

He pumped my hand and told me his name and how amazing I was. I agreed with him until he coasted to a stop. It was easier that way. I was going to be thirty in a few days and probably had less experience than he did but I didn't interrupt my fan.

"He's not the fucking hero, I'm the hero of that story," Ginny McElhone broke in. "I saved his ass."

Actually, that was almost true. That was the problem with Ginny. Her stories were always *almost* true. And she would do anything for a story. Anything. She was a good reporter but if she didn't have the story, she would create, beg, borrow or steal it. As usual, she was dressed to kill, in a flouncy turquoise halter dress thing that only came to mid-thigh, the top open to distract every man in sight—including the senator. In fact, I suspected she was dressing for him these days but, so far, he had declined to be lured to further doom. From what I saw of the two young ladies who slipped into the trade entrance, Ginny was way too uptown for Hardstein's downtown tastes.

"So, Shepherd, how's your veterinarian?" Ginny asked in a flirty voice, petting Skippy, who annoyed me by enjoying it.

"Jane is fine, thanks. Why did you jump to the *Mail*—just when we were on the same side?"

"We'll never be on the same side," Ginny said, confirming my suspicion that she changed papers because she was more comfortable competing with me than playing second fiddle at the same paper. Even when we were both at the *Daily Press*, Ginny spied on me, followed me and stabbed me in the back. If you're going to do that anyway, I guess it looks better if you're on opposite sides of the "newspaper war" in New York.

That phrase always annoys me. After ten years of bombs, ambushes and firefights, I came home and found everyone calling everything a war—except the actual wars we were fighting. The tube was filled with shows that had names like *Mustache Wars*, *Dance Wars*, *Food Wars*, *Song Wars*, *Coupon Wars*, *Storage Wars*. Give me a break. I only had two big resolutions when I got my life back: I was done with guns and I was done with taking orders. That's as far as I've got.

"What have you got on Hard-On today?" Ginny asked casually, like we were buddies and I was as dumb as dirt. Now I knew why she was on her best behavior. She was trying to pump me.

"I told you, I'm not on the story," I told her, truthfully.

"Make sure it stays that way," she warned, walking away.

"Nice to see you, too," I said to her back.

Coming or going, she was impossible to ignore and every conversation with Ginny Mac was a declaration of war.

8

"Were those two girls hookers?" Sparky asked.

"Judging from the clothes, either that or high-school girls," I replied. "But my guess would be hookers because they didn't giggle. Also, they went in the service entrance. I think they were coordinating with Hardstein, an end-run. He's got brass balls."

"But we don't know for sure they were going up to meet Hard-On?"

"No, but I'd say it's a good bet."

He called his desk and told them to send another photographer, telling his editor we got word that Hard-On might sneak out a second entrance and we had to cover both. No mention that two hookers were inside, possibly with Hardstein—or that we were the only ones who knew. That could change. Besides, any reporter or photographer who told their boss that they *might* get an exclusive was very new at this line of work or just plain stupid. It was a scientific fact that editors did not hear certain words. Words like "may" or "might" or "possibly." If you did not produce the exclusive—which, in five minutes your editor will have exaggerated and taken total credit for—you were dead.

The other photographer was there in five minutes and

Sparky made a show in front of our colleagues that this was his relief and he was leaving. If Sparky and I left together, Ginny Mac or another competitor might follow us, assuming we had a hot lead, which we did. Sparky told me where to meet him and wandered off. I slowly cut Orlando out of the herd and we casually strolled out of earshot and faced away, pretending to be talking on our cellphones.

"What's up?" Orlando asked.

I told him about the two young ladies and he almost blew it.

"What!"

Ginny's head turned toward us. I calmed Orlando down and told him to call the desk and get another reporter to the scene to distract our loyal opposition and cover the front. He seemed confused. Ginny turned away.

"Meanwhile, you watch the other entrance for when they come out," I told Orlando. "But don't jump on them right away. If you do, everyone else will be all over them. Follow them discreetly, until you're out of sight of these guys, and call Sparky before you talk to the ladies. He'll want photos."

"Where will you be?" Orlando demanded, still suspicious.

"With Sparky. Then I'm leaving. I just happened to notice the girls. I'm not on this story."

He didn't believe a word of it but agreed because he couldn't figure out how I was going to screw him. Skippy and I casually said goodbye to everyone. Ginny scratched Skippy's head and made baby noises at him, calling him Sparky. He wagged his tail and licked her hand. No judge of character at all.

"Skippy," I corrected her. "Sparky is the photographer."

"Really?" Ginny asked in a fake mistake voice. "I get confused. They sound alike and they both bark."

There was nasty laughter from the ladies and gentlemen of the media.

"That's not nice, Ginny. Sparky can't help having

Tourette's syndrome. But I guess you can't help being the way you are, either."

"Fuck off!" was her elegant reply.

9

I did as Ginny Mac ordered. Skippy and I met Sparky out of sight in the park, in a rocky clearing surrounded by trees. He looked like a space cadet, wearing goggles with a curved piece of plastic over the face. At his foot was an object with two offset black metalwork squares, each about two feet square. At each of four of the eight corners of the metal star was a vertically-mounted model airplane propeller. In the center was an undercarriage platform with a combination video and still digital camera, secured in a swivel and gimbal-mounted sphere. Skippy sniffed it and backed away.

"You have got to be kidding me, Sparky. You are such a geardo. A helicopter drone?"

"My own little air force. Fuck's a geardo?"

"A weirdo who loves gadgets," I explained.

"Oh. Didn't you use these things in Afghanistan?"

"Not like this one," I told him. "Bigger. Mostly big model airplanes. They were great, once we learned not to have them fly back to us, give away our position and draw RPG or mortar fire."

I asked him what he was going to do. He said Hard-On had a penthouse with big picture windows and a patio overlooking the park.

"Let's see what Hard-On and his hookers are up to."

"Is this legal?" I asked.

"Up to four hundred feet. I can run it for a mile at thirty miles an hour. The batteries last about half an hour. I get live wireless feed back to my laptop from all three cameras but it's better to retrieve the drone and download the higher megapixels."

"That little camera is going to get something useable?" I scoffed.

The classified optics on our stealthy army drones were larger and state of the art. This looked like a home video camera strapped to a futuristic milk box with little propellers. Something a hobbyist would put together.

"This Sony videocam has fifty power optical zoom, which is great, and the still camera has twenty power digital zoom, which is not as good. The megapixels on the CCDs is thirty—which means I get every hair on everybody's ass. Also, an image stabilization system compensates for movement, which is amazing. Check it out!"

He picked up a remote control. The whacky whirligig buzzed to life and hummed straight up into the sky. Skippy barked until I told him to be still. At thirty feet, the sound of the tiny props went away. At a hundred feet, I realized why the craft was constructed as an open framework. The thing, mostly space, vanished from sight. Cheap stealth. Sparky was getting real-time video from his airship projected onto the inside of his goggle screen. He pointed to a flat, protruding rock nearby, where his laptop computer lay open. I sat down with Skippy and watched the screen. There were two video boxes on the top and bottom of the left side of the onscreen display, for down-pointing and forward-aimed cameras, so Sparky could navigate by sight. The right side of the screen also had a larger, forward-looking view, for the still and video camera and a fourth box for a GPS map view.

I watched the bird's eye view as the drone rose. It climbed until it was the same height as the top of Hardstein's building, dead ahead. Sparky kept approaching until a shielded water tower on top was clearly visible. The drone dropped slowly until a penthouse balcony patio and windows were in view. It looked like the device was hovering just over the balcony ledge, as if you could step off onto the landscaped rooftop and take a seat at the dining table.

"I thought they would be out on the terrace," Sparky said, disappointed.

"I'm actually relieved this isn't going to work," I told Sparky, turning away from the screen. "We're not spying on the T-Men or al-Qaeda. He's a member of Congress."

"What's the fuckin' difference?" Sparky snorted. "Wait… Hello! Whadda we got here? Holy fucking dickshit!"

I turned back to the screen. It took me a few seconds to understand what I was seeing. It was Hardstein and the two girls. Oh, man. They were naked and going at it on a large bed.

"Wow! Giggity!" Sparky said. "Mother-humpin' butt bucket! They weren't kidding about the fucking Viagra, amigo. Look at the flesh flagpole on the senior senator! Go baby! I could dub the National Anthem over this."

Hardstein was on his back, the darker girl bouncing like a hurdling equestrienne on his hips, her pal straddling the honorable gentleman's face. Clear as day. The one above Hardstein's head was smoking a joint. She had a teddy bear tattoo above one boob. Her friend had a tat on her ass.

"Duck-fuck and upchuck me!" Sparky laughed. "This thing just paid for itself. And a lot more! Shepherd, I love you man! You are the ball-banging bitch best!"

Freelancers got to keep resale money from their photographs. Sparky would make a fortune. The silent trio in the penthouse switched off, changing positions, and went back to work. I turned away.

"Fuck you going, Shepherd?" he asked.

"I have to look for a story."

"What the hell is this?"

"Gossip. I'm starting that other thing tomorrow. I'll let you know."

"You gotta be kidding me. Listen. I owe you big-time, man. You need anything on that other job, whatever it is, it's all free, okay?"

"Okay, thanks. Have fun."

"You bet. I hope his hard-on doesn't last more than four hours. My battery can't handle that. When they see these… whoa! What the hell was that? Hold it, Shepherd. Look at the screen. Something's happening… Seriously. Now!"

I did. Hardstein was sitting on the edge of the bed, clutching his left shoulder and grimacing. He was still visibly aroused and rocking back and forth. One hooker was still puffing on her spliff. The other one was backing away from the bed, clearly afraid. Hardstein stood up, erect as a toy soldier. Now both hands were grabbing at his chest. He fell over backwards. Both girls poked him and shook him. The black girl straddled him again, pounding on his chest, apparently shouting instructions to her friend, who pinched his nose and blew air into his lungs.

"Holy cock-fucking, mother-bumping cunt fuzz!" Sparky yelled next to me, startling Skippy, who barked again. "I didn't know hookers knew CPR. That's handy."

After a minute or two, the girls stopped, exhausted, and looked at each other. Then they began furiously throwing on their clothes.

"Shit tits! Monkey licks!" Skippy said, zooming in on Hardstein's chest.

It wasn't moving.

The panicked girls, now more or less dressed, ran from the room. I made a quick call on my cell.

"Hello? 911? I would like to report a sixty-seven-year-old

man having a heart attack. He may have taken Viagra. We need an ambulance at Fifth Avenue and Sixty-Ninth Street. Top floor penthouse. He appears not to be breathing."

"Shepherd, whatchya doing?"

"I'm just a concerned citizen," I told the emergency operator. "I'm not actually there. I'm not in the building. Well... it doesn't matter. Just get him some help. No, sorry, thanks."

I hung up.

"Did you say his name?" Sparky asked.

"No and I didn't give the actual address but we both know it doesn't matter. The photo editors will hear the call over the radios and they'll go bananas. I can't just let him die, Sparky."

"He's dead already but I know. You're right. I won't tell the desk you called the cops. What about Orlando?"

I made another quick call.

"Orlando? It's Shepherd. Listen to me. Those two girls are probably going to come flying out of there any second. Yes. Repeat after me. Hardstein just had a heart attack upstairs."

Orlando did that, but in a hushed voice.

"Hardstein just had a heart attack upstairs? How do you know that? Wow, is that true?" Orlando whispered.

"Yes it is. But I meant repeat it loudly—like you're fucking up by letting out a secret. If anyone asks you— deny it. Then, when the shit hits the fan, chase those girls with your shooter so no one else sees them. If you're lucky, everyone else will be too busy covering the heart attack to notice where you went. Okay, yell. Do it now."

I heard him yell "Hardstein had a heart attack upstairs?" Then I heard a lot of other voices, followed by sirens and screeching tires. I hung up.

"Is this legal?" I asked.

"Sure," Sparky answered. "Hard-On is out of the picture and I'm taking pictures from a public area."

"That's a stretch," I laughed. "Better withdraw your air force before the NYPD get upstairs, Sparky."

"Not until I get some shots of cops inside with the body," Sparky insisted. "Jeezus squeeze-us, look at that. Poor horny bastard is still at attention. You gotta give it up for Viagra, man. Chubby hubby forever."

The cops and EMS paramedics arrived and swarmed the penthouse. Sparky got his video and stills. I knew I had to call Mel. I told my boss what had happened. It sounded like he was jumping up and down on the other end.

"The sex stuff is folking amazing but are you sure he's dead?" Mel demanded.

"Sparky has the video that shows the ladies doing CPR. He zoomed in and his chest wasn't moving. I'd say he's dead. The paramedics couldn't do anything, either. Maybe they'll revive him at the hospital."

"No, I hear they're not transporting him," Mel said. "It's a flagging crime scene. Great fogging job, Shepherd."

"I didn't do anything," I told him. "I'm not even on the story."

I waved goodbye to Sparky. Skippy and I walked toward the park exit. Dirty clouds were coming in low and fast, from the Hudson. Skippy's head was busy, snapping toward every bird and squirrel. My cheek and temple throbbed softly, my scars responding to the falling barometer. I called Jane at work. Lots of barking in the background. She was too busy to talk, so I said I would see her later at home.

Hell of a day. A friendly chat with my boss, Mel. Stalked by a chameleon lady private eye. A job offer. Stumbling over a story, the charge of beating the competition, beating Ginny Mac. That was all new and not unwelcome. But the secret surveillance mission, the stealthy drone, the death— that was too familiar.

Inescapable.

I took out my phone.

"Siri, am I a pathetic adrenaline junkie?"

After a pause and a double beep, she replied with her usual good breeding.

"I would prefer not to say, Shepherd."

10

I was done but the day wasn't done with me yet. I tried to goof off but it didn't work. Back at Jane's place, I grabbed a beer. Jane's refrigerator only contained designer beers. I wondered if she was gently trying to steer me away from my high-octane arak liquor and onto an unending series of fancy pumpkin ales and wheat stouts or whatever overpriced brew the Manhattan suds snobs were pushing this month. I was channel surfing the fifty-inch on her living room couch and sipping something called Honey Meade Malt when my father's face appeared on CNN.

"Holy crap!"

I turned the sound up. The banner underneath his image read POLITICAL SCIENTIST PROF. JAMES B. SHEPHERD. He looked good, kind of like Santa Claus gone corporate. His silver hair and beard were as long as ever, the chin whiskers almost covering the top of his blue silk tie, Kansas cornflower blue eyes sparkling, his mouth crinkled in amusement. On the table in front of him was his latest book, with a picture of the Statue of Liberty being auctioned off in what looked like a slave market for green goddesses.

SOLD! Wall Street's Coup d'État.

My dad was doing what he always did—railing against

the powers that be. He was calmly saying something about the Tea Party being neo-secessionists intent on imposing neo-slavery. He had no clue that most people had no idea what coup d'état or neo meant. He was rudely interrupted by a nasty voice.

"Shut up!" said the voice, as the camera switched to the famous hawk face of TV pundit Bob O'Malley. "Keep your commie crap to yourself!"

O'Malley routinely invited liberals onto his show, *Free Speech Zone*, to prove how even-handed he was, but usually cut off their mikes and called them names. The show should be called *The Bully Zone*.

"America's economy is run by predatory capitalism but our sacred government is based upon one person, one vote—until now!" my father fought back. "You and your corporate-owned supreme court have officially switched our form of government from democracy to capitalism—we are now a cash-based oligarchy, with a stock market and an army."

"Cut off this clown's mike," O'Malley shouted. "My audience doesn't have to hear this Marxist malarkey."

"Between buying elections and suppressing minority voters, that is the only way you can win the..." My father's measured voice was cut off.

"Go back to Moscow!" O'Malley sneered.

"I'm from Kansas!" my father said in an even but very loud voice, still audible over the air.

My father was polite, soft-spoken and quoted Emerson, about a gentleman not making any noise. But he was from the Planet 1960s and you couldn't silence him.

"I said cut off his mike!" O'Malley yelled again, panic rising in his voice.

"You cannot silence the voice of an informed electorate, no matter how many lies you tell," my father continued calmly—at the top of his lungs.

He sat quite still, the color rising in his round face.

His voice was so loud it was picked up by O'Malley's microphone. The host looked like this had never happened before. It must have been the practice my dad got from all those anti-Vietnam War demonstrations. O'Malley was going berserk. He called for security.

"Only in gun-crazy, money-mad America could activist judges label cash as free speech and certify that a corporation is a human being—but with *more* rights than a person. Americans have lost their voice, just as I have on this show—because a millionaire shut me up. Wake up! There is no free speech on this show or in the country—unless you're rich!"

"Shut the BEEP up!" O'Malley screeched, his obscenity bleeped out. "Cut off my mike, too. Go to BEEP-ing commercial."

Uniformed security guards dragged my smiling dad off-screen. O'Malley threw one of my father's books at him, just before the image froze.

"That was the wild scene last night on FAX TV's Bob O'Malley's *Free Speech Zone*. O'Malley didn't like what his liberal guest was saying, so he cut off his mike and then had him dragged off camera," a gorgeous blonde CNN host said. "CNN has learned that the TV host with the famously short temper had political science professor and author James Shepherd ejected from the studio—and also from the luxury hotel where he had been put up by the show. I guess O'Malley forgot that he named his show the *Free Speech Zone*," the anchor chuckled.

It cut to a catchy musical commercial: a montage of car crashes, ambulances and a blizzard of green cash and dollar signs. A bandaged guy on crutches danced and belted out a happy tune:

"Klaus and Fins, injury attorneys—let us sue to score cash for you!"

I switched to FAX News channel. As usual, former Alaska governor and former vice presidential candidate Miranda Dodge, a right-wing glamor girl, was slamming the president who had defeated her in the last election. Beneath her image, her identification was FORMER AK GOV., AUTHOR OF *WHITE SLAVES UNITE*.

"Well, shoot," Dodge said in her fake folksy tone. "If the election had not been rigged and stolen with voter fraud by all those illegal aliens, I would be in office now—not that mongrel Moslem foreigner. The enemies of our great nation are helped by traitors, who would tear down our precious freedoms, such as the right to bear arms, the right to self-govern and freedom from taxes."

"Are you referring to Speaker of the House, Percy Chesterfield?" the moderator asked her.

"He is one of many but his treason is more painful because he pretends to be one of us," said Dodge. "Well, shoot! First he is *with* us, then he is *against* us."

"That's right!" piped up another voice.

The camera turned to a husky bearded guy with long scraggly hair, wearing full camouflage shirt, vest and jacket. It did not help him blend into the TV studio. The banner below his long beard said TEA PARTY BLOGGER CLAYTON LITTLETON. Who the hell was this guy?

"The pretender president is in league with Chesterfield and the other RINOs and false patriots who are unwilling to do what is necessary to bring down this godless, foreign occupation of sacred Christian America," Littleton said. "It is past time we resorted to Second Amendment measures to take back our country and restore it to one nation under God, so that *real* Americans can rule once more." Dodge nodded her agreement.

This was interesting. Two people on a major TV network like FAX—run by owner of the *New York Mail* Trevor Todd, openly calling an elected official a traitor and suggesting he be shot because of his political views.

In America.

Iraq and Afghanistan are very different from the US in a

lot of ways. But the weird thing about coming home after so long was how similar they had become. It was beginning to look like I couldn't escape the Cult of the Sacred Gun; ruthless, dedicated madmen who worshipped weapons and ached to kill with a sexual fervor stoked by their mullahs and their own movies and TV shows.

I guzzled the rest of my too-sweet near-beer and poured a glass of arak. My father, and probably my mother, were in New York and had not even called me. Typical. I tried other news channels. My father's fight with the conservative talk show host was all over the tube but was quickly replaced by BREAKING NEWS segments about the senator.

"To recap, for those of you just tuning in," one anchor intoned. "The *New York Daily Press* website is reporting exclusively that Senator Richard Hard—uh... Hardstein, is dead of an apparent heart attack inside his Manhattan home. We have been unable to confirm that so far but a large number of police and emergency workers have arrived at Hardstein's home, as you can see from this live shot."

The scene was chaotic, with a crowd held back by cops and TV cameras and press and, in the middle, one really pissed-off redhead.

11

Two araks later, my cellphone rang.

I answered without looking for the caller ID—always a mistake.

"Yeah?"

"Francis?"

"Mom?"

My mother was the only one who ever called me that.

"Hi."

The last time I spoke to my parents was a few weeks earlier, after national stories ran about how I was involved in a massacre of civilians in Afghanistan. They weren't true. Before that, they hadn't spoken to me for most of the past decade—ever since I enlisted after the 9-11 attacks. They never called me or responded to my calls. Three could play at that game.

"Nice to hear from you, Mom," I said casually. "How are you and Dad doing? Enjoying the summer? Any vacation plans?"

"Well, yes, actually, we're here in New York."

"Really? You should have called in advance so I could have taken some time off and shown you the town."

"We would never put you to that trouble, Francis. Um... How are you?"

"You mean other than being a baby-killer and a tool of the corporate-fascist war machine?"

"Your father was upset. When the later stories made it clear that those charges were not true, he regretted saying that."

"Great. I guess he forgot to call and tell me. Not to mention the TV station."

After an awkward silence, she mentioned the new TV appearance. I feigned ignorance.

"It was very amusing," she giggled. "This O'Malley person is quite a tiresome egomaniac."

You didn't have to be a clinical psychologist, like my mother, to figure that out.

"Immature genital fixation. His belief system seems wholly animist."

"That's what I've always said," I told her.

"Are you mocking me, Francis?"

"Never, Mom. You need a place to stay, don't you?"

After a long silence, she responded.

"You saw the show."

"No, but I saw a clip—they kicked you out of your hotel."

She didn't deny it.

My parents are not wealthy. They do not believe in stocks or bonds, although they believe in savings accounts, for some reason. Of course, that was when interest was actually paid by banks. Now the interest rate for the suckers was almost zero—at the vapor-lock point. My parents also do not believe in inflation-causing credit cards. They didn't owe anybody anything but they didn't have much, considering that they had been professors for decades. They had been all over the world but always stayed with friends for nothing. That would mean they had a finite amount of cash with them and no credit cards and were having trouble getting an un-booked hotel room in the tourist season.

"Let me guess, Mom. You want to stay with me?"

"Well, no... actually, we thought perhaps some friends of yours might..."

"Let me get this straight, Mom. You hate my guts but you want me to find you a place to stay, so your low-budget vacation won't be ruined."

"You know I hate ugly phrases like that," she said, coolly.

"But you like cold phrases like 'psychopathy' and 'passive-aggressive,' right?"

"Francis, I'm sorry. I didn't mean to... You're right. This was ill-advised."

"No, Mom. I know someone who moved into his girlfriend's place recently. I have the keys. It's down in TriBeCa. You're welcome to stay there for the week."

"Well, thank you, Francis, that's very considerate of you. Maybe we can get together one night for dinner?"

"That would be nice, Mom."

As if. Maybe Congress would pass a gun-control law. Or any law.

"Yes, I'll... check with your father."

"Great. Get back to me. I'll send the address and the keys over by messenger. Where are you? Hold on. Let me get a pen."

I got the *Yellow Pages* and found a messenger service. I called and a guy on a motorbike arrived ten minutes later. I gave him money, my house keys and a note in an envelope and sent him off to my parents. I sat back down, downed my drink and laughed. Only way to deal with it.

12

By the time Jane got home, it was dark and I was drunk. She seemed upset and I asked her what was wrong. She blew her nose, sat with me and said it was nothing. But I had already figured out that she thought there was something wrong with people who drank alone, especially if they got blasted. She kissed me and gave me a hug, which I returned. Jane thought because I could always tell when she was upset that I was a sensitive person, which was true, and a good listener, which was also accurate. She had also told me she felt I was not a judgmental person. She thought those things meant I was a warm, fuzzy guy and a caring boyfriend. I wasn't so sure that my hyper-vigilance meant I was such a good guy. I had no idea. We were a new couple and I didn't want to dispense advice. Especially advice I would not take myself.

If you didn't care about killing, even as a mercy, you were a killer. I was a killer and I didn't like it. As my calming Lao Tzu Daily Thought app said: "Caring is an invincible shield from heaven against being dead." If it was a shield, why did it hurt so much? I said none of this to Jane.

"Why are you drunk?" she asked pleasantly, but with a little edge.

I pointed at the screen and let her watch. I got her a glass and she had a shot of arak with me, even though she hated the stuff. That way, I wouldn't be drinking alone. We held each other on the couch for a while and watched the news, while Skippy snoozed on the floor, his giant head warming my feet.

"So, when you went out with Skippy this afternoon, you covered that?" Jane asked, pointing at the *Daily Press* website HARDSTEIN HEART ATTACK DEATH headline, displayed on CNN.

"Not really. I saw the girls sneak in and I told Sparky and this other reporter. I tipped them off and they nailed it and ran with it. I left."

"What girls?"

"They haven't used that part yet. Hardstein was having sex with two young ladies when he died."

"Oh, my God! Why isn't your paper going berserk with that juicy morsel?"

"They're trying to get more, trying to talk to the women, saving it for a big splash in the morning paper."

"Oh. Of course."

I told Jane what else had happened.

"Was it the Viagra?" she asked. "Did it cause his heart attack?"

"Maybe. I'm not on the story."

"Okay. So, tomorrow is your first day as a private eye?" Jane asked.

"Looks that way. Sounds more like a security guard job."

"If you don't like it, you can quit."

When a commercial came on, we got up and made dinner together. Jane carefully sautéed a small fish while I made a salad and drizzled on some virgin olive oil with herbs and Trader Joe's Balsamic Glaze. I served Skippy some of his favorite canned wet food, Straw Dogs.

"Something else is bothering you," Jane said when we were done.

"I just sublet my apartment," I explained. "Actually I sub-sublet it. For free. I'm celebrating."

"For free? To who?"

"Total strangers."

She waited.

"Total strangers who are related to me."

I told her about the TV show and my mother's call, while pouring myself another glass of arak. When I told her my parents were staying for only a week, I detected relief. I tried not to take it personally. We had only been dating a month.

"Your parents make mine seem wonderful," Jane said. "Yours sound somewhat abusive."

"Sort of."

I served with guys, some real psycho killers, whose parents had beat the shit out of them. My parents never used anything except words.

"Did they…"

"Never laid a hand on me," I said, truthfully. "Always remembered my birthday. But they… told me terrible things… dangerous lies."

"Like what?"

"That if I was a good person and worked hard, I would be rewarded," I told her. "That people were the most important thing in this world—not money. That I was personally responsible for Justice for everyone, everywhere, every day of my life."

"The bastards," Jane laughed.

"Exactly."

13

The folded front page of the *Daily Press* was lying in wait for me on the front porch at seven the next morning, a brisk, sunny day. I was showered, dressed, clean and feeling good. The last thing I wanted to do was read the paper. I unfolded it cautiously, as Skippy sniffed the fresh air. He was getting his information and I was getting mine. The entire front page was one of Sparky's drone shots of Senator Hardstein, naked and dead on his bed, a lopsided smile on his handsome face. For modesty, a black rectangle had been placed over his aroused crotch, akimbo at a forty-five degree angle—hiding, yet highlighting the spot. The paper had gone for the gusto—the headline in huge bold type, in fire-engine red ink:

HARD-OFF!

Oh, man. I was horrified to see my boldface byline as the first of three names on the EXCLUSIVE! story below, even though I had not filed anything. There was even a postage-stamp-sized photo of me. I cursed under my breath as I scanned the sub-headline and read on.

FATAL ERECTION?

Sex-scandal Senator Richard "Hard-On" Hardstein suffered an apparent heart attack and died yesterday — during kinky three-way sex with two naked women inside his $8 million Fifth Avenue penthouse, the possible result of a popular erection-inducing medication, law enforcement sources said. Exclusive *Daily Press* photos and video show that the married Hardstein, a father of three and grandfather of two, died after engaging in extra-marital hijinks with his young playmates just minutes after he refused to comment to a crowd of media outside his home — uttering his last public words: "Sorry, I have a pressing appointment."

© Copyright, N.Y. DAILY PRESS.

I was still new to newspaper work and had no clue what the word "hijinks" meant. Inside, page after page of huge photographs of the senator and his teen partners, with more black tape over certain body parts to reduce the exposure from X-rated to PG-17. There was also black tape over the ladies' eyes, hiding their identity but not much else.

Wow. And my name was on it. How did that happen? I couldn't put it down.

"PRESSING APPOINTMENT? The Senator Presses the Flesh in His Last Campaign, as one of his admirers sucks on an odd cigarette." The video frame-grabs were numbered in series, like a comic strip, of the action and death and the flight of the ladies, then the arrival of the cops. There was a website listed—a pay-per-view site to view the copyrighted video for $9.99. Further in, two pages were dedicated to exclusive interviews with the two girls.

HARD-ON HARLOTS

"He was, like, really old but he was always cool before. This time, he just friggin' fell over. Maybe he took too much Viagra," said one escort—who asked to be called "Caprice." Her partner, "Swag," said they preferred to be identified as "sex industry workers." They both agreed that if they ever voted they would cast their ballots for Hardstein. Just before the fun turned fatal, they said, the liberal Hardstein asked them to sing "Happy Birthday, Mr. President." Yesterday was not the senator's birthday. "Dickie loved that song," said one of the sex industry workers. "He was totally bonus. I'm, like, totally sad."

The girls revealed their prices and menu for sex, all detailed in a chart on page seven, next to a spread of real estate photos of the penthouse—presumably for sale soon—and speculation on who might buy it and whether Hardstein's widow might get more or less money because of the infamy of his ignominious end there. There was even a shot at Ginny Mac, under a small photo of her pressing her chest against Hardstein. They had air-brushed her cleavage to make it look more revealing and her expression more slutty.

MAIL BOOB JOB FAILS

An unnamed *New York Mail* reporter, left, unethically presses her chest against the doomed senator in a failed bid for an interview. But her shame went largely unnoticed in New York—because no one is reading the *Mail* today. Everyone is getting the whole story, exclusively—only in the *Daily Press*! Don't forget to view the shocking video online. Adults only!

Oh, man. I picked up the warring tabloid from the porch. Ginny had a story on the front page with another big headline:

HARD-ON DEAD

Ginny's piece was very similar—but totally without the girls or the sex or the Viagra. They never saw the pastel ladies, never launched a drone. They were caught flat-footed on the ground, G-rated. Compared to the *Daily Press*, the *Mail* was like a bun without the hotdog. Ginny would be breathing fire. Scooped. I called the paper. Mel picked up right away.

"Great job, Shep!" Mel laughed. "We shucking raped the *Mail*!"

I hate it when people call me Shep.

"Mel, why is my name on the story?"

"You're faking welcome. Sparky told me everything. You set the whole gob-smacking thing up. Without you, we would have zip. You're too modest. I want my star reporter up front and in their faces. Hey, you're flipping famous again."

"Great. Look, I have another thing this morning. I took a part-time job. I'll have the column for you soon."

"What the bark are you talking about? Screw the column. I want you on this story."

"Thanks for the suggestion, Mel, but I'm doing something else that might be a good story. Besides, this has been done to death. It's over now."

"Over? Are you fopping kidding? This is just the lucking beginning. The cops and the DA are downstairs with subpoenas. The faking FBI just called. Everybody but the Department of Agriculture."

"You mean you didn't give the cops the names of the hookers? You made the cops look bad?"

"Hey, if I give cops the names, they'll give it to the *Mail* and end our exclusive. No farting way. Orlando is trying to shanghai the wenches now, get them out of town. The lawyers are on the way over here to deal with the canting cops and the feds. By the way, don't come here: You probably should also stay away from home for a few days, too—on us, of course. You earned it."

"Why?"

"I think those grass-holes may have a grand jury subpoena or an arrest warrant or something for you. Don't worry about it—we'll take care of it."

"Good to know. Thanks for your help, Mel."

I hung up. He tried calling right back but I let it go to voice mail. I dialed Sparky and told him I wasn't happy to be on the story. He apologized. I asked him for the names, ages and addresses of the pastel playmates. I had noticed his photo credit on the clothed pictures of the hookers that went with Orlando's piece. Sparky looked it up on his phone. I wrote it down. He apologized again.

"I thought you deserved credit, man. They were going to cut you out, so I went to the boss. That asshole Orlando told Mel he spotted the girls, not you!"

"That's okay with me," I said.

"Seriously? I don't get you, man. This is a fucking giant story. Why wouldn't you want in—especially after you were the one who nailed it? You might get a book out of this, or a movie."

"I don't like gossip," I explained. "Talking about other people's sex lives is more boring than golf on TV. I know I've been away a long time but whenever they put me on gossip, I have no clue who these assholes are."

"Shit, it's all gossip now, buddy. What else is there?"

"Murder. Somebody's got to catch the bad guy, so the family can sleep at night."

"What? Shepherd, were you in the army or the Boy Scouts?"

"Both, actually."

14

I dialed Major Case Squad Detective Lieutenant Izzy Negron on his cell. I thought my favorite Jewish-Puerto Rican investigator would be happy to hear from his pet columnist pal.

"Oh, no," Izzy groaned as he answered.

"Nice to speak to you, too, Izzy."

"I just saw the fucking paper. I do not want a bite of that," Izzy said.

"How do you know I'm calling about Hardstein?"

"You're not?"

"No, I am, sort of."

"Shit. I am *not* on that case."

"That's what I keep telling my boss."

"I feel bad for Hardstein's family," Izzy said. "Talk about a shonda for the goyim. As my father used to say, '*Lo agarro con las pendejo en la chocha.*' What do you mean you're not on the story? Your name is on the front page, Shepherd."

I didn't speak Yiddish or Spanish and couldn't compete, unless we started speaking Urdu or Pashto.

"As my father used to say, 'Don't believe everything you read in the papers.' Don't your bosses give you credit for things you didn't do?"

"Never," Izzy said. "I can't get credit for the shit I *actually* do."

"Look, off the record, I have the names of the hookers who were with the senator."

"The shameless shiksas? Off the record, so what? The guy had a heart attack, went out with a smile. *A bi gezunt.* This is Major Case, not major hard-on. Call 911, amigo."

"My current paper is going to the mats, protecting the ladies' names, but it's bullshit," I told him. "They're just keeping it from the *Mail*. The DA is also involved, and the feds. Won't you get brownie points for passing the identities on, saving them a big court fight?"

Izzy hesitated again. He kept hesitating. I read him the names, ages and address. The ladies lived together. I explained I didn't want to be hauled before a grand jury to protect an exclusive that was already out.

"The thing is, brownie points don't really count," Izzy protested. "Try cashing them in, sometime. Also, the guys who couldn't get the information end up pissed at you for showing them up. You actually make enemies."

"What a hotbed of intrigue Police Headquarters is," I told him.

"You have no idea. So, where did these pictures come from—you and a photographer out on the balcony, trespassing, sneaking and peeping?"

"You might not believe me."

"Try me."

"Off the record? A drone."

"You're shitting me. You guys have drones now?"

"Not as good as we had in JSOC but pretty damn good. So, what are you up to, Izzy?"

"Phil and I are running with the big dogs, nothing but the biggest cases for us. Much too secret to discuss with a lowly reporter, of course."

"Must have been all your good work on the Hacker case," I said.

"Oh, and I'm supposed to say I owe it all to you?"

"Well, maybe a little."

"Okay, a little. Oh, wait, I get it—you're trying to score brownie points with me."

"Well, maybe a little," I admitted. "I'm starting a part-time gig tomorrow and I may need help."

"That's the other bad thing about brownie points—you also end up owing the guy who gave you the tip. The guys you beat hate you and then you owe somebody else. That's two steps backwards."

For a guy who saw murder victims all the time, Izzy was kind of negative.

"But you'll pass on the sex industry workers' info?"

"Sure. I'll impress my bosses with my omnipotence. I love that euphemism—'sex industry worker.' In the pictures, I don't see the ladies doing any heavy lifting or anything that looks like industry. More like artistry. They got a union yet?"

"Not yet."

"So, Shepherd, what's your new part-time gig?"

"Sorry, it's secret. I can't talk about it."

Izzy chuckled. I braced myself for more Yiddish or Spanish. Instead, I heard a familiar sarcastic voice in the background. Detective Sergeant Phil D'Amico.

"Phil thinks you're becoming a sex industry worker," Izzy laughed. "He says, 'Make sure you wear a hard hat.'"

"Tell him thanks, I will."

15

I walked west in the morning sun, toward Central Park, toward my meeting, with my black backpack on my back. I noticed sporadic staccato patterns of explosions, firecrackers on the day before the Fourth of July. No one paid any attention. A perfect day to shoot someone and get away with it. By the time I reached Fifth Avenue, the back of my neck was itching. Again. Eyes were on me. It was rush hour and the sidewalks were busy. It was hard to isolate my shadow without tipping him off. I pulled out my phone and dialed Amy.

"Amy, it's Shepherd. Are you still following me?"

"What the hell would I do that for?"

"That's what I thought. Forget it. See you soon."

I stopped at the crosswalk at Fifth Avenue, forcing people to move around me, a herd around a tree. I ducked around the light pole on the near corner and snuck a peek back. I couldn't see anyone. I crossed against the light and moved swiftly into the park, the shortcut to my Westside meeting. In the park, I sprinted up a rocky rise and hid inside the nearest clump of thick trees. A group appeared at the entrance—four young, pumped steroid-neck white guys in uniform blue pants. Not uniforms. Pressed skinny jeans, with sharp creases, white silk shirts open halfway down their muscled chests, gold glittering at their necks, collarless black leather jackets, perfect black hair. It was the most formal version of casual clothes I had ever seen. They looked like a retro a cappella singing group. The guy in the lead was wearing a small fedora, also black leather. One of those neo-hipster hats. Sitting atop the brim was an expensive pair of dark plastic sunglasses, the kind that idiots paid a thousand bucks for. Like the hat was wearing shades. Cute.

They were walking fast now, looking around. I slid behind the thickest tree. They approached and passed by. Young voices, stupid. Brooklyn accents and Italian names: Vinnie, Tony, Bobby, Jay-Jay. They were moving faster, clearly panicked they had lost me. The hat kid, Jay-Jay, was getting pissed and was blaming it on the others. I had to chuckle at the bozos in their little outfits. Junior Mafia action figures. A thousand pounds of juiced muscle between them but not one who felt eyes.

Who the hell were they? Or, rather, who had sent them and what did they want? Did they just want to find out where I was going and who I was meeting? Or did they have something nastier in mind? Ginny Mac had followed me before, trying to steal my story. She mugged me once in bed and, when that no longer worked, she sent her two big brothers to beat me up. Did she send these clowns? Or was this how billionaire Trevor Todd was going to take his revenge on me for revealing his newspaper as a criminal racketeering scam that used bugging, spying, theft and even murder to get a story? Whoever wanted a piece of me, I didn't have time for this shit right now. I was running late. Besides, when you have a choice between a victory with violence and a victory with no casualties—it was a no-brainer. When you win, you walk away in one piece and leave your enemy a way out. I left the park and hailed a cab.

I had to use my NYPD Working Press Pass to get into the

brand-new Knickerbocker Convention Center on the West Side; one huge block of luxury high-rise hotel, auditoriums, shops, spas, restaurants, waterfalls, bars, concert halls; a small, self-contained city. The GOP National Convention was about to start and the security was serious. In addition to NYPD cops, there were feds, Homeland Security and lots of plainclothes. The streets around the center were closed, with concrete vehicle barriers, security checkpoints and armored personnel vehicles, bomb trucks, canine units and communications trucks, all gearing up for the nationally televised kickoff tomorrow, on the Fourth of July. The Republicans were again holding their presidential extravaganza in the camp of their supposed enemy—liberal New York City. Of course, Manhattan was media ground zero, so I guess it made sense. It did seem funny that all these law enforcement folks were getting overtime to protect the right-wingers from the left-wing demonstrators, who were sure to show up to protest the Tea Party candidates.

I had not yet been inside the Knickerbocker Convention Center. It was impressive. They had full airport-style body scanners, and a K-9 cop with a sniffer dog was checking bags. After I went through and my backpack was searched, I was asked to turn on my laptop. I took the MacBook out of its case and fired it up. When they saw my computer was real and not a bomb, I was cleared for entry.

Amy, again clad in black Italian fashion, met me in the East Lobby, a ten-story atrium with an Amazon rainforest and waterfall. Like a kid from Kansas, I stared up at the waterfall and the giant fiberglass pterodactyls suspended fifty feet above my head. Clear vertical tubes against the back of the atrium housed large rounded elevators, also transparent, moving up and down. Amy looked askance at my New Balance cross trainers, jeans and blue polo shirt but she said nothing.

"Hi, Amy. Why flying dinosaurs?"

"Prehistoric Manhattan," she replied. "The joke is that the valet parking is at this entrance, so the theme is Jurassic Parking."

We both laughed.

"The other three are also time-travel atriums," Amy said. "Old New York, Future New York, and… I forget the other one. We're over this way. Third floor, Conference Room A, up two levels."

We took a two-person-wide escalator up through the towering foliage to the Manhattan Mezzanine and then a second one up to the Hudson Mezzanine.

"So, you're the reporter, I would like you to take shorthand while we talk with Chesterfield," Amy informed me.

"I would like that too, but I don't know shorthand," I told her, "but I have a good memory. I have a digital recorder, too, and can take notes on my laptop."

Amy scowled at me. Obviously, she had assumed all reporters took shorthand. I explained that I was only a pet columnist. She shrugged.

"You didn't hire me for my secretarial skills, I assume."

She smiled. "What was the deal with your Hardstein pictures in the paper today? A camera drone, right?"

"Yeah," I said, surprised.

"Did you do it?"

"No, a photographer. He's available. Do you use camera drones?"

She just smiled. Upstairs, we had to go through more metal detectors, and a shoe detector—even a "Sniffer" air booth to detect explosives.

We arrived at a set of very large double doors with a bronze plate that identified it as the HUDSON ROOM. A team of plainclothes Executive Protection Service agents were outside. Hands vanished inside suit jackets. Amy identified us and we showed ID but we had to submit our bags for inspection again. My recorder and laptop were also checked out. They took our cellphones, turned them off, removed the batteries and said they would keep them until we were done. This kind of in-depth, hair-trigger security was presidential level. Interesting. How were we supposed to do better? Inside the cavernous, carpeted three-story room, floor-to-ceiling plate-glass windows overlooked the Hudson River. A single, long, large wooden conference table was parallel to the big window, with eighteen cushioned black leather armchairs, most along the side and one at each end. The room was empty. We sat on the near side, close to the left end. I noticed there were lots of boats in the river between Manhattan and New Jersey. An NYPD launch, a Coast Guard cutter, and a giant US Navy destroyer, the USS *John McCain*, equipped with automated five-inch gun turrets, missile launch bays and Phalanx high-speed anti-aircraft, anti-missile Gatling guns. Without doubt the vessel also carried nuclear-tipped Tomahawk and Harpoon missiles.

These people were very serious about security.

16

"Let me do the talking," Amy told me.

"Sure, boss," I said, placing my backpack on the table.

A flying wedge of new security suits burst into the room. Behind them, in an ash-gray suit, white shirt and red power tie, followed the candidate, Speaker of the House Percy Chesterfield; bronzed, bored, and sucking on an unfiltered cigarette. The GOP politician reached for Amy's much smaller hand and pumped it, as she introduced herself and me. The guy who shut down the US government over health insurance and almost sparked a worldwide financial crash to improve our economy—and was threatening to do it again—did not reach for my hand. We sat. Chesterfield fired up a new smoke, the brown tobacco and red glow of flame combined in a burnt-umber orange color that matched his skin. Either this guy used spray tan or he was some kind of new mutant. An agent set down a large cut-glass ashtray within reach. Amy started to talk but Chesterfield cut her off and looked at me.

"Hold it. I served in Congress with Senator Richard Hardstein for many years. Are you the same guy in the *Daily Press* today—the reporter who caught poor Dickie Hardstein with his pants down?" he asked in a deep, raspy smoker's voice.

Uh-oh. It looked like my tabloid work might be a problem.
"Yes, sir."

"That was tragic. Terrible. Where is it?" Chesterfield bellowed to his guards. "The paper I was reading?"

It appeared magically in his hand. He held up the front page. HARD-OFF!

"There you are, on the front page," Chesterfield said. "I knew it! You wrote this!"

This was not going well. Then Chesterfield began laughing hysterically. He pointed to the black box over Hardstein's afterlife erection and laughed until tears came from his eyes. He got up and came over to me. I stood up. He shook my hand firmly and slapped me on the back. As he raised his arm, his suit jacket opened and I could see a black leather holster containing a bejeweled red, white and blue semiautomatic pistol. Not surprising, I suppose, for a gun nut politico from a tobacco state like Virginia. He insisted one of the agents take a selfie of the two of us, with the *Daily Press* front page below us. He was grinning. I wasn't. Amy also stood up, unsure what to do.

"I feel bad for Dickie but this is the funniest thing I have seen in years—Hard-Off!" Chesterfield chortled, exploding into more laughter. "He never could keep it in his pants. He giggled, wiping away tears. "Mr. Holy Liberal gets his dick caught in a sex scandal—and then drops dead before we can use it against him in an election. Nice career move, Dickie!"

He went on like this for a few minutes and then sat down, lit another cigarette, and returned to the business at hand.

"I'll tell you I was very much against this when the National Committee brought this to me—a New York private eye who is also a reporter for a liberal rag—but there is no one I would like better on this than you," Chesterfield told me, slapping my back again. "I think it's bullshit, just a lot of hot air from dickless assholes, but I know I can trust you and Amy. As long as the party pays for this, I'll play ball, providing we keep it quiet. I don't want to look like a pussy. I've got better security than the president, but I will cooperate—whatever you need."

He was spending a lot of time playing this down, this armed super patriot, but I got the impression that somewhere behind the stone face, he was worried.

"Thank you, Mr. Speaker," Amy jumped in. "We need all the threat details. I understand there is a large volume?"

"Only if you think fifty thousand death threats is a large volume." Chesterfield smirked. "Let 'em try."

He called for and introduced us to his chief of staff, Tiffany Mauser, who looked like a Bond girl. In a soft southern lilt, she promised to email us details and follow up by phone. His head of security, a bald man called Karl Bundt, who was wearing yellow Oakley shooting glasses, joined the party. He also exchanged emails and numbers with us, so he could pass on his information.

"I have some stuff from the Secret Service, FBI, and ahh... other agencies you might find interesting. You both have security clearances, right?"

"Yes, of course," Amy said.

Now I was beginning to see why Amy hired me on short notice. I had a security clearance. Or, I did. Why did she have one? She claimed she did no government work. We would have to talk. We all shook hands and set a face-to-face situation report within twenty-four hours, once Amy and I had gone over the material. Chesterfield pulled me aside, arm around my shoulder, his grating yet pleasing voice in my ear, the scent of fresh bourbon in my nose.

"Tell me, buddy, you've seen this sex video?" he drawled.

"No, sir. I saw a feed of it as it happened. I haven't seen the video since."

"So, how did old Dickie do with those two ladies?" he asked.

"He was doing great right up until the part where he dropped dead."

"A shame. But he really fucked himself. He couldn't stop screwin' around—even after he got his dick caught in a newspaper press."

"That's true, sir."

"Why did he do it?" Chesterfield asked.

"I don't know. Compulsion, maybe? You'd have a better idea than I would, Mr. Speaker."

"Why would I know?" he asked, with a nervous glance at Tiffany.

"You knew the man, sir. For years."

"Oh, of course. Right. Compulsion, I'm sure you're right."

Again, he lit up and we lit out. I threw my backpack back on. I never got a chance to take out my laptop or my recorder. A member of the "Chesterfield for America" team gave Amy and me official all-access convention IDs on red, white and blue lanyards. On the way down the escalator, descending into the Jurassic Parking lobby, Amy sighed with relief.

"I thought we were dead there for a second, but we're in. He loves you."

"I think he's peachy, too. I thought you said you don't do government work?"

"I don't."

"I know why I had a security clearance. So I could be sent to jail if I ever revealed any military fuck-ups. Why do you have one?"

"I don't. I meant since you have a security clearance, *we* have a security clearance—the firm. Officially, you are the only one reading this stuff."

"That's sneaky and probably illegal," I told her. "If there is anything you shouldn't see, I won't let you see it."

"For cripes' sake, what a boy scout," she grinned.

"I wish people would stop calling me that. It's not just orders or ethics or morality or whatever."

"What, then?"

"Thirty years in Leavenworth Federal Penitentiary. When do we start?"

"We're on the clock already. We're going back to my townhouse to start going through all this stuff."

"Now?"

"Of course now. All night, if we have to. Your lazy life as a reporter is over. I have a spare room you can crash in."

I told her I needed to pack a few things and tell Jane I was diving into the new case and would be working full bore. Amy gave me two hours to prepare and the address of her Greenwich Village townhouse. It seemed like everybody in New York had a townhouse except me. I walked quickly, looking for a cab, but everybody wanted cabs at lunchtime. You could only get a cab in Manhattan when no one else wanted one—including you. I jogged into the park and ran faster, my backpack bouncing rhythmically. By the time I neared Jane's block, I was sweaty but feeling good from the run.

I stopped in my tracks when I looked toward Jane's townhouse and spotted a dipshit black leather hat—wearing shades.

17

This was annoying. The mafia junior varsity squad was back. Blocking my path. I ducked into the Smart Bean Espresso House and watched the four of them for a few minutes. They had split up into two pairs to cover both ends of the street. It was very suspicious. Maybe I should just wait until one of the rich old ladies on the street called the cops? No. Following me around badly was one thing, staking out Jane's place was another. The good news was the opposition had divided their forces without knowing the disposition of their enemy. Overconfidence was an edge.

Siri, should I run or should I fight?"

"I can't answer that for you," she replied.

I removed my black Kevlar gun gloves from my backpack, the ones I had used for years, and slipped them on. They protected the hands from sharp knives, hot weapons, cold winters and, of course, the heartbreak of psoriasis. I said hi to Amber, one of the baristas behind the counter, and asked her if she would mind watching my bag for a few minutes. As I walked out the door, I noticed the music playing was the Rolling Stones, "Street Fighting Man."

I started breaking the problem down in my head into small, doable tasks. I had no real plan, just a series of goals.

I kept my head low, humming the song softly. I walked up right behind the hat guy, Jay-Jay, and one of his troops.

"Yo! Jay-Jay!" I shouted. "Wait up! How's it hanging, bro?"

To say they were very surprised by my appearance and first-name greeting doesn't really capture the beauty of the moment.

"Fuck is this?" Jay-Jay demanded, as if it was his underling's fault.

"Hey! Jay-Jay! It's him!" the guy said, unnecessarily.

"Fuck you think you doin'?" Jay-Jay demanded, puffing his chest, clenching his fists.

"Playing hide and seek. I won. Your turn. Go hide."

He was genuinely confused but I needed him to move on. I had an appointment.

"So, Jay-Jay, buddy, who asked you to follow me?"

"We ain't following nobody. Fuck you talkin' 'bout?"

"You were following me in the park. Now you're waiting for me. I don't want any problems. Please go away, guys. *I* have a job. I'm busy."

"You don't give orders, fuckhead!" Jay-Jay warned.

"I just did. I asked nicely. *Please* fuck off."

"This place is as good as any, Jay-Jay," said his underling. "Let's tune him up now and be done with it."

"I'm sorry," I said. "You aren't just following me? You have orders to kick my ass?"

"That's right, asshole," Vinnie, Tony or Bobby said.

Okay. Time to move. I could sense the other two mutts jogging in our direction. They looked like boxing assholes who thought you threw one punch at a time, backed up and waited to see what happened, instead of hitting hard and fast as many times as humanly possible.

"The message is you were warned, asshole," Jay-Jay said in a tough voice. "You're catching a beating, 'cause you—"

I flew at Jay-Jay and punched him hard in the throat with my left hand, pulling the punch halfway, so it didn't crush his windpipe, just popped it. At the same time, I hooked five or six fast shots with both fists to his solar plexus, leaning my weight into them. He went down on his knees, gagging and gasping, and twisted onto the pavement in a fetal position and vomited. His fancy hat rolled into the gutter, his hip shades spinning away.

I kept his body between me and the approaching pair, who were close. I spun toward the nearest clown. He had focused his attention on his fallen boss, as I hoped he would. But he saw me, turned, and cocked one of his huge biceps, his left, which was lucky. I pivoted and kicked through hard—into his exposed armpit, a solid hit with the flat of my boot. He staggered back, off balance, his big punch un-thrown, his face showing pain, a hurt look in his eyes that said he felt my armpit kick was unfair.

I didn't wait to see if Number Two was still up. I instantly hopped up and around, one hundred eighty degrees, toward the other two. They advanced side by side, their fists up. I only had one more piece of intelligence to try to rattle them.

"Heeeeey! Tony, Vinnie, Bobby! What's the problem?" I asked.

It broke their rhythm, slightly.

"Fuck you know our names?" one asked.

I reversed, then forward fast, skipping to my right. I jumped into the air and landed with a straight leg onto Number Three's outside knee. It snapped away like a dry log and he went down. I only got one hard shot at his head before staggering away to stay on my feet, keeping the downed guy between me and Number Four, not knowing where Number Two was.

"MOTHERFUCKER!" Number Four roared, charging, his porky paws reaching for my throat.

I put my chin down and my hands up in a hold-it gesture, but quickly slapped my flat palms together as hard as I could—his head in between. They made a sound like bubblewrap popping. His hands, almost on my throat, reflexively jerked back to his ears. He began to scream, his eyes wide. Before he could take another breath to scream some more, I elbowed him at the base of his nose, knocking his head back. Then I clubbed him with fists to either side of his head until he went down.

An arm went around my throat in a chokehold. Number Two, grunting at my back. I stomped on his right instep to give him something to think about, and reached around with both of my hands to grab his fist atop my left shoulder. With my left hand I uncurled his fingers and, with my right, grabbed his thumb. He fought back, making a nice lock for me but did not let go of my neck. I couldn't breathe. I yanked as hard as I could on his thumb, feeling it snap. He yelped and let me go. I turned to face him, doing a quick survey. No one else up but Number Two. He put up his fists, pretending his left still worked. I stepped to my right, away from the good arm. He made a grab for me with his left arm but it was slow and looked very painful after the armpit smash. I raised my arms, waving my hands above my head. His eyes followed them up, like I was going to magically produce a weapon. Presto! I hooked his left ankle with my left ankle and slid it out from under him, giving him a helpful shove on the way down. He landed loudly on the other knee and rolled over onto his right side. I drop-kicked him in the left, bouncing off him like a grunting inner tube, breaking a few ribs. He stayed down. I spun around, ready.

All four down. I caught a few good breaths. Flexed my gloved fists.

Jay-Jay was still in fetal pose on the concrete; coughing, winded.

Number Two was on his right side on the sidewalk, moaning.

Number Three was sprawled on the pavement, hissing and cursing, holding his broken left knee with both hands.

Number Four, broken nose, punctured eardrums, was flat on his back, out cold.

My knees and elbows were scraped. I had blood on my body and face—some of it may be mine. I was wired, pumped high. I still loved it. I looked around. We had gathered a crowd. Half of them had their cellphones up. Sirens were getting closer.

Shit.

I couldn't split and deny I was in this mess, if it was already on YouTube. Now that the thugs were down, the audience inched closer. I peeled off my tight Kevlar gloves and stuck them into my pocket. My hands were a bit sweaty but unmarked. No cuts, no broken knuckles. Not even a bruise.

"Man, you trashed four big lunks—how'd you do that?" a black guy in a suit, still filming on his phone, asked me from a safe distance.

"Special effects," I explained.

18

I tried something new. I told the cops the truth.

It didn't work.

I knew it wasn't going well when the female cop kept calling me "the alleged victim," while watching paramedics load my new acquaintances into ambulances. Jay-Jay was vowing to kill me in a raspy whisper, which is all you can manage for a while after someone has compressed your airway.

I explained to the cop several times that I didn't have any accomplices and that the four guys had been following me, the innocent victim. I asked them nicely to leave me alone but they wouldn't.

"They announced their intention to beat me up," I explained to the NYPD officer. "It was self-defense."

"Okay, so they attacked you first?" she asked. "All four of them?"

This was the tricky part.

"Well, they told me they were going to 'tune me up,' and I was going to get a beating," I said.

"And then they assaulted you first?" the cop asked.

"More or less," I shrugged. "They all engaged."

"Yes or no?" the cop said.

I knew if I said I threw the first punch, I might have a

problem—so I didn't want to say it. That was when the helpful black guy in the suit came over and told the cop he had the whole thing on video.

"You witnessed this?" the officer asked him. "What's your name?"

"George Casey," he told her, holding his phone up. George congratulated me like I had won a cage match and shook my hand. My new fan showed the cop the whole video, doing a Bob Costas play-by-play—in case the officer had failed her eye exam. I also watched.

"See, here is the guy with the hat, threatening him, yelling at him, with the other guy getting ready and then, before they can crush him—boom!—he goes at the hat guy." I became aware of others crowding around us, also looking at the screen action. "Look at this—he does a karate kick to the second guy—in the friggin' armpit! It stopped him dead in his tracks. Really cool!"

It was always nice to get good reviews.

"Holy shit!" the cop said.

"Look, here he breaks the guy's thumb and puts him down hard. Watch this part! He fuckin' does a knee-drop on him! This guy is, like, a pro, man."

"Looks like it. I'll need a copy of that, sir," the cop said. "So... Mr...."

"Shepherd."

"Yes, Mr. Shepherd. You attacked these men first?"

"Technically, maybe. Just before they attacked me."

"That is not self-defense," she said. "And... I see you're wearing some kind of gloves in the video. Where are they? Did you put them on before the fight?"

"Look, if I'd waited until they made their move, I'd be the one in an ambulance right now. I have... experience with this kind of thing."

"Where?" she asked.

"In the service," Detective Lieutenant Izzy Negron answered

her in his usual sarcastic tone. "He's a super soldier and a star reporter. He was a commando. Also thinks he's Mad Max."

I was about to correct Izzy and tell him we didn't call ourselves commandos. COs. Combat Operators. Operators. Mark Ones. I let it go.

Izzy and I did say we would see each other soon. Izzy, about five foot ten, fifty years old, wiry, his jet-black hair combed straight back, was his usual suave self. He looked like a corporate lawyer in a dark navy Brooks Brothers suit, teal dress shirt and mauve silk tie.

Behind him was Detective Sergeant Phil D'Amico, younger, taller, sandy hair, about six foot four, pumped. Phil's fashion sense was strictly off-the-rack Macy's Men's Store, with charcoal-gray slacks, navy blazer with gold buttons, blue shirt, and blue rep tie, looking like a high-school football coach forced to dress up for a sports dinner.

"Lieutenant, he can't go around beating people up," the cop told Izzy.

"If Shepherd says he acted in self-defense, I believe it," Izzy told her. "We'll take it from here, officer."

"The alleged victims are, so far, refusing to file charges," she said. "Why would Major Case Squad care about a possible assault, or maybe a possible nothing?"

"Because the moron with the hat is Jay-Jay Potsoli."

"Oh," the cop replied.

"Who's that?" I asked.

"The grandson of dead mafia don Paulie Potsoli and the son of Faith Potsoli, a best-selling author who also writes a column for the *New York Mail*."

"Really?" I asked.

"Shepherd, why is a halfwit hoodlum prince from Brooklyn trying to put the hurt on you?" Izzy asked.

"I don't know," I answered. "He was about to tell me but I didn't let him finish."

"That was rude," said Phil.

"I had to move fast. He did say I was warned."

"Warned by whom? About what?"

"Didn't get that to that part. I only know of two people who have threatened me recently."

"Only two?" Izzy asked.

"Other than us?" Phil interjected.

"You know them both," I told them.

They both knew that my former editor at the *New York Mail*, Tal "Lucky" Edgar, had threatened to have me killed—but he was helpfully dead. Of course, his billionaire boss, who also probably wanted me killed, was alive and kicking.

"Who else?" Izzy asked.

"Ginny Mac. She told me not to beat her on the Hardstein story but I just did."

"So you suspect a billionaire or your former girlfriend of hiring these junior wiseguy ginzoes to stomp you?" Phil asked.

"I have no idea," I told them. "Both people are connected to the *New York Mail* but maybe it's somebody else. Can I go, guys? I have some work to do."

"What's with the gloves?" Phil asked.

"My old gun gloves. Kevlar."

"Like in our vests?" Izzy asked.

"Yeah but the gloves aren't really bulletproof."

"We call them tactical gloves," said Phil.

"I'm going to charge these thugs with attempted assault," said Izzy.

"That won't stick," Phil pointed out. "Shepherd kicked the shit out of them. And there's video to prove it. Any jury would laugh and set them free."

"I know," Izzy said, "But it also shows them *trying* to kick his ass. This way the charges will be dropped if they agree not to sue."

"Thanks, Izzy," I said. "I appreciate that. You guys want coffee? I left my bag in the Smart Bean so my laptop wouldn't get trashed."

"You knew in advance you were going to take them on," Izzy said. "You had time to put on your fancy kick-ass gloves. It was premeditated. *Meshugga*."

Even I, an out-of-towner, knew the Yiddish word for crazy.

"I knew it was possible, sure, but I was pissed they were at Jane's house," I told them.

"Four to one. Why the hell would you risk that?" Phil asked. "They could have ruined your year. Why not just wait them out or call 911?"

"Where's the fun in that?"

19

Jane was not happy to hear about my fight when I stopped by the Arthur Animal Hospital to explain. I told her it wasn't my fault but she didn't agree.

"You should have called the cops, not taken on some gang," she said.

"Maybe you're right."

"*Maybe*?"

"I'm used to doing things differently," I said lamely. "Hey, I'm fine."

"Fine? Really? You started some kind of blood feud with mobsters on my doorstep and you think you're fine?"

I had no magic gloves for this fight. We had been living day-to-day, not talking about where we were going, just letting it happen. She never asked me to move in with her. Neither did I but that's what had happened.

"Jane, I'm sorry."

"Shepherd, you know I lost... I don't like drama."

Jane had been badly burned by her marriage, a match she thought was perfect, until her lawyer husband Burt dropped dead. Four of his secret girlfriends appeared at his funeral—including his secretary and a neighbor. The grieving girlfriends felt compelled to confess to the freaked-out widow, so *they* could feel better. Once the girlfriends found out about each other, the after-funeral became a hate-the-deceased party. Jane was not interested in marriage again and was especially gun-shy after she found out Ginny Mac and I had a brief thing.

"I'm not causing the drama, Jane," I protested. "Ginny Mac may be the one behind Jay-Jay's interest in me."

"She would send killers after you—over a newspaper story?"

"Maybe. But just to beat me up—not kill me," I said, hoping it was true.

"She is insane," Jane concluded.

"I agree."

I didn't mention the other possibility—that a mob queen columnist for my former newspaper and her thug son were seeking stronger revenge against me at the behest of my least favorite billionaire.

"So, what's your excuse?" Jane demanded. "I know you're not stupid, Shepherd. Please tell me you are not some weird adrenaline junkie who never saw a risk he didn't dig?"

I couldn't tell her that. But I tried, without actually lying. I reminded her I had sworn off guns, without admitting she had hit a bull's eye.

"So, I'm supposed to be thankful you only get into fist fights now—not gun battles? Shepherd, I... I like you. I couldn't take it, if... I don't want you to die."

"Again, I agree."

I told her I might have to spend a few nights at my new boss's place to bear down on the new case. I thought I detected a glimmer of doubt, as if Jane was wondering if I was fooling around with Amy. She didn't say anything, but she seemed secretly relieved that I would be out of her house for a while. That made me sad. I had zero experience with long-term relationships. I was making this up as I went along.

I took Skippy—who had been hanging out at the animal

hospital—back to Jane's place with me and put a few things in a bag. On the way over to Amy Massi's Skippy pulled me along at a brisk pace. I couldn't get a cabbie to allow Skippy inside, so the two of us jogged downtown.

Amy's townhouse, in Greenwich Village, was like an upscale sorority house the day before final exams. People were coming and going up the steps and through the cut glass and wooden doors. There was no sign that this was a private detective business. The place was decorated like a magazine home, with blue and red walls and theme rooms, micro spotlights highlighting paintings and sculptures. On the first floor, women and men were working on computers and phones in various rooms. Others were moving from room to room. There seemed to be one of every kind of person: all colors, ages and clothing styles.

I heard high-pitched barking approaching, with a skittering, claw-on-wood noise. The meeting between Skippy and Dr. Strangelove was like a buddy movie—they became instant pals. The genetically engineered, fuzzy mixed-breed scampered about playfully as the much larger Skippy joined in the fun, moving slower to cover the same ground. Amy appeared, looked down at Skippy, and patted his head. We left the dogs to romp and she led me to her office. It was an impressive antique wood study from the Victorian era, complete with ancient desk, dark leather chairs, couch and dark wooden walls of bookcases. Photos everywhere featured Amy with movie stars, TV stars, rock stars, presidents, alive and dead. She looked different in each photo, a chameleon's vanity wall. This was the impress-the-client room, no doubt. I was impressed. There were also photos of people I didn't recognize, but I knew they were all Amy. The superhero's den, complete with shots of her secret identities.

"I hear you kicked the shit out of that natty Mafia kid and his goons," Amy said. "That was a stupid thing to do. I need you in one piece."

"How did you hear about that?" I asked her.

"You're trending on Twitter and Google," she told me, laughing. "Congratulations."

"You're kidding me?"

"Some undercover you are."

She took her iPad from her desk and showed me the *New York Mail* website.

MOB WAR?
Exclusive! Bad Boy Reporter in Battle with Wiseguys.
By VIRGINIA McELHONE
EXCLUSIVE VIDEO!

Her story implied—without actually libeling me—that a reporter for a competing newspaper was some kind of crook, and that the whole thing might have been faked.

Wonderful. I grabbed my phone. There were long lists of missed calls, emails and voicemails from Mel, from Ginny Mac, and from Jane. Oops. Looks like the witness, George, sold his video to Ginny. Mel would not be happy. I opened an email from my boss. After a lot of threats and mock-cursing, he wrote that the *Daily Press* had also purchased the fight video. I was a hero on our website but he was not happy with me. My phone logs also showed calls from TV and radio reporters.

"Can we get to work or do you need to contact the World Wrestling Federation?" Amy asked.

"Only if they pay more than you do."

20

My cellphone buzzed. I was receiving emails from Speaker Chesterfield's aide, Tiffany Mauser. I told Amy and she set us up in a small room with a desktop computer, a phone, a printer, and TV and police scanners.

I opened the first email from Mauser, expecting top-secret information, and was surprised to see a compilation of emails, newspaper articles and video clips. They only rated a low RESTRICTED classification. Open source chicken feed. At the top was a memo from the Executive Protection Service, stating the nature, volume and sources of the threats against Chesterfield, seeking input. It went to the usual agencies: FBI, OHS, CIA, and the rest. The articles and video clips on the Usual Suspects included GOP-slanted TV talk shows, with guests like conservative cutie Miranda Dodge and her blogger buddy Clayton Littleton. There were also KKK Klansmen, Nazis, white supremacists, Neo-Confederate cowboys, secessionists, Tea Party protesters, armed militia members, and Libertarian loons. There were no threats from Democrats. Three suspects were Republican office-holders, who were also delegates to the convention, including Dodge, who was also running for president, even though Chesterfield had the nomination sewed up.

The next email had a higher security classification and featured more memos, web videos, video blogs, blog posts and even pay-per-view hate sessions for dial-your-enemy. Again, Miranda Dodge and Clayton Littleton were the superstars.

The third email had the meat and was classified as DELTA S.C.I. DO NOT OPEN. I couldn't open it. When I tried, my computer threatened me with federal prison.

I emailed Miss Mauser, who sent me a link to a familiar secret Intranet web—the one the public never saw. It was a clone of America Online, but for spies and the military. About a million people with top-secret clearance logged on every day.

I clicked on the link. My specific file was embedded into the familiar US government website homepage. I took a quick look at what the secret world was up to today. The main website photo was of Special Forces troops in Saharan Africa, assisting local governments in their anti-terror campaign. ISIS insanity took up the usual amount of space. The other big story was a terror alert in Sudan and Mali. Pakistan was also expecting a big Taliban summer push in Waziristan.

I clicked on my enabled link and found a list of surveillance reports, transcripts, audio and video recordings. More than a hundred. I opened an audio file marked OPGUNSMOKE/audio.newyork.88.

I chuckled. The feds picked the perfect name for their investigation, Operation Gunsmoke. Chesterfield carried a gun and smoked like a chimney. I clicked play. A SIGINT logo and phone digits marked the file as a telephone intercept. I instantly recognized the snarky, sexy voice of Miranda Dodge. She was talking about Chesterfield to a man with a southern accent. I realized she was talking to Clayton Littleton, who was obviously dying to get into her pants suit.

"Someone should SAM that friggin' asshole and make things easier for all of us," Dodge said. "If he were out of the picture, we could make it this time around."

Sam? Oh, I get it. Second Amendment Measures. Code for plugging someone. Cute. I'll bet Dodge winked when she said it.

"Damn right, little lady. I talk about that every day. The thing of it is, he's got a better ring around him than the Gorilla-in-Chief."

They both laughed at the racist slur at the black president.

"You should be in the White House," Littleton said.

"Then it will be the *White* House again," Dodge sniggered.

I paused the recording. The FBI was running Operation Gunsmoke and had a warrant to bug an ex-governor, who was also a FAX TV millionaire commentator—and her friend, a rich right-wing blogger who dressed in green camouflage in Manhattan. A federal judge had obviously signed off on the warrant. That meant the politician and the political entrepreneur were suspects in the plot or plots to kill Chesterfield. That fact, not to mention what was on the tape, was more than gunsmoke. It was bombsmoke, a hell of a story. But these guys were the obvious suspects. What were the chances these two creeps were actually plotting to bump off a congressman so one of them could get a shot at 1600 Pennsylvania Avenue?

Dr. Strangelove and his new pal skittered into the room and distracted me. Skippy had his leash in his mouth, asking for a walk. It was an offer I couldn't refuse.

21

Skippy pulled me around Washington Square Park for a while, past chess players and street musicians, as I filled Amy and Dr. Strangelove in on what I had learned. We grabbed hot dogs with mustard from a food cart, which made the animals crazy. I bought two more dogs and gave them to Skippy and DSL. When we returned, I went back to my work in my small room.

There were more recordings of ex-governor Dodge and her buddy Littleton on the phone and even a live link—the FBI apparently had up-and-running coverage. I clicked on that but I did not have the proper clearance. There were also dozens of other suspects, all either right-wing nuts, private armies, racist gun groups, and various militias who wanted to secede from the United States and set up religious-military utopias out in the desert. Three unnamed members of Congress were also mentioned as making apparently threatening statements toward Chesterfield. Too many suspects.

I went back to the Dodge-Littleton recordings and found an interesting one. Littleton was on the phone and told someone that he was coming to New York from his native Idaho for the GOP convention in New York.

"I'm gonna bring my Second Amendment Measures to Jew York but I will be flying in, so I need some ordnance on the ground when I arrive," Littleton said. "Or else I'll be naked."

"Not a problem, brother," a gruff male voice assured him. "Whatever you need. Long or short, semi or full—you got it."

An FBI memo did not identify the mysterious second man but said his phone was a throwaway rental cellphone sold in Brooklyn.

Another FBI memo said an informant alerted them that a Brooklyn cell of the Aryan Purity Nation was preparing for some kind of operation in New York in the near future that involved weapons. The agents could not yet link Littleton's guy to the APN group. If these various plots were linked, it would be bad. The armed-and-dangerous, don't-tread-on-me guys wanted Chesterfield out of the picture for reopening the government and for *not* causing a national economic catastrophe. One very scary anonymous posting on a secessionist billboard called "New Minutemen" read: "We will follow the traitors to the den of sin—New York—to take Second Amendment Measures. We are the New Minutemen. The traitors to Liberty cannot hide from us. First we will strike at the treasonous deal-makers who do the bidding of the Tyrant. Then the Tyrant will fall…"

It was like a letter from John Wilkes Booth before he shot Lincoln. I had a bad feeling about it but I couldn't hard-connect the dots. It seemed Speaker Chesterfield had recently voted for a weak, virtually meaningless gun control measure. That bill was introduced after yet another school massacre—domestic terrorism that Congress refused to do anything about. The legislation was really only window dressing because even the mass murder of children was not allowed to interfere with the business of selling guns and ammo.

One online threat by the New Minutemen said Chesterfield "had fired a shot at our sacred gun rights but Chesterfield and his underlings will discover that the New Minutemen, a well-regulated militia, will defend our birthright to the death."

Why couldn't these idiots just get drunk, murder some helpless deer, and leave the rest of us alone? I noticed that most of these brave warriors stayed safe at home, spent a lot of time at gun ranges and threatened to shoot unarmed people who disagreed with them.

I showed Amy what I had found. She whistled when she heard the recordings of Dodge and Littleton. She asked me for my opinion.

"If two or three of these components are connected, we have a very serious, credible threat. If not, it's still hairy. I would recommend Chesterfield not show a hair in public until the FBI can nail these people down."

"Wait for the FBI? You've got to be kidding? It'll take them a year, minimum. Shepherd, we were not hired for an opinion. We were hired to find out who might be planning to harm Chesterfield—and put them out of business, ASAP. Clear?"

"Okay. The feds identified half of the speakers on FAX TV as possible suspects. I think it's bullshit but we could start there. The problem is, if we question them openly, they'll put it on the air before we can leave the building. It will be a public relations gift to them and to Dodge."

"Yeah, I can hear it now," Amy said. "The president declares war on patriotic Americans."

I told Amy the feds didn't know who the New Minutemen were but they had an informant inside another group, the Aryan Purity Nation cell, the APN.

"That tactical intelligence, about money and weapons, looked like the real deal to me."

"How do we know that for sure?" she asked.

"Only one way to find out—kick in the door and see what you get. At least half of the intelligence I got in the field was bullshit—wrong, too old or disinformation. That APN tip sounded real to me. I need a name and an address in Brooklyn to check it out. I'll start with Chesterfield's people."

"What should we tell Chesterfield?" Amy asked.

"No public appearances, a tightening of security and a roundup of bad guys."

"Okay," Amy agreed. "Tell them and see if you can get an address for that group. Meanwhile, I'm going to meet a source of mine, face to face. He may have something."

I made the call. Tiffany Mauser told me to come right over.

"The same conference room," Mauser said. "Just the two of you."

"Just me. Amy is meeting a source."

"Oh. Okay, fine," Mauser said, before hanging up.

"Okay," Amy said to me. "You go. Do you have any sources in the FBI?"

"No," I told her. "But I know someone in the US Attorney's office, which might be even better. I'll try."

I made the call and left a message on Mary Catherine's cellphone. I didn't mention my name or what I wanted.

"Hi, it's me. Call me."

I told Amy that if my US Attorney friend couldn't help, we might try doing a story in the paper to shake something loose.

"We'll see," Amy said. "What if it really is Dodge and her fan club?"

"Then it will be one hell of a story."

22

The taxi's TV screen, mounted on the barrier between the front and back seats, featured a public service announcement by the billionaire mayor—an appeal for everyone to stop chewing gum—because discarded gum was a nuisance that got under your shoes and made a mess of the sidewalks. The driver, sporting the floppy homespun headgear favored by Tajik tribesmen in northern Afghanistan, muttered to himself in his native tongue—wondering if the mayor's father had perhaps urinated up the mayor's mother's birth canal. I laughed at his crude joke, which caused him to shoot me a look of surprise. I responded in his language that it was unlikely—because that would require an erection. We both laughed. When we arrived at the police barricades outside the Knickerbocker Convention Center, he parked the vehicle and turned to examine me.

"Ranger?" he asked, the leathery gray skin around his eyes tightening.

I shrugged.

"You will go back?"

"No, my friend. I'm home and I'm done with guns. Forever."

He laughed. "So are we all—God willing."

At the barrier, I showed my Working Press Card to the cops. A chanting crowd of anti-Tea Party demonstrators, in their own barricaded enclosure, were waving well-printed protest signs: FACTS DON'T LIE—BUT REPUBLICANS DO! and HOW MANY CHILDREN HAVE TO DIE? Safely across the street, the Tea Party group shouted and waved signs back: TAXED ENOUGH ALREADY! and TAKE OUR COUNTRY BACK FROM FOREIGNERS!

Fire trucks were in front of the Jurassic Parking entrance to the Knickerbocker. I went through security, past the dinosaurs, up the wide jungle escalator toward the mezzanine level. It was more crowded than my first visit. As I stepped off the escalator I saw people sporting red, white and blue three-cornered hats, black Abe Lincoln stovepipe hats, and Uncle Sam toppers. The delegates had arrived, all wearing big red DELEGATE ribbons on their chests, along with big bright buttons that read CHESTERFIELD or DODGE and whoever.

I spotted a man with a weapon and tensed. It was a black AR-15 assault rifle with telescoping stock and telescopic sight, slung over one of the Abe Lincoln's shoulders as he walked by, thumbing his phone. I moved sideways, ready to run, grabbing my backpack by one shoulder strap. Why I did that, I don't know. With my laptop and a water bottle, there was nothing in there that would stop a .223 round. The rifleman kept walking, ignoring me. I scanned around for other exits and realized Abe wasn't the only one toting an assault rifle.

They all were. Hundreds of them.

Every jaunty Abe Lincoln, every goofy Tea Party guy with a tri-corner cap, every scary Uncle Sam, had a shooter. All of them were packing automatic weapons; more AR-15s, some Heckler & Koch assault rifles, Brownings, bolt-action hunting rifles, some AK-47s, and other trendy fire-sticks slung from fancy underarm shoulder rigs or strapped across their backs. They weren't pointing the weapons at anyone, just toting the deadly machine guns around like fashion accessories. It was like hillbilly Disneyland. Looking closer, I noticed several of the heavily armed lunatics also had large buttons: CARRY PROUD, ALWAYS READY TO DEFEND FREEDOM, USE IT OR LOSE IT, and SAM—SECOND AMENDMENT REMEDY.

I watched the half-assed army parade back and forth for a few minutes and then spoke to one of the delegate gunsels, a short guy in a suit, with fuzzy hair and wire-rimmed glasses, who was packing a black Uzi.

"Excuse me. Why are you all carrying rifles?"

"This is an Open Carry convention, son," he said with a loopy grin. "We're making history. We are here to protect the Second Amendment."

I thanked him and dialed Amy.

"Amy? Shepherd. You will not believe what I am looking at."

I described the scene to her. She cursed and laughed.

"Really? All of them are carrying pop guns?"

"Everyone I've seen so far. Magazines in, ready to rock. Anyone with a delegate badge has a banger."

"Wow. Wait, I'm Googling it. Hold on… here it is. Looks like the gun nuts announced they were going to carry weapons at the convention. There was some arguing about it… but after a poll showed that most Christian Tea Party voters thought that walking around with guns was sexy, the sensible Republicans caved in to the National Rifle Association crowd and announced it would be an Open Carry convention. The first."

"Great," I said.

"So, according to the gun lobby, this will be the safest convention ever."

"Amy. These clowns are armed to the teeth. That's what they look like. Clowns with semi-automatic weapons."

I told her I had to change our report, to make it more extreme.

"Okay, Shepherd. I hope you're right."

"If I am, and Chesterfield does what we tell him to do, we'll probably never be able to prove if I was right or wrong."

"And if he *doesn't* do what we tell him to do and nothing happens, we look like panicky pussies."

"Maybe. But, on the other hand, if he ignores us and somebody wastes him, we look great."

"Sometimes, Shepherd, I can't tell when you're kidding."

"Yeah, me too."

23

I found Tiffany Mauser waiting alone in the huge conference room overlooking the Hudson and the naval destroyer. Tiffany looked shipshape, in another tight business-style suit jacket. Except, where a man would have a shirt and tie, she had only a half-shirt of white lace, exposing enough cleavage so no one would mistake her for a man from any distance. Instead of pants, she wore a short matching skirt that showed leg from mid thigh down to her black stiletto heels. Her blonde hair was in a ponytail, with a puffy gather.

I started to say hello but she coldly cut the greeting short and ushered me through the southern door, past guards to an elevator, and took me up to the fourteenth floor. We got to a door and she opened it with a white electronic key card. It turned out to be her hotel suite, which had the main room set up as a living room, with a separate office and Hudson River views. There was also a kitchen area and an open door to a bedroom. The room probably cost $2,000 a day. Tiffany took two glasses from the kitchen and handed me one. It was half-filled with chilled arak. She had one also and took a slug, like she did it every day. She coughed.

"Does everybody say it tastes like candy gasoline?" she asked.

"Everybody says that the first time. Until they realize that's a good thing."

"I'm not there yet but I'll try anything once," Tiffany said in her sexy southern drawl, plopping onto the couch.

"Never do anything for the first time," I warned her.

"What?"

"Nothing. Just something we used to say."

"You mean I should listen to someone who's been there before?"

I smiled back and raised my glass, wondering where she heard what I drink.

"Okay, Shepherd. Shoot. What do you want to tell us?"

"I was all set to give one set of recommendations until I got to this clown convention. Now I have to add more suggestions. If you don't adopt them, I have one final suggestion."

"Hmmmm." Tiffany smiled. "Mysterious."

"Not at all. Which do you want—short or long version?"

She smiled again. "I prefer long," she drawled in a wicked voice. "I've got time."

"Okay," I said, ignoring her flirty tone. "Our first idea was we think the Speaker should not wander around in public unless and until we can nail these threats down. Also, you should take down any bad guys you can. Now."

"So you are taking this seriously?"

"Yes. Very."

"Really? How long have you been a private detective?"

"This is my second day."

"As you can see, the speaker has *very* heavy security."

"All of that means nothing the second he steps out in public."

"Why?"

"Because of equipment like the Barrett M107 sniper rifle and many other weapons that could take a person out from a long distance. All they need is a line of sight and one shot."

"From how far away?"

"A mile. Two, maybe."

"Chance of success?"

"Assuming a professional team? Highly probable. No warning, no sound. The bullet arrives before the sound of the shot. Nothing left but bloody shreds of laundry in the breeze."

She winced and took another drink. So did I.

"You've seen this kind of thing firsthand?" she asked.

"Yes, ma'am."

"We would have to cancel a series of planned events," she snipped. "One with the mayor, a few with local congressmen. It wouldn't look good."

"Him getting shot to death on camera would probably look worse."

"Okay, so, for now, you are recommending that he not appear in public at all?"

"Or in front of any uncovered windows, like that one in the conference room downstairs. That is a gift to a sniper team. Or two or three RPGs from a truck bed—it would be more messy but would also do the trick nicely."

"RPGs?"

"Rocket-propelled grenades. Better than hand grenades. Best infantry weapon ever invented."

"Oh. Those bazooka things? So, you're saying the best security in the country is not good enough?"

"About the window? Yeah, definitely. Glass is not security, it's an invitation."

"What if it's bulletproof?"

"No such thing. At least not yet available. Besides, they can use a bomb. By the way, the cops downstairs are not scouting and searching traffic for two blocks in all directions outside the barriers."

"Why should they?"

"Two words. Truck bomb."

"Okay, which threat are you most worried about?"

"I think it's weird that three members of Congress are suspects in this investigation and two other people in your boss's party are talking openly on TV about popping him. It has a familiar ring to me. According to the FBI intercepts and intelligence you gave us, that TV blogger is arranging for illegal weapons here in New York. Pick him up. Arrange for a 'routine' stop, in which he gets busted. The most credible threat looks like the Brooklyn cell, the APN—the Aryan Power Nation group—with the undercover in place. Sounds like those boys want to make news. Put them in jail first. Today. The New Minutemen online make me very nervous but we have no info on who or where they are. They have to be found because right now we cannot assess whether they are a dedicated group or one blogging schmuck and his hamster. The question is whether any of these three groups are linked. Until we nail that down, fresh air is poison."

"You mean outside of the security zone here at the convention center?"

"Exactly."

"Shoot!" she said, gulping the rest of her drink. "I thought this was mostly a political problem. I thought we might find... other uses for some of that stuff."

"What did you think?" I asked her. "That I'd read that racist transcript of Governor Dodge and her buddy Littleton and just put it into the *Daily Press* to embarrass your opponents?"

"The thought had popped into my head," she said, with a sly smile. "That's still an option."

"I think that would be a major mistake, Tiffany, but I leave the *politics* up to you."

She laughed. It was a hell of a laugh.

"What's so funny?" I asked.

"You say the word 'politics' like it's a disease."

"More fatal than most," I told her.

"So, that's it?"

"No," I said. "I told you everything changed when I got here."

"What?"

"Haven't you noticed that every delegate in this hotel is carrying a loaded assault rifle?"

"Oh, that," Tiffany chuckled. "That's just political theater."

"The props looked real to me. Chesterfield shouldn't be anywhere near these gun fanatics."

"But they are his colleagues in the house and senate, governors, his supporters, his people," she protested.

"At least five of whom are suspects in death threats against him—and who are in this hotel with loaded guns."

"He has to meet with delegates. He can't be seen as fearful. Besides, what are we supposed to do about it?"

"Get the guns out."

"Are you crazy? If the Speaker even suggested that, he would lose the support of…"

"Psychopaths with firearms?"

"I was going to say the NRA, all of the GOP and a lot of voters. It would be political suicide."

"Better than actual suicide," I pointed out. "If he gets up to give a speech before these wingnuts, it would be like talking to an auditorium full of Lee Harvey Oswalds, a convention of killers."

She nodded thoughtfully.

"Okay," I said. "Now that you got the long version—here's the short one. The normal security changes I mentioned, plus no open-carry craziness. The Knickerbocker has to be a gun-free zone. Except for security personnel, of course."

"I agree with you but what if we can't do that?"

"We think he should stay away from the crazy armed people—or leave."

"Are you out of your cotton candy-pickin' brain?"

"I may be the only sane guy in the building," I told her, draining my drink. "Too many ways to die here, Tiffany."

24

A loud, piercing electronic chirping came from the hallway.

"Oh, my lord and savior. Not again," Tiffany groaned.

"Is that the fire alarm?" I asked.

"Yes, of course. This is a no-smoking facility. He keeps setting it off, damn his eyes."

"Chesterfield?"

"Who else? Or one of his other chain-smoking buddies. They've been doing this all day. There are signs all over the place but members of Congress don't think rules apply to them."

"Congressmen think they're above the law? Shocking. They're setting off the smoke detectors in the rooms?" I asked.

"Unfortunately," she said. "Even if you go in the bathroom and turn on the fan. This is the tenth time they've done it. It's a brand-new hotel and all the smoke detectors work perfectly, thank you. The fire marshals are very unhappy. I'm sorry but I've got to deal with this now. You may as well come along."

Tiffany grabbed her bag and walked out the door, stopping on the way to pick up a gold keycard off the kitchen bar. I followed her a few yards to the room next door, as others also converged on the door, including four plainclothes security guys, security chief Karl Bundt, and several hotel employees in maroon and gold uniforms. Tiffany was about to open the door with the gold keycard, when it swung open.

"Sorry, guys," Chesterfield said. "I keep forgetting."

It was obvious he wasn't sorry and had not forgotten. The Speaker was in shirtsleeves, his tie loosened, his fancy pistol on display on his hip. The fire alarm stopped, making it suddenly obvious that we were all talking loudly. Two concierges with brass nameplates that read BRYCE and JONATHAN were assuring Chesterfield that it was okay. The Executive Protection Service security men were talking to two guys in green custodial uniforms and tool belts, one of whom was carrying a step-ladder. Tiffany waded into the fray and gave marching orders to everyone before pulling me inside the room with Chesterfield, security, and the hotel people. It was an even bigger, more luxurious suite than Tiffany's.

"Mr. Speaker, I've informed the EPS agents and the hotel that you cannot use any of the public smoking areas—for security reasons, so adjustments are being made," Tiffany told him. "Meanwhile, Shepherd here can give you and Karl his threat assessment."

Great. I was on my own. I told Chesterfield and his security what I had told Tiffany about unobstructed views and public spaces and rounding up bad guys. They seemed bored— until I mentioned the congressmen with Kalashnikovs and suggested they all surrender their hardware or Chesterfield should steer clear of them—or leave.

Karl just laughed. Chesterfield's eyebrows went up and he took a silent drag on his coffin nail.

"You're joking, right?" Karl asked.

"No, I'm not," I told him. "How can you protect this man in an armed camp, where you are completely outgunned?"

"We've got this," Karl protested. "The gun-carrying thing is just a political stunt."

"Yeah, but with real bullets," I said, staring directly at Chesterfield. "Some of those people are saying the Speaker should be shot—and they're roaming the halls with loaded weapons. You're going to make a speech to a convention hall filled with these people, all locked and loaded. Nothing personal, Karl, but you've got shit. No one could protect this man under these conditions. Change the conditions or go somewhere else."

"Fuck you!" Karl shot back. "I don't need some amateur telling me my job."

"Actually, I've done this sort of thing before," I told him. "I never lost anybody yet. Because they listened to me."

Karl's rejoinder was a suggestion that I attempt sexual reproduction with myself.

"Now, fellas," Speaker Chesterfield chuckled. "Let's not get violent. Shepherd, you're serious about this?"

"Yessir."

"You understand that if I suggest disarming my brethren, my enemies will exploit that and I could lose support, and votes, and maybe the election?"

"To win the election, you have to be alive, sir. I'm not suggesting you take their toys away—just that they stop waving them in our faces and creating an impossible security situation," I told him. "I understand you won't address the convention for three days, so you have some time. Have somebody else order the guns out—NYPD, for example. You could even lead the protest against the cops, as long as the guns go back in the closet. Or even the bullets. Otherwise, you are under constant risk. Please consider it."

"Alright, Shepherd, I will," Chesterfield agreed, offering his hand. "I'll sleep on it."

Karl Bundt bristled at being second-guessed by me. When he began to protest that they had it all covered, I just pointed at the big picture window in the living room of the suite, with its lovely view of Manhattan. The window covers, the sheer, translucent one and the heavier blackout curtains, were pulled back to either side. Bundt angrily walked over and pulled the heavy curtains closed.

"I agree with Shepherd's statement," Tiffany said, finally taking a side.

"I thought so," Chesterfield said.

The discussion was over. The handymen disconnected the smoke alarms and left, after the concierges made sure Chesterfield was happy and did not want any more fruit baskets. Bundt took his leave. When it was just Tiffany, Chesterfield and me, the Speaker lit up and took a deep drag. He inhaled a blast of blue smoke toward the smoke alarm on the ceiling. Nothing happened and we all relaxed. Tiffany waved the smoke away with her hand. Chesterfield picked up a cut-crystal glass half-full of ice and Scotch and took a belt. Mr. Alcohol, Tobacco and Firearms.

"That's better," he said. "Good job, kids. I'll text Bob and Abner."

In response to my quizzical look, Tiffany explained that they were at least two other congressional chain-smokers who had been causing the same problems all day by setting off smoke alarms. The handymen would be busy all night.

"Don't start any forest fires," I jokingly warned Chesterfield.

He chuckled. "Your security recommendations have made it possible for me to engage in my nasty habit with impunity in the comfort and safety of my room, Shepherd. I am indebted to you," he said.

"Well, that was not our reason," I smiled. "I'm just trying to keep you alive, sir."

"A noble cause and I thank you."

"You're welcome, sir. Please keep those drapes closed, okay?"

"I will. That would allow me to parade around naked as well."

"A bonus, sir."

"Just kidding. I have some informal meetings tonight and a few ideas on how to make former Governor Dodge go so loco she'll shove her head up her twat and yodel 'Dixie.' I think I'll do all of the meetings here, not downstairs, now that the room has been made safe."

"Whatever you like, Mr. Speaker," Tiffany said. "Security will like that. They can just guard the elevator and stairs and the hallway. I'll inform everyone to come here, instead," she said, her thumbs flying over her iPhone. "Will you need me for those meetings now?"

"Nope. Unless you like Bob pinching your butt when he gets loaded?"

"No thank you, I'll speak to you later. Call if you need me."

"Sure," Chesterfield waved his cigarette. "You two run along."

25

Tiffany went into robot mode for a few minutes at her desk in her suite, as I watched. She made calls, texts, emails. Food arrived at nine. Two steak dinners. She poured more cold arak for us and headed for the door.

"Please wait here. I've got to deal with a minor issue. I'll be back as soon as I can. Please don't let your food get cold."

I ate my steak and mashed potatoes in half an hour, washed down with some more arak. Mary Catherine called me back.

"Shepherd," Mary Catherine groaned. "I was hoping you had lost my number."

"Sorry, I need some help."

"Don't say any more. I'll meet you in the morning. You know where."

She hung up. I dialed Jane. I wanted to tell her it was my birthday. I could hear barking.

"Hi, Jane."

"Hi, Shepherd. I'm really busy tonight. I've got two emergencies and the Catmobile is out on calls."

"You okay?"

"We have to talk," she said. "I think... I think it might not be a bad idea if we... slowed things down for a while."

"What? Okay… What does that mean?"

"I… I'm not sure. A break for a few days, maybe. I can't talk right now. You're going to be at Amy's tonight? Can we talk tomorrow? I have to go."

"Okay, Jane. Wait, I…"

She was gone. Damn. That was the last thing I wanted to hear. I was confused, hurt, pissed off. I reached for my arak. Jane was not the first girlfriend to break up with me by phone or text. It was a tradition. I was with Jane a month and that wasn't even close to the record for short romances. I thought we were different.

Tiffany breezed back in a few minutes later, smelling of cigars and whiskey.

"Sorry it took so long. The head of security had to be stroked but Karl agreed, no more clear windows, no more open air events," she said, triumphantly.

"Good. Okay, thanks for dinner. I'll take off and get back to work."

"No way. We have a lot to arrange. If the Speaker agrees with you and we have to ban the guns, we have to figure a way to have someone else do it, so my boss's fingerprints aren't on it. Just hold on while I change. Be right back," she said, pulling her hair loose so it fell over her shoulders. She left the room and closed the bedroom door. I heard a shower running.

I called Amy and told her that some of our suggestions had already been acted upon but Chesterfield was sleeping on the gun ban request and we were trying to come up with a political cover plan. I also told her about my meeting with Mary Catherine in the morning. Amy told me she was on another line and would see me later.

What was Tiffany doing behind that closed door? Was she hitting on me or was I a male egomaniac? The worst thing I could do now was drink more. I poured another arak and tossed it down easy. Buzzed, I took out my phone.

"What can I help you with, Shepherd?" Siri asked.

"Siri, should I go for it?"

"I'm sure I don't know, Shepherd."

I was sure I detected disapproval in Siri's terse tone.

When Tiffany came out, the stilettos were gone but she stomped me. She was shorter, barefoot, wearing only a giant Chesterfield t-shirt that came to her knees and hung off one shoulder, exposing amazingly smooth, tanned skin. She attacked her rare steak hungrily with knife and fork. Every time she leaned over her plate, I tried not to notice she was completely naked underneath the goddamn shirt. She looked at me and smiled innocently. It blew me away. She took me by the hand and led me to the couch.

"What time is it?" I asked her.

"After midnight," she replied. "Happy Fourth of July."

"It's my birthday," I told her. "I'm thirty today."

I realized I had never told Jane my birthday but here I was, telling a stranger.

"Happy birthday, Shepherd," Tiffany said, moving closer, smelling like flammable candy. "What do you want for your birthday?"

I couldn't think of a single lie and she grinned wider.

"What was that thing you said about never doing anything for the first time?" she whispered, her hand soft on my face.

I had stopped drinking by the time Tiffany made her move but it was too late.

I was fucked.

26

I woke up on my birthday in my birthday suit, to the tune of "Hail to the Chief" playing on Tiffany's phone. She answered the phone and slipped out of bed, striding gloriously nude around the room. Tiffany was something to look at. I was a Yankee Doodle Dandy filled with patriotic lust. This was hands-down the best rebound sex in history.

Then the triple trolls of guilt, fear and doubt arrived with a hangover for me.

What if Jane found out about Tiffany and me? Was Jane done with me for good? Would she take me back if she knew about Tiffany? What if she didn't? Was my new buddy, Percy Chesterfield, also sleeping with Tiffany? Would he still like me if he knew where I had spent last night? Would my new boss, Amy? Would the Speaker agree to banning guns from the convention? I didn't try asking Siri any of the questions. I looked at the bedside clock: 7:02 a.m.

"That was the FBI," Tiffany explained, slipping on her too-big t-shirt. "They and the NYPD raided that Aryan Purity Nation cell in Brooklyn. They got a lot of guns but no bad guys yet. They also picked up Clayton Littleton on a weapons charge." She giggled and turned on the flatscreen wall TV to FAX News. Predictably, there was nothing about

Littleton's arrest on the channel where he was a paid pundit. Tiffany switched to CNN, who were doing the Littleton story big.

BREAKING NEWS! FAX TV FIGURE ARRESTED ON GUN CHARGES.

They reported that Littleton had been busted by the NYPD and the FBI in his Manhattan hotel room. They were assisted by the Bureau of Alcohol, Tobacco, Firearms and Explosives. There was video of a smirking Littleton in handcuffs, outside a police precinct. The station had nothing about the APN raid yet.

"Fast work, Tiffany," I told her.

"Your wish is my command, Shepherd," she said, plopping on the bed and kissing me. She kissed my left temple on my three-scar slash. She pulled back the covers and began planting kisses on my left arm, on the pale spidery scars that wrapped up and down my flesh. When she moved to my legs and kissed the red rippling scars there, I pulled my legs away.

"All better," I said.

"Lord-a-mighty, what happened to you, sugar?" she asked. "The war?"

"Some of it," I admitted.

"And the rest?"

"Flat tire," I told her with a straight face, sitting up. "A blowout."

"I read about that," she said.

"Let's talk about your scar, instead," I countered, licking a small, faint crescent on the side of her right breast. "The war?"

"No," she laughed. "Doubles tennis."

"Why did this happen last night?" I asked.

"Why did what happen?"

"Us. My birthday present."

"Why not?" Tiffany giggled. "You're a tad banged-up, Shepherd, but a certifiable hottie. Maybe it was my patriotic duty. I wanted it, you wanted it. We're not breaking any laws, are we?"

"That simple?" I asked.

"Some of the things we did were not so simple," she laughed.

In the shower, we kept it simple. Breakfast was set up in the living room by the time we were dressed. Tiffany was calling, texting and tweeting as she nibbled on the room-service breakfast spread and flipped through TV channels. I told her she had done a good job, having the Tea Party guy busted. "You slapped Littleton down and he's Governor Dodge's buddy. That was a sharp political move."

"Like you said, you left that part up to me. Just being a good citizen," Tiffany grinned.

"But the APN guys are in the wind. That was the important part," I told her. "We don't want them walking around."

"I know," she said. "The FBI says they've got some hot leads on who and where those guys are."

"In my experience, that's what they say when they've got zip," I replied.

"I hope that's not true."

"I've got to go back to… my office and get back to work," I told her. "Tell me what Chesterfield decides."

I felt vaguely slutty and had a guilty teenage urge to escape the scene of the sex crime.

"You don't have to run off," Tiffany said.

"Actually, I do. I have to meet a source to try and nail down those Aryan Purity Nation guys. It would be a lot easier if you would just get their address from the feds, although it sounds like they scared them off."

"Oh, okay, great. But we'll meet later?"

"Sure, as soon as one of us has something to report."

"That's not what I meant, darlin'."

"Oh, right. Absolutely, Tiffany. Later."

We kissed. For a while. On the way out, I made a guilt call to Jane at home but fortunately she had already gone to work. Or wasn't answering my calls. I tried the animal hospital but she hadn't yet arrived. I called Amy.

"Where the hell have you been, Shepherd? You haven't answered your damn phone."

"The uh… charge ran out and I fell asleep," I lied.

"Where?"

"Where what?"

"Where did you sleep? It wasn't here. I just got back from walking Skippy and Dr. Strangelove. Your bed was not slept in."

"Ahhh… at home," I told her, vaguely.

"At home with Jane or at home in your apartment?" she asked in a much too friendly voice.

Shit.

"Do you already know the answer to that question, Amy?"

"I do," she replied in that same, chipper voice.

"Then why ask me?"

"Educational purposes," she said.

Shit.

"So, you called Jane and my apartment last night?"

"You bet I did. Don't worry, I pretended to be someone else. I told Jane I was someone at your paper. She gave me your cellphone and said you were at my house. When I called your apartment and did the same thing, it was strange. A woman who identified herself as your mother answered."

"Why is that strange?"

"Well, she also gave me your cellphone number but she seemed to think I was someone from the Bureau. She said the FBI was waiting outside your place."

"Oh, yeah. Right. That's probably because of that story

about Hardstein. Nothing to do with our case."

"Oh, okay. So, you're working. Where are you now?"

"Amy, do you know where I am?"

"Well, your GPS is still at the Knickerbocker. I assume you're in the same place. Did you and Tiffany have a pleasant evening?"

"I drank too much. You hacked my phone?"

"It's not really hacking," Amy protested. "I just accessed your GPS locator."

"I'm leaving now," I told her. "I'm back on the job."

"Are you going to meet your fed source?" Amy asked.

"On my way."

"Okay, talk to you soon."

As I went through the Jurassic Parking exit, the loud chants of the dueling demonstrators drowned out the noise of the city traffic, even at that early hour. As I crossed the street amid the shouting voices, I again felt twinges of guilt, the echoes of a distant Catholic childhood. I even imagined I heard my mother's voice calling me. I laughed and walked faster.

"Francis! Francis! Over here!"

I turned toward the voice.

Guilt, hell. It *was* my mother.

27

My parents were holding signs and shouting from the crowd, the anti-Tea Party group, of course. They were in their full civil disobedience outfits: sneakers, jeans, protest t-shirts, swimming goggles and bicycle helmets—in case of tear gas or clubs. Mom was sporting a large CORPORATIONS ARE NOT PEOPLE! sign. Dad held a smaller JAIL THE WALL STREET CRIMINALS placard.

This was my parents' idea of a fun-filled vacation in the Big Apple.

I approached cautiously. A cop told me to move on. I took out my press card, clipped it to my shirt, and he backed off.

"What are you doing here?" my mom asked.

"Working."

"The FBI is looking for you," my father said. "I think they only have a subpoena because they didn't come in and search your apartment."

I was momentarily stunned my dad had actually spoken to me.

"I know. My editor warned me. I'm avoiding them."

Most parents would be upset if their sons told them they were withholding information from the FBI. My father seemed proud of me, for the first time in more than ten years. I didn't tell him it was about Senator Hard-On. Or that I was working with the FBI on another case.

He asked what I was doing inside the convention center. The last thing I was going to say to him was that I had just slept with a Republican. I told them I was working on a story about the convention. About threats against Speaker Chesterfield. That was pretty much true.

"Everything okay with the apartment?" I asked, just to have something to say.

"It's *your* apartment," my mother said. "We saw the mail. Why did you tell me it was a friend's place?"

"I'm only subletting. I knew you wouldn't take it if you knew it was mine. So, are you going to be demonstrating here long?"

"Between here and 740 Park Avenue, for a few days," my mom said.

"740 Park Avenue?"

"740 Park Avenue," my dad said, as if correcting a dull student. "The richest apartment building in the world— home of the billionaire Roehm brothers, the main architects of the vast right-wing conspiracy against democracy."

"Oh, *that* 740 Park Avenue," I said, causing my dad's bushy eyebrows to lower. "Aren't those the guys who bankroll the Tea Party?"

"Exactly," my dad said. "They bought Congress, and are now engineering the largest voter disenfranchisement scheme in history."

I became aware of someone edging in closer to us, listening.

"Who are we talking about?" Ginny Mac asked.

"Buzz off, Ginny!" I told her.

"I was here first, Shepherd," she laughed. "What are you keeping from me? Who are these lovely people? Do they know Littleton?"

"Littleton? No, we're his parents," my mom volunteered.

146

"Really? You're Shepherd's parents? Wow. I'm very happy to meet you," she said, shaking hands in a demonstration of how unmitigated her gall was.

"Well, aren't you pretty," my mom said, turning on the charm. "Are you Jane?"

"No, I'm his *other* girlfriend. I'm Ginny Mac."

"Other girlfriend?" my dad asked.

"She's not my girlfriend," I protested. "She's a reporter for a competing newspaper. She's crazy. She sent mob thugs to beat me up."

"She did what?" my dad asked.

"I don't know what he's talking about," Ginny cackled, giving me a quick kiss on the cheek. "He's always making up lies about me. It must have been somebody else he screwed over who sent those guys to tune him up. I hear they are very unhappy with him. Tell your sonny boy to watch his back. Nice meeting you, Mr. and Mrs. Shepherd. Hope to see you again soon."

Ginny strolled off, with a toodle-oo wave. What the hell was she doing here? Had she been assigned to get reactions from the political crowds to Littleton's arrest? Or was she stalking me again? Did she send Jay-Jay and his pals? I saw Ginny make a call on her cellphone.

"Francis, what was that all about?" my mom asked. "Is she your girlfriend or not?"

"Not. We… dated… briefly—before I realized she was a dangerous psychopath."

"I thought she was a journalist?"

"What's the difference?"

"But you're with Jane now?" my mom pressed.

"Yes. I don't know. I may have screwed that up too, Mom. Look, I've got to get to work. Maybe we can talk later?"

They both smiled politely but I was sure they were relieved to get rid of me. As I turned and walked away, I spotted Ginny hovering behind some cops. I was afraid she was going to follow me but after a few steps, I noticed she turned back toward the demonstrators. My phone rang. It was Tiffany.

"Hi, Tiffany, what's so…"

She was sobbing and gasping for breath.

"Tiffany, what's wrong?"

"Shepherd, it's Percy… Just get back here now! I don't know what to do. I'm in his room… He's dead!"

28

I told Tiffany I was on the way, and she hung up. Looking back, I saw that Ginny Mac was talking to my parents again. This time she was writing in her notebook and she had a photographer taking their picture. Damn. She was so distracted she didn't see me slip past and back into the Knickerbocker Convention Center.

I dialed Amy on the run and gave her the news. On the fourteenth floor, all was quiet. Where was everybody? I approached Chesterfield's door and knocked.

"Who is it?" Tiffany asked from the other side.

"It's Shepherd."

She opened the door and hugged me, her face pale, her eyes red and wet. She was dressed in another executive dress suit, this time dark gray. The room was filled with sunlight. The picture window curtains were wide open. The smell hit me in the face. Gunpowder. Tiffany took my hand and led me down the short hallway to the living room.

"Wait!" I said, grabbing her hand. "Tiffany, why are you here alone? Is anyone else here?"

"No. I don't think so. I don't know. I just called you."

We seemed to be the only ones in the room except the Speaker of the House, Percy Chesterfield. His speaking days were over. The guy I was supposed to keep alive was on his back, dressed in creased suit pants, black dress shoes, a powder-blue dress shirt, and a red tie. The dead man who would never be president wore a frozen look of surprise, his eyebrows up, his mouth slightly agape.

Unlike Taliban KIAs or the victims of the Hacker, I had met this man before he was killed. It made it more difficult to be objective, more like when my own guys got whacked.

The politician's deep tan was gone, his skin ashen. His expensive handgun was undisturbed in its holster on his left hip. A cigarette was still held between the first two fingers of his right hand, which rested on the carpet, but it had burned itself out. There was a bloody concave wound the size of a fist in his chest. In the center of the wound was a neat hole, about the diameter of a large grape. The crater and hole was surrounded by blackened, burned shirt. It looked like he had been killed by a heavy weapon, maybe a .50 caliber, at close range.

"This can't be happening," Tiffany said, still crying. "He didn't answer, so I came over and... he was just lying there... I didn't hear anything. Was it a bomb?"

"I'm not sure. It's weird. It looks like a few different things. Did you call the cops? His security?"

"No... just you."

"Do you want me to call NYPD?"

"Of course. I'll call security. I just..."

"Tiffany, did you touch anything?"

"No. Wait, I came and I saw him and I rushed over and shook him... He was... cold... I'm not sure."

She was in shock. I took a closer look at her. She had a smear of blood on her right cheek and one of her knees. She had knelt down and kissed the guy. Did she love him? I took out my phone and did a quick video of the room and the body and I began backing out. In the hall, I took a look in the bathroom and shot more footage. It was white, immaculate. I pulled Tiffany out into the hall and dialed Izzy Negron. I told him what I was looking at.

"What is it with you, Shepherd?" Izzy asked. "What makes you a shit magnet?"

"I think he's been there for hours, Izzy."

"Can you tell what did it?"

"Not sure. Maybe a shotgun. Big-ass hole, lots of blood and lots of powder burns."

"Shotgun, point-blank?"

"Maybe," I said. "I'm not sure. It's weird. More like an IED." I hung up.

Tiffany sat down on the hallway carpet and began crying again. I walked down to the checkpoint and hailed two of the EPS suits.

"Yessir?" one asked.

"You have a security situation, gentlemen. Percy Chesterfield is dead in his room. Call out the troops."

They both looked at me blankly.

"What are you talking about?" the same guy said. "The last shift has him logged into his room for the night at twenty-three thirty hours last night. Wakeup set for zero nine hundred. In twenty-three minutes."

"How long have you been here?" I asked them.

"Zero six hundred."

"Change of plan, fellas. You guys are in the clear. He's been dead for a long time, probably before you came on. I'm Shepherd, the guy from the private security firm. I suggest you get down there, secure the scene—but stay out—and call your bosses. All of them. NYPD is on the way."

They looked at each other and dashed down the hallway. I went back to Tiffany.

"Jesus Christ!" one of the security men shouted.

"What the fuck?" his partner asked.

They began keying their radios, issuing very agitated reports, as if Chesterfield had only just been killed. The callbacks said they were locking the place down. I suggested to Tiffany we open her door. She rummaged numbly through her purse and handed me a gold keycard. I tried it in the lock but it didn't work. I told her that was Chesterfield's key. She handed me a white one and that worked. I sat her down in her living room.

"I thought he was going to be the next president of the United States," Tiffany said.

"A lot of people thought he might become president," I agreed. "At least one of them didn't like the idea."

"I told him he would be safe if he stayed inside the hotel," Tiffany said.

"I was the one who had you do that," I reminded her.

"And now he's dead," Tiffany concluded. "Who did this?"

"I don't know yet. But I will find out. I promise you."

She began to cry again. I turned away, took out my phone.

"What can I help you with, Shepherd?" Siri asked.

"Siri, who did it?"

"I don't know, Shepherd. Who?"

29

Tiffany slowly came out of her fog and began making phone calls to alert staff, arranging for others to intercept and notify Chesterfield's wife and family before they left Virginia to come to the convention.

"This is a valuable media chip, before the news breaks," Tiffany told me. "Do you want to break it in the *Daily Press* so we can cash that in whenever we need it?"

"Sure," I said. "I guess. Okay, I'll do it now."

I quickly interviewed Tiffany, typing her quotes into my phone. She talked about finding the body. I reminded her that I would quote her as a source, not by name.

"Of course," she said, her eyes far away.

It was a clever public relations move but Tiffany was running on autopilot and did not seem to realize her job no longer existed. I called Mel at the paper.

"Mel, I need rewrite. We need to break something exclusive on the web. It won't keep until morning. But it's a contract. The source wants a chip for when she needs it."

"Yeah? Nice of you to check in, your majesty. If you're calling about your girlfriend Ginny Mac's cork-sacking story that just popped up on the *Mail*'s website—you're too damn late!"

"What story?"

"It's on your flapping phone, if you bother to look," Mel said.

I looked and opened the email.

"I HATE NEW YORK"
Daily Press Reporter's Lefty Parents Hate Us

It was a twisted interview with my parents, in which their political views were skewed to make it seem like they hated the city, as opposed to the Tea Party radicals currently in residence. It was trash; routine Ginny Mac and *New York Mail* character assassination. The pen is nastier than the sword.

"Well, that's garbage, Mel, but I don't have time for that now. I need rewrite."

"Yeah? What's the big dastardly deal? New pole-packing pet column? Poodles mess toward Mecca?"

"Speaker of the House Percy Chesterfield, the next GOP presidential candidate, has been murdered in his luxury Manhattan hotel suite on the eve of the convention."

"Fork my grandmother!" Mel wailed. "Don't humping hang up!"

I didn't. I repeated my sentence and a lot more to a rewrite reporter before the noise of approaching cops invaded Tiffany's room and I had to hang up. I emailed my video of the crime scene to myself. Just in case.

I hung out in the hallway while the police cleared the rest of the murder suite, the bedroom and bathroom, and backed out to allow the CSI guys in. I noticed Izzy Negron had arrived, along with Phil D'Amico, and they were talking to other NYPD detectives about video and pointing to security cameras in the hall.

"That's the guy," one of the security suits said, pointing at me.

"Yeah, I know who he is," Izzy said. "I doubt he's a

suspect, but if I find out he is, it will be my pleasure to pass it on."

"Hey, Izzy."

"Well, Shepherd, here we are again."

"This isn't the same," I told him. "I wasn't working on a story. I'm working as a private detective. With Amy Massi."

"For the murder victim?" Izzy asked.

"Actually, they're working for the GOP, for the party," said Tiffany.

"Okay," Izzy replied. "And you are?"

I introduced Tiffany to Izzy. He nodded to his partner Phil, who also introduced himself. Izzy took me out into the hall.

"Okay, Sherlock. Walk me through it while CSI does their thing," Izzy said.

I explained how Tiffany had called me and when I arrived at the scene I had realized she was alone, and that I had called him and alerted security, who had no clue, thinking Chesterfield was safe inside the security zone.

"Where were you before you got the call from Tiffany?" Izzy asked.

"I was outside, talking to my parents," I told him.

"When did you see Chesterfield last?"

"The night before, with Tiffany, in his room, with the security team." I noticed evidence techs were in Tiffany's room now. They took pictures of her and samples from her cheek and knee. Then they took her pocketbook and began going through it.

"Why were you hired?" Izzy asked.

I took a breath. Before I could tell him to wait for my new boss, I was interrupted.

"To run down a shitload of death threats," Phil answered, fresh from talking to Tiffany. "And there may be a link to that Brooklyn militia crew the feds are looking for—top of the Hot Sheet this morning, boss. And maybe even some asshole we just locked up for weapons possession—a political star on FAX TV. Littleton."

"That's true," I agreed.

"Oh, man. Why can't it be simple?" Izzy asked. "Why can't it just be a jealous wife, standing there with the gun in her hand?"

"Maybe it's all on the security video?" Phil suggested. "As soon as we get that—"

"Don't jinx it," Izzy cut him off.

30

When the CSI guys had done their bit, they cleared out of Chesterfield's room and Izzy and Phil went in. Izzy always insisted on being at the scene alone—just himself and Phil—before the full evidence collection process began. I put on a pair of gloves and followed them in.

"Where the hell are you going?" Izzy snapped, turning his head. "I need privacy."

"I was admitted to your secret crime scene sessions on the last case—and this time I was hired by the victim."

Izzy looked at Phil, who shrugged. Izzy grunted and turned away. Phil put his finger to his lips. I shut the door behind us.

"Okay, Percy," Izzy began, addressing the corpse. "You were probably in here alone and someone came to the door, right? You didn't bother putting on your jacket or putting out your cigarette, no emergency."

Izzy was always on a first-name basis with his dead people.

"Maybe you looked through the door peephole, maybe you didn't because you're well-protected. But once you open the door, you're still cool with whoever it is, right? You stroll nice and easy back into the living room, puffing on your coffin nail, having a nice chat. Whatever happens,

happens so fast you never drop your butt, never reach for that expensive forty-five in your holster there. Percy, why the fuck did you just stand there while someone shot you?"

Speaker of the House Percy Chesterfield did not respond.

"*Grasa, muda y feliz*," Izzy said to the dead man. "Somebody put a big fucking hole in you, amigo. Why? One of your patriotic Anglo compadres?"

The dead man remained silent. The bloody hole in Chesterfield's chest, and the crater around it, made it look like he had been hit by a small asteroid.

"What did he use? A shotgun?" Izzy asked without answer. "The muzzle blast torched your tie and shirt. Looks like your blood put out the fire, right?"

I looked the remains up and down. The victim seemed completely unharmed everywhere else. I looked at his shoes; polished, pointing straight up. But the carpeting was raked in a few ridges below the heels. I moved closer and craned my neck to get a better view.

"What?" Phil whispered.

I pointed wordlessly to the carpeting. It looked as if Chesterfield had been dragged backwards for an inch or two, his heels leaving marks in the rug.

"What is this?" Izzy asked.

Phil and I knew he wasn't talking to us. Izzy squatted down at Chesterfield's feet and eyeballed the carpet marks, the shoes, the soles, the heels, the socks. He stopped and gently lifted the hemmed cuff of the right trouser, carefully folding it up. He looked at the socks some more, took out a pen and poked in various places, as if he was defusing a bomb. When he finished, he did the other leg, leaving the socks under the cuffs exposed. He nodded to Phil, who took pictures.

"Percy, it's hard to tell with your socks and pants on but your heels are just out of your shoes. Was whatever hit you so strong it partially knocked you out of your shoes? What the hell was it?"

Izzy didn't wait for a reply. He turned toward Phil and made a flip-flop motion with his hand. They both crouched down and lifted the body until they could see the back before gently replacing the corpse on the carpet.

"No exit wound," Izzy noted. "Whatever killed you is still inside you, Percy. Good man. We need that." He examined the shattered chest, particularly the dozens of burn marks on the skin, including the neck and face.

"What's with all these powder burns?" Izzy asked.

Phil and I remained quiet, waiting. Izzy turned to us, annoyed.

"Hey, I asked you guys a question. What's with all this stippling? Looks like a hell of a lot to me."

"Sorry," I said. "Didn't think you were talking to us. I'm not sure. I agree, it's a lot for a civilian weapon."

"What? You think this is military?" Izzy asked. "Like what? Like, a grenade?"

"Don't think so. Not sure. Possible, I guess. More like a fifty cal, but…"

"What about a fifty-caliber rifle?" Izzy asked.

"A fifty would have gone right through Chesterfield and through the wall. Also, probably ripped him in half," I told him. "Unless someone lightened up on the charge. But the size of the gun… Plus no one heard a shot."

"Not exactly a concealable weapon," Izzy admitted. "And given that everyone seems to be carrying guns in this place… Doesn't matter. Percy's got the bullet, we'll get it. The lab will tell us. We should have security videos. The killer will be the one carrying the fifty-caliber monster gun, Watson."

31

I looked at Chesterfield's cigarette hand. You couldn't smell the burned flesh where it had fried his skin but you could still detect the fireworks odor lingering in the air. I looked at the smoke detector on the ceiling. The shot should have set it off but it had been deactivated. Hell of a coincidence.

"Listen, Izzy," I said, as we left the room, "there's a few weird things you should know about."

"Like what?"

"Like we just convinced Chesterfield and his security team to keep him out of the public eye because we were worried about snipers and other things."

"What other things?"

"Like anything militia-type people could arrange—snipers, bombs, RPGs. Then, when I saw all these bozos in the hotel with assault rifles, we told Chesterfield he wasn't safe here. He had to get rid of the heavy metal or leave."

"What did he say?"

"He was sleeping on it. Never got his answer."

"Somebody sent him a message first," Phil said.

"Chesterfield got killed here, behind all the security, in his room—with his gun untouched on his hip. I don't believe in coincidences any more than you guys do. They shut off the

161

smoke detectors in his room last night. I was there."

"That's against the fire code," Phil said.

"Interesting. Why did they do that?" Izzy asked.

"I think it was his idea. He kept setting it off because he was too busy and famous to go to a public smoking area."

"So?" Izzy asked.

"He was dead for hours," I said. "That means whatever weapon killed him did not set off his smoke alarm—because it was shut off. The question is did they know in advance that the alarm was off?"

"Oh, man. I smell the gunpowder," Izzy said.

"Right, gunpowder, not cordite, like in ammo. Weird. There's more."

"Why can't you just stick to pets?" Izzy asked.

"I'm here as a private detective, not as a reporter," I said. "Well, also as a reporter."

"You have a state PI license?" Izzy asked.

"Ahh… it's pending. Hold it. I just thought of something."

We went back to Tiffany's room and I asked her who Bob and Abner were.

"Remember? The Speaker said he would text them about his smoke alarm being disconnected so they could do the same?"

"Yes," she answered. "Bob Blanchette of Alabama and Abner Hatfield from South Carolina. They all have the same arrangement in the Capitol building—so they can smoke."

"They did the same thing in Washington?"

"Yes."

"Was that well known?" Izzy asked.

"No, not to the public, just to… oh, I see what you mean. Any Capitol insiders would know."

"Exactly," I said. "But did the others also have their smoke alarms here disconnected last night?"

"I… I don't know. Maybe. Why?"

"Where are they right now?" I asked her. "Have you

spoken to them today? Where are their rooms?"

"Uh… somewhere on the fifteenth floor, I think. Let me look them up."

"Shepherd, are you saying we may have a problem?" Izzy demanded, catching my drift.

"I'm not saying anything yet. I just think we have to locate Congressmen Blanchette and Hatfield. Like, right now."

"What's going on?" asked Karl Bundt, the Executive Protection Service boss, joining us.

"Oh my God," Tiffany said. "Yes, rooms 1509 and 1511."

Izzy turned to Karl. "Come with us. Let's keep it low key, okay?"

"Izzy, you know I'm very discreet," I said, as we left the room.

"Bullshit," Izzy said. "Every time you say that, some shit blows up on the front page."

32

In the elevator I got an email and I sneaked a look. It was from Mel—a link to the front page of the *Daily Press* website:

CHESTERFIELD ASSASSINATED
Presidential Hopeful Slain
in NY Convention Mystery
EXCLUSIVE By F.X. Shepherd

Next to my byline was a small box with my face in it. We're in it now, I realized. Every one of the thousands of reporters and photographers here for the convention would be breathing down our necks, with more to come. A media clusterfuck of epic proportions. I groaned, as I spotted another headline:

ONCE IN THE CHESTERFIELD

"Shepherd," Izzy asked me softly. "What the hell do you think the weapon is?"

"Not sure. It kinda looked like a fifty but it didn't go through. That makes no sense, unless you took half the powder out of the shell."

"So the muzzle flash did all that stippling?" Izzy asked.

"I guess. But if somebody pointed a motherfucking fifty-caliber monster at you, wouldn't you at least try to pull your piece?"

"I would. But maybe it was really fast—a sawn-off shotgun, maybe?"

"Maybe."

When we got out on the fifteenth floor, we found two of Karl's agents—who he had summoned by radio—waiting for us with their guns drawn.

"How are we going to get in?" I asked.

"The hotel people are on their way up," Karl answered. "In case."

There was a concierge waiting by the rooms, which were next to each other. A dozen more security suits arrived, also ready to rumble. Bundt rang the bells to both suites several times. Couldn't just kick them in. These were congressmen, after all. Then he nodded at the concierge, who handed him two keycards.

"Ready?" Bundt asked his troops. "Go!"

The agents stacked up in two single files, nuts to butts. He flung both doors open. In three seconds, the conga lines of suits stopped short and concertinaed. Bundt was already giving orders to back out. I could smell the gunpowder.

"Okay," Izzy announced. "We got two more. Secure these rooms. No entry. Set up a sign-in sheet now for anyone who went in. Phil, get Crime Scene up here. Call the boss, the commissioner's office. He needs to call the friggin' mayor."

"It's the same damn mess as downstairs," Bundt groaned, holstering his weapon. "Three of them!"

He began to shake with rage, his fists clenched. That made me think.

"The same as downstairs, Izzy?" I asked.

"Yeah, carbon copies," Izzy agreed.

"A hell of a lot of carbon," Phil observed. "I agree with

the pet detective—it's strange. Smells funny."

"And no weapon found?" I asked.

"Doesn't look like it," Izzy said. "Oh, moth-er-fuck-er!"

Bundt looked confused. I turned to one of the hotel security people.

"Tell us about the smoke detectors."

"Oh. Well… um… officially, that didn't happen," she said.

"We don't give a shit. We're not fire marshals," I told her. "What I mean is, was it *only* three rooms?"

"Oh. I don't know," she admitted.

"Find out now!" Izzy ordered.

"Oh, no…" Bundt said softly, as if he didn't mean to say it out loud. "No. No. No."

The woman got on her radio. "Maintenance say that—for, uh, security reasons—they shut off twelve smoke detectors last night—two each in six different rooms."

"Oh, Christ!" wailed Bundt, grabbing the radio from her. "Three more? Where? What are the fucking room numbers?"

Once he had them he told Izzy that he and his men would do entries on the remaining rooms immediately. He left one of his guys with us to safeguard the scenes and they rushed off.

"Poor bastard," Izzy said.

"Yeah," Phil agreed.

"He's a good man," the EPS security guy said. "He doesn't deserve this."

"Deserve's got nothin' ta do with it," said Phil, who liked to quote movie lines.

"I'm no different from Karl," I told Izzy. "I was getting paid to keep someone safe and I fucked up."

"You weren't guarding the Speaker or the others," Tiffany said. "And you've only been on this for one day. The other agencies have been on it for months."

"She's right, Shepherd," Izzy said.

"No way," I said.

Nobody said anything for a while. Izzy and I stood at the entrance to one of the rooms and looked in. A bald man in a white terrycloth bathrobe was on his back, his hairy pink legs sticking out. His wound was more on his left side than Chesterfield's; his ribs seemed bent inwards around the bloody hole. The bathrobe had burned more than the polyester shirt and silk tie of the Speaker—the flames had also damaged this man's face. The spray pattern of carbon, the powder burns and charcoal embedded in the skin, could still be seen where there was less blood. This also seemed hours old.

"Which one is this?" Izzy asked Tiffany, who was sniffling quietly.

I resisted the urge to hold her.

"Congressman Abner Hatfield," Tiffany said, in a shaky voice.

We moved to the adjacent open door. A younger man, with a full head of black hair, dressed in a silver three-piece suit and tie. The wound was very similar to Chesterfield's. A glass lay on the carpet, where it had fallen from his hand.

"Senator Robert Blanchette," Tiffany informed us.

"They knew or trusted whoever did this," I said.

"Looks like it," Izzy agreed. "The doors all have peepholes. They all let the killer in."

The EPS security man touched a finger to one ear and then spoke into his sleeve. He shook his head in disgust.

"Two more homicides," he said. "Virtually the same as these three. The sixth room is empty, no signs of violence. No weapon recovered, no suspect. They are confirming the identities of the other deceased and looking for the missing person now. Lockdown continues. Evacuation and search of adjacent structures. Securing hotel security video. Notifications are FBI, CIA, NSA, Homeland Security, White House, FAA, TSA, Pentagon. Secret Service is barring all civilian weapons from the premises. All protectees are being secured."

"Oh my God," Tiffany gasped in realization. "Five?"

In deference to the lady, Izzy cursed in Spanish very softly. Phil and I echoed him in English. I suggested to the EPS agent that they do a head count of politicos, VIPs, and delegates as soon as possible—to see who was still alive. He got on his radio.

This was bad, even for America. Everyone carrying automatic weapons and five members of Congress, including one of the next two presidential candidates, assassinated at a political convention.

Talk about smoke-filled rooms.

33

I updated Mel at the paper. He had trouble believing me.

"Are you flicking sure about this, Shepherd? Nobody else has this."

"Mel, I'm looking at two of the five bodies as we speak, Congressman Abner Hatfield and Senator Bob Blanchette. Same method as Chesterfield—apparently shot at point-blank range."

I took more phone shots and sent them to Mel but ordered him not to publish them.

"Christ on a crutch," Mel said when he saw them. "With Chesterfield dead, who will the coke-sucking Republicans put up for pumping president?"

"No clue, Mel. I'll let you know. Don't you have a reporter at the Knickerbocker?"

"Yeah, right, of course. Lane Barnett. Rich, filching trust-fund brat who can't find his wiener with a bun. All he's good for is reading mucking media releases and going to puking press conferences, especially if they're catered."

Mel said literally the whole office was working on my story, cranking out sidebar stories on Chesterfield's career and the presidential race—who might go for the gold now. I told Mel that the Knickerbocker was locked down and

I would have to stay in the building. He told me he had Sparky Clarke sneaking in and Sparky would contact me. I said I would get back to him when I had the names of the other victims.

I FaceTimed Mary Catherine. My former commander, now a federal prosecutor, appeared to be seated at a Starbucks downtown, near Federal Circle where she worked. Sipping one of those highly enriched uranium-caffeine blends that fueled her, Mary Catherine was in her dark power suit and power ponytail.

"Hey, Shepherd," Mary Catherine said. "Okay, your new boss, Speaker Chesterfield, threw his weight around with a call to Washington, and the FBI agents got orders to bust the Aryan Purity Nation cell pretty damn quick—and they came up empty."

"Why didn't they wait until they had some people before springing the trap?" I asked.

"Political orders. Results now. Screw the case, damn the torpedoes, full speed ahead."

"How many bad guys in the breeze?"

"Three in the cell, other than the informant. Several more at either end of the guns and explosives pipeline but we know less about them. If we got all their weapons and fireworks, then it was a good bust."

"There are always more guns."

"Time will tell."

"Terrific. I need the address of the bust."

Mary Catherine said it was in a Hasidic neighborhood, Williamsburg, in Brooklyn, and she gave me the street address.

"So, Shepherd, how's Jane?" she asked.

When I didn't respond immediately, she asked what was wrong. Just what I needed. Another mom.

"It's okay, Mary Catherine. I think I just scared her a little bit. She thinks I'm a twisted adrenaline junkie."

"Oh, crud," she said. "She found out already?"

She asked why Jane would get that impression and I told her of my run-in with Jay-Jay and his minions.

"You idiot," Mary Catherine said. "You really do have a death wish. And a mobster's kid? Nice choice. Do you want me to talk to Jane?"

Maybe a very sexy, slightly older woman would be the absolute wrong person to talk to Jane about me at this point.

"I'll let you know, thanks."

"Okay. So, how's the new private eye job so far? Lots of danger, secret intrigue and kinky casual sex?"

"You have no idea."

"What?"

"You haven't heard the news?"

"No."

I told her.

"Oh my God. You're in it now, Shepherd."

"Yeah, so are you. C'mon in, the adrenaline's fine."

"Watch your tight ass, Shepherd."

I called Amy and brought her up to date.

"Well, I guess we're dead in the water," Amy said. "The feds will find out who did this. The party doesn't need us anymore. Come back and walk your dog. Our contract died with Chesterfield."

"I don't give a damn. I'm on this 'til we get the bastards," I told her. "And right now NYPD is on it."

"Hey, that's the spirit, Shepherd. Okay, I'll have somebody walk Skippy. Put Tiffany on."

I went and found Tiffany. The women spoke for a few minutes, then Tiffany ended the call and handed me my phone back.

"You're still on the case until the election is over or until you get the killer," Tiffany said.

"Can you do that?" I asked.

"Sure," she said. "Unless the party committee overrules me later. I may have to work for them soon. Shoot, Percy is…" She began to tear up again.

"Okay. It doesn't matter. Money or not, I'm on this."

"Old-fashioned work ethic?" Tiffany smiled. "Talk about family values."

"Nope. Business. Who would hire a pathetic private detective who not only lost his first client but then couldn't even get the bastard who did it?"

"Right," she agreed. "So you'll find out who it was and lock them up."

"I'm not really trained in law enforcement," I shrugged. "I prefer to settle out of court."

34

My phone vibrated. An incoming email, marked urgent.

NEW MINUTEMEN COMMUNIQUE

Hello. I clicked on the message and showed it to Tiffany.

> The new minutemen have fired the shots heard round the world. We, the people, here in occupied jew york territory, have fired the first volley in the war of re-independence. Don't tread on us. Collaborator percy chesterfield and five henchmen and women have been felled by the second amendment measures of our forefathers. More will follow until we have taken back our country from foreigners for we, the people.

Jew York? Morons.

"Oh, my God," Tiffany gasped. "The bastards. This is unreal."

"Yeah, especially about the women and five henchmen. They shot Percy and four others. Not six. And no women."

"Perhaps they mean they *will* shoot more, including women," she said.

"Maybe," I said.

I found Izzy and showed him the message, which was from newminutemen1@freedomhack.com.

"Oh, man," Izzy groaned. "How do we know these guys are real? Anybody could put this crap out."

"Okay," I agreed. "Let's see what they know."

I replied to the email, asking for "non-public details" of the attacks. They bumped right back. Izzy and I read the response together.

> All twelve smoke alarms in six rooms were shut off by the targets. Chesterfield had a cigarette in his right hand and blanchette was drinking when we the people administered the sentences of death. In all future communication we will use code phrase: oldnorthchurch4181775.

Old North Church. Minutemen. 4181775. The Midnight Ride of Paul Revere and the date—April eighteenth, seventeen seventy-five. Cute.

"Jesus, these guys act like pros," Izzy said. "That's not good. None of that stuff is public."

"Yeah but they already made mistakes," I pointed out. "They said six victims and included women. There are only five victims and they're all male."

"That's true, amigo. I wonder why? Don't correct them yet, until we find out."

"What about the sixth room—the one that was empty? Who was supposed to be there? Do we have a dead congresswoman somewhere?"

"Let's find out."

In a few minutes, Izzy had the sixth room number and we went there. It was blocked off and a shaken Karl Bundt was on his cellphone.

"No, escort her back up," Bundt was saying. "Heavy security. Now."

Bundt glared at me with hatred and didn't answer when I asked him whose room this was. Izzy asked the same question.

"Senator Katharine Carroll of Minnesota. She's on the way up under guard," Karl said.

"Was she in her room last night?" Izzy pressed.

"We'll find out in a minute," Karl snipped.

We all waited until we heard an elevator opening and an attractive middle-aged blonde in a red power suit strode around the corner, surrounded by nervous security suits. She had a hunting rifle in a camouflage pattern that complemented her outfit, slung over her shoulder. I noticed there was no magazine in the weapon. Next to the senator was a thin, pretty young girl with the same hair and face, about fourteen years old—obviously her daughter.

Karl moved forward but Izzy and Phil stepped in front of him. He looked furious.

"Senator Carroll? I'm Detective Lieutenant Izzy Negron of NYPD's Major Case Squad. We have a few questions for you, please."

"Of course, Lieutenant," she said, entering her suite. "You're investigating these terrible murders?"

"Yes, ma'am. Were you in this room last night?"

"Yes, I was here with my daughter Allyson. She arrived late yesterday evening, a bit of a surprise. She's writing a report for school."

"So, your daughter was unexpected?" I asked.

"Yes," the senator said.

"Senator, did you have the smoke alarm shut off in your rooms last night?"

"The smoke alarm?" she asked, nervously. "No. Why would I do that? I don't smoke. Isn't that illegal?"

I took a deep breath through my nose. There was no smell of gunpowder. Other faint odors lingered in the air— cigarette smoke. On the ceiling, there was no flashing green light on the smoke detector. It was still off.

"Did anyone knock on your door last night?" asked Izzy. "Did anything out of the ordinary happen?"

"No. No one. Nothing. It was very quiet, wasn't it, Allyson?"

"Yup," Allyson agreed.

The senator expressed her sadness over the slayings and said she had no idea why anyone would want to harm her. She had not received any recent threats.

"Of course, we all get threats in our line of country but I don't recall anything unusual. Is there anything else? I have more meetings and I have to change. I have to rethink my speech, in light of this tragedy. These are difficult times," she said.

"Yes, ma'am," Izzy said.

"She's lying," I told Izzy in the hallway, as soon as the door had shut behind us.

"I know," he said.

35

We stood in the corridor.

"Now what?" Tiffany asked. I looked at Izzy and Phil.

"The security video," said Izzy, looking meaningfully at our guardian EPS agent, whose name was Thatcher.

The agent got on his radio to call his boss.

"I want to look at Chesterfield's room again," I said, as we waited. "Are the Crime Scene guys done there yet?"

"Yeah," said Phil. "They're going up to start on the fifteenth floor rooms."

Thatcher spoke on his radio again, and then turned to Izzy. "They're almost ready with the surveillance video. You need to go to the security office near the lobby."

"Video first, rooms after," Izzy said to me.

Tiffany and I followed Izzy, Phil and Karl Bundt to the elevator. Downstairs we crossed the lobby, surrounded by flashing lights and screaming reporters. A crowd of my colleagues were penned behind NYPD barriers. I spotted Ginny Mac and Sparky in the crush of press. We ignored the unintelligible questions and crammed into the security office. There was standing room only and a wall of big video screens above a long counter with computers and phones, manned by several uniformed security guards. Live feed flashed backwards and forwards on the screens above them.

"Can we do this?" a very cranky Karl Bundt snapped. He tapped the shoulder of one of the seated security guys at the control panel, and three large screens, each showing four different camera playback views, began rolling. We watched armed delegates, security personnel, and hotel workers walk up and down hallways and enter and leave rooms.

"On the left screen, we have the views outside Speaker Chesterfield's room," Bundt explained. "The middle screen has the cameras outside Senator Blanchette and Congressman Hatfield's rooms. The one on the right has the other two rooms, of course, victims four and five, Congressman—"

"What time is this?" Izzy interrupted.

"I had them start all playbacks twelve hours before we found the first body," Bundt replied.

We?

I shook my head but said nothing. Izzy snorted in derision. "Are you fucking kidding me? You think we're going to spend hours watching this shit while the killers leave town? Start with the discovery of the body and rewind from there."

"We will fast forward, of course," Bundt said, flustered. "I thought we would—"

"You will do what I just told you to do or you will get your ass out of this room," Izzy fired back. "You, security guy. What's your name?"

"Indogo," he answered.

"Okay, Indogo, the first body was found about eight this morning. Punch in oh-eight-hundred and hit play on all of these now. Please."

The security guard didn't even look at Bundt. The screens wiped, went to black, and new images of the same halls appeared.

"Eight o'clock," Indogo announced. "Running forward."

Nothing happened. A man and a woman walked down the hall and up the hall outside Chesterfield's room; the coming and going illusion caused by cameras at opposite ends of the hall. Everyone leaned forward, tense. The couple vanished from the screens. A hotel employee, pushing a breakfast tray, appeared and then vanished on the right screen. More people passed on the middle screen. No one opened any doors. Then Tiffany appeared on the left screen. She knocked on Chesterfield's door and waited. Her mouth was moving but there was no sound. She produced a room card, inserted it in the door slot and opened the door. She vanished inside. Nothing happened.

"Hold them all, Indogo," Izzy ordered. "That's you, right, Miss Mauser?"

"Yes," she sniffed. "That's when I... found him."

"Okay." Izzy paused. "Wait. You found him alone? I thought you were with Shepherd?"

"Umm... I was... that is, he came... shortly after that."

Izzy looked at me but let it go.

"All right. Indogo, please rewind at regular speed please."

Everything started moving backwards. No one went in or out of any of the target hotel rooms. It got boring. After twenty minutes, Izzy ordered fast rewind. Nothing began happening backwards again—but faster. I located the time counter in the lower left of each frame to keep track. It was in military time: hours, minutes, seconds and hundreds of seconds. 07:49:43:12... 07:30:22:59... 07:00:00:00... 06:45:21:04... 06:12:10:05... 06:00:00:00...

"You have to watch carefully on fast rewind," Indogo warned. "Keep your eyes on the doors. You might miss something."

We didn't miss it.

All three screens exploded into snow. Backwards snow.

"What the hell is that?" Izzy demanded.

"I don't know," Indogo said. "Pressing play."

The snow didn't look much different at normal speed, just slower.

"Something is wrong," Indogo said. "I have never seen this before."

"How much of this is there?" Izzy asked.

Indogo did a very fast rewind and jotted numbers down on a pad. Then he used a separate keyboard to access some kind of software with logs and lists and menus. He said angry words in a language I didn't know. I assumed they were curses.

"Nine hours," he concluded. "And not just on these cameras. On all cameras."

"Someone erased the data?" Bundt asked.

"No. Not erased. The cameras never recorded. They were shut off at nine p.m. last night. In real-time, from the outside. Only came back on again at six this morning. We've been hacked."

This time it was an exasperated Izzy who cursed, in Spanish. "*Cuanto mas remueves la mierda, peor huele,*" he sighed.

Tiffany, apparently a Spanish speaker, nodded in agreement. I looked to her for a translation.

"The more you tromp on a turd, the wider it gets."

36

The convention started while we were in the security office. We realized it when Indogo restored the live camera feeds, including the ones in the huge convention auditorium. The armed delegates were pledging allegiance to the flag. Or at least *some* of them pledged allegiance to Old Glory. Almost one out of four delegates pointedly did not take part.

"Boy, that really pisses me off," Phil said. "If they don't believe those words, what the hell are they doing *in* the government?"

"Makes you wonder," Izzy agreed.

"They don't like the fact that it says 'and to the Republic, for which it stands.' Also they object to the word 'indivisible,'" Tiffany said. "Some of them are secessionists."

"Not to mention the part about 'Liberty and Justice for *all*,'" I added.

"This is just the opening," Tiffany said. "First the pledge, then a prayer by the chaplain, and after that the Sergeant at Arms will make a motion to adjourn to committee until later."

A minister appeared at the podium, saying a prayer "for the victims of evil in our midst," and asking for heavenly guidance for their deliberations.

"This will be over in a minute," Tiffany began, "and we will have meetings because I have no idea what the hell is going to…"

Tiffany froze. The padre was gone and Senator Katharine Carroll, slim, dignified, with fire in her eyes, her now-loaded rifle hanging at her side, was at the podium.

"Wait," Tiffany said. "That's not right. What is she doing up there? She's not scheduled to speak until… Can we have audio please?"

Indogo flipped a switch.

"…Speaker Chesterfield and the others were, indeed, cut down by an evil in our midst—foreign or domestic," Carroll declared darkly. "I have been told I was also targeted by the killers. I cannot yet tell you whether they are traitors among us or enemy combatants. Either way, can we allow the assassin in the night to hijack our sacred American democracy?"

"NO!" the crowd thundered, on its feet.

"Do you have the courage to battle this cowardly enemy and restore freedom to our country?"

"YES!" they cried.

"I am not afraid," Carroll said, parking the butt of her rifle akimbo on her hip. "Will you fight with me?" She reached out her hand to the throng, as if to take theirs.

"YES!"

"Will we honor these men—who fell in the cause of Liberty, our God-given cause?"

"YES!"

"Percy Chesterfield had a dream that he could reunite this broken land and restore respect and confidence to a tarnished White House," she told the crowd. "I share his dream, as I know you do. That dream must not fail, cannot fail—if our great nation is to prosper. But first, we must honor the memories of our martyrs. My fellow delegates, as a gesture of support and a memorial for these great men, I move that this convention—by acclamation—vote Speaker

Percy Chesterfield as our honorary interim nominee for president of the United States, until this convention chooses another candidate."

"What the fuck?" Izzy laughed.

"She can't do this!" Tiffany shrieked.

"She's doing it," I pointed out.

"Second the motion!" someone shouted from the floor, followed by many others.

"All in favor?" the senator shouted.

There was a massive showing of hands and sign-waving.

"Opposed?" she shouted over the din. A vocal minority were shouted down. "Motion carried!" Carroll concluded, producing a wooden gavel. "God bless you and God bless the United States of America! This convention stands in recess until two o'clock this afternoon."

She banged the gavel on the podium dramatically and threw both hands into the air, hoisting her weapon high. The crowd went berserk, clapping, stomping and yelling. "God Bless America" blasted out from hidden speakers.

"What just happened?" Izzy asked. "They're putting a dead guy up for president?"

"Only temporarily," I pointed out. "I think the senator has someone still living in mind for the spot. All presidential candidates say 'God bless you and God bless America.'"

"The senator who is lying to us—the only one who wasn't blown away last night—just hijacked the convention," Phil said. "Interesting. She's got my vote."

"I can't believe this," Tiffany groaned. "She had no right. How did she do this?"

"It doesn't matter anymore," I told her. "She must have seen her chance and rushed to the podium right after we left her room. This just went out over the TV networks live, right?"

"Oh, my God, yes," she agreed.

"I think it's safe to say Senator Carroll is now officially running for president and isn't waiting for an invitation," I said. "At two o'clock, my guess is she will be nominated."

"That was… like a keynote speech," Tiffany said. "I've never seen anything like it. It was incredible, but how could she be so cold?"

"Not cold," I told her. "Cool. If she was a guy, we'd be saying she's got guts, balls—a hell of a leader."

"No," Tiffany said. "I meant cold about the Speaker—trying to take his place so soon after his death. They were close. Are you questioning my feminism, Shepherd?"

"No," I answered. "The questions are why she didn't get popped along with the others, why she's lying to us and whether that rousing speech we just saw was improvised or written in advance."

"Well," Izzy said, "she's either a hell of a politician or a hell of a psychopath. Maybe both."

37

Tiffany rushed out of the security office to meet with her "Chesterfield for America" team in her room. That would not be a happy get-together. Their presidential candidate was dead, they were jobless, and one of his pals was elbowing onto his place on the ballot. On the video screens, the convention floor was chaotic, a lot of yelling and screaming. Several fistfights broke out over control of the podium and microphone. People began pointing their weapons at each other but no shots were heard. Democracy in action.

I followed Izzy and Phil back up to Chesterfield's room, where the crime scene crew was still bagging and tagging. By phone, Izzy delivered the bad news to One Police Plaza and to City Hall that hacking had robbed them of a record of the killing and that he was exactly nowhere. Of course, he didn't say that.

"Yes, Commissioner, I understand. Please tell him we have numerous good leads and we are actively in the process of including and eliminating suspects as we speak, sir."

Phil turned to me and silently mouthed the word "Bullshit."

"Yessir, we will absolutely catch the shooter. Well... it's very early in the case. Of course the APN cell are at the top of the list and they are still in the wind. With current manpower, it will take us twenty-four hours just to... Yessir, that would be helpful. Right away. Thank you, sir," Izzy said, disengaging.

"You tell him we have dozens of armed suspects and no fucking clue?" Phil asked.

"Not in those words," Izzy smirked. "He's sending us assistance."

"Who?" I asked.

"Everybody," Izzy replied. "We've got twelve hours to close this out."

We all laughed.

"It'll take weeks just to interview all these assholes," Phil pointed out.

"I know," Izzy agreed. "Everything is fast-tracked. As soon as the troops arrive, detectives from our squad and every homicide squad in the city, we'll assign them and observe the autopsy of Chesterfield at the ME's office. Then we come back and do re-interviews, lock up our suspect and have a beer."

After Izzy and Phil made a few more calls, about fifty suits arrived, with more on the way. We went to a meeting room downstairs and Izzy and Phil set up a command structure to interview suspects and lock them into alibis and timelines, for later comparison with evidence that either confirmed or contradicted them.

Phil gave the assembled detectives a short version of the murders, including victims' names, estimated times of death, wounds, possible weapons and the situation concerning the smoke alarm and video shutoffs. He emphasized that the murdered appeared to be the result of an organized, premeditated conspiracy, probably carried out by multiple suspects, all of whom were to be considered armed and dangerous.

"We will be gathering evidence from each and every suspect's hand and clothing worn at the time of the homicides for a GSR test, to determine if they recently fired a weapon," Izzy added. A hand shot up and Izzy pointed to the detective, a chubby, silver-haired veteran with his tie askew.

"Lieutenant, as you know, GSR testing is only good for maybe four hours and they can wash it off or clean their clothes."

"Yes, *I* know that but many of our subjects may not. Also, it can't tell if they fired a gun or were just near a gunshot. Doesn't matter. It's like asking a suspect to submit to a polygraph exam—the most important result may be that he refuses, displaying consciousness of guilt. If a suspect refuses to submit to a GSR test or surrender their clothing or weapon, they will go to the top of our suspect list and we will bird-dog with warrants. Call it in to our field office here."

He explained that there were more than four thousand delegates to the convention, and so, as a practical matter, they would start questioning those who threatened or opposed Chesterfield. The first inner circle would include former governor Miranda Dodge and the blogger Clayton Littleton. Izzy said that the next group in the expanding circle would be elimination interviews and tests on those who had access to Chesterfield and the other victims, including staff. He estimated that was at least fifty subjects. Full departmental paperwork would be completed later. The Manhattan DA's office would expedite subpoenas and search warrants for the gunshot residue tests, room searches and firearm ballistics testing. Phil handed out assignments to teams of investigators, who received a computer printout of their subject, with photo, state, name and room number.

"You're first," Izzy told me.

"What?"

"You have the right to remain silent," Phil said.

"Oh, okay. Right," I said, sitting down.

They asked me my whereabouts between six p.m. last night and nine a.m. this morning. I told them everything. Almost.

"So, you came to the Knickerbocker Convention Center for the second time last night," Phil said. "You'd already had a conference about Chesterfield's safety earlier in the day?"

"Yup."

"Then the smoke alarm went off and you went to Chesterfield's room, saw them get disconnected, then had dinner?"

"Correct."

"How did he seem?" Izzy asked.

"The same as before. Nothing unusual."

"How did she seem?"

"Who?"

"Tiffany."

"The same. She was a little annoyed with Chesterfield over the smoke alarm thing. He pulled the same shit in Washington."

"How annoyed?" Phil asked.

"Not enough to blow a hole in his chest... I feel bad for her."

"Yeah," said Izzy, turning toward me. "Nice kid. Wait a second... who did you have dinner with?"

"You know, the GOP people."

"Like Tiffany?" Phil asked, as they both edged in closer, smelling a half-lie.

"Yeah."

"Anybody *other* than her?" Izzy demanded.

"Nope, just us," I admitted.

"After this alarm rhubarb, you spent the night in the hotel?" Phil asked.

"I was there all night. I left early."

"He didn't ask you when you left," Izzy said. "Where did you sleep?"

"Who says I slept in a room?"

"Are you... Shepherd, are you and Tiffany...?"

"What?" I asked, as innocently as possible.

"You're my hero, Shepherd," Phil added.

"You guys are nuts. Give me a break."

Sometimes hanging out with detectives was a pain in the ass.

"So Tiffany is your alibi and vice-versa?" Phil asked.

"Yeah."

After a few more questions, they called over a surgically gloved CSU officer from NYPD, a thin woman in a lab coat, who used a clear adhesive tape on the back of my hands, like a lint brush. Then she also used the sticky tape on my shirt before putting it into a plastic bag, which she labeled with my name and date of birth.

"Have you fired a weapon today, sir?" she asked me.

"No. Not today."

She also wrote that down, asked me to sign a label, and gave me a numbered and dated receipt.

"Give this to your defense lawyer," she told me, with a smile.

38

My phone buzzed with emails. I left the meeting room and leaned against the hallway wall. My office was sending me fresh website front pages and also demands for more news.

Our new webline was "DEAD HEAT: Ballots or Bullets?" My story was updated with delegates of the Grand Old Party voting Chesterfield the temporary, honorary nominee: "The GOP has voted a dead man as their standard-bearer in the upcoming presidential election. The move is allegedly a temporary honor but the struggle within the party, which appears to have become an actual shooting war, threatens to detonate the convention before a living candidate can be voted on."

Our competition, the *New York Mail*, called events "ELEPHANT WAR," and, as usual, had its own unique approach to the crisis: "HEADLESS PARTY TAPS LIFELESS BODY. Panicked GOP delegates continue to vote for a dead man and failed policies, rather than back viable candidates, such as Governor Dodge—who can take the fight to the enemy in November."

"Siri, would a dead man make a good president?" I asked my phone.

"Hmm," Siri responded, "let me think. I'm sorry, but I can't do that."

"Siri, I didn't mean you should kill somebody."

"Oh, no," she said. "Sorry."

This was getting weird because I didn't want Siri to think ill of me or to hurt her feelings.

"Siri, don't be sorry."

"I'm sorry."

"You have no reason to be sorry, Siri."

"Is that so?"

"Yes, Siri, unless you're making a joke. Unless you're smarter than me?"

"Who, me?"

I was wondering what to say to her next, when Izzy and Phil told me things were getting hairy on the convention floor and we should head there.

"We'll interview this governor woman and the blogger guy, if you want to tag along," Izzy said in the elevator.

"Okay."

"Were you talking to your phone?" Izzy asked me.

"You talk to dead people," I pointed out. "At least Siri answers me."

"You're both nuts," Phil observed.

The convention floor, an echoing vault ten stories high, was a huge, red-white-and-blue zoo—populated by about 5,000 costumed delegates, separated into screaming armed camps. Many of the men and women, ranging from sitting congressmen to aspiring dog catchers, were leveling their assault rifles at each other and cursing. TV crews, scrambling to cover the chaos, scurried from one confrontation to another. Some intrepid reporters were wearing bulletproof vests and combat helmets. Several people with delegate ID cards were exiting the floor. They were all rolling carry-on travel bags and hard rifle cases. One told us that about twenty per cent of the delegates had sided with Governor Miranda Dodge and her Tea Party stalwarts, who were demanding Dodge get the nomination.

"Where are you going?" I asked one man.

"Home," he said, and headed for the exit.

"Don't you have to nominate somebody for president?" I shouted after him.

"Some gunfighters. Fucking pussies are afraid of being shot," Phil sniffed.

"Aren't you?" Izzy asked him.

"Yeah, but this isn't my convention."

At the front, an elevated stage featured a podium and a large CHESTERFIELD FOR AMERICA banner. Above that, a mammoth vertical screen pleaded: PLEASE COME TO ORDER. I spotted Senator Carroll and Tiffany—plus their respective staffs—behind the podium, locked in intense argument.

"Holy shit!" Phil said.

"You live long enough, you see everything," Izzy grinned.

"I used to think politics was boring," I told them.

"Let's get down there," Izzy ordered.

Onstage, I pulled Tiffany away from her discussions with Carroll and asked her what was happening.

"See for yourself, Shepherd. Delegates are running away, not even waiting to do their job," she snarled. "Carroll and Dodge both want the top spot and have placed their names in nomination. Carroll offered Dodge the vice presidency but she refused. Now Carroll wants to put it to a straight up or down vote between the two of them. But Dodge knows she will lose that contest, so she has threatened to leave the party with her people unless she gets her own, personal, unopposed vote first."

"Why does Dodge want a first ballot vote alone if she doesn't have the votes to win?" I wondered.

"We don't know," Tiffany said. "We don't trust her. She acts like she has something up her sleeve. She might have proxies from fleeing delegates."

"Don't give her her own ballot," I warned. "Maybe that's part of a plan that included the killings."

"I agree," she said. "We're deadlocked and every minute, another coward turns tail and runs for home."

"Who's leaving?" Izzy asked. "Your people or hers?"

"Both. Especially our people. No one feels safe. The longer this goes on, the closer we get to losing a quorum—and then we won't be able to do anything. A dead man will be our candidate."

"Voters have elected dead men before," Phil pointed out.

"True, but never for president," Tiffany agreed. "At this point, that may be our best option. If Percy's ghost wins in November, the Electoral College will *appoint* a president. It's better than having Dodge in office."

"That's just dumb-ass stupid," Izzy said.

"I'm the head of the Rules Committee. I'm open to suggestion," Tiffany said.

"Dodge says her crew will quit the party if she doesn't get her way?" I asked.

"Yes, then we won't even have a quorum, a minimum needed to take action."

"Call her bluff," I suggested. "Tell Dodge to fuck off."

"What?" Tiffany shouted.

A network camera crew had noticed our lively discussion and moved closer, pointing the lens at Tiffany. She grabbed my elbow and moved us away from the newsies until we were alone.

"I have to get back," Tiffany told me. "I'll see what Carroll thinks."

"So, you're with her now?" I asked Tiffany.

"Maybe," she sighed, before turning and striding away.

"We better interview this moose killer lady and that blogger before they secede or they all shoot each other or whatever," Izzy said.

"I second the motion," I agreed.

"Let me guess," Phil said. "You were a Student Council government nerd in high school?"

"No. I learned dirty politics at the Shura Council in Khost."

"The what in where?" Izzy laughed.

"Ask your phone," Phil told him.

39

Former Governor of Alaska Miranda Dodge, dressed in a form-fitting red dress—which accentuated her prominent breasts—was on the convention floor, surrounded by a loyal mob of Tea Baggers, rifles at the ready. She was giving a speech to several TV cameras, whose lights made her matching necklace and earrings—in the shape of polar bears—sparkle. Behind her, her skulking husband Fred Dodge was whispering key words to her, which then came out of her mouth as mangled, disjointed non-sentences.

"Did us a favor…" Fred murmured.

"Whoever exercised their Second Amendment Measures against these RINOs, these Republicans In Name Only, may or may not have committed a crime but they sure did America a favor—taking action against socialist tyranny is what I'm talkin' about!" Dodge declared loudly, with a sexy wink.

There was a smattering of applause from her supporters and she raised her black assault rifle—which had a fancy rhinestone US flag on the stock—over her head, pumping it like a hockey player after scoring a goal. Her speech was oddly slurred, as if she was stoned.

"*We the people…*" Fred whispered.

"Now, We the People of this great land of patriotism for

each other have the opportunity to really act in a way that we all can praise God now that we are on the right path for all real Americans, all the precious children, ready to fire against godless perversion…"

"So, you called on people to shoot Speaker Chesterfield and now you're celebrating that shooting?" one of the reporters asked.

"Divine will…"

"Our prayers are for the victims and their families but divine will is what will be seen in the future as having happened now," Dodge said. "God, not me, has decreed that these things have happened and the Lord does not make mistakes, which is what people make because they are 'We the People'…"

"The hour of freedom…"

"The hour of freedom is coming." She tossed her shiny chestnut brown hair. "Shoot, this election is about freedom and God wants us to be real free and clear about our choices, which we have done and will do on election day. Just ask God in your heart and he will for sure guide your hand."

"So, are you saying the murders of five members of Congress was a good thing and was ordained by God and you should be nominated?" a confused TV reporter asked.

"Murder not good but…"

"Murder is not good, of course, not for you to put words into my mouth, that's also not good to trick the American People with lamestream media mumbo-jumbo, and we have no control over that and must do what he ordains because we have free will because we are a free people who must carry on and make the best of a bad situation and make no mistake that we will make the best that it can be and will be made, you betcha."

"Umm… okay, thanks," another reporter said, turning away.

"What a putz," Izzy muttered. "*El tonel vacio mete mas ruido.*"

"What?" I asked him.

"An empty cask makes the most noise," Izzy translated.

Next to Dodge, waiting his turn, was Clayton Littleton, obviously sprung on bail. We worked our way through the crowd of delegates until we got to the inner ring, with half a dozen men holding their rifles at port arms across their chests.

Izzy held his gold badge up and called out to Dodge.

"NYPD, ma'am. We need a few moments of your time, please."

The gunman closest to Izzy swung his barrel toward him. Phil closed the distance until he was on Izzy's left, almost touching the guy.

"Ease your finger off that trigger, pal," the taller Phil said clearly and calmly. "You're a daisy if you do."

The rifleman opened his mouth to speak but his chin fell when he looked down at Phil's nine-millimeter Beretta, which was inches from his gut.

"Now, please, sir," Phil told him. "We don't want any mishaps."

"Thank you for your help," Phil told him, elbowing him aside with a smile.

Izzy repeated his spiel to Dodge and her husband, explaining they were investigating the homicides.

"Of course, we fully support law enforcement," Dodge told him. "They are our first line of defense."

"That's great," Izzy said. "We just need you and your friend Mr. Littleton to cooperate in our investigation, as all of your other colleagues are doing."

"What can we help you with, officer?" Fred Dodge asked, trying to get in between Izzy and his wife.

"Where were you between nine last night and nine this morning?" Izzy asked, standing his ground.

"In my room, with my husband and my family," she said.

"Great," Izzy said. "We just need a quick test on your hands and clothing and also on that rifle you have and we can let you get back to your convention."

"*What*?" Littleton piped up, outraged.

"You friggin' kidding me?" Fred Dodge shouted. "The government has finally come for our guns!"

"I don't want to keep your weapons," Izzy explained. "We just have to test for gunshot residue and ballistics."

"I said it would happen and here it is!" the former governor declared in a loud voice, causing the TV crews to scurry back to her. "The mongrel Moslem administration has come for our god-given guns."

"Lady, I'm investigating five murders and we are asking everyone who…"

"The time has come!" Littleton shouted, not to be upstaged. "First gun control and now this!"

I noticed Phil still had his piece out, swiveling it around, watching the gunmen, especially their hands. The cameras were back, the lights on. Izzy had his friendliest smile on, his most easygoing tone.

"Mrs. Dodge, many of the other delegates have already agreed to help us solve these terrible murders, by eliminating all of you good people," he said. "But you can refuse to speak to us, that's your right. It's cool, because, hey, anything you tell us can be used if there is a trial. You could get a lawyer. I know they're expensive, so, if you like, we could ask a judge to get a free one for you. Do you understand that?" Izzy handed her a white card.

"Umm… sure, I guess… but…"

"Did you just read my wife her rights?" Fred asked, dumbfounded.

"I don't have to read them. I know them by heart. Mrs. Dodge, now that you understand your rights, are you willing to speak to us and to cooperate?"

"How dare you?" Fred asked. "Who the hell do you think you are?"

"NYPD. And you're in my city. Well, Mrs. Dodge? Will

you speak to us and submit to testing?"

"No way!" Fred shouted.

"I didn't commit any crime," the bejeweled politician protested. "I didn't kill anybody."

"Mandy!" Her husband shouted. He was clearly aware that she had just given the media a new lead story.

"Okay, that's fine," Izzy told her. "We'll be in touch. Soon. Have a nice day. How about you, Mr. Littleton? Are you willing to speak with us and submit to—"

"I will never submit to the Zionist Occupation Government and their jack-booted thugs," Littleton announced.

"You're the one wearing combat boots, pal," Phil said. "These are cop Oxfords. Aren't we your first line of defense anymore?"

"So, to be clear, ma'am," Izzy said for the cameras, "you are refusing to cooperate in this homicide investigation."

"That's right, I will never surrender my guns," Mrs. Dodge added, recovering.

"Cold, dead…"

"You can have my gun," she shouted dramatically, directly at Izzy, with an exaggerated hair flip, "When you pry it from my cold, dead hands!"

She tried to stare Izzy down. He glared calmly back at her until the applause ended.

"Hold on," Izzy told Dodge. "I'm thinking."

40

Miranda Dodge blinked but Izzy didn't. Her husband pulled her away and the convention resumed around us. Tiffany was at the podium, and informed Dodge that her motion to have her own nomination ballot was denied. Dodge's supporters booed, hooted and hollered for ten minutes, waving DODGE FOR PRESIDENT signs, before running out of steam. Dodge stepped to a microphone stand at her native Alaska delegation area and demanded to be recognized.

"The chair is not recognizing delegates at this time," Tiffany announced. "We will proceed with the vote on the nomination of Senator Katharine Carroll for President of the United States. Please come to order for the calling of the role."

"NO!" Dodge protested. "You don't have enough votes! Without us, you won't even have a quorum! You won't have a candidate—you won't be able to do anything. I want my vote first or we walk!"

"Again, the chair is not recognizing delegates until after the vote."

"That's it! We're leaving!"

"Is the delegate from Alaska informing the chair that she and her pledged delegates are resigning from this convention, under rule 22 point 9, section F?"

"Shoot yeah! We resign, we secede!"

Her crew went wild, making it difficult to hear Tiffany at the podium.

"Very well, the chair acknowledges your irrevocable resignations and wishes the delegates the best of luck."

Dodge and her large block of Tea Party delegates swarmed for the main exit, pumping her signs, chanting her name. She led the exodus, waving and smiling for the camera crews, who went with them. It took another ten minutes for them all to exit and gather in a tight crowd in the main gallery outside where a podium had already been set up for her. Dodge gave TV interviews about her move, explaining that she had stopped the convention, which could not achieve a seventy-five per cent quorum needed for any action. Izzy, Phil and I followed from a distance and watched from the exit arch. Tiffany began quickly calling the names of the states, asking how many in each delegation voted for Carroll.

"Madam Chairwoman, the great state of Alabama is proud to cast its six remaining delegate votes for Katharine Carroll for President of the United States!"

Tiffany continued at a very fast pace, alphabetically polling the states. Some seemed to have a lot of remaining votes; Alaska did not answer when called. Some state delegations had only a few left but all the votes cast were for Carroll. We strolled over to the edge of Dodge's mob to listen to her interviews.

"So you control the convention because you control the quorum?" a reporter asked her.

Dodge's husband leaned toward her but we couldn't hear his prompt.

"That's correct, Diana, it's all about Parliamenting Procedure and vote counting," Dodge responded, obviously trying to sound brainy.

"Perhaps you can explain to me what rule 22 point 9, section F is?"

Dodge's eyes bugged, as if someone had squeezed her ass. She obviously had no clue. She tilted an ear toward her husband and then dodged the question.

"*We* know what it is, Diana, but that's far too technical and boring for everybody. The point is, this convention must recognize me as the rightful candidate or everything will stay deadlocked."

"No, I really don't know what it means. What *is* rule 22 point 9, section F?"

"We are too busy with the country's business to waste time on tech-support, kinda gotcha questions, Diana. Let's keep message discipline here."

"Okay, why do you think you deserve the nomination when you only have, at most, twenty-five per cent of the delegates?"

"Because I am the only candidate who can beat that liberal liar Amelia Calhoun in November! All the polls show that I will beat that Democrat fat cat."

"Actually, the only poll that shows that result was your poll."

"Next question," Dodge snapped.

A lot of cellphones sounded in the press gaggle. One by one they stopped waving their hands to ask questions and ran back into the convention hall. Within a minute or so, Dodge was standing alone, confused. Without the press noise I could now hear what was going in the main hall. Tiffany was well along in the alphabet and the applause by the remaining delegates was building as more and more votes piled up for Katharine Carroll.

Dodge looked at her husband, confused. He mirrored her expression. Dodge's delegates drifted back toward the hall, as she and her husband and their team huddled. They broke and walked as fast as they could back toward the convention floor. They were stopped at the entrance by a wall of security. Inside, Tiffany had reached the end of her hurried roll call.

"Wyoming?" Tiffany asked.

"Madam Chairwoman, the cowboys and cowgirls of Wyoming, the Equality State, is proud to cast all of their votes for the next president of the United States. Senator Katharine Carroll!"

Everyone except Dodge's people went berserk. The convention chanted Carroll's name, stamped their feet and cheered. Dodge and her group hurled curses and threats—even their signs—but were denied access and ordered to leave as they had resigned from the party and from their delegate status. The quorum was no longer an issue—because their departure meant they needed fewer delegates in order to take action. Rule 22 transferred the seceding votes to whoever received the most votes, which was Carroll.

"This convention stands in recess until the acceptance speech at seven p.m. this evening," Tiffany announced, banging the gavel and leaving the stage.

"They can't do this!" Dodge moaned. "They will pay for this! I will kill those motherfuckers!"

I transcribed her words into my phone and sent them to the newspaper. Dodge didn't notice or didn't care that a few TV crews were back, shooting her tantrum. Her husband was glaring directly at me. The ventriloquist was furious, as the dummy flailed in the spotlight.

"This isn't over! Payback's a bitch," Dodge spat. "I will destroy every one of them! Who fucked up? What the hell was rule 22 whatever?"

Rule 22 was mathematics. When Dodge pulled out, her delegates' slots were voided for the rest of the convention, lowering the number of votes needed for a quorum or to pass a nomination. I couldn't resist.

"Something you probably should have read before shooting your mouth off," I told Dodge before walking away.

41

My stomach growled. I realized it was two in the afternoon. I hadn't eaten breakfast yet and was starving. There was a food and beverage table backstage, where Tiffany was orchestrating TV interviews with the new candidate on a small, brightly lit set with traditional furniture that looked suspiciously like the White House Oval Office. I loaded a plate with mysterious finger foods: green dumplings, red eggrolls, mini sandwiches and the best food in the world—those little pigs in blankets with mustard. Izzy and Phil joined me but ate fast and rushed back to Chesterfield's room, to supervise the removal of his body to the Medical Examiner's office.

As I chowed down, I was amazed how quickly the names on the signs were changed and how fast the back-benchers had come forward. I watched Senator Katharine Carroll explain to one interviewer what happened on the floor prior to her nomination and then quickly launched into her political talking points, already campaigning against the Democratic nominee. Her hair and makeup were perfect, her words polished. Maybe too polished.

"My liberal opponent, Senator Amelia Calhoun, failed to protect the people under her command in the State

Department and they were defenseless against the terrorists who killed them," Carroll declared. "That would never happen on my watch."

Boring.

"You were right, Shepherd," Tiffany said, sliding up to me as I finished my food. "Dodge and her people never bothered to read the rules. They walked right into the trap."

"Your new boss is walking into a trap of her own right now," I warned.

"What are you talking about?"

"Five of her guys were murdered on her watch and she didn't prevent it. And it happened right here, under her nose, in the good 'ol USA, not in some terror spot in the Middle East. She even had a rifle loaded for terrorist bear and didn't use it."

"Jesus, you're right," Tiffany agreed. "Shoot! The Calhoun campaign will probably come out blasting on that one. See, Shepherd, I really could use your help on this campaign. It's crazy—jumping in like this. I need you."

"You've already got me—I'm onboard until we nail the killers."

"No, let the cops and the feds do that. Come work with me on the campaign trail. You're a natural."

"Actually work in politics?" I laughed. "No way. When it's not boring, it's stupid or disgusting."

"That's the only way I'll get to see you for the next four months," she said, moving closer, slipping her hand in mine. "I would like that. You could work directly under me." She smirked wickedly.

"Yeah, I'd like that too, but I've got this job to do first."

"A man of your word?"

"What else is there?"

"Adventure? Destiny? Sex?"

"You forgot food and booze. Listen, can I grab your new boss for a few moments? I just have a few more questions for her."

"I thought you were done with her?" Tiffany replied coolly, withdrawing her hand from mine.

"Are you kidding?"

"Not now, Shepherd. This is her moment. Tell me what you need, I'll ask her during a break and get back to you."

"That's not the way it works, Tiffany, you know that. You were there when she lied to us."

"Hold it! I don't know any such thing."

I reminded Tiffany about Carroll's disconnected smoke detector in her suite, the smell of cigarette smoke lingering in the air there and how she lied to us in front of her daughter.

"You can't possibly think she had anything to do with this," Tiffany said.

"I don't know. She seems to be the only politician targeted by the killer who survived. Why? She is certainly the one who benefitted from this mass murder. Yesterday she was Senator Who? Today, she's running for the White House with mountains of money that was supposed to elect your old boss. Why is she lying? Maybe she made it happen."

"That's not funny, Shepherd."

"I wasn't trying to be."

"Okay," she snapped. "I'll ask her as soon as this live segment is over."

While Tiffany returned to her candidate, I called Izzy and told him what was happening. He said the bodies of Chesterfield and the others had been removed for autopsies but the murder rooms were still sealed crime scenes, as was Carroll's. I checked my paper's website.

MIRANDA WARNING
Prez Hopeful Read Her Rights
In Quint Slay Mystery

It's not her day. Within minutes of becoming a murder suspect in the slayings of five members of Congress,

Tea Party Darling Miranda Dodge was outfoxed by GOP
stalwarts and left out in the cold. Spouting profanity, the
family values politician vowed to run a spoiler campaign
that... (Continued...)

Tiffany delayed for ten minutes and then told me it would
be at least an hour until the senator could speak to me. Maybe.

"We'll try to fit you in then," she said, with a lovely smile.

"Super," I told her, returning her fake smile.

When Izzy and Phil arrived, we chatted and then
approached Tiffany. They were all business. Tiffany also
tried to stall them, saying her boss was speaking on live TV
with FAX News.

"Miss Mauser," Izzy told Tiffany. "This is a multiple
murder investigation. Either you make the senator available
to us right now or I will join her on the couch and ask my
questions live on FAX News."

That worked. Five minutes later we were in a dressing
room with Katharine Carroll. Izzy kicked off proceedings.

"Senator Carroll, I don't think you were being completely
honest with us earlier, at your suite, when you said you did
not have your smoke detectors disconnected."

"Of course I was, Lieutenant. Why would you think
otherwise?"

"Because your detector *was* disconnected. The hotel
says your people asked them to do it. You also said you
had not been smoking in there but we smelled tobacco.
Want to try again?"

The senator, ruffled at Izzy's lack of awe, stared at us for
quite a while.

"I apologize, Lieutenant. May we speak in confidence?"

"Of course."

"My daughter is fourteen years old and she thinks I have
given up smoking. Sometimes... actually very often... I still
smoke, at the office and elsewhere. I didn't want her to

know. It would be embarrassing."

"Not as embarrassing as being busted for five murders," I pointed out.

"You can't seriously think I had anything to do with that?"

"Is your daughter here?" I asked. "So she can confirm that? And it also doesn't explain why you were the only one of the smokers who is still breathing."

Tiffany glared at me.

"I have no idea, Mr. Shepherd. I hope the police will find out and tell me. Good luck. And no, you may not interview my daughter. Now, if we're done, I have quite a few more interviews and a campaign to plan."

Izzy shrugged. "We'll be in touch."

As we left, I saw Carroll shoot a glance at me and whisper something to Tiffany, who nodded and followed us out.

Outside the dressing room, Phil stated the obvious: "There's no evidence against her."

"Nice job," Tiffany said to me.

"Thanks," I replied.

"You're fired," she said. "I'm sorry, Shepherd. I tried to stop you. Will you leave now or do I have to call security?"

"I'm fired? So I guess I won't have the pleasure of serving under you?"

She walked away without answering.

"First fight?" Phil asked.

42

Phil was right. I'd never been fired before. It felt weird.

"Hey," Izzy said. "You were going after her new employer. Did you see Carroll whisper something to her? If your friend ignored a direct order from her boss to can you, she would also be out on her ass."

"Tiffany signed onto this new candidate pretty quick," Phil countered.

"I was wondering the same thing," I told him. "We don't know who did this yet."

"This kind of thing happens all the time in politics," Izzy said.

"But that's when candidates drop out—not drop dead," I pointed out. "Carroll lied about the smoke alarm and won't let us talk to her daughter. Why is the senator still alive?"

"Are you saying you like her for it?" Izzy asked. "That Carroll and maybe Tiffany planned this whole thing?"

"I'm not saying anything yet," I said. I had a sudden thought. "Do you guys know anything about Karl Bundt?"

"The security guy who looks like a jerk?" Izzy asked. "No. Why? You think he was too dumb to be true?"

"I'm not saying anything," I repeated myself. "I'm just asking."

"We'll check him out, but a few more facts to rub together would be nice," Phil said. "While the troops continue interviews here, we're going over to the ME's office for the post on Chesterfield. You coming, Shepherd?"

My trendy lunch shifted in my stomach. An autopsy would round out my perfect day.

"Sure. I just need to change clothes and check in with Amy. I'll meet you over there."

As I dialed Amy's number, I saw dozens of delegates fleeing, ducking into limos, glancing around nervously—presumably trying to spot assassins. At this rate of retreat, there'd be no Republicans in town to hear Carroll's acceptance speech at seven tonight, just before the big fireworks display.

"You got fired?" Amy asked when I reached her. "They can't fire us. We have a contract."

"That was with the previous management," I pointed out. "He's on the slab over on First Avenue."

"Well, the good news is they've already paid us in full," Amy told me. "But I don't see how we can file for new expenses."

"Does this mean I don't have to save receipts anymore?"

"No. I still need them. So, you're coming back here? Your dog is eating me into bankruptcy."

"Skippy has a healthy appetite. Yeah, I need to change and then I'm meeting Izzy and Phil over at the Medical Examiner's office for the post-mortem on Chesterfield."

"But we don't work for the Republicans anymore."

"I'm on this 'til we get the bastards. If I still have my job with you, that is. We have to save our rep."

"Yes, you still have your job. And I agree with you... up to a point."

"Up to what point?"

"I don't know. I'll let you know when we get there," she said, and hung up.

Aces. The sunshine outside was hot, a blue sky filled with Disney-white clouds. In twenty-four hours I was dumped by my girlfriend, found a new girlfriend—who then fired me and kicked me out of her bed—after the guy I was supposed to keep alive was murdered, along with four others. The day couldn't get worse.

That was when I spotted my parents, still at the barricade. My mother was autographing a copy of the *New York Mail*—the one that labeled them commies—and having her photo taken with a fan. My father was a few yards away, giving an MSNBC TV interview about the political violence. My parents had Liberal groupies. Just shoot me.

I walked over. If my father used the phrase "the violence inherent in the capitalistic system," I would shoot him. If I still shot people.

"So? Was it Miranda Dodge and her neo-confederate trash?" my mother demanded. "Did they do it?"

"I don't know," I told her. "It's possible."

My father was happy. He was on TV and he'd predicted something that came true. The war inside the party he hated was a gift for him. He loved being right more than anything. My mother smiled fondly at him.

"Several TV stations have interviewed him already. Soon we'll take the message to Park Avenue, to the evil billionaires behind the Tea Party," she said.

"I'm glad you're enjoying your vacation," I said. "But I have to get back to work."

Walking east across the park, I thought about the events of the night before. It was hard to concentrate; I kept getting sidetracked onto the sex. I remembered that she ducked out for a while. That was about nine, right after the steaks arrived. She was gone more than half an hour. Where did she go? What did she do? She never said. Did she have time to run around the hotel, blasting politicos, who opened their doors to the titillating, on-task Tiffany? If so, where was the weapon or weapons? How come no one saw her or heard five separate shots? She was questioned, just like I was. And she was given a Gunshot Residue Test. She had an alibi and the test must have come up negative, like mine, because she had not fired a gun. Or had she? Why didn't I mention to Izzy and Phil that she was not with me for a period of time during the security video blackout, during the murders? Because she fucked me silly? Because it never occurred that she would have anything to do with something like this? I was her alibi and I never mentioned that she was missing for more than thirty minutes after nine—the time the security video system was shut down by the hacker. A lot of damage can happen in half an hour. Hell, even half a minute. As soon as she got back, Tiffany took a shower and changed her clothes, which would have erased traces of gunpowder. I wondered if Tiffany mentioned her mysterious evening errand to the detectives. Or did she just tell them about her time in bed with me? She gave me one hell of a birthday present but, if she also left out her little evening stroll, I had given her something much more valuable—an alibi.

43

Skippy almost knocked me over when I walked into Amy's place. It took ten minutes to get past all the licking and invitations to play before I could have a talk with Amy, take a shower in an upstairs bathroom and change. The walls were bright purple and the style was Victorian oak and white marble. I noticed the ceiling was a painted, starry heaven with golden, floating cherubs. As I was getting dressed in clean clothes, Jane called my cell.

"Hey," I said, unsure what to say. "What's up?"

"If you want to talk to me about what happened over at the convention center, I'm available," Jane said.

What the hell?

"Umm... okay..."

My stomach twisted into a knot. Did Jane know about Tiffany?

"It's very upsetting," she said.

Damn. How did she find out?

I just made a non-committal grunt; stalling, hoping for a way out.

"But you had only just met," Jane continued.

"True," I agreed, evenly.

"Still, it has to be very painful to have your first client murdered."

219

What?

"Yes. Painful," I stumbled, hoping I was through the minefield. "Exactly. Chesterfield seemed like a nice guy, for a politician."

"And the others, too," she said. "Very scary."

"Yes," I concurred. "That was very scary."

Jane talked for a bit, as I tried to pretend I was as upset as she seemed to be. She made a vague apology for being on edge recently and asked when I would be home. Home. She wanted to see me. I told her I would be at her place after I met Izzy and Phil at the autopsy. She paused, maybe wondering how upset I could be if I were going to an autopsy. Then she surprised me.

"Can I come along?"

How could I say no? Quality time at the morgue. Skippy was upset that I was leaving so soon but I knew he would not like my destination and would probably not be allowed in anyway. I hopped in a cab, which had a video of the mayor, Irving Flowers, welcoming me to the Big Apple. I picked Jane up outside her office. She was wearing her white lab coat with the "Dr. Jane" nameplate and a stethoscope around her neck. We kissed on the back seat.

"Well, this is quite a lovely date," Jane giggled, as we went to the office of the Chief Medical Examiner, a blue-bricked rectangular building on First Avenue at East 30th Street, between Bellevue Hospital and New York University Hospital.

"Hey, this was your idea," I pointed out.

"Maybe I can help you," Jane said. "I'm not a pathologist but I have training and experience that may be useful."

"Also you're wicked smart," I agreed. "And a hottie."

"Correct."

I paid the cab, got a printed receipt, walked up the steps into a glassed-in lobby and told a woman behind a counter why we were there. I was still wearing the GOP ID card from the convention around my neck and Jane had her own plastic ID card on her lab coat. We were directed downstairs, to "The Pit." It looked like a hospital, but without any of the equipment needed to monitor or sustain life. It smelled like formaldehyde. The long white room had eight rectangular stainless-steel autopsy tables lined up across one wall. Each table had a gray metal tray set into the tabletop and five of the eight slabs hosted familiar congressional corpses. The farthest one held a naked Percy Chesterfield and around him stood Phil, Izzy, and an unfamiliar man and woman. An older male pathologist, his face the color of dark chocolate, wearing blue scrubs, blue gloves and headgear with a clear plastic face shield, was doing the post-mortem. An assistant moved about, busy with organs and equipment.

Izzy and Phil greeted us with muted cordiality.

"Just in time," Izzy said to me. "Cleaning and photos are done. X-rays show what Dr. Warner says looks like a ball bearing lodged in the spine."

"I said it *could* be a ball bearing, especially if this was an explosive device," said the pathologist. "But, from what you tell me, it is more likely to be a musket ball, fired by black powder. Certainly smells like it. We'll see."

"A musket ball?" Jane asked, intrigued.

"Give me a friggin' break," Izzy groaned. "A musket? Couldn't be anything simple?"

"That makes sense," I told Jane. "These are gun nuts, who worship weapons and the Second Amendment. Also, they're calling themselves the New Minutemen—you know, like the Revolutionary War guys with muskets. This is a political statement. 'We're using the Founding Fathers' firearms to kill you'? Very cute. That might explain the gunpowder smell. Old-fashioned black powder. You gotta give it to these guys, Izzy. They have style."

"And maybe a sense of humor," Jane added.

Izzy responded with a string of obscenities that did not include any props to the killer for style or wit.

Dr. Warner opened the chest, probing while speaking his findings out loud into a tiny wire microphone. His words appeared magically on a flat-screen TV above the table, obviously a speech-to-word-processing program.

"Okay," Warner said, "there is a red ecchymosis ring around the point of apparent entry. Referencing the earlier charring of clothing, extensive and pronounced stippling of the skin, probably with propellant. We have a small section of fabric embedded in the main wound, possibly consistent with the victim's clothing. The wound tracks slightly upward from front to back. As we explore the wound track, the skin and musculature of the chest was forced inward from the concussion wave of the blast, several ribs were fractured from this force... the heart is ruptured and perforated."

He listed the specific ribs and the organs struck by the metal ball. "The projectile is lodged into the inside of the anterior spine with considerable force at the T5 level. There is extensive comminution of the backbone, with displacement of bone spicula."

Izzy gave him a look. Warner sighed.

"The backbone was fractured. Lots of bone fragments blown around everywhere."

It took a pair of pliers and some serious yanking to remove the shiny sphere from Chesterfield's spine. The pathologist placed it in a metal tray and hosed off the blood.

"The ball shot is barely deformed," Warner said. "Measuring approximately three quarters of an inch. No evidence of ballistic lands and grooves markings on the projectile. Heavy, possibly stainless steel. Looks like a musket ball to me but not lead. We will test to determine what kind of metal it is."

"With my luck, it's plutonium," Izzy grumbled.

"The force of impact would likely have knocked the victim over," Warner continued. "Death was virtually instantaneous."

His assistant used a caliper to measure the metal sphere

and announced for the record that the diameter was slightly smaller than three quarters of an inch—point six nine inches. The ball looked heavier than a fifty-caliber slug. Dr. Warner used forceps to remove another small bloody object from the open body cavity.

"From the musculature, I have removed what appears to be a small two-inch square of fabric, possibly more clothing contaminating the wound," Warner said.

He rinsed it off at the adjacent sink and declared the rough material was green in color, and charred. It was bagged and Izzy and Phil peered at it.

"Doesn't look like it came from Chesterfield's tie or shirt," said Phil. Jane and I stepped in closer to see for ourselves.

"That looks like silk or linen," Jane said.

"It's wadding," I said. "Musketeers used patches to wedge the musket ball into the barrel."

"You may have something there, Sherlock," Izzy agreed. "But how the hell do we do a ballistic match on this ball, without identifying marks?"

"You don't have to," I told him. "Just look for guys with muzzle-loading antiques, like Revolutionary War re-enacters or gun collectors. How many can there be?"

"A lot," Izzy countered. "You can buy muzzle-loaders, new single-shot flintlocks and percussion cap weapons through the mail, as kits or fully assembled replicas. Black powder and musket balls, too. It's legal. And, thanks to our wonderful gun laws, not only can anyone buy them but they are not registered and don't even have serial numbers."

"Oh," I said. "So anyone using a musket to kill someone is, basically, using an unlisted gun—an untraceable murder weapon."

"Maybe," Dr. Warner responded. "We are going to do testing on everything—the powder, the musket ball, the clothing—and we might find a distinctive signature of some kind to compare to a suspected weapon."

"If we find one," Izzy pointed out. "Which we haven't, so far."

"Think positive," Warner suggested.

"Where the hell could they hide a friggin' musket?" Phil wondered. "Some of those things are five or six feet long."

"The same place you would hide a tree, maybe," I told him. "In a forest of long guns."

"One of the assholes carrying rifles at the convention?" Izzy asked.

"Just a thought."

Izzy smiled and nodded. Phil made a call to the team at the convention and asked them to find out who was carrying what type of weapon—especially anyone carrying an antique.

"A lot of the delegates have already split," Phil informed Izzy. "We'll have to track them down."

"*Pluma a pluma, se pela la grulla,*" Izzy sighed.

"Feather by feather, the goose is plucked," Jane translated, with a smile.

I forgot that she spoke Spanish.

44

The morgue got crowded. A mob of detectives in suits arrived first, led by the Chief of Detectives and feds in chinos and FBI windbreakers. Next to join the crew were men and women wearing Department of Homeland Security uniforms; agents from the Bureau of Alcohol, Tobacco, Firearms and Explosives, wearing ATF jackets; and more men and women in plainclothes, harder to peg. Then the Mounties arrived—at least they looked like Mounties—New York State troopers with Smokey Bear hats, cross-chest gun belts and tall black leather boots. Izzy pointed out a few from the State Attorney General's office, and Manhattan District Attorney Krystal Ryan.

"Wonder which ones are from Scotland Yard?" I asked.

Phil and Izzy chuckled but kept their mouths shut. Izzy reported to his boss, who didn't look very happy about what Izzy told him.

"What the fuck?" the Chief of Detectives erupted. "A musket?"

The killer's little joke was having its effect. The news buzzed through the law enforcement horde in seconds like weird wildfire.

"The chief tells me we are going to keep the musket thing under our hats," Izzy said when he returned. "We're waiting

225

for three more pathologists to arrive and autopsy the other four bodies, this time with a larger audience. Some of these guys are pissed off that Chesterfield's was done without them present."

"Weren't they all killed the same way?" Jane asked.

"Yup. But there's hope that one of the other bodies will yield some new evidence." He lowered his voice to a whisper. "The real reason we're here is to hold onto our case. Because all of these Staties, feds and spooks want to steal it. We are probably going to become that terrible thing—a multi-departmental task force."

"Let the feds have it," Phil protested. "This is a disaster, a toxic clusterfuck that already has out-of-state connections."

"I'm with you, Phil, but the boss is holding onto this and we have orders to fight to keep the cases. We get to keep them—or we get some major favors if we give them up."

"So he can be commissioner?" Phil asked.

"Actually, I think he wants to be the next mayor. For now, we still own it."

"Don't forget, Izzy," Phil warned, "when the elephants fuck, the mice get squashed."

"We ain't no mice," Izzy shot back.

Amy called and I filled her in on the autopsy.

"A musket? You are pulling my dick."

"No, Amy, I'm not pulling your dick. Wait, my editor is calling. I'll talk to you later. Hey, Mel, what's up?"

"That's what you're supposed to flapping tell me," he snapped. "Kaplan at the cop shop just called. He said some kind of antique blunderbuss was used to kill these guys?"

Jesus, that was fast. The news about the musket had travelled from this room, to One Police Plaza, to our reporter, to my editor, and back to me in just five minutes. The shot heard round the world.

"That's off the record," I told Mel. "They don't want that out."

"Tough titmouse," Mel snarked. "If we got it, the *Mail* will get it soon. Frigate—we're going with the soaking story."

He was gone. I gave the bad news to Izzy, who relayed it to his boss, who went, well, ballistic.

"The next asshole who leaks anything to the media from my investigation is going to get his pension shoved up his ass so far he'll be able to read the fine print when he looks in the mirror!" he shouted.

I asked Izzy who the couple were that had observed Chesterfield's examination with us.

"No clue," Izzy responded. "They were very polite but I couldn't get a fucking thing out of them."

"Department of Agriculture?" Phil wondered, sarcastically.

I checked the *New York Mail* website, but they hadn't got the musket story yet, and were covering the mass exit from the convention.

ELEPHANT GRAVEYARD
Patriot Lames Pack Trunks, Turn Tail

The story described the "gun-shy" Republican convention as "a circular firing squad." My paper's webline had already updated. I showed Izzy and the others.

BLAST FROM THE PAST
MUSKETEER FEAR
Cops Seek Antique Arms in GOP Massacre

There was a picture of a flintlock musket and an inset file photo of a generic musket ball. There was also another file shot of Miranda Dodge, wearing a Tea Party three-cornered hat and firing a flintlock.

"Case solved," Phil said.

After standing around in the autopsy room for a while, I got bored. I asked Izzy if I could go back and look over the murder scenes, now that the Crime Scene Unit was done with them.

"You're leaving our little cop convention? Why?"

"I didn't really get a chance to get a good look at Chesterfield's room, or the other scenes, and it might help me think."

He made a face at the word "think," shrugged and had Phil make another call "You can do walk-throughs but under police escort, and for God's sake wear gloves."

I turned to Jane. "You want to come?"

She shook her head. "This is too fascinating. I'll see you at home later, okay?"

I shrugged and kissed her, which raised a few eyebrows, not least from Izzy and Phil—they were no doubt thinking of my private time with Tiffany. Apparently none of the others in the police posse were on kissing terms. I carefully threaded my way through the crowd of cops, agents, lawyers, spies—and one gorgeous veterinarian—and left.

45

I used my GOP ID to get back through security at the convention center. It was so deserted, the only thing missing was tumbleweed. The cops at Chesterfield's room insisted on calling Izzy again before they would give me blue surgical gloves and paper booties to put over my shoes. A uniformed female NYPD sergeant, whose nameplate identified her as REED, dropped the bright yellow NYPD CRIME SCENE DO NOT CROSS tape and unlocked a new shiny padlock, which was fixed onto a new hasp screwed into the doorframe.

When she opened the door, you could still detect the fireworks smell, the black powder odor. The sergeant walked in front of me down the short hallway and stood blocking the bloodstains on the rug where Chesterfield fell. The small burned area on the left was still there but his cigarette butt had been bagged and removed.

The color scheme in the Presidential Suite was red and gold, including gilded furniture, which gave it a regal look. Even the wall-mounted TV screen was framed in gold. Fingerprint powder was brushed over every surface, including his crystal whiskey glass on a table.

"Don't step on the rug here," Reed said, pointing toward the blood. "Our guys have been here but the FBI evidence crew won't get here until later—they're doing the other scenes upstairs first."

I walked around the spot and looked at the large window I had warned Chesterfield about. The drapes were wide open and the Hudson River was still occupied by the giant warship. I moved closer and looked at the glass but couldn't find any holes. The round didn't come through there. The window was sealed tight. I looked for Chesterfield's belongings on the coffee table—the unfinished drink, a cellphone, a pack of Lucky Strikes and a gold lighter—but it, too, had been tagged as evidence and removed.

The bedroom was palatial, with a huge gold canopy bed and a sitting area and another giant TV. I looked at the large gilded windows, which were also sealed shut. Hotels did not like people to commit suicide by jumping out their windows, so they did not open.

"Quite a nice whorehouse," I said aloud.

"Nice to be the king," Reed laughed.

"Until someone else wants to be king," I said.

"Right."

I noticed more dark fingerprint powder everywhere, including on the surfaces of a large dresser and two night tables flanking the royal bed. One of the night tables had a book on it about Ronald Reagan that looked untouched. I began opening drawers. One night table was empty. The one with the book on it had a Gideon Bible inside, also unopened. I moved on to the dresser. There was a large bulky lamp in the shape of a fluted column. I tried to move it but it was obviously bolted to the top of the dresser. I opened a drawer.

"Careful," Reed cautioned.

"His clothes are still in here?"

"Yup."

"Anybody go through everything?" I asked her.

"Yup. All photographed, videoed, checked out. The stuff

here will have to be removed after the FBI is done. No touch."

"And?"

"Who are you again?"

I told her I had been hired by Chesterfield to investigate the death threats against him. I neglected to mention that I had sort of been fired.

"Nothing major. Some rubbers. Unused. Prescription meds."

"Okay. Where were the rubbers?"

"Next to the Bible."

Where else? The bathroom décor was not Louis XVI style but Roman emperor, with black and white floor tiles forming a mosaic. The tub, toilet and sink were large, rounded white porcelain, as was a statue of the Venus de Milo in the huge shower area. Everything in the bathroom gleamed, clean as a whistle. I noticed a small gold button in the shape of a flower on top of the toilet, about the size of a small strawberry. There was a little hexagonal hole on top. I pushed the gold flower, tried to slide it, then unscrew it, but nothing happened.

"The flush is the gold dolphin on the side," Reed told me.

"Oh. What's this?"

"Top lock," Reed explained.

"They lock the toilet top on?" I asked her. "I understand they nail the lamps down so nobody will steal them—but a toilet top?"

"Yeah, some jails and mental hospitals do it too, so nobody uses it as a weapon. It's really heavy. You can bash someone's brains out with one of those. Maybe even smash out a window."

"Oh. Never thought of that. Right."

The medicine cabinet had been cleaned out, only black fingerprint powder smears remaining. The shower floor had a nice mosaic of a porpoise. The spigots in the shower, tub and sink were matching gold-plated dolphins. Draped over the side of the tub was a floor mat, which had suction cups on one side—so guests wouldn't slip and fall and sue the hotel. The bathroom alone must have cost twice what my apartment was worth—and I couldn't afford that either.

"He should have been safe," I told Reed. "He was locked in a soundproof room, he was armed, his majesty couldn't slip in the bath and no one could brain him with a potty top or a lamp or shove him out a window."

"Yeah," Reed agreed. "Too bad he opened the door."

"Speaking of which, the hotel must be bugged that all these fancy rooms are still crime scenes?"

"Tell me about it," Reed laughed. "Those guys are up here every hour on the hour, batshit, telling us how much coin they're losing every day. They claim they'll go to a judge if we don't leave soon but I think they're just huffing and puffing."

Chesterfield's suite alone cost $5,000 a day. With the other rooms at lower rates, it had to be fifteen or twenty grand a day the hotel was losing.

"What kind of asshole blows people away with a flintlock anyway?" Reed asked.

"An asshole who owns a flintlock and wants to make a really stupid point."

"I guess. How the hell did they get it in and out of here?"

"This place was a gun convention," I said.

"Yeah, I guess."

"Also, it doesn't have to be huge—it might have been a pistol," I suggested.

"You mean like a pirate pistol?"

"Yeah, or a dueling pistol. I think that might have the same effect."

"Okay. So, this is the Tea Party guys bumping off their own people who are in their way?"

"Maybe. Not sure yet."

"Don't muzzle-loaders take, like, five minutes to reload?" she asked.

It was a good point. Did the killer waste one person, reload for several minutes, and then proceed to the next room to do it again—until all five were dead? That would mean a lot of exposure for a single gunman.

"I think you're right. Maybe there was one rifle—or pistol—for each hit."

"So you could be looking for five guys with one gun each, or one guy with five guns?"

"Or six—looks like they wanted to whack Senator Carroll, too, but maybe something went wrong."

If Carroll really was an intended target.

"So there was probably a crew of half a dozen or more, who offed armed, highly protected politicians inside a security fortress and got away clean, along with an arsenal, and you have to find them?"

"Uhhh... yeah."

"Better you than me, pal. Watch your ass."

"Thanks."

46

It was already dark when I left the convention center, walking south on Seventh Avenue, the hot, humid air rumbling everywhere with the sharp sounds of combat—firecrackers, heavy fireworks exploding like small arms fire, artillery and missile strikes, near and far, echoing off the buildings. It sounded like the whole world was at war. I could feel the larger detonations in my gut, the adrenaline building. My senses began to speed up at the familiar noises, my heartbeat matching the battle rattle, gearing up mentally for attack.

The crowds of demonstrators and counter-demonstrators were gone but the barricades were still up. My parents were nowhere in sight. Manhattan seemed normal after the incredible events at the convention, or as normal as Manhattan ever got. The crowds were light, probably because of the holiday.

I thought about what Sergeant Reed had said. It felt like an inside job, of course. The most logical conclusion was that the politicians got whacked as a result of a power struggle within the party. What she said also felt like a warning. The victims all opened their doors to their murderers, which meant the killers looked like good guys. Also, if these guys could do this to powerful men and get away with it, I was a bug. I suddenly needed dinner badly—I was dying of thirst.

That was when the eye in my neck blinked again. I spun around but no one was there. I walked back the way I came but saw no familiar or suspicious faces. I continued south toward Amy's place. Every few blocks, I would try to shake out a possible tail but I couldn't find anybody. Nobody paid attention to the paranoid guy whirling around and charging backwards, then turning back on his original course. Just another psycho on the streets of the City That Never Sleeps. All the way, the eye blinked. Maybe it was *on* the blink? Maybe the fireworks were freaking me out. Where could I go for a repair job? My best idea was arak. Booze and food and then sleep. Couldn't hurt.

"Siri, where can I get the eye in the back of my head repaired?"

"I don't know what that means, Shepherd."

"Neither do I."

Skippy went berserk again when I arrived back at Amy's place. I brought Amy up to speed, while wrestling with Skippy.

The sensation of being followed was gone. Amy invited me for a barbecue but I told her Skippy and I were going back to Jane's. I would work from there.

"Good," Amy responded, as she followed me upstairs, followed by bounding Skippy and his playmate, Dr. Strangelove. "Glad to hear it."

"You know, Amy, you come off as a tough chameleon, a hard-ass professional, but it turns out you're just a goopy blob of warm feelings."

"Don't be a dick. I'm trying to like you."

We laughed.

"Seriously, Shepherd. That's the last time you fuck a client of mine. Bad for business."

"Tiffany wasn't really the client," I pointed out.

"If you can't follow my rules, there's the door."

"Okay, Amy. You got it. Shouldn't be a problem—anyway, she blew me off."

"Yeah, like you wouldn't jump through hoops naked if she changed her mind tomorrow."

It always felt great to be a predictable male moron. I couldn't argue.

"Either way, no hanky-panky or I spanky," Amy concluded.

"Okay," I agreed.

I fastened his leash onto Skippy's collar and apologized to him. He hated the leash but I had already gotten a ticket for having him off it. In the City That Never Sleeps, neither did the people who gave out tickets. I turned to my new boss.

"Group hug?" I asked.

"Fuck off and get back to work," she said, slamming the front door.

Skippy had some business to take care of in a local park, which was why I carried plastic bags in my knapsack along with the computer. When he was done, I called Jane.

"Hi," Jane answered. "I'm still at the morgue. This is taking forever."

"So leave and we can get some dinner," I told her.

"I'm going to hang in for a while because the lab results should be ready in an hour or two and we'll be done. Then we'll get something to eat."

"You're really taking this seriously," I told her.

"I said I wanted to help. I'm curious about the lab results."

"Anything new?" I asked.

"Well, so far, nothing new except Congressman Abner Hatfield has a tattoo on his groin just above his penis of a little red devil guy pointing his pitchfork and the words 'HOT STUFF.'"

"Sweet. Abner, we hardly knew ya. Okay. I got Skippy. Maybe we'll get a snack or something and see you later."

"Okay, Shepherd. See you at home."

Again, she called it home. Our home? I found a deserted

upscale deli, got a bottle of fancy water from a glass cooler and ordered a turkey sandwich on whole wheat bread from the man behind a high, food-jammed glass counter. I also asked him for a plastic soup bowl.

"What kind of soup do you want, sir?"

"No soup, just the empty bowl, please."

He made a face.

"Can you cut that sandwich in half and only put mustard on one half, please?"

"Yessir. Only half?" the guy asked, confused.

"Yeah."

"What do you want on the other half?"

"Nothing."

"No mustard?"

"Right."

I watched him make the sandwich, cut it in half, and pick up a knife from a mustard bowl.

"Which half?" he asked, pointing the mustard knife.

I looked at him but couldn't tell if he was serious.

"You pick."

47

Skippy got the half without mustard. We wolfed down our food on the sidewalk. He even ate half of the pickle. I poured half the contents of the water bottle into the empty soup bowl and put it on the pavement for him. We both drank from our respective containers and I made a satisfied "ahhhh" sound. Skippy did the same. It tasted better that way. We walked for a few minutes and I decided that, since Jane was still busy, I'd do a little more work.

"What do you say, Skippy—shall we go hunting in the bowels of Brooklyn?"

"Wowf!"

"Okay."

I scanned the street at the corner but I couldn't find a yellow cab. I preferred to use official medallion cabs but it was often hard or impossible to find one when you needed it. Also more expensive. After a while, I took out my phone, and opened the Uber app.

In five minutes, a black SUV pulled up. A guy with a beret lowered the window.

"Hi, I'm Raymond. Are you Shepherd?"

He was listening to jazz.

"I am. My dog okay?"

"Sure, but if he makes a mess, you get charged a hundred bucks."

"You don't mean fur, right?"

"No, I mean solid or liquid waste."

"Not an issue," I assured Raymond, giving him the address in Brooklyn of the APN, the Aryan Purity Nation, which had been raided by the FBI.

We crossed over the East River on the Williamsburg Bridge, a huge monster that looked like a giant child had pasted it together out of rusty popsicle sticks. As we crossed, a subway was also crossing next to us, rumbling and screeching toward the City of Churches.

I was surprised how quickly we were there, the dim streets filled with groups of Hassidic men in long black coats, long beards and black hats. Williamsburg was almost entirely an Orthodox Jewish neighborhood.

"Do you want me to wait?" Raymond asked.

"Nope, thanks, Raymond. I'm going back soon but I'm not sure how long I'll be."

"Okay, take care."

He drove away with a friendly wave. Having him wait would be expensive. Also, I might not want a witness.

The raided building was a converted storefront with bricks where the large plate glass had been. There was yellow crime scene tape across a steel door, and a blue-and-white NYPD car out front with two cops inside. Some businesses seemed to be still functioning but were closed at this hour.

I walked toward the entrance of the white supremacists' headquarters, Skippy pulling at his leash. There was a small sign on the door that read "APN," but nothing that identified it as a right-wing terror group. The two cops popped out of their car, hands on their pistols.

"Can we help you, sir?" one of them asked, suspiciously eyeing Skippy.

"Yeah, thanks," I replied.

I gave them my name, the fact that I had just come from the convention center, and was investigating the homicides. One of them clicked a flashlight onto my GOP ID card and looked at my face.

"Okay, but this is a crime scene and we can't let you in unless one of our bosses says it's a go," the cop said. "They pretty much cleaned the place out, anyway. We're just babysitting."

"Oh. Okay. I'll just ask around the neighborhood."

"Good luck with that."

Across the street, there were several townhouses with lights on inside. I went up the steps to the closest one, as the cops got back inside their patrol car. Neither ringing the doorbell nor knocking on the door got any answer. Same thing at the second house. At the third, a peephole in the door flashed. Someone was looking out. Slowly, cautiously, the door opened. I smelled food. I wasn't sure what kind of food but it smelled good and probably wasn't pork. I told Skippy to sit. A teenaged girl opened the door wider.

"You another detective?" she asked. "Are you a canine cop?"

"I'm Shepherd. I'm investigating the people down the block." I stuck out my hand to shake, but a large, bearded man stepped in between us, sweeping his daughter back with one arm—horrified that I was about to touch her. Oops. Obviously the Hassidim did not approve of inter-gender touching. Sort of like the Amish, but Jewish and in Brooklyn.

"What do you want?" he demanded.

I started to tell him but he cut me off.

"We know nothing, thank you. Good night."

Slam.

Skippy and I continued down the block toward the river but that was the best I got. I came to an apartment building but there was a uniformed doorman who started scowling at me from one hundred paces out. After that the street got darker and there were more dark, silent factories than homes.

I rounded the corner, just curious. Skippy sniffed the air.

"Foof!"

The street here was down to the original cobblestones, paving that had been placed down more than a century earlier. Most of the streetlights were out or missing. From here, the bridge loomed above, arching out over dark industrial buildings and across the river. The dark bridgework began shaking and thumping, as arcing electrical sparks flashed inside its lattice. The vibrations shook the ground under me like an earthquake but it was just an elevated train rattling into Brooklyn.

After the noise faded, Skippy snapped his head right, toward something I could not hear or see. As my eyes got used to the darkness, I realized Skippy was looking at three men with long beards, long black coats and wide-brimmed hats, clustered in the shadows, their faces dark. Kosher vampires? I approached them but they turned and walked away. Shy vampires. It occurred to me that the Orthodox uniform was an excellent criminal disguise because it made them all look alike—beards and glasses and hats and long black clothing that hid faces and shapes and age.

I stopped and called Izzy.

"Yeah?"

"Hey, Izzy, I'm in Brooklyn, where they raided the APN cell."

"Why?"

"Just nosing around," I told him.

"Not much to see. My landsmen welcoming you?"

"What's a landsman?" I asked.

"It's Yiddish for countryman, a fellow Jew."

"Oh. Not so much."

"A goy in the hood," Izzy chuckled. "I thought you weren't getting paid anymore?"

"I'm not. What's new?"

"Guess what one of the congressmen had tattooed below the belt."

"A little devil?"

"Jane told you."

"Yup. Anything else major?"

"Not really. No new leads. Time to call it a night."

"Okay, talk to you in the morning."

I looked around the corner from where I had come. Lights from cars and streetlights beckoned from a few blocks away, through a dead zone of warehouses and empty lots and fences and abandoned vehicles. Fireworks exploded and cascaded above the river. As I walked over the uneven cobblestones toward the light, I activated the Uber app again.

Skippy suddenly jerked me around, a low growl in his chest. Three figures were following us at a distance, a block away; long black coats, long dark beards, dark brimmed hats. The same guys? I considered waiting for them and trying to chat but my gut rejected that. I kept walking toward civilization. *Better in the light*, I thought, quickening my step.

They stepped up their pace, too, now half a block behind me. I noticed they were spreading out. One went straight down the middle of the deserted street and the other two took to the gutters on either side. There were no sidewalks. Why would three friends do that? I'd only do that if I was going to do something and was worried about the dog. Wouldn't it be funny if I was mugged while hunting for killers? I headed for the closest working streetlight, stopped under it and turned around, an excellent target. Skippy was tensed, his fur rippling. The three men also stopped, staying out of the light. Weird. I had a strange vibe that they were armed but I didn't think many Hassidic types packed heat. Of course, I was new in town. I began putting on my gun gloves.

"Good evening, landsmen," I said loudly.

They did not reply. Headlights came down the block behind them, temporarily wiping out my night vision. A dark SUV pulled right up to me.

"Hi, Shepherd," Raymond said, through his open window.

"I was nearby and got the return call."

We got in but Skippy kept his eyes on the dark street behind us, where the trio had been skulking. The three men seemed to have vanished. Raymond asked if it was okay if we picked up another passenger on Delancey Street in Manhattan. Somebody going to Radio City Music Hall.

"Of course, that means your fare is reduced," Raymond explained.

"Fine with us," I agreed.

On the way, my phone rang but no one was on the line. I looked at the screen, which said NUMBER BLOCKED. I texted Jane, in case it was her, and said we would be home soon. On the other side of the bridge, back in Manhattan, a chunky older guy got in the front with Raymond. He did a double-take at Skippy but settled in for the ride. Apparently he didn't speak much English. When we got to the music hall, on Avenue of the Americas at 50th Street, near Rockefeller Center, I told Raymond I wasn't far from home and Skippy needed a walk. I thanked him and said goodnight.

"You got a real cool dog," Raymond said, as we got out. "You trained him well."

"Thanks," I agreed, reaching for the door handle. "But I didn't train him."

"Who did?"

"I don't know."

48

Skippy took care of his business quickly and we started to jog north toward Jane's, Skippy barking at fireworks. The third eye feeling I had earlier returned, the itchy shoulder blades, like a switch had been toggled on. Fuck. If I couldn't trust my third eye, I had no edge. I was just another fat, dumb and happy Jethro waiting for impact. Skippy's ears were working overtime, like fuzzy radar dishes, swiveling left and right as the explosions went off around us.

"It's just fireworks, Skippy. Maintain an even strain."

He stopped in his tracks, tensed and looked up at the dark starless city sky between the tall buildings flanking Avenue of the Americas near the Hilton Hotel. His head bobbled randomly, like he was watching a fly near his nose. Then his head stopped and tilted, then tracked around again. I looked up again and saw nothing.

"What is it, Lassie?" I asked Skippy. "The Dogstar?"

He made a whining noise that sounded like he was trying to talk, his snout sniffing the air at a high-rise building a hundred feet away, on the other side of a little plaza with a fountain and a few benches. He led me to the building, under a third-story overhang, an empty lobby visible behind large plate-glass windows. The building was obviously closed for the night and there was no door on our side. I heard something and looked up at the underside of the building overhang.

In the dim light, feathery gray, white and black shapes were clustered on ledges. I looked at my feet under the crowded eaves, white splatters on the cement.

Pigeons. Hundreds of them, sleeping. I always wondered where they went at night. I took a few sidesteps to avoid being dumped on by dreaming pigeons.

"Since when do you like pigeons?" I asked Skippy.

Usually Skippy went after bigger game: other dogs, cats, carriage horses. But I noticed he wasn't looking up at the drowsy birds. He was looking out over the avenue, again intent on the empty sky, like he spotted a squirrel on a lamppost. I didn't see any pigeons out there. Obviously they weren't nocturnal.

Skippy tensed his muscles, as if he was going to lunge. I held the leash tightly. He could pull me over if he did that. I looked up again. I saw some of the Big Brother video camera bubbles mounted on poles and buildings, part of the expanding surveillance culture that terrorism had forced on us. Nothing else.

"Skippy, buddy, there's nothing up there. Let these guys sleep. They have a busy day tomorrow. I'm hungry, let's get…"

I saw it. A dark shape flashed across a light steel building checkered with reflective glass, like a spider sliding over a web. Then it vanished upwards. Fast.

What. The. Fuck.

"Easy, buddy. Sit. Good boy."

He sat. I never taught Skippy anything but he came to me already highly trained, from a murdered reality show host. Someday, I would have to find out who had instructed my dog.

My rear eye was winking wild. I took out my phone and pretended to take a call. Then I switched on the camera, so it was pointing over my shoulder. I took a shot. Then

I slowly traversed and did it again and again. I looked at the pictures. Nothing. I flipped through them faster, like a movie, and spotted something. I enlarged the spot. Fuck me if it didn't look like a little spider in the sky. Goddamn. Every nerve in my body told me to move. Skippy growled low and kept looking over his shoulder, showing his teeth. My shoulder blades felt like someone was tickling them with a feather duster.

"Good dog!" I yelled. "Let's run!"

Skippy and I took off and I changed course, tugging his leash back toward the building, under the eaves. I yelled loudly upwards; no words, just a throat-ripping Wolfman roar. Skippy began barking loudly.

"Good dog!" I yelled.

The flock of pigeons exploded down and then up into the open air, with a blast of wings all around us. We ran with them. The mass of panicked birds overhead was still climbing, shifting shape upwards, as it funneled around itself. Thumping, snapping noises and the brood changed direction, and disappeared. I heard buzzing, a crash and breaking glass, as something bounced off a parked car a hundred feet away. The car's alarm sounded, whooping loudly.

"Damn! Skippy, stay," I ordered him.

I left him in the plaza with a loose leash and raced over. It was big, maybe three feet across, like Sparky's drone but bigger, and had bounced off the hood and windshield of the car. Half a dozen shredded pigeons were scattered all over. I felt bad. The poor birds had trashed at least four of the propellers. Several of the props on the eight-motored drone were still spinning, trying to fly, a huge, wounded spider with an angry wasp voice. In the center, a black camera with a long lens was still swiveling and zooming. Then I saw the familiar orange plastic-covered flat brick and wires underneath. It looked like a pound of cheddar cheese but smelled sweet, like marzipan. I didn't think. I pulled out

247

every wire as fast as I could, starting with the ones going to the soft brick, as if my life depended on it. One wire lead was attached to a silvery tube that looked familiar. One end of the detonator tube was stuck into the orange material, which had the consistency of firm clay. I tugged it from the brick and then ripped the other end out of a junction box. I carried it over to a sewer storm drain and tossed in the tube and attached wires. As I turned back to the crash site, there was a loud bang. I yanked the brick package and it popped out of its slot. When I was sure there were no more wires connected, I shoved it back in. It took me a few more tugs to disconnect the rotors. The wasp humming stopped. Everything stopped. Several curious people approached on the sidewalk. I called Skippy and he came running, cautiously sniffing the drone.

"Foof!" Skippy said. Then he froze, pointing his snout directly at the orange slab in the drone, his eyes glued to it.

"Holy shit!" I said.

"What happened?" a skinny guy asked me.

"Some kind of fireworks thing landed on somebody's car," I lied, picking up the whole apparatus with my gloved hands and walking away. "Skippy! Heel!"

I began moving as quickly as I could without breaking into a run across Seventh Avenue, with Skippy trotting at my side, before any asshole could whip out his cellphone camera.

I heard voices behind me, indecisive, confused. Someone called out but I ignored it and hurried around the corner at 58th Street, a one-way street. I thought I heard screeching tires behind me. Of course. They'd be in a vehicle with the remote control video rig. I broke into a full run. When I heard a distant siren a few minutes later, I ran faster for a few blocks north and went into the park. I was out of shape. After only ten minutes of running, I dropped my trophy on the ground and took a break on an empty bench. Skippy alerted on the drone again, in case I was completely stupid, and then lay on the bench next to me, nervous.

"Skippy, you are a pro," I told him. "It's okay, boy."

I made a call.

"Sparky? It's Shepherd. Yeah I know. A fuckin' musket, right? Listen, pal, something just fell into my lap and I think it's right up your alley... this could get hairy but you're the only twidget I know who knows this stuff. I need your help... and your van. This thing is heavy. Yeah... right now... Central Park... uh... wait, hold on... North of the Plaza Hotel on 59th Street, there's an entrance to the park at Fifth Avenue with a sculpture... not sure... yeah it might have been Alice in Wonderland. Yeah. That's about the size of it. We're down the fucking rabbithole now. Okay. How long? I'll wait."

As my rush receded, I had to smile. My third eye was working just fine after all. It was closed for now but the eye in the sky was closed. Who did it belong to? When they remotely blew the detonator, was that to kill me or were they just trying to destroy the drone so it wouldn't lead to them? It seemed like they were more interested in watching me than wasting me. I tried not to take it personally.

When Sparky's van screeched to a halt in the street nearby, he got out and made a face at me because I was laughing out loud. I had run with a broken spy drone through the middle of Manhattan and nobody looked twice. Then I sat on a public Central Park bench—with a trashed black drone covered with bloody pigeon feathers and a block of Semtex plastic explosive tucked inside—for more than twenty minutes. Not one person challenged me, bothered me or even suggested that was odd.

I love this crazy town.

49

I explained to Sparky what happened and told him not to touch the drone without gloves.

"Holy fat fuck-a-doodle-doo," Sparky observed, raising a camera and taking shots of the defeated drone. "You think the goddamn *Mail* did this?"

That hadn't occurred to me. Would my competition follow me with a drone? Yes. But a brick of Semtex seemed a bit extreme, even for my favorite journalistic psychopath, Ginny McElhone. She had a hell of a temper. It would not be good if she had her own air force. I told Sparky I assumed the evil flying spider belonged to the bad guys. Hopefully, we would know soon.

"This is nice," Sparky said, now shooting video. "What's with the feathers?"

I told him how Skippy and I had sent the pigeons on their suicide mission. Sparky laughed his ass off.

"Nice camera," he said. "Can I take out the card and download their video?"

"The cops will wrap my nuts with my guts if we do that."

"I'll put it back—they don't have to know," Sparky said.

"How fast can you do that?" I asked. "Without leaving fingerprints?"

He giggled and showed me it was very fast. When he was done, he asked where the drone was brought down and I told him.

"Sparky, don't use anything from their camera unless I say, okay."

"You got it, Shepherd. You da man."

I dialed Izzy's cell.

"Izzy? Shepherd. You still at the morgue? Got something for you."

"Well, speak of the devil," Izzy said. "No, we're back at the convention center. Turns out I've got a question for you."

"Okay, me first," I said. "I've got somebody's little toy and you need to check it out, especially for fingerprints. Where do you want me to bring this?"

"Bring what?"

I told him but he interrupted me when I got to the birds.

"You shot down a drone using pigeons?" he asked.

"Yeah. I feel really bad about that part. I just thought it would confuse the drone and I could escape."

I resumed my story but when I got to the Semtex payload part, he interrupted me again.

"Hold it, Shepherd—you have a drone you claim was following you and it's got a chunk of high explosive attached?"

"De-activated high explosive, Izzy. I told you. Just one brick, only big enough to take out a truck. But it's safe now. Trust me."

"Well, that may be a problem right now. Where are you?"

I told him.

"What do you mean that might be a problem right now?"

"Who is with you?" Izzy asked.

I did not like his tone.

"Umm... nobody," I lied.

"Okay," Izzy said. "I'm going to leave now but some people are going to get there before me. Do us all a big favor and don't argue with them."

"Oh, shit, Izzy. You're hitting the panic button. I told you it's safe. This is dumb."

"No, Shepherd, playing around with plastic explosives in public is dumb. I have no option here."

"I had no choice, Izzy. If I left it there, the bad guys would still have their flying monkey-bomb drone. Or the ordnance would be lying around in public."

"Maybe. We'll see. Sorry, but my advice to you, Shepherd, is to be really, really cool. No sudden moves, amigo. See you soon."

"Fuck me!"

"Who was that?" Sparky asked.

"The cops," I told him, picking up Skippy's leash and walking toward Sparky's van. "Damn. I need you to take Skippy and get the hell out of here until I call you back, okay?"

We put Skippy in the van.

"Get out of here as fast as you can," I said, shoving him toward the driver's side.

"Who is coming?"

"Everyone. Go!"

He drove away. I called Mel's cellphone. He was not happy to get a nighttime call at home.

"What the sock do you want?" he demanded.

I told him I had captured an enemy drone that was carrying a surveillance camera and bomb.

"Christ, I knew you'd frosting crack," Mel said. "Are you drunk? Don't you guys take some kind of mother-fighting medication for flashbacks?"

I ignored him and said I would send him a text. I started typing a text to Mel but I stopped and sent what I had when I heard an unwelcome sound approaching.

"This is stupid," I said out loud.

"What?" a passing woman jogger in red shorts and tank top asked me.

"Sorry, I wasn't talking to you. You shouldn't be here."

"Why?" she asked, doing that silly jogging in place people do when they think they're in the Olympics and don't want to stop.

"A lot of cops are coming," I told her.

"Why?"

"Alien spacecraft," I told her, pointing at the broken drone on the sidewalk nearby.

She gave out with a knowing New York chuckle and jogged on. I walked a few yards down the path, away from the drone, to be more visible from the street. Maybe I should just jog to the subway? I took out my phone and dialed Jane.

"Where are you?" Jane asked. "I have some interesting details to tell you. I'm home. I ordered in Mongolian barbecue. When will you be here?"

"Yummy. Listen, I just heard from Izzy and we are meeting to go over a few things I found out tonight. You and I can compare notes later."

"The food will get cold."

"You eat, I'll nuke it later when I get home. Hey, what do you know about Skippy's background? Was he trained as a military or police dog?"

"No, not as far as I know but we know almost nothing. Some man in a car asked a neighborhood woman to watch Skippy while he did an errand. He tied the leash to a sign and drove away. She brought Skippy to us. Later, he went to your favorite reality show host. That's it. Obviously he was well trained but I don't know anything about *police* training. Why?"

"Just curious, thanks."

Sirens were converging on me from every direction. I heard a helicopter. Crap.

"Gotta go, Jane. My ride's here."

50

I sat down on the hot pavement and waited as the sounds of cars, screeching brakes, slamming doors and yelling cops multiplied. Then I lay flat, put my hands behind my head, and waited. I was ordered to freeze by several nervous voices. Someone asked where the bomb was. I tried answering but they were all making too much noise to hear me.

"There's no bomb," I explained. "It's safe. I removed the detonator. There's just the plastique, the drone and the camera."

They weren't listening. I was searched and handcuffed, hand and foot. They removed my gloves and took my phone. I stayed still, knowing a lot of guns were pointed at me.

"Here it is!" someone shouted. "Looks like a drone. Don't see any bomb."

The Bomb Squad, when they arrived, disagreed, and forced an evacuation to a wider perimeter when they spotted the Semtex. I was told to stand up.

"I can't. You handcuffed my ankles."

Someone reluctantly took them off. Two guys helped me up and turkey-trotted me into the rear seat of a nearby squad car, which was then moved because they feared they were too close to the explosive. It took half an hour for a cop in blue overalls and an NYPD baseball cap to open the rear car door and tell me he was from the Bomb Squad.

"How is it rigged to go off?" he asked me.

"They had it on a radio remote but I ripped all that out. It's just the brick—totally safe. How many times do I have to tell you guys that?"

"Because we don't just trust guys who get caught with a bomb," he told me.

"I didn't get caught, jackass, I called it in."

"So you claim. But actually, Major Case called it in and your gloves field-tested positive for RDX. You have been handling explosives."

"Duh. I just told you. I ripped out the det and checked the payload for a backup. You are wasting the lead time I gave you with all this bullshit. They probably didn't leave prints but the Semtex and the camera might be traceable. Also the video card in the camera may lead you back to these pricks. My guess is they're in Williamsburg, in Brooklyn, probably the APN, the Aryan Purity Nation group."

"So who did you want to blow up?"

I laughed.

"You think this is my explosive drone? Look, either ask Izzy about this—and me—or come back with somebody smarter than you. And get me some food. I'm hungry."

"If you're with the good guys, why did you run off with the device?" he demanded. "Why not just leave it at the original scene and notify us?"

"Because they were obviously somewhere close, in a car, Einstein. If I hung about, I wouldn't be around to have this chat now and you wouldn't have the drone for forensics. Hey, come back when you have some food."

"Even if we believe you, they could have some kind of hidden failsafe trigger in the brick."

"Negative. They triggered their detonator after I took it out. Obviously to trash the drone because I brought it down. That was it. If they had another way of remotely detonating it, they would have done it already. Stop wasting time."

"Not that simple," he said. "There's also a camera and a sealed GPS and command module. How did you bring this thing down?"

"Pigeons."

He laughed.

"How fucking stupid do you think I am?"

"I refuse to answer that question, on the grounds that I am handcuffed."

Later, I found out they used their rolling robot to check out the drone, wasting more than an hour. I understand they have to be careful but if you're too cautious, you lose. If there was video stored on the SIM card in the videocam that led to these APN motherfuckers, Sparky may already be looking at it—but I couldn't call him.

They drove me to Police Headquarters downtown, and marched me to a large room upstairs. A TV in a corner was playing CNN News on mute. They sat me in a chair that was welded alongside a metal desk. A cop opened my left cuff and secured it to the chair. I looked around. I was now alone. There were rows of similar desks and a view of the Brooklyn Bridge and the river. It was difficult to get comfortable while chained to a chair. The desk next to me was neat, IN and OUT boxes both empty. There was only a phone console, a stapler and a pencil cup with a few pens stuck in it. I reached over with my un-cuffed right hand and pulled out a plastic ballpoint pen with a shiny, inch-long aluminum pocket clip. The metal clip snapped off cleanly and I stuck the flat end of the strip into the hole where the handcuff ratchet went into the cuff lock around my wrist—at the same time pushing the cuff teeth tighter into the lock area. The cuff popped open. I sat back more comfortably to wait.

51

Izzy arrived with Phil, who was carrying a case folder. I stood and shook their hands. They looked at me and at each other.

"You were supposed to be cuffed," Izzy said.

"Maybe they forgot," I told them. "That whole show was really stupid, Izzy. You wasted a lot of time and probably blew our edge."

"I had no choice," he protested. "I can't take a chance with bomb shit. You tied my hands. I've got the commissioner, the mayor, the governor and the president looking over my shoulder."

"More reason not to drop the ball," I told him.

"We also have to deal with that question I have for you. Sit down and tell me again what you did the night Chesterfield and his pals were killed."

I asked him if he was kidding. He wasn't. He said he had to ask.

"Why?"

"You want a lawyer?"

"No. Tell me why."

"Why did you have a key to Chesterfield's room?"

"What? I didn't."

"You sure?" Phil asked.

"Yeah, I'm sure. I didn't have any key. I wasn't a guest there."

"Exactly," said Phil, placing the folder on the desk and extracting a plastic evidence bag with a gold keycard, smudged with black fingerprint powder.

"Do you know what this is?" Izzy asked.

"Looks like a keycard."

"Yes, it is. In fact, it is a coded key to Chesterfield's suite. It was found inside his room, on the rug behind the door during the CSU search."

"And?"

"Is this yours?"

"No."

"Then can you tell us how your index finger and thumbprint got on this card found at the scene of the homicide?"

"What? You're serious?"

"Oh, yeah."

This shit was falling apart, a soup sandwich.

"Izzy, Phil, I didn't have any room keys. The only... wait... When Tiffany and I went out after the smoke alarm went off that night, to Chesterfield's room... she left her copy of his room key on the counter and asked me to grab it. I did and handed it to her. That could be it!"

"Why didn't you tell us this before?" Izzy asked.

"You never asked before. I didn't know it was a thing. Tiffany took that card from me and I never touched it— or any other room key—again. That's the truth. Take it or leave it. What does Tiffany say?"

"She admits that she had a key to Chesterfield's room but she doesn't know where it went," Phil said. "She said she used it to get into his room when she found the body and then she lost track of it."

"Okay, there you go. She opened the door, found her boss blown away and dropped the card. You said it was found on the rug behind the door?"

"Yeah," Izzy admitted, "but she doesn't remember dropping it."

"Okay," I said. "The key is the same color as the rug. If Tiffany dropped it when she found Chesterfield, it could have been swept behind the door when she let me in. You asked her if I had a key?"

They looked at each other.

"She said you had no key," Phil admitted. "As far as she knew. Of course, she could be protecting you."

"Ha. But my prints were on the card you found. Were her prints on the card?"

"We have some partials, nothing definitive. The problem with women is that so many use hand lotions that can smudge prints. We need her to come in for full prints of the sides of her fingers, hands and palms," Izzy said. "Also DNA."

"That's her card and I handed it to her. She dropped it. Get her in here now so we can settle this."

"Can't," Izzy said. "She's out of town. Back in Washington."

"Oh, okay. Meanwhile, the APN bad guys are skating because you're investigating me. What about prints on the drone and camera?"

"Wiped clean, under all that pigeon mess," Izzy said. "Identifying marks on the whirlybird have been removed. We're trying to trace the purchase history of the drone and the camera but nothing yet. We're waiting for TARU to set up a screening of the SIM card video from the digital camera. They said they'd be ready in about ten minutes."

I asked and was told that TARU was the NYPD's Technical Assistance Response Unit.

"Dinner and a movie sounds good, after what you did to me, Izzy. Maybe flowers and candy, too. Can I have my cellphone back now? I have to call Jane. Where are you taking us to dinner?"

"I'm taking you to dinner?" Izzy asked, handing me back my phone.

"Goddamn right you are," I replied.

"I hear Katz's Delicatessen has a great shredded squab special," Phil suggested.

52

While Izzy took a call, I asked Phil if they had turned up anything on Karl Bundt, the EPS security guy.

"Oh, yeah. Turns out he used to be in the Secret Service until he violated regs on public speaking on the web. That's how he ended up at the EPS."

"Let me guess," I said. "He did a Tea Party rant?"

"You saw it?"

"No, but that's interesting."

"Doesn't prove anything. He's not a suspect," said Phil. "Leave the poor guy alone."

I phoned Jane and apologized for the delay, explaining what happened. She got quiet after I got to the part about the explosive. I could hear computer keys clicking, as she accessed the *Daily Press* story. I quickly explained that there was no real danger but she knew I was lying.

"I had a good excuse for not calling," I told her, attempting humor. "I was handcuffed."

"A better excuse would have been if you were dead," she replied coolly.

I looked at my paper's newest stories—most with my byline—about my close encounter with the drone. The part with the detonator being triggered and exploding in the sewer was all in the copy. I was credited with "averting a deadly blast by just seconds with quick thinking."

KILLER DRONE
Daily Press Reporter Captures Buzz Bomb

Killer? The story put together by a rewrite person—from my notes and Sparky's photos—also made it clear that I was bringing down the spy drone to help police solve the political assassinations. But, looking around at Phil and Izzy, who were staring at the TV where CNN was displaying my headlines behind a red breaking news banner, I didn't detect any gratitude. After the KILLER DRONE headline, the TV showed another headline on a sidebar story asking who was controlling the drone—the Aryan Purity Nation or someone else?

Sparky's photos of the drone and me in the park were included with the story. He also took a shot of the smashed car back on Seventh Avenue. I told Jane I would call her back. Even when I wasn't trying, I couldn't do anything without pissing everybody off. I called Mel at the paper.

"What now?" Mel joked. "You bring down a mother-jumping satellite?"

"Why did you call it a killer drone, Mel?" I asked. "You're scaring my girlfriend. Nobody was killed."

"Aren't you forgetting those pigeons? It was obviously set up to be a flying bomb, to fogging kill people. It was probably sent by the killers. The dork-wads tried to blow you up, didn't they?"

"They probably wanted to blow up the drone, not necessarily me. The problem is that it makes it look like they're out to bomb the public."

"We never actually said that," Mel was quick to point out. "It was a frikking bomb. It was flagging flying. Don't piss on your own story, Shepherd."

"But you have some random woman in the fourth graf, saying she is terrified that the killers are now out to blow us up."

"Public reaction," Mel said. "Completely routine. Mrs. Nussbaum is entitled to her gong-banging opinion. This is America, anthole."

"I gotta go, Mel. The cops want to yell at me for all my help."

My phone rang again.

"Hi, Sparky. What's up?"

"What happened?" he asked. "Where are you?"

I told him about my brief incarceration. "Did you look at the video from the drone yet?" I asked him.

"No, not yet. Had to get the pictures and your story online first. The cops still giving you a hard time?"

"Yup."

"Skippy wants to know where you are."

"Okay, c'mon down. I need a ride," I said, taking a second call on hold. "Hi, Amy."

I had to go through everything again for her and she wasn't happy.

"When were you going to tell me about this drone?" she demanded.

"Amy, they handcuffed me."

"Those ungrateful assholes."

"I agree. Listen, can I call back? These guys are giving me the stink-eye."

"You need to decide which side you're on," Izzy informed me.

"Your bosses are embarrassed," I guessed, putting my phone away.

"Sure," Izzy said. "They wanted you to keep it quiet so they could take credit for it at a press conference. But it's more than that. Aside from the chain of evidence thing, nobody wants a glory hog running around bragging about how he's solving the case alone."

"Yeah, that's our boss's job," Phil said.

"It's not my call, Shepherd," Izzy continued. "We are a team and you are not. You got fired from your GOP gig but you're still working for the private eye firm and your newspaper. And you want to work with us and have us help you. You can't work for everybody at the same time, Shepherd. Pick a side."

"Actually I *can* work for everybody. And they're not sides—we're all after the same thing. The drone thing just happened and I did the best I could. I bring you guys a break in the case. All your superiors care about is who gets credit in the paper. I'm not redeploying again. This is why I won't take orders anymore."

"Sorry, Shepherd. I've still got orders," Izzy said. "You're a great detective but a royal pain in the ass. Either you agree to become an unofficial—and very silent—part of the chain of command or we escort you from the building now and release a statement that you have nothing to do with the investigation."

It looked like I was getting fired for the second time that day. "Do your bosses realize that if I decline the offer it means I won't give them any more information?"

"I think they are prepared to take the risk that they won't care about anything you come up with on your own," Izzy replied.

"Does that mean they're giving me back the drone and the Semtex? I'm going to keep at it until I get the people who killed Chesterfield and the others," I told Izzy. "So, no deal."

Izzy and Phil walked me to the elevator and out of One Police Plaza into the warm evening air.

"Does this mean you're not taking me out to dinner?"

53

Skippy was sitting up front in the van next to Sparky, his head out the open window. He barked at me as I approached. I shot a quick glance at the sky but didn't spot another drone.

"Skippy and Sparky—the A-Team," I grinned, getting into the back seat.

"More like Scooby-Doo," Sparky laughed. "If he's some kind of Eskimo hound, shouldn't he like whale blubber or something? This monster ate three double cheeseburgers in, like, ten seconds. And an apple pie and most of my fries."

Skippy almost never met a food he didn't like. All this eating talk was making me hungry. I called Jane and told her I was on my way. My phone vibrated in my hand with an arriving text.

It was my New Minutemen friends with a new message, which was preceded by the OLDNORTHCHURCH4181775 verification code:

> As we depart, the New Minutemen deny the libelous charge in the *New York Daily Press* that we intended to cause harm to citizens on the streets of Jew York. We struck only at enemies of the people—not We, the People. At the time of the unplanned incident, NM was in exfiltration mode, in preparation for Phase Two, national redeployment downrange, which will commence directly.

I did not like the sound of the last part. I forwarded the message to Mel, so he could slap it on the web. It was a non-denial denial. They didn't claim the drone wasn't theirs or that it didn't have explosives attached—just that they weren't going to commit random terrorism. Gee, thanks.

Mel called right away.

"What the hell does this cup-stroking crap mean?"

"The first part means they deny they were out to bomb people. The second part is both good and bad. The good news is that they say they're leaving New York and going home. Bad news? They're on their way to a national Phase Two, wherever and whatever that is."

"Which could be bad bugging news for someone, somewhere else, right? Best guess when?" Mel asked.

"I would say within a day or two and I would assume it will be kinetic."

"Kinetic?"

"Yeah, ballistic, like in bullets. Violence."

"Umm... we'll watch the wires, okay, I'll goose it and juice it. Shepherd, you think *they* think you're an enemy of the porking people?"

"I've gotta go, Mel. Long day."

I was going to forward the message to Izzy but I hesitated. I sent it to my US Attorney friend Mary Catherine first. After I thought about it, I copied the message to Izzy, since he was just following orders. Another message hit my phone. Again, from my psycho drone masters, complete with authentication code.

> MESSAGE TO F.X. SHEPHERD. CEASE AND DESIST IMMEDIATELY. FIRST AND FINAL WARNING.

Nice to be singled out in dispatches. I wondered who else might be getting warnings. I called around quickly. No one. Just me.

Sparky parked his NYP press plate van right in front of Jane's place. As we walked toward the door, my third eye twitched. I instinctively looked up, ready for another kamikaze drone in the sky but saw nothing.

"What?" Sparky asked.

"Nothing, I guess."

As we walked up the steps, I turned suddenly and just caught a lithe black figure topped in red ducking behind a tree across the street.

"Hi, Ginny," I yelled.

She didn't respond.

"Hold on a second," I told Sparky.

Ginny McElhone gave up her stealthy act as I crossed the street. Skippy wagged his tail. Ginny scratched his head.

"Please stop following me, Ginny."

"I'm not following you. I'm staking you out," she corrected me, with a cute smirk.

"Where are your thugs?"

"Look, Shepherd, I wanted to talk to you about that."

"You're going to deny you sent them?"

"Yes. No... Look, I'm not the one you have to... Shepherd, they really want you back. They asked me to ask you. You know, because we used to..."

"Your gang pals want me back?" I asked, confused.

"No, asshole. The *Mail*. They want to hire you back. Now. Tonight—for more money."

"Who does?"

"The paper, I told you."

"No, I mean, who at the paper told you to ask me? Most of the guys I worked for when I was there... aren't there anymore. They aren't anywhere."

"The new editor."

269

"Who's the new editor?"

"We're not supposed to use the editor's name. You have to understand that they have had it with you beating us on this story. Will you come back for more money? We could work closely together again. I'd like that." Ginny took my hand. "*You'd* like that. You did before."

Sex with Ginny was hot but I'd learned the hard way you couldn't take it personally.

"Pass," I told her, disengaging. "See you 'round."

"Wait! Please, Shepherd. I'm asking you not to say no. Seriously. I like you. I don't want to see you... C'mon, be smart. Take the money. What's the difference? You have to trust me."

I laughed all the way into Jane's house.

"What did Queen Maleficent want?" Sparky asked.

"She's still hot for my bod."

"Yeah, right."

I turned for a quick look. Ginny was in the same spot. I expected her to talk smack at me but she didn't look like her usual angry self. I had never seen this expression on her face before.

Ginny looked scared.

54

Skippy and I could smell the Mongolian barbecue, which Jane had reheated in the microwave: bowls of stir-fried chicken, beef and vegetables, with sides of brown rice. It was a close thing but I actually ate almost half of the beef bowl before Skippy got to it. While I chewed, I told Jane about my in-custody experience.

"So, the cops have fired you, too?" she asked.

"Well, NYPD never hired me," I pointed out.

"I don't know, Shepherd." Jane smirked. "Sounds like you can't keep a job."

"I still work for the paper and for Amy. I only lost two out of four of my jobs."

When Amy arrived, I brought her up to speed. Then she fired me.

"You're kidding, right?" I asked.

"Think about it, Shepherd. On the record I have to terminate you—so I can continue my relationships with the GOP, NYPD, the feds and everybody else who doesn't like you. You're a freelancer. I can't fire someone I never hired. I'll stay in touch. Unofficially, of course," she assured me.

"Does that mean I still get paid?" I asked. "Unofficially?"

She thought for a bit. "You'll get paid in cash. For now."

Sparky got out his laptop and set it up on Jane's kitchen table. He said the drone camera copy contained a big file and it would take a few minutes to upload.

Jane took out a small notebook and told us what she had learned at the other autopsies earlier in the day.

"I think I told you about our friend Congressman Hatfield's strategic 'HOT STUFF' tattoo?"

Neither Amy nor Sparky had heard of the groin art and got a big laugh out of it. Jane explained that the post-mortems were weirdly similar, with each victim slain by one powerful blast of a musket ball to the chest. She joked that they were carbon copies, each victim's flesh and clothing burned and singed by the discharge of old-fashioned black powder. The square patches of cloth, the wadding, had been identified as some kind of silk. Most interesting were various chemical testing results.

"Okay," Jane said. "Every one of these guys had been drinking, with blood alcohol levels ranging from Chesterfield's point zero nine up to the tattooed guy's point one nine reading. They were all legally drunk. Your government at work."

"Well, it's not like they were driving or anything," Amy said.

"Yeah," Jane replied. "Just carrying around loaded firearms. Robert Blanchette goes to the head of the class because he also had a hefty recreational amount of cocaine hydrochloride in his bloodstream."

"Alright, Bob!" Sparky cheered.

"But that's not what I found weird," Jane said. "Get this. The identical heavy metal musket balls, almost six tenths of an inch in diameter, are not lead or stainless steel. They're almost pure silver."

"Silver?" Amy asked. "Seriously?"

Nobody used silver for bullets.

"Yes, according to the tests, the balls are about ninety per cent pure... Wait... 'eighty-nine point two four per cent pure silver' and 'seventy-six point one per cent copper.' Each ball was heavy and weighed about twenty-six point nine six grams—which is about three-fiftieths of a pound."

"What the hell?" I asked no one in particular.

"I got it!" Sparky whooped. "The congressmen were all werewolves! That is fucking awesome! A slamming story! They can only be killed with silver bullets!"

"We get it, Sparky," I groaned.

"Who are you again?" Amy asked Sparky, one of her eyebrows arching suspiciously.

"There's more weird," Jane informed us, glancing at Sparky.

"The cost," Amy volunteered.

"Correct," Jane said. "I looked it up and did the math. The price of Chesterfield's murder, almost twenty-seven grams of silver, at today's market price is a bullet that cost the bad guys one hundred and sixty-three dollars and eighty-seven cents."

"Times five," I added. "Money to burn."

"Exactly," Jane echoed. "Total cost in bullets, not counting guns, gunpowder or sales tax, is eight hundred and nineteen dollars and thirty-five cents."

"That is just nuts," I said.

"But, when you consider they have changed the course of history, a bargain," Amy concluded.

We were silent for a moment.

"So... you guys don't like my werewolf idea?" Sparky asked.

55

We crowded behind Sparky's laptop as he started the video playback of the drone brought down by the pigeons.

The screen flashed and then went dark, a barely visible line of vehicles on a dark street, receding as the drone rose above a black van and into the air. Day, date and time numbers in the lower right corner showed the video was filmed that night.

"Damn. No license plate visible on the van," Amy observed.

"Bad angle," Sparky agreed. "So, you think that's Williamsburg, Shepherd?"

"Think so."

Three dark figures were visible in the street below for a second before the drone angled away towards dark buildings silhouetted by light.

"Wait, go back to those guys," I ordered Sparky, who rewound the video and froze on the trio of black hats and coats in the roadway.

"Are they Hassidic?" Jane asked.

"Maybe," I replied. "Not sure. They're in an Hassidic neighborhood, dressed like the locals..."

"Why would Hasidic Jews be part of an anti-Semitic plot

to kill members of Congress?" Jane asked.

"That makes no sense," Amy agreed.

We watched as the screen became lighter and the drone flew over several well-lit Brooklyn intersections. Sparky pointed out a nearby structure that looked like an aqueduct made from a lattice of dark steel.

"Broadway and the elevated line," Sparky said. "The drone is following that SUV with a small, blinking targeting square superimposed on the roof. Looks like it's getting onto the Williamsburg Bridge back to Manhattan."

The shot became more distant, as the drone climbed vertically and then optically zoomed back through the bridge structure, tracking the SUV.

"That's the Uber car," I explained. "I'm in that vehicle."

"Nice," Amy said.

We watched as the vehicle emerged from the bridge maze and stopped to pick up a figure, the other passenger who got in at Delancey Street. The drone smoothly glided between buildings, never losing the target. It followed uptown to Radio City, where I also got off. The camera zoomed in as the drone descended for a better angle on my face. The craft fixed on me and Skippy on the street. Then the pigeons exploded in a blast of bright feathers and the drone wobbled, veered and crashed.

"Hey, man. That's you," Sparky laughed, as the camera caught me descending on the downed drone like a deranged giant, all hands and face.

The screen went black.

"The end," Sparky announced. "If there were earlier missions, they erased them before blastoff."

"So we've got exactly nothing," I concluded.

"Not quite," Sparky said. "They forgot to erase everything. Check this out."

He brought up a control screen that featured several icons: GPS, VIDEO, HOME, WAYPOINTS, REGISTRATION and MISSIONS. "I can't find anything under any of these—

except the video we've just seen, under MISSIONS, and a few things under WAYPOINTS." He opened WAYPOINTS and an interactive map of New York appeared. There were red push-pins stuck into the map at specific spots.

"The first one I noticed was this one in Brooklyn—the headquarters of your pals, the Aryan Purity Nation in Williamsburg," Sparky said. "Then I found this," he smiled, putting the pointer on a Manhattan red spot.

"Hey," Jane said. "That's here. That's my home address."

"Yeah. They also got Shepherd's apartment and the address of our paper, the *Daily Press*, and the convention center on the West Side."

"Makes sense if they're watching me," I said. "They would have places I go to listed."

"That is incredibly creepy," Jane said. "How can you be so calm about this?"

I shrugged.

"Not sure about a couple, though," Sparky continued, clicking on another spot downtown.

"That's my address in the Village," Amy enlightened him. "Nice to be included."

"Oh, okay," Sparky responded. "What's this last one?"

We looked at the address. 740 Park Avenue. Nobody answered.

"I don't think I've been there," I offered. "Oh, wait. I know people who were going there. People I spoke to at the convention center."

"Who?" Jane asked.

"My parents. They were going to demonstrate there against those Tea Party billionaire brothers who bankroll all the right-wing causes, the Roehm brothers. All the Conservative candidates go there to kiss their asses and get big oil bucks for their campaigns—including Miranda Dodge."

"So you think our opponents are also tracking your parents?" Amy asked.

"Looks that way. My mom and dad are staying at my place and they said they were going to this place on Park Avenue to demonstrate against the Roehms. Remember, my dad was trashing Dodge and the others on the TV. He was already their enemy. Or, they picked my parents up at my apartment."

"So, we're back to square one," Amy said.

"Maybe not," I told her. "If they're not tracking my parents, maybe there's another reason 740 Park Avenue is listed as an important location."

"Like what?" Sparky asked.

"Maybe it's their real headquarters," I said.

"Meaning they sent the drone out from that spot before?" he asked.

"Maybe."

"How can we prove that?" Jane asked.

"The cops trace the drone and the camera and the explosive and they all point to the Roehm brothers," Amy suggested, hopefully.

"Or not," I countered.

"Then what?" Jane asked.

"Then tomorrow we stroll over to Park Avenue for tea," I said. "And maybe a party."

56

My phone buzzed with new *Daily Press* stories, which I shared with Amy and Jane:

MORE MUSKETEER MAYHEM
Worms bite Big Apple, squirm away—vowing wider terror

Sparky tried to convince me to give the new drone video to the paper but I wanted to wait. He gave me a USB thumb drive with a copy of the file.

"Why not upload it?" Sparky whined. "This will go viral faster than a bastard. We can make some serious money if we slap it on my site. You don't owe the cops nothing."

"Actually, I think I do. The new video doesn't really add much. I just want to wait and see what happens."

"Like what?" Amy asked.

"Like what Phase Two is and where."

"Makes sense," Amy agreed.

"You're not going to go running around the country chasing bad guys," Jane said. "Let these lunatics move on and find someone else to follow. We can continue to investigate here."

Sparky laughed sarcastically. Amy rolled her eyes. Neither one had ever backed off a big case. Ever.

"I agree," I told Jane.

Sparky and Amy looked at me with shocked pity, as if my testicles had fallen off. To save face, I announced I would be on the case at 740 Park Avenue in the morning. They left, unsmiling.

When we were alone, with a yawning Skippy, Jane zeroed in.

"Were you serious about not following those psychos all over the country?"

"Sure."

"Why?"

"This case makes you very nervous and I don't want to stress you out. You're more important to me than any case."

"Good," she said, kissing me, pulling me close.

"Good," I said, kissing back. "So, I'm rehired?"

"What?"

"You fired me."

"You mean the night you were at the convention center and stayed at Amy's place?"

I hoped that wasn't a trick question.

"Right."

"I forgot about that. I'm sorry. I was upset and I got scared... I apologize."

I told her she had nothing to be sorry for but I didn't mention I did.

Later, in bed, she went channel surfing and stopped at an old movie, *Greystoke*, about a Victorian-era English lord who was raised by apes in Africa and rescues a beautiful lost English girl named Jane from the savage jungle—who teaches him her name.

"I love this movie," Jane said.

I should have thought of this. A good chick flick or romantic comedy was the equivalent of at least two drinks.

She smiled at me, pointed at herself, said her name, and waited.

"Jane," she said again, pointing to herself and then to me.
"Shepherd?" I asked, jerking my thumb at my chest.

Jane shook her head no until I admitted her name was
Jane and my name was Tarzan. And then proved it.

In the morning, my phone went berserk. There were
emails, news alerts, bulletins, and calls from everyone. The
paper had refreshed the website yet again, this time with a
headline screaming:

MORE BIG BORE GORE
HOLE IN POL ON BOWL

Another Republican congressman had been perforated
by a musket ball—this time in a men's bathroom stall at the
Minneapolis Airport in Minnesota. Representative Brad
"Blue" Bunyan had been returning from the less-than-
triumphant GOP convention in New York, the story said.
Allegedly, a call of nature caused him to stop in the john
to take care of some business before proceeding home to
his wife and three children. A person or persons unknown
had blasted Bunyan into eternity at an embarrassingly
infamous homosexual haunt, sources said.

Our disloyal opposition, the *New York Mail*, trumpeted
Congressman Bunyan's demise with its usual tasteful
diplomacy:

COMING OR GOING?
MUSKET BALL GAY SLAY?
Tea Party Animals Strike Again

Tea Party Animals? Guess the killers had a name now.

In addition to Bunyan's murder, other members of
Congress had received death threats in at least ten other

states. The feds were stepping in. It looked like the New Minutemen's Phase Two had begun.

Mel called and wanted me to get on a plane as fast as possible with Sparky. I said no, as Jane was listening. Mel told me I was crazy but he didn't immediately fire me. Sparky and Amy also called again to pressure me to chase the big story all over the map. They thought I was whipped. Jane gave me a kiss and a smile. I was supposed to get on the 740 Park Avenue lead right away but I wasn't in any hurry to talk to my parents. Jane made an egg-white omelet with cheese, mushrooms and tomatoes—with a dash of salsa. I slapped mine on wholewheat toast and ate it as a sandwich, Jane looking on with amusement.

"What?" I asked, with a full mouth.

"Nothing," she giggled. "I forgot how much I like watching a man eat."

"I forgot how much I like watching a woman cook. Let's get a farm," I laughed.

I resigned myself to hanging back and letting someone else take the point, for a change. I had a feeling that the key to the case was what had happened in New York, no matter where these clowns actually came from or wherever they did more carbon copy killings. I might be wrong about that but I was still glowing and relaxed after last night in the treehouse with Jane and looking forward to bedtime.

Jane didn't wait until bedtime. After lunch, Skippy went to sleep on Jane's bed and she jumped my bones in the kitchen.

I ignored my calls, emails and texts. I wasn't worried about what Mel or the others thought.

I didn't care.

I was Tarzan.

King of the Jungle.

57

I was back in-country, at the head of my team, outside a night target location, weighed down by full battle-rattle. I was cleared hot—staring into darkness. My left side throbbed a quiet warning, the gloved hand of the operator behind me squeezing my left shoulder, signaling go, go, go.

But my PEC-Fours were no-go. Dead, the batteries of the infrared night-vision goggles failing at exactly the wrong fucking time. I flipped them back up onto my helmet, now using just my useless eyes, blind inside the black. Before I could relay my problem, the dark lit up with banging white strobes of muzzle flashes and screaming tracers—first the long fire bulbs of rapid AK-47 rifle blasts, returned by our M-4s on full auto. My left side burned with pain as I fell.

I fucked up. Ambush.

I pulled my M-4's trigger. Nothing.

We were all going down.

I woke up, snatching for my weapon. I grabbed a fistful of sheet.

After a deep breath I was glad to be awake, naked in bed with a naked Jane, and not there. I concentrated on my breathing and let the thoughts come and go, rolling off me like rain, as I had been taught. My heart slowed down. The details of the dream were always different but they all had the same ending.

The sky visible over the townhouses across the street was gray, cloudy. Hot, sunny weather put me on edge. Bad weather always calmed me. Snowstorms made me positively purr. For most of my years in uniform, the Taliban never attacked in winter. The passes were snowed in and we were the only ones initiating kinetic operations. That's why I spent a year in the Caribbean. An army shrink, who thought I had become sun-phobic, said she thought it would help me readjust to life. I don't know if it helped, but it was great. I flushed out my headgear and acquired a minor taste for dark rum because there was no arak.

"What's wrong?" Jane mumbled, rolling toward me.

"Nothing. My scars pinch when the weather changes, you know, with the barometer," I explained. "When I'm asleep, my mind makes up reasons for that."

"You had a nightmare."

"Everybody does."

"Not like yours, I bet," she said, yawning and stretching. "In my nightmares, I didn't study for a test or I'm in a play and I don't know the lines."

"Same with me."

"I thought we were going to talk to each other?"

I took a deep breath and told her my dream but it's hard to convey to a civilian the terror, insanity and addictive rush of combat.

"Did that ever happen?" she asked.

"What? Me dying? Let me think."

"No," she laughed, swatting me with her pillow. "Did you ever fuck up, let your men down?"

"Men and women," I corrected her.

"You were in combat with women?"

"Sometimes, yes."

"Where?"

I shook my head. Not going there.

"And a dog," she added.

"Yeah. Fatimah."

"The dog who saved you, who blew up with the bomb that injured you."

"Yeah."

"Whose bones hit you, gave you those scars on your face?"

"Yeah."

"But that wasn't your fault."

"You mean logically."

"Of course. I understand… Survivor's guilt."

"I'm glad you do."

She crawled onto my chest and hugged me. I pretended the sheet, now covering us both, was a quiet layer of snow. I closed my eyes.

"If you want something to worry about," Jane began, "worry about me meeting your parents today."

"Who says you're meeting my parents today?"

"I do."

"Thanks, Jane. Maybe you should stop trying to help me."

"I'm a doctor. And I do house calls."

"You're an animal doctor. Are you calling me an animal?"

"No, but I think you have excess stress, energy that needs to be released with physical activity."

"Does this involve a gym?" I asked, pulling her closer.

"No."

"Good."

58

After breakfast I took a shower and got ready to leave for Park Avenue with Skippy, who was prancing around, eager to get outside. I pulled on my backpack and called my mother to ask her if she was demonstrating at the Park Avenue home of the Tea Party billionaires. The chanting in the background made her "yes" redundant. I told her I was going to stop by and hung up before she could ask me why. I noticed Jane had sent me an email with her notes on the autopsies, the tests on the dead politicians' blood, the silk patches and the silver musket balls. As I thanked her, I realized she was getting ready to come with me.

"Can we walk you to the office?" I asked.

"I told you. I'm coming with you," Jane informed me.

"Don't you have work?"

"You're not getting rid of me. I've reshuffled things and had the staff take the emergencies so I can come with you," she explained. "I want to meet your parents."

"I don't want you to meet my parents."

"Why not?" she asked. "Is there something wrong with me?"

I decided to cling to honesty, no matter how much all my senses warned me of danger.

"No. There's something wrong with them," I explained. "Also, they think there's something wrong with me and most people, and they're not shy about sharing their opinions. On everything."

"You think I'll break up with you after talking to your mom and dad?" she chuckled.

"Maybe. They might insult you. Why should you be different?"

"What's the worst that could happen?" Jane asked.

I didn't answer. Skippy and I led the way. I noticed Skippy now occasionally watched the sky, alert for any more possible enemy aircraft.

"Good boy," I told him.

"So, you think the killers—these Tea Party Animals— are ultra-conservatives murdering slightly more moderate Republicans?" Jane asked.

"Looks that way," I said. "One thing is for sure— whoever is doing it has lots of money. Antique muskets? Silver bullets?"

"Like the Roehm brothers, whose house we're going to?" she asked.

"Right. Deep pockets and deep hatred."

I asked Siri to give me information on oil billionaire Hans Roehm and his brother Gert Roehm at 740 Park Avenue in Manhattan. More than a million hits popped up. The two were also paper moguls. Oil and toilet paper, the ass-wipe kings. One story credited the brothers with actually creating the Tea Party by setting up dozens of "astroturf" political groups claiming to be grass roots organizations that spontaneously appeared in response to the election of the first black president in US history. The camera-shy twins, one a coin collector, the other a stamp collector, were identical. The gaunt septuagenarian siblings had silver hair and thick, arched black eyebrows, and looked like clones of Count Dooku from *Star Wars*, without the beard.

"This is a dark time in our beloved country," Hans said in one video interview. "We have to put these *people* back in their place and take back *our* country—for the *real* Americans—no matter what the cost."

The two Roehms were awash in oil money and also ruled Wall Street. They required congressional and even presidential hopefuls to travel to their Park Avenue tower to kiss their rings and beg for support from what one Liberal columnist called "the twin Darth Vaders."

"Siri, are the Roehm brothers trying to take over the planet?"

"I can't answer that, Shepherd," Siri replied.

"Talking to Siri again?" Jane asked. "I'm beginning to get jealous."

"Jane, you have nothing to worry about—unless Siri learns how to make house calls like you."

Jane blushed and slugged me on the arm. Skippy jumped and pulled at the leash. He liked hanging with us but he needed to run. I knew the feeling.

59

A white limo glided to the curb ahead of us and parked. The driver door opened and a husky Asian guy in a tight black suit and thin black tie popped out. Skippy stopped and tensed. I kept the leash taut. The driver opened the rear door and stood behind it, then gestured into the dark interior of the limousine.

"Mr. Shepherd?" the driver asked.

"Yeah?"

"Mrs. Anthony would like a quick word with you."

Jane and I looked at each other, clueless.

"Who?" I asked.

"Faith Anthony, sweetie," a high, raspy female voice echoed from inside the car, a voice both sweet and sharp, like chocolate syrup poured over a pile of broken glass. "Don't be afraid, I won't bite. At least, not too hard. Hop in!"

Skippy and I peered inside. An aging diva, dressed in a pink silk gown at ten on a Tuesday morning, was ensconced in the white leather rear seat. Her elevated cheekbones screamed high-end plastic surgery. Her impressive platinum-blonde hair and perfect makeup job bespoke a fancy salon. She was wearing pearls, real ones probably, around her neck. A wooden breakfast-in-bed table, which had been converted into a small desk, was propped above her lap, cluttered with two cellphones, a small computer and a notepad and pen. She looked like a well-preserved fifty but it was a lie. Her perfume was no doubt expensive but the aroma irritated my nose.

"Please come in," she said. "If you don't mind, Ad will keep your friend company outside while we have a quick chat, Francis."

Jane shrugged. I handed her the leash. Skippy sat.

"I don't like my first name," I told her. "I prefer just Shepherd, thanks."

"Okay, Shepherd," she said, extending her hand like a duchess.

I couldn't shake her hand, so I just tugged at her thin, hard fingers, topped with gleaming pink nails. One had a diamond ring with a faceted shiny rock the size of an ice cube. Her hand smelled of musky perfume and Marlboros.

"Just call me Faith. Everybody does."

"Okay, Faith. Look, I usually use Uber cars or one of those rental bikes to get around. I can't afford to travel in these things."

"Sure you can afford it, dear boy," she chuckled. "The *Daily Press* pays you very well."

Then she told me my exact salary.

"So you're *not* a car service?"

"You're joking but you really don't know who I am, do you?"

"You're a rich lady in a big white limo," I answered.

"Amazing," Faith said, shaking her head in wonderment at my vast ignorance.

"Among other things, I write page nine every day in the *New York Mail*. You used to work there, I would think you would have noticed."

"I wasn't there for long. I quit after my bosses decided to lay me off in an unusual way."

"Yes, I heard those allegations," Faith said. "Hard to believe."

My memory told me I had heard something about her but I couldn't remember what it was.

"Believe it. So you're the gossip girl at the *Mail*? What can I do for you?"

"You can come home, dear boy. All is forgiven. The editor would like to hire you back at double your current salary at the *Press*."

"I'm a popular guy," I told her.

"You're a very effective guy. You're kicking our ass and we will pay you a lot more to leave the *Press* and start kicking *their* ass. That is the power of the free market in action."

"Ginny Mac just offered me this deal last night and I said no."

"Yes, I know."

Her perfume finally got to me. I sneezed.

"Bless you," she said.

"Thanks. Why do we say that when someone sneezes?" I wondered aloud.

"It's an old thing," Faith explained. "Your soul is sneezed out of your body and the devil can jump down your throat and take your soul unless someone says 'God Bless You' in time. At least, that what the nuns told us."

"Huh. So, you just saved my soul?"

"I'm trying, Shepherd."

"I didn't say yes to Ginny Mac, why would I say yes to you?"

"Because I am much more persuasive," she said. "I am a powerful friend and a very bad enemy. I know everybody and everybody knows me."

"I didn't know you," I pointed out.

"But you do now," she said, the friendly tone becoming slightly harder. "And I know you now. If you continue to fight against us, you'll force us to cut you down to size.

Nobody wants that. If you come back to the *Mail*, we will make you rich and famous. That's a promise."

"From you or from this shy editor?"

"Both."

"What's his name?"

"Come with me to the office and you can meet your new boss. We can have a lot of fun together, Shepherd. You'll be a celebrity. I will *make* you."

"I'm already made, thanks."

"I heard about your little fistfight the other day," she said, her Upper-East-Side voice suddenly veering downtown. "You think you're tough but you were just lucky. Maybe next time you won't be so fortunate. We can protect you."

"You're going to protect me? Is the paper still owned by the same man? Is Trevor Todd still hiding out in New Zealand?"

"What do you care who owns it?"

"Because I don't like that guy," I told her. "I didn't like a lot of people who worked for him. Let me know when Trevor Todd is in jail where he belongs and somebody else owns the rag." I reached for the door. "Nice meeting you, Faith,"

"You really do not want to say no to me, Shepherd."

"I just did."

"Change your mind," she said, offering me a business card between her bony fingers.

"Change your perfume," I suggested. I was out of the order-taking business.

"What was that all about?" Jane asked, after the limo zipped away.

"Fucked if I know."

"Do you know who she is?"

"Of course," I protested, as we resumed walking with Skippy. "Faith Anthony. Gossip columnist for the *New York Mail*."

"Among other things. How mad was she?"

"Who said she was mad?" I asked. "In fact, she offered

me a job back at the *Mail* for twice as much money."

"Really? What did you say?"

"No, of course. You know I won't work with those people."

"So she wasn't mad about her son?"

"What son?"

Jane looked at me like Faith had. Like I was the dumbest tourist in New York.

"You idiot. You beat the hell out of her son Jay-Jay. Her full name is Faith Potsoli Anthony. She's the daughter of the Godfather, Paulie Potsoli."

"Oh. I thought he was dead?"

"He is," Jane agreed.

"Well, she did mention the fight but she didn't mention Jay-Jay was her son."

"What *did* she say?" Jane demanded.

I told her.

"You jerk. She made you an offer you can't refuse and you *refused* it."

"I thought she was just a gossip columnist?"

"Sure. Never arrested. But the men in her family have different jobs. Don't you read the papers? Her son, her husband, her uncles, her cousins are all mobsters; thieves, bookies, pimps, drug dealers. Killers."

"She seemed nice."

60

My parents were front and center at 740 Park Avenue, behind blue metal NYPD barricades that had been placed beyond egg-throwing distance from the ornate entrance to the building. My mother's sign read BILLIONS FOR BILLIONAIRES BUT NOT ONE CENT FOR HUNGRY KIDS? My dad's message was GREED BREEDS EVIL DEEDS.

A small group of their fellow demonstrators were weakly chanting my father's slogan. We squeezed into the protesters' pen and greeted my parents. Skippy, happily sniffing and jumping, always ready to make new friends, introduced himself.

"This must be Jane." My mom actually smiled, extending her hand for a formal shake. "I'm Amanda. Wow, aren't you gorgeous."

Jane blushed. I could see my dad agreed. I couldn't help thinking that they were surprised Jane was beautiful because I didn't deserve it. My dad also shook hands, like we were going to discuss a used car.

"Aren't I gorgeous, Mom?" I asked.

Jane laughed. My parents didn't break a smile. In the awkward silence that followed, Jane asked why they were demonstrating against the Roehm brothers and I cringed, knowing my dad would give a full lecture on the subject. If you asked Professor James B. Shepherd what time it was, you got an hour on the history of clocks.

"The recent publicity surrounding Senator Hardstein is a case in point," my father told Jane. "I don't care who he was—pardon my French—screwing, only that he was screwing the taxpayers. Hardstein was posing as a liberal democrat but he helped ram the law through Congress that allows hedge fund managers and billionaires to pay only twelve per cent tax, while their minimum-wage workers pay forty. In this country we have now come full circle, from having the wealthy pay high tax rates, to giving billionaires a free ride while the dying middle class and working class pay the freight but get no bank interest to build savings. The economic game is criminally rigged."

He went on for a bit and I interrupted with questions about the Roehm brothers' political opinions. My father cut right to the chase.

"If your question is are the Roehm brothers the Tea Party Animals behind this latest coup attempt, my answer is very possibly but you'll never prove it," he said. "The obscene system of massive bribery we call campaign contributions already makes it almost impossible to discover who gave what cash to which candidate or even if foreign countries are buying congressmen."

"This kind of thing would be even more secret, I would think, since it is openly criminal and involves murder," my mom added.

"Exactly," my father agreed. "If the Roehm brothers are not behind this conspiracy, they would certainly agree with it."

The demonstrators began buzzing as a black limo pulled up in front of the entrance. All signs went up and a chant began but then died out after a handsome gray-haired man emerged. It wasn't one of the Roehm brothers but apparently another resident. He looked at us, bounded over with a beaming smile and began shaking hands of the protesters like a politician. My parents rushed to clasp his hand. He looked familiar.

"Who's that?" I asked my mom.

"Don't you recognize Walter Cantor?"

She intoned his name with reverence. I had a vague memory of a liberal billionaire who believed successful people did not give back enough to the people and wanted them to pay more taxes. Can't be many of him. He lived in the same building as the evil Tea Party twins?

"Professor Shepherd," Cantor said, pumping my dad's hand and then my mom's.

"This is our son, Francis, Mr. Cantor," my mom told him. They called him "mister." Cantor grabbed my hand.

"F.X. Shepherd, right? I've been reading your stuff."

My parents seemed stunned. At our feet, Skippy nuzzled Cantor's leg, then sat and presented his paw. Cantor laughed and shook it. Jesus. Everybody loves a lord.

"Keep up the good work," Cantor said, with a final wave. "Take care, everyone."

He strode inside. The other protesters congratulated us. A liberal billionaire had singled us out. He said he read my stuff. My parents were bursting with pride. Weird.

"You got here just in time," my father said.

"That was amazing," my mom said, in a reverential tone.

"I got a shot," one of the protestors said, waving his phone.

I hadn't seen my parents so awed since we visited the Lincoln Memorial in Washington, D.C. when I was twelve. My parents didn't believe in organized religion. For them, democracy, the idea of America, *was* a religion.

"If he wants to give back so much, he could have at least asked us all in for lunch," I joked. "It's hot out here."

My parents weren't amused. Jane elbowed me in the ribs.

"Jane, tell me about your practice. I understand you're a vet?"

Jane gave my mom a short version of her life and work. My dad seemed to be pouting for some unknown reason.

"So, you know Cantor?" I asked him.

"Not really," my dad replied modestly. "I met him at a conference a few months ago. He gave a speech and afterwards I gave him a copy of my book."

"He might be able to help you," I said, instantly regretting it.

"Help me?" my father asked sharply. "You think I need help?"

In Kansas, some asshole was always trying to take away my parents' tenure at the university or threatening to fire them or calling them communists.

"No, I just meant, with a friend like that, maybe he could put in a word at a better school or foundation or something, that's all. I wasn't…"

"A *better* school?" he snapped back. "It was good enough for your mother and myself, although I recall you weren't able to complete your coursework there, were you?"

"I dropped out, Dad."

"In the sixties, one dropped out. You just disappeared down a black hole of secrecy."

"Whatever. Look, could we not do this? I don't want to…"

"Why did you come here?" he demanded.

"I wanted to see the Roehm brothers. Jane came because she wanted to meet you."

"Didn't *you* want to see us?" my mother asked, always my dad's wingman.

"Sure I did. It's always a blast. Especially when dad gets jealous because his tame billionaire also knows my name."

All of us spoke at once. Jane tried to interrupt with a change of subject. My mom's shrink eyebrows were up and she began to analyze the group dynamic. James was scolding me about maturity, while practicing making me evaporate with his eyes. I was asking if we could skip this part.

Skippy silenced us by barking at us. We noticed the other protesters were watching us. First the billionaire flesh-pressing and now a family feud with fur flying.

"The real reason I came here was to ask for your help," I blurted out.

What? Why did I say that?

"You want our help?" Dad asked, as Mom's eyebrows danced again.

I noticed Jane was also confused.

"Yes," I continued. "From political and psychological points of view, I thought you guys might help me figure this whole thing out."

"*You* want help?" my mom wondered.

"From *us*?" Dad asked.

"Yes. Maybe tonight at dinner. Think about it and we can all put our heads together, okay?"

They didn't protest. I told them we had someplace we had to go and would call them later. We left before they could recover.

"What just happened?" Jane asked.

"You met Amanda and James. Have fun?"

"Loads. Were you serious about needing their help or were you just trying to escape in one piece?"

"Yes."

61

Jane went back to work and Skippy and I went back to her place for lunch. I sat at the kitchen table and logged onto the University of Google. Apparently the patriotic billionaires invested millions in Revolutionary and Civil War weapons and coins, beside their more well-known purchases of oil and large companies. Of course, whatever they touched turned to gold, including gold, and its value always went up. Even their hobbies had to be for profit.

I called up Jane's notes on the autopsy and test results. According to the lab, the silver in the musket balls assayed out at mostly silver, at 89.24 per cent pure with only 10.76 copper. I fed those exact numbers into Google and got an avalanche of rare coin websites. I hadn't told the search engine to look up coins but several searches earlier, I did ask about the Roehm brothers and coin collecting. Opening the top website, "US Silver Dollars, 1794, a Buying Guide," there were pictures of coins with a profile of a woman who vaguely resembled the Statue of Liberty. The word "Liberty" and a ring of small stars circled her head. It was a Flowing Hair dollar, whatever that was.

Damn. In the detailed description, the search engine had highlighted a sentence that noted the coin consisted of 89.24

per cent pure silver and 10.76 per cent copper, the exact proportions as the musket balls. It also said each coin weighed 26.96 grams. I checked back to Jane's notes on the bullets. That was the exact weight. Not only was the killer or killers using expensive silver to dispatch his victims, it looked like each slug was a melted rare coin. I scrolled down to the end of the listing. That particular coin, the first of the American Revolution, was for sale for the low price of $25,000.

Sweet. And apparently these were the bargain-priced ones. Years earlier, one of these coins had sold to an unidentified bidder for a record $10 million. Maybe George Washington kept that one in his loafers? After some searching down-market, the cheapest one I could find online was $6,000 for a worn-down specimen. So my original estimate of under a thousand bucks per bullet would have to be scaled upwards to six grand or more. If the victims knew how much their slug had cost, they might have felt honored to be bumped off. Who the hell would do this? A lunatic? A billionaire? Both, maybe? Sparky was wrong. This wasn't about silver bullets to kill werewolves, this was a loaded Lone Ranger who was convinced he was shooting for some higher purpose. What was it? Love of country? The perfect crime? History's most expensive murders?

I searched past auctions but couldn't find lists of who bought what. I put on my reporter hat and called a few auction houses but they wouldn't tell me squat. I went back to Jane's notes but couldn't find anything else helpful. I kept reading about the silk patches used to wad the shots. The lab said analysis showed the silk was also not new—it was about 300 years old. More antiques. It included descriptions of the weave and weft and how the damask silk was originally bright green but had faded to light yellow over the centuries. I began a new search, feeding all the silk analysis into the white rectangle of the search box. One click later I had lots of sites. Silk manufacturers, antique clothing collections, lots of museums displaying old clothing and flags, including something called the "Gadsden Flag," which turned out to be a variation on the familiar 1775 "Don't Tread On Me" flag revived by the new Tea Party in 2009. I learned that Ben Franklin suggested a coiled serpent as a symbol because England sent convicts to the colonies and Ben thought they should ship rattlesnakes to the mother country, in order to return the favor.

The search engine had also brought up something called the "Delaware Militia Colors, 1776." Pictured was a bright green flag, with red and white in the top left corner, where the stars are in today's US flag. Apparently the Delaware rebels covered Washington's retreat at the Battle of Long Island, saving his army and the revolution, at great cost. It was one of the first flags to feature the stripes. There were a few specimens in museums and several in anonymous private hands, and the record price for one was $15 million a few years back. The weave and faded color looked similar to the five one-inch-square wads used by the Tea Party Animals. This latest addition to the murder package bumped up the price tag—if the killer actually cut squares off a valuable historical flag. I called two museums, one in Dover, Delaware and the other in Brooklyn. I couldn't get a live person in Delaware but someone picked up at the Brooklyn Museum.

"I'm sorry," the woman in the curator's office responded. "You're asking me if anybody has cut strips off our Delaware Militia flag? Of course not. It's behind glass and pretty high up on the wall. Why?"

I asked if she knew of any private person who might have bought one of the flags. She didn't.

"What's your best guess on who might be a buyer?" I asked.

"A rich white person," she told me.

"Thanks."

62

I printed out my various revelations from the web, called Amy and Sparky to invite them over for dinner with my parents, and then Izzy. I left Skippy napping on the couch and set up a car service ride to Police Headquarters. Phil came down to the main entrance and escorted me upstairs, without signing me in at the security desk.

"So. We're friends again," I asked Phil in the elevator.

"Not officially," Phil replied. "The feds are leading the case now, so nobody cares about you as long as we don't rub you in anybody's faces."

"There he is, the Private Eye and the Public Mouth," Izzy intoned, as I entered the Major Case room. He was sitting at his desk; on the wall behind him was a WANTED FOR MURDER poster of a lanky man in a fringed buckskin jacket and coonskin fur cap, holding a flintlock rifle.

"Daniel Boone, right?"

"No," Izzy snapped, "It's Fess Parker as Davy Crockett."

"Oh. Okay. Who's Fess Parker?" I asked.

Izzy and Phil groaned. I handed Izzy my printouts, knowing he responded to hard copy better than digital. I told him about the rare coins matching the analysis of the musket balls.

"Hmm. Thanks. It's interesting, I guess," Izzy said, tossing the printouts onto his cluttered desk. "Normally, that would be great, but we have nothing to compare it to, no coins belonging to a suspect."

"It's totally insane," Phil added. "Who would spend thousands on this?"

"Crazy billionaires. One of the Roehm brothers is a coin collector."

"And you think it's them?" Izzy asked, picking up my printouts again and looking at them.

"It's all over TV," Phil said. "I like 'em for it, too."

"Any real evidence yet?" Izzy asked, not looking up. "No? Then I'm not going hard against anybody without any hard fucking proof. Especially against motherfucking billionaires."

I had been pumped by my discoveries but my cop friends were so negative, I didn't tell them about the flag, which was even more tenuous.

"Okay, what've *you* guys got?" I asked.

They hesitated but Izzy nodded. Phil said so far the drone I had downed was a dead end because all serial numbers had been removed from the whirlybird and the cameras. Working with the FBI, they were looking at drone manufacturers, gunpowder suppliers and gun dealers, trying to trace the explosive from the drone, processing the murder scenes, and waiting for more test results.

"I've got more than you do," I bragged. They didn't deny it. "So, where are the murder weapons?"

"The killers may have just walked in with them and then just walked," said Phil. "Trees in a forest. They're probably in the wind. Gone, maybe destroyed. The feds are trying to track them down but most of the politicos fled the jurisdiction after the shootings. Not that it matters."

"Why not?"

Izzy handed me some paperwork. "Ballistics report," he said. "Bottom line, there are no lands and grooves, no markings to match with a weapon if we ever find one."

"Because muskets have no rifling to spin the bullet?" I asked.

"Correct," Izzy replied. "Our little silver balls are as smooth as a baby's nuts."

Terrific. I asked Izzy if the feds were running down all the threats made to still-living politicians around the country. They were trying. The hotel rooms at the convention center were still crime scenes, because the FBI was slower than post office snail mail. They had not yet found any trace of the three bearded men who had followed me, and who were possibly from the APN militia in Brooklyn—which was still deserted—although the cops were still staking out the building for the feds. Meanwhile, NYPD was also still stuck guarding the crime scenes, while the hotel staff went slowly berserk, threatening to sue NYPD for lost revenue every day.

"The feds haven't found the shooter of the other congressman in the crapper in Minnesota and half of the Senate is applying to the Witness Relocation program." Izzy laughed. "The FBI has us babysitting the hotel, doing a few routine checks and door-knocks and not much else. I think they're just trying to keep the secrets of dead congressmen. I don't give a damn. If they let us loose, we'd get these motherfuckers."

"Everything is awesome," Phil sang in an odd voice. "Everything is cool when you're part of a team."

"What the hell was that?"

"*The Lego Movie*," Phil answered.

"He's got young kids," Izzy explained.

"Speaking of the hotel, do you mind if I go back to the crime scenes and look around one more time this week?" I asked.

"Why?" Izzy asked, suspiciously.

I shrugged. "I must have missed something. And I've got nothing else to do. Except a column I'm supposed to write on how dogs can sense the earth's magnetic field and only poop north to south."

He said it was okay, as long as I kept it low key, wore gloves and was watched by the cops there at all times.

"No problem, thanks."

"Sounds like you're onto something with that magnetic crap idea," Phil said, with a straight face.

We ran out of things to talk about. I asked casually if they had ever heard of Faith Potsoli Anthony. They laughed.

"What?"

"The last time you asked me about a girl, it was Ginny Mac," Izzy said. "You didn't listen to us about her and we all know how well that worked out."

"I'm not dating Faith. She's, like, twice my age. I just met her and I have a girlfriend," I protested.

"And Tiffany has left town," Phil added.

I ignored him.

"The latest I hear on Faith is that she is running your old newspaper while the boss Trevor Todd hides in New Zealand," Izzy told me. "La Madrina is a very busy lady."

"La Madrina?"

"The Godmother. After her dad croaked in jail, she took over the family business but we haven't been able to prove that yet. Allegedly she now runs two organized crime groups; the Potsoli Family and the *New York Mail*. Why are you asking about her?"

"She offered me my job back. With a big raise."

"And you didn't take it?" Izzy asked.

"Nope."

"What did I tell you, Phil? This guy is the gift that keeps on giving."

"Totally awesome," Phil said.

"Hey, Shepherd, don't worry," Izzy told me, lapsing into Spanish. "*Hombre prevenido vale por dos.*"

"Which means?"

"Threatened men live long."

63

I wanted to order pizza but Jane insisted on cooking a real meal, some kind of chicken casserole and French potatoes with cheese. She was a bit miffed that I had also invited Amy and Sparky. She thought this would be a quiet dinner with my family but I knew it would only be quiet if there were other people around. I didn't tell her I also invited Izzy and Phil but they were busy. The meal was terrific. I opened some wine and broke out a bottle of arak. Sparky and I did a few shots with the hors d'oeuvres and more with dinner. If Jane thought she was going to impress my mom, she was wasting her time. I never knew my mother to cook. My dad could do simple barbecue but he was also not a homebody. He never took me fishing or taught me baseball or changed a light bulb. You could say they rejected traditional gender and parental roles. Also, you could say they were completely absorbed in their own careers and spent more time with their students than with their only son. Jane gently drew out my dad, asking about his TV appearance and duel with the Conservative talk show host. He talked about his book and Jane seemed genuinely impressed.

After two glasses of wine, Jane told her story about the woman's dog at the animal hospital who regurgitated the condom, which led the woman's husband to conclude his wife was cheating on him. Surprisingly, my parents actually laughed out loud. Amy, who had also sampled the arak, giggled. Sparky roared with laughter, until tears rolled down his cheeks. He asked if we could do the dog/condom story for the newspaper.

"No way," Jane told Sparky.

"But that's a front page," Sparky whined. "Dog fetches divorce! Hubby spies proof that hound found on ground!"

I had to change the subject to prevent him from blurting out other possible obscene headlines. It bugged Amy but I interested everyone with my discoveries about the silver coins. Everybody agreed that the obvious suspects were the Roehm brothers, along with their hired militia guns. Then I shared my frustrating chat with the cops, who had almost zilch.

"But if these brothers are going to finance a secret plan to kill their rivals and rig the election," I asked, "why also donate huge sums to competing candidates, even some of the ones who were killed?"

"To allay suspicion now, so they can point to that when anyone questions them," my father pointed out.

"Exactly," my mother chimed in.

"I'm going to go over the scenes again," I said. "Maybe we missed something."

"Have the police and FBI already searched them for all possible evidence?" my father asked.

"Yes."

"Then what will you achieve by going back there?" His voice was tinged with doubt. "Do you think *you* can find some vital clue they missed?"

His implication was obvious but I didn't go for the bait.

"No, of course not," I lied with a smile. "I just need to go over the ground again to get it all straight in my head."

"That's a good idea," my mother surprised me by saying. With her next breath, she managed to turn it into a condescending statement.

"That's very mindful. You're a visual learner. It may help you reconstruct scenarios."

"Then what?" Amy asked, sipping her wine.

"Then I talk to the Roehm brothers, as a *Daily Press* reporter," I said. "And ask them if they're the Tea Party Animals."

"Francis, I hope your approach will be a bit more subtle." My mother smiled.

"Oh yeah, I'll ask him his favorite color first."

"They'll never talk to you," Jane said.

"Only one way to find out," I replied.

I was stunned to see my father help Jane clear the table and set up for coffee and dessert. My mom and Amy chatted in the living room. I had the odd feeling that they were all talking about me. I took Skippy outside for a walk and Sparky came along. It was a warm, calm night. I looked around—and up—but couldn't spot any surveillance.

"Doesn't mean anything," Sparky pointed out. "Hey, check this out," he said, opening the back doors of his van. "New toys."

There were two large horizontal racks to hold two gigantic black octo-copter drones with mounted cameras.

"Wow," I said.

"I've been making mega bucks from the pictures of Senator Hard-on. Thanks to you, amigo. I'm expanding my business, even hired a guy to run the van when I'm asleep. And these drones—they can lift almost a hundred pounds beyond their payloads. State of the fucking art, man."

He pulled out his phone and showed me an incredible video taken by one of the drones—inside the Fourth of July fireworks over the East River. It was like nothing I had ever seen before and told him so.

"How big a deal is it to run a night mission with one of your drones?" I asked.

"Not a big deal at all, why?"

"Could you send one to 740 Park Avenue? I'd like to take

a peek in the Roehm brothers' penthouse."

"Seriously?"

"Totally."

Five minutes later, one of the drones was out of the van, onto the pavement and up, up and away. We got into the back of the van, into two swivel bucket seats. Skippy curled up underfoot. Sparky had multiple screens built in and we watched the sparkling skyline fly by in front of us.

"Don't you have to keep it in sight?" I asked.

"Not with these beauties. They have three-dimensional GPS databases, ultrasound, night vision, collision avoidance, and lots more and are completely programmable. It knows where we are, where 740 Park Avenue is, the altitude of the building, everything. By the way, there is no other drone nearby. The system already looked. Here's the building now."

On the screens, there were views down to the street hundreds of feet below, where car and cab headlights moved, and also video ahead, of wide, stacked terraces of penthouses atop the building. One screen had data readouts of the address, latitude and longitude numbers, and the height of the structure at two hundred and fifty-six feet.

"The bird will hover over the street and never trespass," Sparky said. "Let's zoom in."

The forward video zoomed in on the large penthouse windows, which were lit from within. I saw high ceilings, Scandinavian-style living rooms, dining areas, and an indoor fountain. In a large study, the wall was crowded with long brown tubes. He zoomed in more. Muskets, dozens of them, including flintlock pistols.

All the lights were on but nobody seemed to be home. Sparky circled around the building and scoped out the matching penthouse on the other side, which belonged to the other twin. The décor was different: glittering gold accents and crystal chandeliers. We couldn't spot any coins until Sparky moved the drone upwards and shot downward.

In the study there were rows of dark wood cabinets and gleaming glass tables. Inside, thousands of gold and silver discs. His coin collection. Again, no one was home.

Sparky sent the drone to the penthouse below, but all the lights were off, the curtains drawn. The penthouse above was lit, revealing early American furniture but modern paintings on the walls, a combination that to my eye didn't work. Just because you had money didn't mean you had taste.

When Jane came out to see what had become of us, we shut the recon mission down. "I recorded that, in case it was helpful," Sparky told me.

"I don't think so but hold onto it. It confirmed what I already knew they collected—rare guns and rare coins. And ugly furnishings."

"Man, you may not like it but I bet every piece of furniture is worth more than we make in a year."

"Yeah but remember, Sparky, money can't buy happiness."

"The fuck it can't. You ever notice rich people never say bullshit like that? Only poor people."

64

Jane was right. The Roehm brothers would not see me the next morning. They did business out of a giant skyscraper on Fifth Avenue with its own subway stop. It was easy to find, even for a new private detective like me, because three sides of the stone structure had ROEHM BUILDING chiseled into it in giant letters. After going through airport-level security and a search of my backpack, my Working Press pass only got me into a third-floor public relations office after waiting an hour. I told them I wanted to interview the brothers about current events. After a lot of BS, a very nice young blonde lady handed me a printed sheet with instructions on how to email my questions in advance to Roehm International. I asked her if it was worth the trouble. She looked around before answering in a hush.

"Not really. I've been here four years and they don't talk to the press at all, unless they want to and then *they* call *you*. I've never actually met them. But it can't hurt to leave your information. Maybe they'll call."

She made it sound like winning the Lotto. She handed me some glossy pamphlets on how Roehm International was a giant oil and toilet paper octopus spanning the globe but was run by two great down-to-earth guys who just wanted to help working Americans by creating cool jobs.

After that, I hiked back to 740 Park Avenue and tried to get in. Silly me. My parents were not among the three-person crowd protesting the Roehm brothers today. A bit too much wine last night, maybe? The doorman told me no one by the name of Roehm lived there. I laughed. Then he told me they were out of the country. Then he told me to leave. I left.

On West 59th Street, near the park, I passed a teacher with little preppy girls in starched school uniforms and pigtails. Like in the children's book *Madeline*, but with a lot more money. A passing truck backfired loudly.

"Poachers!" exclaimed one little girl, pointing into the trees.

After I passed them, the eye in the back of my neck twitched. I headed west, across town. I called Izzy and asked him if he knew where the brothers were. He asked why I was asking. I told him I wanted to interview them.

"Yes, I can't but you can," Izzy said. "Hold on."

He came back on the line after a minute and told me the address of their office.

"I just came from there. They're there now?"

"Unofficially? Yes."

I wondered how he knew that but thanked him. As I walked, I fought the urge to look back and see who was on my ass. I continued west toward the convention center. It occurred to me I didn't want to bring whoever it was who was following me to the hotel, so I diverted into Central Park to flush out my tail first. I picked up my pace and jogged until I saw an empty bench I liked on a rise near a boulder, with lots of open space around it. The bench was about thirty feet long and curved outward, along the path. The vertical structure of the outdoor seating was cement, anchored into the ground. The horizontal slats were green, possibly wood. Behind the bench, the open ground looked level and firm. I sat, took off my backpack and started placing items on the bench while I waited.

When I spotted a black leather hipster's hat and shades approaching with three other guys, I pulled on my gun gloves. Improvising, I wrapped my white charger cord twice around the inside hinge of my MacBook. It gave me just enough cord at the outside ends for me to get an outside grip onto the square white transformer box at one end of the charge and a little plug at the other end by running the cord through my gloves between the fingers on both hands. That left my thumbs free to flip the laptop computer open or closed. I put my mostly empty ballistic nylon backpack back on. Then I sat there with my wire-wrapped MacBook open on my lap, but facing away from me, like I was just another guy wearing gloves and surfing porno websites on a park bench on a hot summer day.

They fanned out around the front of the bench. I wondered if Jay-Jay got a new hat and sunglasses or whether he had just cleaned up his original ones.

"Hey, shitbird," Jay-Jay said in a hoarse voice I had given him with my throat punch the last time we met.

I looked at Jay-Jay and his crew and smiled. I never knew which one was Vinnie or Tony or Bobby but they were funny to look at. They were wearing the same uniform of designer jeans and blue silk shirts. One was wearing a big black knee brace. Another had white tape across his bent nose and his left eye was still swollen black and blue. The last guy had a cast on one hand, where I had snapped his thumb. I laughed. This seemed to infuriate them.

"Laugh, now, motherfucker," said Jay-Jay, pulling out a six-inch hunting knife.

"Thank you, sir, may I have another?" I chuckled. "Seriously?"

The others, hesitant, also pulled out matching blades. How cute.

"We are going to cut you down to size," Jay-Jay announced, echoing his mom's expression.

"Not as small as you, I hope."

"Shut the fuck up!" said Busted Nose.

"What's with the little laptop, shithead?" Knee Brace demanded. "Why'd you bring a computer to a knife fight?"

"You gonna email the cops, dickwad?" Broken Thumb asked.

They started to close in.

I jumped vertically from a sitting position to standing on the seat under me.

They stopped, stunned. I was holding my wired-up laptop defensively, like a small shield in front of me, half-open, like a sharp silver clamshell.

It was their turn to laugh.

"What? You gonna, like, Google us to death?" Jay-Jay sneered, hanging back. "I'm, like, twittering with fear, man."

He was. The smartest of the dim quartet, I caught him eying the sharp steel edges of my notebook. I jumped again, landing on top of the bench. I had the high ground, difficult to get at. I jumped back again, landing behind the bench, the solid structure now between us. I closed the laptop, making it one solid metal rectangle.

Busted Nose lunged onto and over the bench first, leading with his knife. I just moved back and slapped his blade aside. It went dangerously wild, barely missing my arm. The outer surface of the notebook was too smooth for fencing. I slammed both edges of the computer hard onto the bridge of his nose. He made a high-pitched screech like a monkey and dropped his knife, blood gushing from his nose. I popped him again harder in the mouth with the laptop. Something crunched. He wailed again, louder, and went down.

One.

Broken Thumb dove in but his legs hit the bench seat. He stabbed at me but this time I used the open laptop to snag and parry his blade, which caught in the keyboard. Before he could strike again, I followed through and swung the glass screen flat into his face. I could feel things cracking. I raked it tight against his face as I pulled away. His knife vanished as his good hand went to his eyes. He grunted, clutching his bloody face, which was now streaked with a dozen bleeding lines. He looked like a wild animal had been at him. I whacked him again firmly on the back of the head for good luck.

Two.

I heard him go down as I swung toward the others. Jay-Jay was hanging back but Knee Brace was in the air above the bench. He landed on my side of the bench, too close, as Jay-Jay slowly moved in, on the original side of the bench.

Knee Brace was clutching his knife as I held open my laptop, clamshell-ready, edging away. He rushed me, bringing his blade up toward my gut. I fed him my keyboard, slammed it shut with his weapon inside and twisted hard toward the bench. His hand slammed a cement vertical. I twisted his snagged blade back the other way and he lost his grip. I flipped the knife to my right, opening the laptop to set it free before snapping it closed again. As the hunting knife flew away he clipped me in the chest with his other fist. I straight-armed the closed computer into his chin and he staggered onto the bench. I spun in a complete circle to the left, feeling something scrape my back. The laptop opened and I impacted a hard edge right under Knee Brace's nose, upwards. He yelled and swung at me again, wild. I immediately sliced back the other way, one of the cutting edges getting him in the throat. I kicked at his injured knee as he fell backwards again.

Three.

Jay-Jay was angling to stab me over the bench. I lunged and banged my weapon flat on top of his hand. He wailed, lost his knife, stumbled backwards and sat down hard on the sidewalk. I vaulted over the bench, gave Jay-Jay one more whack on his knucklehead with my computer. He obviously wanted to run but knew he wouldn't get far. I put my weird weapon down on the bench and removed my backpack. It was shredded. Chickenshit Jay-Jay, slashing at my back, came the closest to getting me, and I barely felt it.

"Won't you need that knife to cut me down to size, Jay-Jay?" I asked, pointing at his dropped blade, daring him to pick it up.

"I wanted to use guns," he whined. "But she wouldn't... Next time..."

"There won't be a next time, dickless," I told him.

I checked out my MacBook. It was only slightly dented, scratched and scraped on the outside and along the edges. Some keys had been popped out of the keyboard. The screen was badly cracked but only missing a few slices of glass. Curious, I hit the power button. The laptop turned on. I was impressed.

I glanced at my slashed backpack and at the shit-weasel on the ground.

"In answer to your earlier question, Jay-Jay. I didn't Google you to death. I fucking Facebooked you."

65

Jay-Jay's cellphone speaker amplified the call. I had scrolled through his contacts and found "Mom."

"So?" she asked.

"Hi, Faith," I said. "It's not Jay-Jay. F.X. Shepherd here. How are you this morning?"

"Fine, thank you, Shepherd... Why are you calling from my son's phone?"

"Because he can't make the call."

"What does that mean?"

"You know exactly what it means, Faith. You gave your little boy two shots at manhood and it was twice too many. What would you do if someone came to hurt you or kill you—twice? You would end the problem permanently, right? I'd rather not say it on a phone. You never know who's listening these days."

"What? No, no, no! You filthy son of a... They were only... If you... I'll kill you!"

"Exactly. That's what you would do. Would you blame me if I did the same thing? In self-defense?"

"You're a dead man," she hissed.

"What a strange thing for a law-abiding gossip columnist to say."

"I have no choice," she said. "If you hadn't… I know Jay-Jay is a… he's a…"

She was crying. Some Godmother.

"I know what you're feeling, Faith. I've been there. If only you hadn't sent your ass-clown son on this stupid mission. If only you could go back and do things differently and bring him back to life—you'd give anything."

"You sick bastard!"

"I also understand wanting revenge, Faith. Sending more guys out to annihilate the people who did this."

"Yes."

"But nothing you do can bring him back, Faith. Nothing. Every person you kill just makes it worse and worse and you disgust yourself. Then all those people you kill have friends and family and they come after you, thinking the exact same thing as you, wanting revenge. Your life becomes nothing but hatred. But all you really wanted was for it never to have happened. You just want to see him, talk to him again, but all your money and power are useless. Did I mention this was all your fault?"

"You motherfucking…"

"Please focus, Faith, we have to negotiate and I have things to do. I'm a busy guy."

"Negotiate? You must be crazy…"

"Nope. I want something, you want something—let's make a deal, that's what negotiation is all about. For example, I don't want to kill you, I just want you and your dumbass family and your moronic newspaper to leave me the fuck alone so I don't have to do this anymore. That's all I want. Very simple. What do *you* want at this moment?"

"Unless you can bring my son back, friend, we have nothing to talk about."

"Okay, if you stop bugging me, we have a deal. Yes or no?"

"What the hell are you talking about?"

"Will you leave me alone if I can bring Jay-Jay back from the dead? Yes or no?"

"What? I'm going to…"

"Last time. Last chance, lady—yes or no?"

She was quiet for a change.

"Yes?"

"Okay, that was easy, wasn't it? I will hold you to your word. I hope you keep your bargains better than the other guys in your business I've met. Here."

I took the leather hipster's hat out of Jay-Jay's mouth, where I had stuffed it, and handed him back his phone. He whined for a while and I heard her crying. I packed up my dinged laptop, noticing there was some blood on it. Yuk. Moron germs. I wondered if my power cord still worked. Meanwhile, I made an anonymous call to 911 about three injured guys in the park. As I walked away, the mafia brat called me back.

"Hey, she wants to talk to you again," he said, holding the phone toward me.

"You tricked me," she said.

"No. I helped you see the error of your ways. I just talked you through it, so we can all move on and be awesome. Unless you intend to break your word?"

Another pause.

"No. We have an agreement," she said.

"Okay. Good. Sorry about the perfume crack," I said, turning away a second time.

"Wait," she persisted. "What if I had said no? Would you actually have killed Jay-Jay?"

Jay-Jay looked at me. He also wanted to know the answer. I grinned at him.

"Have an awesome day," I said, giving him my best Miranda Dodge wink before walking away.

66

I started walking toward the convention center but I stopped and did a one-eighty. I saw cop cars and ambulances, lights and sirens going, heading into the park to take the re-injured lugs to the hospital. I went back east to Fifth Avenue. I was taking my computer to the hospital. I entered the Apple store, where half of the hip staff were chatting amongst themselves, probably about artisanal bread and jazz poetry. I brought my battered laptop to the service desk.

"What happened to this unit?" a guy with green spiky hair and a "Genius" nameplate that read MAXIMUS asked me.

"I used it to knock the crap out of four guys who were annoying me. You guys make a nice weapon. Does it slice cheese?"

Maximus laughed. He told me my full insurance would pay for a brand new machine, which would arrive in a day or so, but I would have to buy a new charger. I did so, using my *New York Daily Press* American Express card.

"Anything else I can help you with?" Maximus asked.

"Yeah. How do you sharpen this thing?"

He laughed again, to show he thought I was a really funny guy, and I left. I put my new power cord in my backpack, which was pretty badly sliced up, another casualty of my battle with the bozos. Also, evidence of our encounter. I diverted to an outdoor store, picked up an identical replacement, switched my combat computer, gloves and other belongings into the new backpack, and was back on the street in ten minutes. My phone rang.

"Hi, Amy."

"So? Anything?"

"Oh, sorry. I didn't get to the convention center yet. I was delayed."

"Are you working on this case or not? What are you up to?"

"I stopped to say hi to some guys and we worked out. I also had to order a new computer, and buy a new backpack."

"You're *shopping*? You're too much. Well, what do you expect to find at the crime scenes at this late date?"

"No idea. I'm trying to backtrack, find out if I *missed* something. It feels like it."

"Like what?"

"You know, like a secret treasure map. And there's good shopping over there."

"Goodbye, already."

I reminded myself to tell Amy later—when we weren't on the phone—what really happened. I started to walk west again. My rear-eye was not sensing any company. I was thinking about when I first saw Chesterfield's body: the singed face, neck and chest; the smell of gunpowder; the soundproof suite; the unused pistol still sitting on Chesterfield's hip; his startled expression of surprise; his burned-down cigarette; his whiskey glass. I remembered the smoke detector, disabled by the handyman, the open curtains, the nailed down paintings and lamps, the fancy bathroom, the gold faucets and fixtures, the sealed windows, the locked toilet, the keycard on the floor behind the front door. After the murder, the victim's room was sealed, like the toilets, and guarded until now. Routine. There were four other identical killings, a total of five victims in five rooms—dispatched by a magician who vanished, along with his musket or muskets. But there were six sealed crime scenes, counting Senator Carroll's room, also with a disabled smoke detector, where nothing happened. Six crime scenes, not five.

Magic.

But I knew there was no such thing as magic. Only preparation and misdirection. How far in advance did this magician prepare his illusion? Long enough to plan a hack of the hotel video security system. Who—or what—was it the cameras couldn't see? The Tea Party Animal magicians obviously knew about the smoke detectors being disconnected. Somehow, he—or they—was able to get past security and into five rooms. Who let them in, never reached for their hardware and were wasted before they could say "What the fuck?" A close colleague? Tiffany? Karl? A cop or security guard? Perhaps the dead congressmen didn't go for their weapons because they were reaching for their rods, opening their doors to an attractive woman.

How did they get a murder weapon or five murder weapons out of the security ring at the convention center? Everything was searched and logged on the way out and in. Either they smuggled it out or they didn't. So, it's gone or it's still there. Where? Only one possible spot. Or six. Maybe. Worth a shot.

"Siri, where's the closest hardware store?"

She told me there was one on Ninth Avenue.

"Thanks, Siri."

"My pleasure, Shepherd."

The store clerk said there was probably a customized industry item for what I wanted but they didn't carry it. He hooked me up with a ratchet screwdriver, called an Easy-Driver, and a few attachments that might do the job, along with some gallon-sized plastic sandwich bags. I paid with the newspaper's credit card, stashed everything in my new backpack and continued on my way.

The security was diminished at the Knickerbocker Convention Center after the departure of the political circus. A car show was setting up. I went upstairs on the escalator, caught an elevator and ran into NYPD officers outside one of the crime scenes. I told them who I was and that they could call Izzy for approval. In five minutes, my buddy Sergeant Reed arrived. She asked what I was doing and I told her. She called Izzy and told me it was okay but she would go with me and I had to wear gloves at all times.

"No problem, Sarge."

Before we could enter the suite I had chosen, one of the young hotel workers from that night, Bryce, showed up with a clipboard and demanded to know when the six suites would finally be released for rental.

"Tonight's the last night," Sergeant Reed told her.

"Great, terrific," Bryce exulted, shaking the sergeant's hand and then mine. "My boss will be very happy."

When I squeezed her hand back, she visibly winced.

"Sorry," I said. "You okay?"

"I'll live. I hurt my hand the other day. Slammed it in a drawer."

"Ouch," I said, looking closer.

She displayed her open palm. The heel of her right hand was bruised and there was a dark red U-shaped mark.

"You should ice that," I told her.

"I will, thanks," she said, flashing a smile.

She thanked us again, wrote something on her clipboard with her left hand and took off.

"You going to flirt with the staff or check out the room?" Reed asked.

"Can't I do both?"

The sergeant put on blue surgical gloves, I put my gun

gloves on, and we entered Senator Carroll's former suite. I walked back into the hallway and asked Reed to shut the door and yell loudly, then reopen the door.

"Okay."

She shut the door. I heard nothing. I walked up to the door and put my ear to it. No sound. She opened the door.

"I couldn't hear a thing," I told her.

"I yelled," she said.

"They're all the same," I concluded. "Soundproof."

"I guess they spared no expense. Good thing for a bridal suite," she said with a chuckle.

"You got that right."

I went all around the room, looking at the curtains, the windows, touching the lamps and paintings, looking in empty drawers. I peered at the smoke alarm in the ceiling. After a while, I took off my gloves and told her I was done. As she moved to the door, I asked her if I could use the bathroom. I told her I really had to go. She hesitated.

"You want to come in with me?" I asked.

"Hurry up," she said. "And put your gloves back on."

67

I put my gloves back on, shut and locked the bathroom door from the inside and quickly went to work. I pulled out the ratchet screwdriver from my bag and found the closest diameter attachment to fit the octagonal hole in the metal nipple in the top of the toilet tank. The metal moved and I felt something unlock. I carefully lifted top off and looked inside the water tank.

Damn. Nothing, just the usual pipes and copper plumbing.

Wait.

One of the vertical pipes on the left inside wall looked out of place and didn't seem to be connected to anything.

Yes!

Preparation and misdirection. But what the hell was it? It was an octagonal gray plastic tube about an inch and a half in diameter and maybe nine inches long. It was held in place by two metal brackets protruding from the inside wall of the tank. The top of the pipe was tightly sealed with taut metallic foil. A pipe bomb? I peered at it from every angle but I didn't see any exposed wires that might blow me up. I carefully touched the cylinder with both gloved hands, got a grip and gently pulled. It came free. The other end of the pipe had an octagonal cap, covered by a thin rubber pad. The tube was textured and featureless, except for one side, closer to the padded end, where there was a thin, raised rectangular box with some kind of hinge, like it could flip open. What the hell was it? Maybe it was a bomb after all. Jesus, I think it might be a…

The door banged three times.

"Yo, Shepherd! You fall in?" Sergeant Reed shouted, pounding on the door some more. "Let's go!"

Damn.

"No! Sorry, Sarge, be right out."

No time. I quickly put my mystery find in one of my large sandwich bags and dropped it into my knapsack. I flushed the toilet to cover up the noise of replacing the tank top. When I emerged, Reed was waiting by the door. She locked the suite and nodded to the cop on duty outside. In the hall, as we walked to the elevator, I hesitated over what to do.

"Did you say you guys are closing down these crime scenes tonight?" I asked.

"Yup. Finally, we'll be out of here," she said.

It looked like I had no choice. I almost cursed out loud when I remembered that I did not re-lock the top of the toilet tank. There was no way I could ask to go back to that bathroom now.

"Look, sorry, but I just realized I also have to check out Chesterfield's suite before I go."

She grumbled but took me there. I did my Sherlock Holmes act again as the sergeant watched, clearly bored. I was stuck. I opened the bathroom door and looked inside. I dialed Izzy on my cell.

"Hey, Izzy. Listen, I've got a… Yeah, I'm there now… in Chesterfield's suite. Right. Yes, she's here with me now. Wait…"

"Just the guy I want to talk to," Izzy told me. "Where were you earlier this morning?"

Uh oh.

"I was at the Roehm Building. I also went to the Apple store, did some shopping and then walked to the convention center."

"So you weren't in Central Park busting up the same guys you knocked around last week, you know, that mutt Jay-Jay Potsoli and his pals?"

"What? Why? Do they say that?"

"No. They claim they were doing a kickboxing workout that got out of hand but I don't believe that and neither do the witnesses, who said they got their asses handed to them by a ninja."

"Oh. Everybody okay?"

"You worried about them? They'll live, although one of the idiots got such a bad concussion he's still in the hospital. What was it you wanted?"

"What did I want? Oh yeah. Did you guys take off the tops of the toilet tanks at the crime scenes here?"

There was a long pause.

"Not sure," he answered. "Not like we were looking for anything that might fit in there. It's not a drug investigation. Weren't they locked with some kind of doohickey? So, no, I don't think we did but the feds took over pretty fast. They probably did it. Why?"

I suggested he might want to come over and check—before the scenes were released.

"I'm not going over there to stick my head in a toilet for a reporter's hunch."

"What if Sergeant Reed took a quick look—just to be sure?"

Izzy cursed and I could hear him talking to Phil.

"What are you up to?" Izzy demanded.

"Nothing," I lied. "I just thought you should be the one to discover the murder weapons—if there are any to be found. Hey, you never know."

There was more discussion.

"Phil says he thinks you're running a number on us, for some reason. Okay, we'll be there soon. But if we don't find anything, Shepherd, you are going bowl surfing."

They made good time. Izzy stormed in, saw I was wearing

my gloves, and ordered me to lift off the top. I made a gallant effort but, of course, it was locked. I shrugged helplessly and suggested calling the hotel maintenance staff.

"They've probably got the doohickey to open it."

"No," Izzy said. "Let's keep this quiet—either way."

He asked Sergeant Reed for help. She pulled out a steel multi-tool and had it open in thirty seconds. She and I lifted the porcelain off and onto the toilet seat. I could smell gunpowder as soon as we took it off.

"So?" Izzy demanded, peering inside.

"What the hell is that?" Phil asked, pointing to another gray plastic tube clipped vertically to the inside of the tank, identical to the one I had found. But on this tube, the foil at the top was missing. The ugly gray pipe was empty, charred black around the muzzle, which stank of black powder.

"Yeah," I said, peering over their shoulders. "What the hell is that?"

They looked at me. Hard. I looked back with sincerity. I think.

"Crap. Preserve this for prints and get Crime Scene over here now; pictures, the whole nine yards," Izzy ordered Reed.

She got on her radio. I asked again what it might be.

"You know what it is," Izzy told me. "It's some kind of tube gun. The Tea Party Animal blasted Percy and then hid this popgun in here. It's probably some kind of one-shot zip gun—while we've been beating the bushes, hunting for a motherfucking musket."

"I think you're right, Izzy. This might be a big break in the case for you. Hey, leave me out of it. You think the other toilets might have these, too?"

"Maybe, if they're single shot. But, if they can be reloaded, this could be the only one." Izzy grinned. "Shepherd, I don't fucking know whether to kiss you or kick you in the nuts."

"Do I get a vote?"

68

Izzy and Phil found four more octagonal plastic tubes secreted in the other victims' commodes. I didn't ask anyone if they had thought of looking inside Senator Carroll's potty. Izzy thanked me with a manly handshake and a pat on the back, then asked me nicely to leave.

"Again, you're welcome," I said.

"A lot more cops are on the way, including, literally, a busload of feds. Best you make yourself scarce."

"I get it. No problem. But I have to file this."

They looked at each other.

"I owe you that much," Izzy said, "but give us a few hours before you do and don't quote me by name, okay, buddy?"

"You got it. I just need a non-attributed quote about finding the murder weapons."

"Uh... how about... 'Pending ballistics testing, we suspect these are the murder weapons. The, uh, nature of the custom assassination devices, and other factors, points to very sophisticated killers with access to large amounts of money and technology.'"

"Excellent. You're getting good at this."

I wanted to tell them everything but I was in a bind. If I admitted I had stolen evidence, he might still send me bowl surfing. I left. On the way out, in the hall, Sergeant Reed was giving me the stink-eye, like maybe she regretted not accompanying me into the john. I gave her a friendly wave and took off. It didn't matter, I told myself. Finders, keepers. I had removed crucial evidence but, if Reed went looking, there was nothing to incriminate me.

Except the metal clips affixed to the inside of the toilet tank wall—identical to the others. Oops. Okay, if they find them, it could mean the bad guys had planned to bump off the senator but, for some reason, they did not. Ergo, no empty plastic blunderbuss. But what if the presence of the gray tube actually meant that the senator was a part of the plot and had one put there to deflect suspicion? Why did I take the unfired weapon? Ego? Maybe, but I needed to get a closer look. And I might have a use for it.

In the lobby, I found Bryce at the concierge desk, on her cellphone. She got off as I approached.

"Yessir, Mr. Shepherd, how may I help you?"

"Get a chance to ice your hand?" I asked.

"Not yet. Kinda busy. Thanks for asking."

I noticed for the first time that her voice was somewhat musical, her eyes sparkling.

"You know who I am?" I asked, surprised.

"Of course. I've been reading your stories online. They're great."

"Okay, cool. I just have a few quick questions for you, Bryce...?"

"Bryce Martha Draper."

"Bryce Martha Draper, what a lovely name."

"Thank you. What questions?"

"Well, are you married?"

She laughed. "No."

"Boyfriend?"

"With this job and school? I'm working on my masters. Not at the moment, no."

"How old are you?"

"Twenty-three. What does this have to do with the murders?"

"Nothing," I confessed, giving her my best you-caught-me smile. "Look, I really want to take you to dinner tonight and pick your brain for some background for my stories—strictly off the record. How about eight at L'Éveil?"

"Wow. Probably the most expensive French restaurant in town," she noted. "That's the place that slow-cooks for a week and does all kinds of weird scientific things to food, right? You must have some expense account."

"Yeah, unlimited. Please say yes, Bryce. I think you're a very interesting person. To be honest, I suddenly can't stop thinking about you. I hope that doesn't creep you out?"

"No, it doesn't, actually," she said, rewarding me with a big-eyed look. "I think you're interesting, too, and I also want to pick *your* brain about the case. I just heard the cops are back in lockdown indefinitely and we won't get our suites back tonight. They won't tell me what's happening. Did you find something new up there?"

I gave her a sly smile. "I promise to tell all at dinner—before I put it in the paper. Please say yes, Bryce."

"Okay, Shepherd. It's a date. Do you know what 'L'Éveil' means in French?"

"No," I lied. "Evil?"

"No." She leaned slowly over her counter, giving me a better view of her cleavage and a sweet whiff of something floral, to whisper in my reddening ear.

"Arousal."

Oh, man. I retreated before she could wipe the floor with me.

69

It was three when I got outside. I called Amy and told her I was stopping by.

"Now is not good, Shepherd. I have to sell crack to a movie star in thirty minutes."

"Is it an emergency?"

"Yes. No, it's a case. Undercover sting, insurance job."

"What movie star?"

"I can't tell you on the phone."

"Reschedule it, please. I just got out of the convention center. I'll be right over. Oh, and make sure no one else is in the house."

"What? I told you…"

"Amy, I'll be right over. Be there."

"Okay, okay. Bye."

When I got to Amy's townhouse, I told her what really happened in the park and produced my surprise in the plastic bag.

"This better be important, Shepherd. A ten-million-dollar performance bond is on the line. What the hell is that?" she asked, staring at the tube.

"That," I replied, "is a musket without the flintlock."

"What? It looks like a pipe bomb."

"I know but it's one of at least six identical weapons secreted inside the locked toilets of the rooms of the Tea Party Animal assassination victims."

"You're shitting me?" she said, moving closer, peering at the gray cylinder.

"I shit you not. I found this one inside Senator Carroll's throne. It hasn't been fired. The others, in the victims' rooms, had been used. Izzy said they look like single-shot zip guns."

"I'll be damned."

I put on my gloves and Amy donned surgical gloves. I opened the bag and gently placed the firearm on top of it. I used my phone to take still pictures from every angle, then carefully flipped it over and did the same on that side. Then I did video, as Amy held the tube and displayed all aspects.

"This is different from a zip gun," Amy said. "They use rubber bands and a nail to hit a center-fire cartridge that you load into the back of the pipe. This thing is sealed at both ends."

"Yeah. But I think the round fires through that foil on the top. That thin box on one side, closer to the padded bottom than the top, has a hinge."

I held the pipe in one hand and gently tugged at the top side of the assembly. It swung out toward the rear at a right angle to the tube and kept going for another forty-five degrees until I met resistance. I didn't force it. The box was hollow, like the top of an old Zippo cigarette lighter.

"Be careful," Amy warned, moving away.

"My middle name, Amy. It's a trigger assembly," I told her. "Look, under the box is a small sliding switch. That tiny bubble on the tube next to it looks like an LED."

"Exactly, it's a bomb," she said. "Please don't blow up my house. I just got a new espresso machine."

"Nobody got de-res'd. This is a firearm, although it's been completely reinvented. I think it's electrical or maybe piezoelectric."

"De-res'd?"

"De-resolution. Blown to bits."

"Oh. Sounds bad. You're sure it's not an explosive device?"

"Not unless this copy of the others is a Shanghai Surprise and is rigged to blow up when we find it and play with it. I think it's a hand cannon."

I reached over and slid the tiny switch. The tiny LED glowed red.

"Jesus," Amy gasped.

I slid it back and the red light went off again. Amy started breathing again. I folded the trigger assembly back to the initial safe position and picked it up. I put my right hand around the tube, over the trigger area, and used the butt of my left hand to brace the end of the weapon for recoil.

I pointed the gray muzzle away from us, holding both arms straight out.

"There's a small triangle of metal on the upper end," I told her, "a fixed gunsight. Except for the switch and fold-down trigger assembly, there are no moving parts, no bullets, no shells, no firing pin, no ejector mechanism. I think all you have to do is squeeze with the trigger hand to send a charge to the black powder in the tube, which discharges a silver ball and silk wadding into the chest of the victim at point-blank range. Then, all you'd have to do is hide it and walk away."

"Wow," Amy said. "You brought this here so I could tell my GOP customers the real deal and alert them to possible future danger?"

"Of course. With pictures. I'm emailing them to you now. I still work for you, right?"

"Right."

"You have a few hours to do that before I file it with the *Daily Press*. I also still work for them."

"What are you going to do with this thing?" Amy asked. "You know it's a state felony to steal evidence and it's a federal crime to possess this gadget? It's also not a nice thing to do to your cop buddies."

"Yeah, I feel bad about that but I may find a use for it. I've helped them a lot more than I'm hurting them, if at all. They'll get it eventually, but I wasn't here and you never saw it, okay?"

"For sure. I don't intend to join you in jail. If you live that long. The cops were here earlier. You know they think you assaulted those mafia goons again?"

"Yeah, thanks. Jail is the least of my problems," I told her, heading for the door. "I have to go home and change and go out on a date with one of the concierges at the hotel and eat a $2,000 dinner that's been cooking for the past month."

"Does Jane know about this?"

"Not yet."

"Shepherd, I know you're a young guy but don't be an asshole. Jane is a wonderful girl. You'll regret this later."

"Maybe but at least my paper will be paying for it. Oh, you mean with Jane? Relax, Amy, everything's cool. As Phil would say, everything is awesome."

70

Jane wasn't home but Skippy was glad to see me. I took him out for a walk and called Jane. She said she was trying to catch up and was booked until at least nine. Perfect.

"That's okay," I told her. "I've got a business dinner at eight. When I get home, I'll tell you about what I found at the hotel."

"What? Tell me now."

"Not on the phone, okay?"

"Really?"

"Yes, really."

"Text me."

"Nothing on the phone or online."

"This is unfair. Now I'm dying to know. Who are you eating with? Izzy and Phil?"

"Actually, yes. Plus someone from the hotel, which reminds me, I have to call and make reservations."

"Okay. See you later."

I looked at the time: after five. I called L'Éveil. I asked to speak to the executive chef, whom I had met before, a man named Henri Plouffe, and told him I needed a custom order for dinner.

"This evening?" he asked, doubtfully. "This is very close, Shepherd, not many hours."

"Yes. It doesn't matter what it costs, Henri. The paper will pay. It's very important and it's a surprise. I'm sending you the pictures and measurements now."

"This is business or pleasure?" he asked.

"I guess you could say it's both but what it really is, is preparation and misdirection."

"I do not understand."

"Magic, Henri. I'm asking for some of your magic. On short notice."

"I make art, okay, Shepherd?"

"Yeah, sure, but you use science to make magic, which is an art. Great art."

"Yes, thank you, this is true."

French chefs are so sensitive.

When Skippy and I got back home, I fed him, took a shower and changed into my one suit: a navy-blue two-button jacket number, a pink short-sleeve dress shirt and purple power tie. It didn't feel powerful, just tight and sweaty. I felt overdressed, and underequipped without my backpack. My cell rang.

Tiffany Mauser was calling.

"Hi, Tiffany. Long time, no see. How's the weather in D.C.?"

"Quit it, Shepherd. I just heard about the pipe pistols in the toilets from the security people. You found those damn things, didn't you?"

"Off the record, yeah. On the record, the cops found them."

"Bless your heart. I just called to thank you for continuing to work on the case after the way we treated you. You are amazing. The senator…"

"I'm awesome," I corrected her. "Are we still talking about my work or…"

She responded with a naughty laugh. What was I doing?

"Seriously, you're a good man."

"And they're hard to find," I reminded her.

"This is not why I called… Okay it's not the only reason I called… I'm back in town for a day. I was wondering if you were free tonight. I'd like to see you. I also have something to tell you. It's important."

"I'd like to see you, too," I heard myself saying.

I told myself I was just being polite. I told her I had a business dinner at eight but I'd meet her for a late dinner at ten at Park It, a cool little bistro near the park.

"Great, that's right near my hotel," she said, I'm sure for no reason at all. "You're going to eat two dinners?"

"I'm a growing boy. Besides, I'm chowing down at a very fancy, trendy spot, an artistic, artisanal eatery for RWPs, so I'll probably be starved."

Looked like it was going to be a busy night. After Tiffany hung up, I tried to ignore the guilty Jiminy Cricket voice in my head, slut-shaming me with a man-whore lecture. Fuck the little bug.

I pulled my beat-up MacBook out of my new backpack but the shattered screen made it impossible to work on. My new one wouldn't arrive until tomorrow. I wrote my story on Jane's home office desktop and called Sparky. I told him about the pictures I had taken of the mini-musket inside Senator Carroll's crapper and the stills and video I had taken later. I told him to take credit for the shots and video and say it was a secret source.

"Fucking hey, man. These are great! I'm popping a woody. This shit is exclusive?"

"Totally. But the cops and others have them so we have to file tonight, in case there's a leak."

"No problem, amigo. You rule. This time, I'll split the photo resales with you, right? No argument."

I agreed. I walked him through the murder device description and operation.

"Okay, Sparky. I'll send you a copy of my story, so you

can write your captions. It's past six o'clock, I've got to call Mel now."

First I called Izzy's cell and told him I was going to pull the trigger on my story on the toilet tubes at eight. I also requested that he and Phil do me an interesting favor. He agreed without questions.

I then got my boss on the line and predictably, because it was close to deadline, Mel Greenbaum cursed at me. At least, as close to cursing as Mel the Mild got.

"I got an exclusive break in the Tea Party Animal story, Mel, with exclusive photos and video—use it or lose it."

"What friggin' story? Why don't I know about this shih-tzu?"

"You know now," I told him. "I sent you my story, Sparky is sending pictures. You should have both by now."

I read the top of my copy out loud to him:

After assassinating presidential candidate Percy Chesterfield and four other top GOP pols, the Tea Party Animals hid their smoking murder weapons—five high-tech mini-muskets—inside the sealed toilet tanks of their dying victims, the *Press* has learned exclusively.

The bizarre gadgets—electrically fired plastic tubes—remained secreted inside the opulent bathrooms, under the noses of an army of local, state and federal investigators since the killings—until the elite NYPD Major Crimes Squad discovered them today. The crucial find came just hours before the suites of the five victims were to be opened again to the public.

I continued, reading Izzy's anonymous quote about the guns. Mel stopped me before I got to the background copy.

"Yeah, I got the cheese-licking thing in front of me. Nice of you to finally do some more fuggin' work," Mel complained.

"You don't want the story, Mel? I know someone who

does. I spoke to Faith today. The *New York Mail* wants me back at twice my current salary."

"No, no, no! I want the mother-trucking story—I'm just sayin'. Don't be an asshat, okay, Shepherd? The story is good, nice pictures. How did you get all this?"

"I found them."

"No spit? The *Press* found the evidence? You buried your forking lead, dumbnuts—that has to go up top."

"No, Mel. Sorry, but I've got a deal with the cops. They get the credit and I get the exclusive. Just hold it until eight o'clock and then blow it out on the web, okay?"

"Don't make Coke-sipping deals like that!"

One thing I had noticed about newspaper work, during my brief time in the racket, was that no matter how good it was—it was never good enough.

"Too late, Mel. I made the deal and can't break it. Any problems or questions? I've got a dinner date... with some important sources."

"Sources? Dock me! I assume that means the parsing paper will be paying for this forking dinner?"

"You bet."

"Well, thanks for a few moments of your precious porking time, Mr. Shepherd, it's been a freaking honor."

"The freaking honor is all mine."

"Remember to get a mother-mugging receipt."

"My mother-mugging pleasure."

71

I still had an hour and a half before meeting Bryce, so I grabbed a cab over to Park Avenue. My parents had apparently knocked off for the night, along with the other demonstrators. Only a few signs were strung from the saw horses in their pen on the opposite sidewalk. I thought maybe my nice suit might get me in the door. I went up to the doorman, a different one this time, and asked if I could see the Roehm brothers.

"Which one, sir?"

"Whichever one is home."

Wrong answer. He asked if I had an appointment. I didn't lie.

"You'll have to contact their office, sir," he told me.

"Okay, thanks. Umm... is Walter home?"

"Mr. Cantor?"

"Yes. I'm F.X. Shepherd. We're friends. Could you call him and ask if he's got a quick minute to see me?"

He looked me up and down. He obviously thought I was some random guy but the suit and tie and my fancy initials forced him to give me the benefit of the doubt.

"Very well, sir. Please step inside and I'll inquire."

He pushed the heavy glass and brass revolving door and

I entered the sacred precincts of the gods. The lobby was opulent, with plush red carpeting. I waited as the doorman spoke to someone on a wallphone.

"What is your name again, sir?"

"F.X. Shepherd," I said, as if my name had launched a thousand ships.

The doorman listened to a voice on his intercom and then asked me if I was F.X. Shepherd from the *Daily Press*. I decided to keep trying the truth.

"Yes."

The doorman listened again, nodding. Were they telling him which bones to break?

"Please have a seat in the lobby, sir. Someone will be right down."

"Thank you."

I was still inside. I sat in a comfy armchair, wondering if they had called the cops and I was about to be arrested for trespassing. I sweated it out for ten minutes. If I were a betting man... The large elevator across the lobby opened, giving a flash of mahogany paneling, a velvet bench and a small crystal chandelier inside.

Walter Cantor, in tan cargo shorts, sandals and a turquoise Caribbean reef shirt, walked out and came over to shake my hand. Son of a bitch.

"Thank you, Eddie," he said to the doorman. "Hi, Shepherd. How are your parents? What can I do for you? Sorry I'm all wet. I just finished my laps."

Of course he had a pool. Nice.

"Hello, sir. They're fine, thanks. I just wanted to quickly run something past you, off the record, in confidence, if that's okay?"

"Off the record? Sure. Call me Walter. Let's sit down."

We sat on the couch. I quickly shared what I knew about the Tea Party Animal killings, including the silver musket balls and the hidden zip guns, presumably very expensive custom items. I realized I was showing off for the rich guy. I couldn't mention that the silver probably came from melted antique coins.

"Why haven't I read about any of this?" Walter asked.

I told him the hidden tube guns story would break at eight but the fact that the bullets were made of silver was a police holdback.

"A holdback?"

"A vest card, something only the bad guy and the cops know about. It gives them a gauge of guilty knowledge and eliminates the fakers. I also think the killers used squares of a rare Revolutionary War flag to wad the silver shot."

"A flag?"

I explained about the yellow silk, which had originally been bright green, and how the silk patches had been used.

"Why would someone use pieces of an historic flag?"

"I don't know," I told him. "Maybe to literally wrap the whole plot in Old Glory."

"Fascinating," Walter said. "Oh... I get it. You're here because you think Hans and Gert might be the bad guys, because they're rich and right wing."

"Yeah, maybe. And one collects Revolutionary War muskets."

"True. Anything's possible but I doubt it," Walter chuckled. "Hans and Gert are gentlemen. Why would they do something like that?"

"To change history, to be king-makers?"

"They already have and they already are," Walter pointed out. "Courtesy of the Supreme Court, their corporations are now officially people and their cash is considered free speech. But I haven't heard a shred of proof against them yet, Shepherd. This is still America. I certainly haven't seen my neighbors ripping up flags." He laughed.

"Okay, thanks for your time."

"Eddie said you were on your way to dinner?"

"Yeah, I'm meeting a lady at L'Éveil over on the park," I told him, bragging again.

"Great place, amazing. Enjoy," Walter said. "Eddie can get you a cab. I'm sorry I couldn't be more helpful."

"I just wanted your opinion and you *have* been helpful. Thanks again, Walter."

"Any time," he said, shaking my hand.

72

I was more than half an hour early to L'Éveil on Central Park South. I rode a glass elevator up to the eighth floor duplex restaurant overlooking the park. My phone chimed. Mel had sent me the headlines that would be used on my exclusive, about to break on the website.

HIDDEN HOT RODS
Cops Flush Out Secret Stubby Shooters
Tea Party Animal Arsenal of Mini Muskets

I shut off my phone, knowing the restaurant had reception-blocking technology to cut off all communications. Henri would not allow anything to compete with his fabulous food. His place was world famous for cutting-edge sous vide cooking—vacuum-packed preparation at low, slow temperatures and other radical culinary techniques, including 3D food printers. The science behind it all concluded that traditional oven and stove cooking dried out food and destroyed the cells of meat and vegetables. But the cellular structure could be preserved by slowly heating food in a vacuum-sealed plastic bag at an exact temperature between one hundred twenty and one hundred fifty degrees for many hours. It sounded ridiculous but tasted much better than anything I had ever tasted before. Unfortunately, Henri charged $2,000 a plate, and that didn't include liquor.

The cocktail lounge of the restaurant was an ultra-modern affair with a dozen tables and chairs on a shiny black marble floor, with a black marble bar on the right wall. Six bartenders were mixing colorful drinks overflowing with white fog and rippling with blue flames. Over the bar, three large screens displayed a live feed from the kitchen, famous movie food scenes—currently *Tom Jones*—and an informational video on scientific cooking. A glass wall featured a view into the busy kitchen, which looked like the engine room of the *Starship Enterprise*. The chefs worked at strange machines, which had brass labels on them like "Carbon Dioxide Foam Machine," "Liquid Nitrogen Chamber," "Cryo-Griddle," "Immersion Blender," "Thermal Immersion Circulator," "Centrifuge," and "Ultrasound Oven." A large piece of equipment, labeled "3D Printer," had arms that darted quickly left and right and back and forth, like a map plotter. On a tray, small sculptures of bright green artichokes were magically growing, as computerized nozzles built them.

I strode to the bar and ordered an arak. A pretty bartender asked my name. She went away, spoke into a phone and returned with my favorite liquor. I wished I could afford to eat here.

"Mr. Shepherd, Henri asked me to welcome you and tell you that everything is prepared."

"Thank you."

I took a slug of arak. Some of the other customers, especially a young lady with a flaming blue martini, looked familiar. I looked back toward the entrance. Next to that was the exit to the dining room, a grand staircase down one floor.

Henri appeared in whites and kissed me on both cheeks.

"So, Shepherd, everything is in place for you, my friend. What are we doing this evening?"

"Just a little Shanghai Surprise, Henri. I really appreciate you doing this on short notice."

"Shanghai?"

"Just an expression. Make sure all dinners and drinks go on my paper's card."

"Okay, no problem. Please, what is a Shanghai Surprise?"

"A joke with two people. Like when you think a bomb is a fake but it isn't."

"This is a joke?"

"For one of them."

73

Bryce arrived on time, in a snug black V-neck cocktail dress and black stiletto heels. She kissed me on the cheek and slid onto the bar stool by my side. She ordered a London Fog, a frosted concoction that overflowed with what looked like dry ice. She asked what we had found at the hotel but I told her it would have to wait until dessert.

The maître d' appeared with two menus and Bryce slid her hand into the crook of my elbow as we followed him down the grand staircase. The lower floor of the restaurant was decked out like a movie set, with giant potted palms, huge red velvet drapes, large Ming vases, round tables covered with white cloths, and burgundy leather chairs. It was done up like a Victorian gentlemen's supper club, set inside a giant greenhouse.

The waiter seated us in comfortable armchairs and left us with the menus. I noticed several familiar faces. Random celebs.

"This place is amazing," Bryce said. "It smells great in here."

"That may be your menu. It's edible."

I took a nibble off the corner of my menu. It tasted like French cheese, but crunchy. God knows what it really was. I sampled some of the green lettering and got a taste of basil pesto. Inside, there were sections for sous vide. It was best not to think about your shrink-wrapped duck entrée being bathed in lukewarm water for a few days before you got there. Better to just let your mouth enjoy the orgy.

We had a caviar appetizer of translucent red globes, with tiny egg white balls in the center. The salads were crunchy green pine cones that tasted like arugula and were topped with maple ginger sauce and fruit. Maybe. I had a duck that was incredible. The fat had been removed between the skin and the muscle and replaced with bittersweet chutney potato foam. Bryce went wild for her salmon and said it was the best she had ever eaten. We had more drinks. I talked about my big stories. She talked about the famous people who came to her hotel.

"This is totally swag but I can't wait anymore," Bryce said. "What did you find in the rooms today?"

"Hold on one minute," I told her, waving to a nearby table. "I see someone I know."

Izzy and Phil, already on their coffee, waved back and came over. Bryce looked confused. I quickly signaled our waiter, who nodded.

"Bryce, you remember Lieutenant Izzy Negron and Detective Sergeant Phil D'Amico?"

"Yes, I think so," she said, her eyes narrowing in suspicion.

"What's new, guys?" I asked them.

We were interrupted by the magical arrival of our coffee and desserts. Each chocolate dessert was a perfect replica on a white plate—an octagonal gray tube, artfully garnished by a little square of yellow silky material, a neat pile of black granules and a shiny silver ball. On the white plate rim, spelled out in blood red letters, was her name.

Bryce jumped out of her chair, her napkin falling from her lap.

"What is that?" she tried.

"You tell us," Izzy suggested. "You reacted as if it were a rattlesnake."

"I don't know what it is."

"Sorry I frightened you, Bryce, just a little joke," I said, reaching out across the tabletop for her hand. I took her by the wrist and turned her hand over. With my other hand, I grabbed my chocolate tube and fitted the butt end perfectly into the injured pattern on the heel of her hand. She jerked her hand back.

"We found five weapons just like that today," I told her. "Except they weren't made out of chocolate."

"I don't know what you're talking about," she snipped, her cool returning.

"So you say," Izzy said. "We've been questioning a guy named Norton Pyle. You may know him, Miss Draper—he's a handyman at your hotel."

"Oh… yes, the name does sound familiar. Why are you questioning him?"

"Because he had access to the toilets at the crime scenes, of course. He lied at first but he quickly admitted installing six sets of double clips inside the toilet tanks," Izzy told her.

"So you're saying some kind of weapon was hidden in the bathrooms and one of our people was involved? That's awful. I should inform management."

"We already have, Miss Draper," Izzy said. "We understand you were working the overnight shift at the hotel the night Chesterfield and the others were murdered?"

"Yes, I was," she said, digging into her tubular treat.

"Anything unusual happen that night, Miss Draper?"

"You mean other than five murders?" Her cool was totally restored. "Shepherd, this is really yummy."

"How many breaks do you get on your shift?" Phil asked.

"Two," she answered, "at three and six. Why?"

"Where did you go on your breaks?" Phil pressed. "What did you do?"

"I don't remember. Probably to the bathroom, the lunchroom."

"Have any witnesses?"

"Correct me if I'm wrong but aren't you supposed to prove people guilty, as opposed to people proving they are innocent?"

"So you have no witnesses," Izzy snapped. "What are your politics, Miss Draper?"

"I'm a registered Independent," she said, rolling the silver ball in the red sauce. "I'm currently undecided. This crunchy gunpowder is amazing. The green square is banana and something else. Is the silver ball white chocolate and amaretto?"

"Miss Draper, do you have any information about these killings?"

"Me? Not guilty." She scraped the plate clean. "Obviously, if I did, as a good citizen I would have told you immediately. Shepherd, thanks for a lovely evening but did you bring me here just to spring this elaborate prank?"

"Guilty."

"I'm disappointed. Unless you gentlemen need any more of my help tonight, I'm going home. Again, Shepherd, thanks for a memorable evening."

She blotted her red lips with her napkin and stood up, smoothing her skirt. Bryce kissed me on the cheek and walked away. She was quite a dish.

"She is guilty as shit," Izzy declared. "Almost jumped out of her panties."

"Second the motion," Phil agreed. "She knew exactly what that was."

"Yeah. Be nice to have some proof," I ventured. "But that missing security footage is gone forever, I think."

"Yes, and the handyman didn't implicate Bryce in any way," said Izzy. "Pyle claimed the job was set up by phone, by somebody who knew about his criminal record. The man—a man not a woman—threatened to get him fired unless he cooperated. He said he met a guy on a dark street and was given an envelope with ten thousand bucks in hundreds. He swore he only installed the clips and had no clue what they were for."

"Where is he now?" I asked.

"Still being questioned downtown. And we've got nothing concrete on Bryce. She's never been arrested, nothing shady in her past, grew up in Connecticut, attended all the right schools."

"Terrific. So, how did you guys like your gourmet meal, courtesy of the *Daily Press*?" I asked.

"Two thumbs up," said Phil. "Are you going to eat your chocolate musket?"

74

Izzy and Phil gave me a ride home in the back seat of their unmarked car and we talked about how to go at Bryce. Phone taps were ordered into place, surveillance begun and further background checks arranged, plus routine shoe leather, like talking to her neighbors, family, friends, co-workers.

"Shepherd, I gotta say that was the most ridiculous piece of police work I ever saw," Izzy told me from the front passenger seat. "Also, maybe the best."

"Also delicious, expensive and fattening," Phil added from behind the wheel. "But next time, let us in on the gag from the beginning. It might have been better to build a case slow. Like that food."

I told them I figured if they started grilling her co-workers and neighbors, Bryce would have found out quickly and the element of surprise would have vanished, especially since my story was hitting the website. They didn't dispute that. I suggested we discuss Bryce in the morning and got out at Jane's house.

"Just so we're clear," Phil told me through the open window, "anytime you want to pay to question suspects at that fancy joint, I'm in."

I went inside to say hello to Skippy, who was wild from

being cooped up inside. Jane was still not home. I checked my phone, which was stuffed with messages: Mel wanted to know what new follow-up lead I had for the morning. Jane apologized for an emergency that was keeping her late. Ginny Mac begged me to call her. There were lots of other messages from my colleagues in TV and radio, who saw my latest scoop and wanted to get more out of me. I called Jane first.

"Sorry, Shepherd, I had an emergency surgery," she told me. "I was worried about you. Give me another half hour to make sure the patient comes around in recovery okay, then I can come home. We had pizza here. How was your dinner?"

"Sweet. Izzy and Phil loved it but our guest was shocked by dessert. I'll tell you later. I'm taking Skippy out for a run now. Why were you worried about me?"

"I don't know, I just had a scary feeling before but you're fine. See you soon."

Skippy and I took off, toward my meeting with Tiffany at ten. I called Mel and told him we could go with another exclusive—Tea Party Animal suspects being questioned by cops. I made his night.

"You Fokker, that's what I'm talking about! Yes!"

I called Ginny Mac. Because I'm such a nice guy.

"Thank God you called!" Ginny said. "I gotta see you, tonight!"

"No thanks, Ginny. It was fun, in a masochistic sort of way, but we're done, okay?"

"You don't understand, Shepherd. You have to back off. I'm trying to help you."

"Why would you suddenly start doing that?"

"I can't talk on the phone."

"Tell me now or forget it."

"Damn you, okay. Look, Faith told her son to get you and—"

"Thanks, Ginny, but that's old news. I took care of that. Seeya."

"No, asshole, let me talk. I heard her talking about you. She said she and you were even-up. She was done with you."

"There you go."

"No, there *you* go. Then she said that was okay because she heard somebody else out there was going to punch your ticket."

"Who?"

"I have no clue. You should back off, be careful."

"She's probably talking about the Tea Party Animals but how would she know?"

"I don't know but… you know her family business… and one thing criminals do is sell illegal guns. Maybe she heard something."

"That's it?"

"Yeah."

"Okay, thanks, Ginny."

"You're welcome. Maybe sometime we could just hang out?"

"Sure, I gotta run, okay?"

She was trying to scare me.

Skippy and I ran toward my second dinner date. The bistro had a short white picket fence around its open-air dining area, topped by strings of little white fairy lights. Tiffany was sitting at a round table outside. A red citronella candle warmed her face, a chilled pink cosmo in one hand. She was wearing white shorts, tight lavender tank top and straw-colored sandals. Wow. I waved. She and Skippy hit it off and she petted him while I ordered a beer, an assorted appetizer platter and a burger for Skippy. Tiffany and I worked on the appetizers and fed Skippy.

"Do you always order dog burgers here?"

"They're Skippy's favorite, although he hasn't met a food he doesn't like yet."

We laughed and pretended there was no tension in the warm night air.

"So is your boss ready to confess her part in the murders?" I asked.

"That's bull and you know it," Tiffany said.

"She lied about her smoke detector and she is the only one who mysteriously survived. She's at the top of the menu of suspects."

"Bull. You can pop turds in the oven—that don't make 'em biscuits," Tiffany smiled. "You already know Katharine was just lying to hide her nicotine addiction from her kid—she told you already."

"The girl showed up unexpectedly?"

"Yes, the senator expected her the next morning but the father got rid of her early."

A United States senator lied to police and the FBI and misled a major investigation because she didn't want her teenager to know her mom had lied about smoking?

"That may explain it," I said. "What if the Tea Party Animal knocked on her door, but decided not to blow the senator away in front of her daughter? Also, the mini-muskets are single-shot."

"Nice try," Tiffany said. "But nobody knocked on the door. I asked them both repeatedly."

"Nobody?"

"Right. Only hotel people."

"Exactly," I said. "Was one of them named Bryce, a nice-looking blonde?"

"I have no idea. Shall I ask? That's why I'm here. Full cooperation."

"Okay. Yeah, ask them that right now. Please."

She pulled out her phone. Skippy finished his burger and looked at my plate hungrily.

"Okay," Tiffany told me, still on the phone, "the senator's daughter answered the door to a female hotel staffer. She was pretty and blonde but she doesn't remember the woman's name. She checked the towels or something and left."

"Would she recognize this person if she saw her again?"

"Maybe," was the answer.

I sent Tiffany a photograph of the lovely Bryce Martha Draper and she forwarded it to the senator. The confirmation came quickly.

"That's the woman," Tiffany said.

I texted the new info and the identification of Bryce to Izzy, who, along with the feds, could make the identification official. A piece of the puzzle.

"What's the significance?" Tiffany asked.

"I've been sworn to secrecy. It was the musket that did not go boom in the night," I explained.

"Come again, darlin'?"

"I think the senator is still alive only because her daughter arrived early. I'm not sure if it was a practical issue of not enough bullets or some vestige of humanity. What was the other thing, Tiffany?"

"Oh, my God! What? What other thing? Oh... You know what it is. You felt something, too, didn't you?"

"Yeah but my situation... suddenly being single... turned out to be temporary."

"Well, bless your heart, Shepherd, aren't you the shy gentleman? Go back to your girlfriend. I'm just fine. I just... I was just hoping you felt the way I did, is all."

"I ... I wish I could."

"Well, honey, the world will turn. Come see me in the White House. You never know."

"You are... something."

"You bet your ass I am, sugar."

75

On the way home, Skippy and I had an informal chat about the case as we walked along the west side of Fifth Avenue, the park and its 150-year-old stone wall on our left. As usual, Skippy was a good listener and made supportive noises, which consisted of mewling, yowling and burbling sounds. I asked him why I had kept the unfired zip musket. If I turned the Tea Party Animal's weapon on him or her, would that break my no-gun vow? Skippy just huffed. Of course it would.

"Did I do the right thing, breaking it off with Tiffany?" I asked him.

Skippy responded with a sarcastic chortle. I was asking a male dog if I should be faithful to one female. I told him I would check out Bryce in the morning. How long had she worked at the hotel? How long had she and the New Minutemen been planning the killings? Long enough to make arrangements for the toilet tank hiding places, long enough to set up the video security system hacking, long enough to construct custom firearms designed specifically for the job, long enough to find a hotel with soundproof rooms... Weeks, months of planning...

Maybe the New Minutemen weren't just hired guns or

political extremists, but experienced covert operatives. Like me. It was a new hotel, opened this year. What if billionaires built the hotel, with large toilets, soundproofed suites and a specific security system—just so the murders could take place there?

Skippy scoffed at that.

Ridiculous, absurd. A massive right-wing conspiracy. They would've had to know in advance where the GOP convention would be held. Impossible. Yeah, but what if? Who owned the hotel? I didn't know. Skippy didn't know. It couldn't hurt to check.

Skippy pulled the leash, a low rumble in his throat. He spun around fast. I'd been distracted, in my own little world, ignoring my surroundings. Suddenly, the back of my neck was bristling with dark eyes. I pivoted around.

Oh shit.

Four men in long leather duster coats, hats and beards. Like the ones who had followed me before. Were these the New Minutemen? They moved faster now, two on the sidewalk in front of me and two in the street, flanking me on my left. A classic, L-shaped deployment, so they would not shoot each other. Each was maybe thirty feet away, close enough not to miss but not close enough for me to do anything. They were pros. There was a garbage can and trees near and behind me but nothing big enough to hide behind. The four-foot-high stone wall of the park, ten feet away, blocked escape to my right and there was a sharp drop to the unseen ground on the other side. I knew the sidewalk behind me was open but I wouldn't get three steps.

One by one, they racked their pieces, black tactical bastards with what looked like three barrels. Shotguns. Short 12-gauge Bullpups. They had fifteen rounds each, times four. I didn't need to do the math. It equaled death. I knew I should move fast but I didn't.

"The Aryan Purity Nation, I presume? Or is it the New

Minutemen? Don't I get a smoke and a blindfold?"

"You were warned," one of the shadowed faces in front of me replied. "Embrace the suck."

I remembered the cease-and-desist message on my phone from the New Minutemen. I let go of Skippy's leash. I decided to go over the wall, a hundred-to-one shot but my only chance at cover.

"Run, Skippy!"

He didn't run. I gave the order again but Skippy, usually so obedient, started advancing on them, snarling.

"No, dammit, Skippy! Run!"

The first blast exploded in a horizontal fountain of fire and blinding white sparks fifty feet long. What the fuck? It roared past, singing my right side. Something shattered behind me. I moved involuntarily to the left, away from the wall. All four weapons opened up and I was bathed in thundering sparks. I felt impacts, burning, blinding, yelling at Skippy to run. I couldn't see him but, in between booms, I heard his ferocious roar. I dove toward his voice. The night was on fire. I couldn't hear Skippy anymore. I fell and the world went dark, my vision blurred with after-images of the arcing electric flames. My ears were ringing, things flame-red around me. Garbage can, trees, all burning like torches. Still alive. I saw a pale shape and scrambled toward it. Skippy on the ground—not moving. His fur was wet and smoldering.

NO!

I howled, picked him up in my arms and staggered toward the park. My legs had just enough strength to propel us onto and over the angled chest-high stone wall.

76

The fall knocked the wind out of me but I stumbled around in the dark woods, keeping the wall on my right. I could feel Skippy's heart beating against my chest, fast, but he wouldn't respond to my whispered questions. I could smell blood and burned hair. I put him down, used my shirt to wipe his bloody fur and saw more blood come from his abdomen. I wadded my shirt against the wound and hugged him tight to stop the flow. I pulled out my phone, hit a number, and ran. A walkway led to the right, out of the park. I stopped and peeked around the wall but saw only a few cars. The New Minutemen were not there. I sprinted east. Skippy's heartbeat was slowing down. I ran faster. Why was I still alive? Jane answered the phone. I yelled at her to stay there, that Skippy had been shot and she had to save him.

When I arrived at the animal hospital, Jane and a male assistant were waiting at the door.

In the light, there was so much red blood. I yelled that it was Skippy's blood not mine but she kept looking at me and Skippy and crying.

"Jane, he has a wound in the side. He's losing blood. They were firing shotguns that blasted fire and probably buckshot. You have to operate now."

"Yes, we've got him. Andy called the police."

I carried Skippy to the rear surgery area and placed him on a stainless steel table. I was shaking with rage and fear. There was a mirror on one wall, with a bloody, dirty zombie in it. I looked undead. Sections of my hair and my eyebrows had been burned off. My pants were scorched and blackened. I was smeared with Skippy's blood and dirt. I had maybe a dozen random cuts. From what? Ricochets? Why am I still alive? Skippy and I should be blown apart. They couldn't be such bad shots. I went into an exam room and reached for paper towels to wipe off the blood.

I stopped.

A better idea occurred to me. I called Sparky and told him what had happened.

"I'm not cleaning up until you take pictures. Get your ass over here."

When I returned to the operating room, they were working on Skippy.

"Stay over there," Jane warned, calmly. "You're filthy. Skippy's got a perforated wound through one side and out the other. His signs are dropping. We're warming up a unit of blood for transfusion but not until I can stop his bleeding. Okay, oxygen mask? Good… Starting anesthesia now, Andy?"

"Yes, I'm keeping it light," he said.

I called Izzy and left a message, pacing nervously, as they worked on Skippy. I remembered my paramedic training, ABC. First, clear the Airway, then check Breathing and then Circulation.

I called the paper and got an editor on the overnight City Desk, told her what had happened and that my photographer was on the way. She gave me a rewrite reporter, who took my notes and said they'd have it on the web in half an hour.

Jane hosed Skippy off and then painted him with antiseptic before cutting him open. His belly was full of dark blood. I clenched my fists. This was my fault.

"A lot of blood," Jane said. "Towels, please. Looks like the spleen was hit. Andy set up that unit of blood, please." She reached inside. "The spleen is ruptured, through and through," Jane concluded. "I'm clipping off the blood supply and then I'll take the spleen. Let's hope it missed the intestines. Okay, tied off. I'm running the bowel now… It's okay, no damage. Andy we need more towels and irrigation—lots of dirt and hair in here. Okay, better… I'm removing the spleen. More irrigation, please. Clean that up, okay? Okay, finish up… I'm getting the stapler to close up both sides. Okay one… wow, big hole… okay, there. Two. Okay, paint it again… now gauze… yes… Can you help me with the belly wrap bandage? He's heavy… Great… okay, now the Ace Bandages… one more… great. Heart sounds good." She stroked Skippy's neck. "Let's get the Ringer's and antibiotic IVs going, please."

Skippy was still alive. We should both be dead. Jane washed up and came over.

"Skippy is going to be fine," she told me.

I let out a breath.

"He has to stay here on IVs for three days. He'll be weak but in a few days he'll be walking. In a month, I expect he'll be his old self again."

"Can I touch him?"

"Yes, of course. If you wash your hands."

I washed my hands, apologized to Skippy, even though he was unconscious, and gently stroked his head. His eyes were mostly closed, his mouth agape. His teeth were red. So was his fur.

"Why is there blood on his muzzle?"

"There's no injury there but it's probably his own blood."

What if it wasn't?

"Maybe. Can you preserve a good sample for Izzy?"

"Okay. You think he got a piece of one of those bastards?"

"Yeah. He wouldn't leave me," I said. "I ordered him to run but he attacked."

"Shepherd, this has to stop," Jane said, hugging me. "Please. Can all this ugliness end?"

I didn't know what to say. I wanted to tell her that I would do my best to finish it soon but I knew that was not a good answer. Fortunately, Sparky arrived to take pictures and Izzy arrived and saved me with questions of his own.

77

"They're called 'Dragon Breath' shells, custom ammo, a new one on me," Izzy explained. Izzy, Phil and I were at the scene of the shooting, the rising sun just visible. "They were firing 12-gauge combo-rounds with phosphorous and single .69 caliber balls—just like the ones used in the murders—but these are lead, not silver. Maybe they ran out of money?"

"Or I'm just not worth the expensive kind," I suggested. "They weren't trying to kill me—a blindfolded baby could have blown me away with those cannons."

"They were teaching you a lesson," Izzy agreed. "'Cause you don't listen so good."

"Somebody up there likes me," I told him.

"God?"

"No. Their boss. But why?"

"You're the luckiest fucking guy in New York, Shepherd," Phil said. "Thank every god you can think of, kiss your girlfriend and your dog—and go forth and sin no more."

"This wasn't luck," I told him. "Somebody wants me to *know* it wasn't luck."

There were dozens of shotgun shell casings amid the charred, chipped cobblestones. My cuts came from fragments of granite. The Crime Scene Investigators were bagging and tagging the shells, which would be checked for fingerprints. I knew these guys weren't dumb enough to leave evidence on shell casings.

The fire department had already been there to extinguish three burning trees and one garbage can. There were large holes in several tree trunks and a bus stop sign.

"They shot all around you," Izzy continued. "Amazing you're still in one piece. You should look like Chesterfield, but worse. What was it like, being inside that firestorm?"

It was like being in Sparky's Fourth of July fireworks explosions, but not so pretty.

"The motherfuckers shot Skippy," I said. "Leaving me alive is the last fucking mistake they'll ever make."

"You're beautiful when you're angry," Izzy laughed. "So, you think the pooch bit one of them?"

"You've got the blood sample Jane took from his muzzle—you tell me."

"Still waiting on that," Phil said. "If we get lucky, it might match someone in the DNA database."

"That would be nice," I agreed. "Either way, they go down."

"You do know murder is still against the law, right?"

Sparky came over, having finished shooting stills and video of the scene. He whispered in my ear. I whispered back. We did this for a bit, until Izzy demanded to know what the hell we were talking about.

"Sparky is a good citizen," I told Izzy. "He would like to report that a nearby apartment building has a video surveillance camera that recorded the attack. He thought you might be interested."

Sparky pointed the way and Izzy and Phil went off to check it out. Meanwhile, Sparky showed me the security footage, which he had emailed to himself. From across Fifth Avenue, there was a night-vision image of Skippy and me being followed by the New Minutemen and surrounded. When the pyrotechnics began it was spectacular: the white-hot light from the muzzle flashes temporarily wiped out the resolution of the video. My stomach and my fists clenched. There was no sound but you could see my mouth moving, ordering Skippy to run, and then Skippy flying at one of the shooters, going for his throat. The guy went down but his partner swung his bullpup toward Skippy—who was swallowed up in an avalanche of silver fire.

"Motherfuckers," I spat.

I saw myself dive into the sea of sparks and then the video went darker for a bit, as the bastards flipped their selector switches to access the other half of their ammo. At that point, they had to have fired more than thirty shots. I watched myself scoop up Skippy and wobble like a drunk to the wall and go over. The guy on the right front, the one who had spoken to me, had his hand up and his crew didn't fire at my back, an easy target. They let me live.

Sparky sent me a copy of the footage. Izzy and Phil returned with the impounded security equipment as we were watching the playback again.

"That's going to go viral," Sparky predicted. "It's awesome."

"But you can't see faces," Izzy pointed out. "I can't even recognize you—too far away. Unless they were morons and left their prints on the ejected shells, we're back to the mystery blood from the pooch."

I checked my phone and saw our new front-page story— TEA PARTY ANIMALS ATTACK PRESS REPORTER— with details of the shooting. There was a photo of me, looking like I was nuked, and a sleeping Skippy, all bandaged up. His photo was much bigger than mine, of course, since tabloid readers care more about pets than people.

As we watched, Izzy made a call, talked, listened, cursed and hung up.

"No joy on the mystery blood," Phil announced. "Contaminated. Lab says they detected components of human DNA, animal DNA, insect DNA and avian DNA.

Nothing clean enough for a database hit. Game over."

"Avian DNA?" I asked.

"Pigeons, probably," Izzy said.

"Don't let on that the DNA from Skippy is no good," I said.

"You want the bad guys to sweat?" Izzy asked. "So they make a mistake, do something crazy?"

"Right," I agreed. "I'm going to do a story about the DNA and the footage and say you know who they are and you're about to bust them."

"Don't use my name on that bullshit."

"He wants them to try again," Phil told Izzy.

"What? He's not that crazy. You're not that crazy, are you, Shepherd?"

"You bet your ass he is."

78

I went back to check on Skippy, who was still asleep but doing fine. Jane told me she was taking me home and we would be back later. At Jane's, I showered and we grabbed breakfast. Jane crashed on her bed but I had work to do and guzzled some coffee. My head was fuzzy. I needed sleep but I kept trying to think about what I was mulling over before the New Minutemen rattled my brains. The Revolutionary War flag used as wadding for the musket balls, maybe? I had no luck trying to trace whoever bought that at auction. A massive right-wing conspiracy? Yeah, that was it. The totally paranoid, insane-ass thought that the Tea Party Animal killings were planned not days or weeks ahead but months or years in advance. Ridiculous.

But why not? Billionaires and businessmen planned projects involving many people and events years ahead of time. Why wouldn't they evince the same, careful advance approach with the perfect murder? Or, rather, the perfect mass murders. Cops looking for one or a few bad guys would miss the big picture, the corporate sweep of many non-criminal individual and multiple routine actions—divided up into discrete tasks. The handyman, who had a convenient secret criminal record that opened him to blackmail, installed the clips to hold the custom reinvented firearms—which were conceived and manufactured by someone else. Another person to hack the computer surveillance system, Bryce, and maybe as many as five others to use the weapons and hide them in the toilets. Possibly others to collect the evidence later and destroy it? But they had to wait because the suites were still guarded crime scenes. There had to be at least one additional person to operate the drone and maybe obtain explosives. And, of course, my friends the New Minutemen—the enforcers—blew them away. The Tea Party Animals weren't a guy or a small group—they were a whole company. The Supreme Court, as Walter Cantor said, has ruled that corporations are people. In this case, an efficient covert team unaware of the existence of the others outside their roles—their strings being pulled by... who? This was beginning to sound very familiar. The Minuteman who spoke to me. Probably from observation, he knew I didn't smoke. He said, "Embrace the suck," a very common phrase among my colleagues in my former line of work. Definitely ex-military. Nice to see American business giving my fellow vets jobs.

I used Jane's computer to do another search on old flags but I still couldn't track down any anonymous buyers at auctions. A plan was forming in my head and I used Google Earth to check out sites on the Hudson River that looked promising.

I hadn't had a chance to check on my favorite concierge, so I googled Bryce Martha Draper. Not too much. One hit had a reference to someone of that name as a master's degree candidate in political science at New York University. No photo. A debate at some fancy prep school six years earlier had a photo of a group with someone who might have been Bryce. Too small to tell. Further down there was a link to the D.A.R.'s website, the historically right-wing Daughters of the American Revolution. I clicked and there was Bryce, a red, white and blue blonde in the junior auxiliary. She had an ancestor who fought in the War of Independence, somebody named Draper who helped finance the rebels. Very interesting. I printed the page. I thought a moment and went to the Knickerbocker Convention Center website and checked their Staff pages. I found Bryce under Concierge Staff, along with a familiar face—the other staffer who was with her in Chesterfield's room on the night of the murders. His name was Jonathan Cooper Morris, from New Jersey. I clicked back to the D.A.R. page and used their search engine to plug in Jonathan's name. Bingo. He was also in the student auxiliary, with a rebel ancestor. I printed the page. It took me half an hour to locate four other staffers at the hotel from the northeast who were in the D.A.R. and had notable revolutionary predecessors. They all worked at the same hotel. This wasn't a coincidence—this was a star-spangled firing squad.

"Smile now, motherfuckers!"

I called Izzy and told him.

"Motherfuckers!"

"That's exactly what I said."

"You crazy asshole, you just split this shit wide open."

"Maybe. These are blue-blooded suspects but I don't think they're the mastermind, or the banker, do you?"

"Ask me in forty-eight hours," Izzy told me. "Look, don't print their names or any of this D.A.R. shit until we get them, okay? Otherwise, they'll be farts in the wind. Thanks, Shepherd. Hey, man, now your bullshit story about us being ready to bust the bad guys is actually true."

I asked him for a quote, as a source. He gave it to me and hung up so he could go back to work. I was too jazzed to sleep. I banged out a new story on Jane's computer, proofed it and then called Mel at the paper to tell him my new piece. I dialed but he wasn't in. It was only nine in the morning, too early for Mel. I called his cell and he answered after multiple rings, obviously asleep. I told him I was excited because I had come up with five new suspects. Mel mumbled that was great. I told him about the D.A.R. connection but that we couldn't use it yet, or their names.

"We already flagging printed that cops were questioning some bunting suspects," Mel grumbled. "How does this advance the cheese-picking story?"

"Well, it's more of them, a bigger conspiracy," I stammered.

"Ball-mitt," Mel snapped. "Don't joke me off! The only new things are the nit-knocking names and the goose-bagging D.A.R. thing."

I hated him because he was right. I had a good story but I couldn't write it yet. Another idea I had was openly libelous—hinting that the mastermind lived at 740 Park Avenue and collected antique muskets.

"You made another feckless deal to do yourself out of a good groping story, Shepherd. Anything else?"

I frantically searched for a way to get the story I needed in tomorrow's paper. There had to be a way.

"Umm… No… I'm just going to file my pet column for tomorrow."

"The one on clipping crapping toward Mecca? Okay, so what? File it—but don't chomping wake me up until you have a hard story that really shucks my cob."

79

I rewrote my story as a column after I got off with Mel and filed it by email. Then I did another version of the story with the hotel employees and the D.A.R. in it, holding it for later. I got a call from someone named Naomi in features to confirm the column was slotted for the morning paper, which actually came out at the stroke of midnight.

"I know my column will be in the printed paper in the morning, Naomi, but what's the earliest you can throw it up on the website?" I asked.

"Hard news has to wait until the Witching Hour but a feature like your pet column can run any time after nine tonight," Naomi informed me.

"Run that puppy at nine, please," I told her. "May I suggest a headline?"

"Sure, go ahead."

"Park Avenue Guttersnipe," I told her.

"Okay, you got it."

It was time to call Amy and ask for her help. She agreed. I put on a pair of black bathing suit shorts, a black Lycra water shirt and a pair of black Teva water sandals. Just another guy ready for a warm July night in the city. My gun gloves and a wad of cash went into one zipper-shut shorts pocket and my keys and iPhone fit into the other. I caught a quick glimpse of the spider webs of scars on my legs in the mirror.

I snuggled up to the sleeping Jane on her bed, kissed her gently and told her it was time for me to go out and we'd meet at her office later. She groaned that I had to get some sleep.

"I'll nap at your office. I want to be there when Skippy wakes up."

Amy texted me that she was ready. I needed someone good to watch my back, keeping an eye out for a drone or anyone following me—especially the New Minutemen. I dialed her cell.

"Hi, Amy. So you'll call to warn me if I pick up a tail?"

"No. Too slow. You'll be toast. I brought a little air horn, loud as a motherfucker."

"One if by land and two if by sea?"

"No, schmuck. One, if the bearded bastards are on your ass. Two, if their air force is flying. Got it?"

"Got it. Either way, blow your horn and split. If I make it to the waypoint, stop in and I'll slip you my phone and my keys. You know what to do."

"Let the cops handle this, Shepherd."

"You know if I do that we'll end up with dead cops. These bad guys are topline pros."

"Okay, hot shot. See you at the coffee shop."

I walked out the door and left my backpack—containing my mini-musket souvenir—on top of the dresser, where it would not be disturbed until I returned. On the way to see Skippy, I stopped off to buy a cheap burner cellphone. I couldn't spot Amy on the street but I knew she was there somewhere.

Already awake in his large wire cage, Skippy was very excited to see me. Andy said he couldn't bounce around too much, so we opened the door and I sat in the open cage. I gently petted Skippy and he nuzzled me. After a while, Andy brought a blanket and a cushion for me. Skippy fell asleep first and then I did.

* * *

Jane woke me up to let me know it was twenty past nine at night. I'd slept nearly twelve hours. I texted Amy I was leaving the animal hospital. She texted: READY.

"I have to go meet Izzy," I told Jane. "He might be making arrests tonight."

"You shouldn't go unless it's safe."

"It's perfectly safe."

I slinked off like a liar. Okay, I am a liar. Outside, scanning around, there were people on the street but none that looked like Amy. As I walked, I used my iPhone to call Izzy.

"Hey, Shepherd. We got all but one of your D.A.R. shooters. I think the last one is on his way to Venezuela or some damn place. Nobody's talking. If you want to go with the D.A.R. connection in the paper, be my guest. Thanks again."

I emailed the full arrest story that I had been holding in reserve to Mel at the desk. He called right away.

"You cap-sacking beauty! I love you, you son-of-a-biscuit!" Mel gushed. "I fopping love the 'Star-Spangled Firing Squad' Schlitz! A roundup of rich trust-fund Fokkers, including a hot wench. Great freaking yarn, Shepherd. All downhill from here. Too bad this mugger-thumping story can't last forever, right, Shepherd?"

"Mugger-thumping right, Mel."

I hung up before he could take the fun out of any more obscenities.

For my purposes, I needed a real blitz and called some colleagues, TV and radio reporters—to alert them, so they would pick up my story fast. I wanted everybody to know. The last call was to Ginny Mac at the *Mail*, who still worked for La Madrina.

"I told you, you dumb, stubborn bastard!" Ginny Mac greeted me. "Almost got your ass shot off, didn't you?"

"They weren't trying to kill me," I explained. "Seen the *Daily Press* website lately?"

I heard keyboard keys clacking.

"You guys still have all this stuff about the attack on you. Nice video. So what? Nothing new. That was up before lunch today."

"Today the good stuff is inside. In my column."

"You still write that pet thing? Okay…"

I waited.

"Holy shit!" Ginny observed. "Wow. Park Avenue Guttersnipe. Are you totally insane? They'll sue your ass off."

"Better than having it *shot* off."

"What is all this other stuff? Oh, I get it, you're doing a column pretending to be a dog. This is Skippy, a dog detective, working on a murder case with a German Shepherd? Ha! That's you. I see. Funny… oh crap—you give the actual address on Park Avenue of the Tea Party Twins? You're totally nuts—they'll sue you. At least one billionaire German Schnauzer is the prime suspect in the murders of five Tea Party Terriers? You mean the Roehm brothers, right? The four bearded Dobermans are the guys who attacked you, okay… got it… What is this stuff about pedigrees and ancestry and six patriotic killer dogs working at a pet hotel?"

"Read it on our website, Ginny. We're moving the real deal to the front of the paper. I just wanted to give you a heads up, so you don't look so bad."

"Don't do me any favors, asshole. I'm going to kick your butt."

"As if… Ginny, I have to get off. I gotta get over to the Knickerbocker right now."

I hung up before she could ask me why. Now for the other part. The Internet café, Webfoot, was on the West Side, across from the convention center's entrance. I paid for a doughnut and coffee and found a stool at a counter where I could watch the street with my back to a wall. Using one of the communal laptops, it was a snap to post dire warnings of violence and commit several felonies, including terroristic threats. All in a day's work.

I waited, watching the street, hoping no explosive drone would fly in through the window and strike me dead.

Thinking back, I realized I had forgotten about tracing the hotel's ownership. My pal Siri told me the convention center was owned by an international consortium of corporations and registered in Dubai. She supplied the names of the corporations from Gibraltar and Costa Rica, and newspaper stories and websites in multiple languages, including Russian and Arabic. Wonderful. A tangled web of godlike wealth but not one actual individual name. I asked Siri for names, people, in the firms. There were hundreds of them but it was just uncovering lower layers of shell companies, without a clear owner.

"Siri, I need the names of the people behind this."

"Behind the convention center, Shepherd?" she asked.

"Yes, Siri."

"The convention center has four entrances and exits, Shepherd. Which one would be behind?"

Siri was very literal tonight. I tried again.

"Siri, is there one man or two men who provided some or all of the money, a controlling interest in the convention center?"

Without comment, she displayed more than a million hits about a very familiar name—not one of the Roehm brothers. This guy seemed to have nothing to do with the Knickerbocker but at least we were getting closer. Actually very close, I realized, looking at an interior decorating magazine story about his Park Avenue penthouse. I wondered if I was at the point where the search engine couldn't locate what I wanted and moved down to a lesser detail and displayed items on that. For some reason, Siri seemed to think this was the guy who secretly owned the hotel. Maybe somewhere in those million plus stories, websites and links was the proof, but several other tries at refining the search also failed to come up with the goods—no actual linkage between the name and the convention center.

Weird.

Or not.

Maybe this *was* the answer? Somewhere I remembered another conversation from last night and wondered if there was a connection to events later that evening. It was possible. In fact, it would explain how they knew where I would be. It made no sense but Siri thought it did. The more I thought about it, the more I had the feeling she was right. Why not? If true, even one of my mistakes in my column wasn't actually a mistake. In fact, it might be helping things on their way. In some mysterious web way, Siri had figured it all out. I idly clicked again on the decorating article—and there was a lovely color shot of the kindly gentleman smiling—in front of a large green painting on his wall. No, it wasn't a goddamn canvas. It was a huge fucking flag.

"Siri, I love you," I told her.

"You are the wind beneath my wings, Shepherd."

"Siri, did I ever tell you you're my hero?"

"Who, *me*?"

"Yes, you, Siri."

"And *you*, Shepherd."

"Siri, you're great."

"I'm good but not *great*, Shepherd."

"No, you're *great*."

"You're certainly entitled to that opinion, Shepherd."

"Siri, you're my closest friend."

"I really don't like these arbitrary categories," she scolded.

"Want to be my girlfriend?"

"This is about *you*, Shepherd, not me," she pointed out.

"But you're my friend?"

"Okay, Shepherd, I'll be your friend in fair weather and foul."

"A friend."

"Yes, Shepherd, a person you regard with affection and trust."

"But, Siri, you're not a person."

"I'm not? Huh."

"Siri, you're smart and funny."

"Flatterer."

80

I wondered if I needed to go through with this. But we still couldn't prove who was behind all of it or even who the New Minutemen were. No evidence—at least none a human could see. If I turned it over to the cops, I was sure there'd be casualties. Or nothing would happen. Izzy and Phil were great but they and all other cops were hampered by laws and regulations. The New Minutemen weren't. They were gunned up and ready to rock and weren't going down without a firefight. I was tempted to split but, now that I had forced their hand, it was too late to retreat.

A shapely young lady with an afro, in tight mocha yoga pants, bright red high-top sneakers, and a tight pink Mexican wedding blouse, bopped into the shop and went to the counter. She got a latte and sat near me, looking away.

"Hi, Amy. Hot outfit. You bring new meaning to the term plainclothes."

"You were clean all the way here," she said, ignoring my comment. "No tail, no drone. At least, nothing I could spot."

"Sounds like we did all of this for nothing."

"Nope. I came in because a black van just arrived and circled around the block. Several men inside. I didn't get close enough yet to confirm it's your trigger-happy friends.

That's why I didn't use my air horn. Check it out."

The traffic was thin. A black van with tinted windows rolled by. It cruised by two more times. It was all no-parking zones here, so I knew they weren't circling looking for a spot. It looked like it might be the New Minutemen's ride, but was it? I had certainly left enough of a trail. Moment of truth—call Izzy or go through with it? It didn't matter. I used my burner phone to arrange an Uber car to pick me up. Leaving my iPhone and keys on the table, I stood up.

"Okay, Amy, thanks. When I leave, take my phone and keys and let yourself into Jane's place. Call yourself on my phone and stay on until I get back, okay?"

"I got it. Why? What are you going to be doing?"

"Nothing."

"Shepherd, wait. I've got two nine millimeters on me. Let's take the bastards now."

"I will—but my way, okay? There are too many people on the street and we can't beat their firepower. Besides, I don't pull triggers anymore, remember?"

"You can't go up against them without any weapon."

"I still have my brain. Wait," I said, eyeing her outfit. "Where the hell do you have two handguns?"

"You actually think my boobs are this big?"

My throwaway cellphone buzzed with a text from a guy named Oscar, who said he was picking me up in a red Volkswagen Jetta. One pulled to the curb outside the coffee shop. I waited for the New Minutemen's vehicle to drive past one more time and disappear around the corner.

Moving quickly out the coffee shop and onto the pavement, Amy not far behind, I opened the car's back door, leaned in and began to chat with the driver, Oscar; a thin bald guy with a Latino accent in a Hawaiian shirt. When I saw the dark van appear at the other end of the block again, I let them spot me and ducked into the car, sliding low in the back seat. As Oscar pulled away I distinctly heard one loud blast on an air horn. One, if by land. Amy was confirming my four hairy hunters were on me.

Then I clearly heard two more air horn blasts behind me, like a cold hand on my back. Two, if by air. Their fucking drone was also on my ass. It would have night vision—a real bummer for a plan that depended on darkness. The only question was did it have another brick of Semtex? I had to assume it did. I was boned.

Oscar was babbling about something up front, as he drove me just four blocks to a pier on the Hudson. I made one last call on my burner phone, using the anonymous voice-disguising app.

"Hello, police emergency? I would like to report four heavily armed men with beards at Pier 95 in Manhattan, at Forty-Seventh Street. Get some cops here. They're pointing some kind of black tubes out over the river at a big boat. Yes, hello? I'm losing you."

I removed the battery from the disposable phone and tossed it out the back window.

"Hey! What was that? Why you throw your phone away?" Oscar demanded. "Who you talking to?"

He began to slow down. I ignored his questions and told him not to stop at the brightly lit entertainment pier on our right. Behind the pier, moored in the dark river, a string of white lights atop the USS *John S. McCain* were visible, strung from stem to stern.

"The next one, please. Yes, the deserted pier."

"Why you want a deserted pier?" he asked suspiciously.

"Meeting some friends. Thanks, man."

I jumped out and dashed for the safety of the rusty old green metal structure.

"Hey, don't do it!" the driver yelled after me.

Don't do what? It was mostly open inside the pier, a lattice of ancient steel beams above a crumbling concrete surface. I had to move slowly around vertical I-beams, trying not to stumble over chunks of loose cement.

A screech of tires behind me, slamming doors.

The black van.

I couldn't hear it but also behind me would be the all-seeing eye mounted on the explosive drone. Moving faster through the rubble toward the far right corner of the pier, I gambled I wouldn't trip and fall. If I did, that would be it. I had to draw fire but, with the drone, they would find me and kill me much quicker than I had planned. I was almost there when flashlight beams began sweeping the dark behind me. Maglites attached to their shotguns. No more warnings. This time they were going to blow me away, one way or the other.

I moved faster. Barely visible, as I got closer to the edge, random holes appeared in the floor, a twenty-foot drop to the water below. It might have been helpful to check the tide tables. At the edge, I ducked behind a pillar and looked at the destroyer, its nose pointing to the right, north, upriver. There was a lot of activity on deck, people moving around. I heard a voice on a loudspeaker. Feeling around on the floor, I found a rusty bolt and a fist-sized chunk of stone. I lobbed the bolt to the other side of the platform, where it loudly connected with a steel beam.

They opened up, firing at the sound—four fifty-foot blasts of fireworks through the space and out over the water—right toward the giant warship. They stopped shooting and racked their slides, ready, moving closer for the kill.

Any second now, the drone would find me. Being de-res'd by plastic explosive wasn't a bad way to go. The blast bubble travelled at more than twenty-six thousand feet per second. Instantaneous. One second you were here and the next second you weren't.

Out over the river, I heard a loud klaxon.

Time to go. I tossed my concrete chunk and the assholes fired again, very close this time, illuminating everything like monster flashbulbs, the musket balls ricocheting around like an open-air pinball machine.

Fuck it. It was either watch what was about to happen or stay alive. I couldn't do both. Turning, I broad-jumped as far as possible out into the open air. I caught more flashing sparks and one lone male voice, drowned out—desperately yelling an unheeded warning.

I hit the water, shockingly cold for summer, and let myself sink deep into the cold, quiet darkness. Above me, the water lit up like someone had flicked a light switch but the brightness was mostly streaming from the other direction. The water around me throbbed with the tremendous blasting bellow of a giant beast, spitting a huge stream of dotted red fire over my head, into the pier above me. The steel girders rattled as thousands of twenty-millimeter depleted uranium slugs from the USS *John S. McCain*'s Phalanx guns ripped the pier apart. I tried swimming away underwater but I ran out of time. Mammoth chunks of metal and concrete pounded into the frothing water all around, a seaquake trying to crush me. I surfaced into a racket of shrieking metal and distant yelling. Again, I could watch—or live.

I swam for my life.

Later, I clawed my way up a rotting wooden bulkhead and collapsed in a dark parking lot. A stiff cool breeze off the river chilled me. I could hear sirens and helicopters to the south, lights on the river. I looked around. I was alone. Mission accomplished.

I hoped the drone went down. It was unlikely the Semtex was set off by the shooting but I hoped the bird was hit by rounds or crushed in the collapse. Objectively, it was a very dangerous thing to do, but damn, I was tingling with adrenaline from my toes to my fingertips, pulsing with life and death-cheating power. I howled up at the moon, even though there wasn't one.

I felt blue and cold as Papa Smurf. I stripped off my

shirt and wrung the water out of it before putting it back on. I took out my wad of cash. I squeezed the money and salty brine dripped out. A lot of water also came out of my bathing suit shorts and, finally, my gun gloves. I got re-dressed, smoothed my hair back, replaced the cash and gloves in my pockets and sat down to catch my breath. It felt good to be alive.

The New Minutemen would ride no longer. I didn't take any orders and I didn't fire a gun. Of course, I helped them provoke the dragon, or, at least, a Phalanx. The assholes who hurt Skippy were dead—because they brought shotguns to a Gatling gun fight.

81

Amy was surprised to see me alive, although a bit damp, but asked no questions. She handed me my keys and my iPhone, which was still connected to her cellphone, with unlimited voicemail.

I ended the call and told Amy I would see her in the morning. She left for home, to complete the loop of the lie and then reschedule her fake dope deal. It was a shame Jane would not see her in her get-up. I should have demanded a quick-draw demonstration from her bra holsters. Instead, I fed Skippy, took a shower and changed into dry clothes, including long pants. When I got out, Jane was home. She was tired but not surprised to see me. She asked questions and I lied shamelessly. We heated up some leftovers. I ate like a condemned man and had a few araks. Jane had some wine and I offered a toast.

"To the U.S. Navy—a global force for good. Cheers!"

We clinked glasses and drank. I turned on the TV. CNN was in a red-letter breaking-news frenzy over "TERROR ATTACK IN MANHATTAN?"

Ahh, the almighty question mark. Apparently a group of bearded men, possibly Islamist terrorists, had tried to sink a battleship in the Hudson River, possibly with rockets, sparking a wild firefight. Hmm. Jane and I watched with interest, as they aired videos of tongues of flame from the ship, tracer rounds zipping across the water and demolishing the pier. Cool.

I hoped it was too dark and all the video cameras were too distant to detect a lone guy jumping into the drink.

I dialed Izzy's cellphone.

"What?" a harried Izzy answered, a lot of noise in the background.

"I'm watching CNN. What's with this attack on the river?"

"That's what we're trying to nail down," Izzy replied. "First there were internet threats—from your Tea Party pals the New Minutemen—vowing to destroy the symbol of Zionist-American aggression, the USS *John S. McCain*."

"No shit? That's crazy. Wow, I'd better get on this."

"There was a lot of chatter over the last few hours. Our terror alerts, NYPD and the military's, got ramped up. Also, we got a 911 call that four bearded men were pointing tubes at the destroyer from Pier 95 on the Hudson. Before we could respond, the ship detected and fired on what they say were multiple sources of heavy hostile fire from shore—directed at the vessel."

"Incredible. So, is it the New Minutemen, my New Minutemen?"

"Looks that way," Izzy said. "Whoever was stupid enough to attack a destroyer was shredded into thousands of pieces. The ME is trying to separate small body parts, weapon fragments, hair, blood, bone and leather but no IDs yet. This is going to be done slowly and carefully with DNA and a spoon."

"Wow. Well, it couldn't happen to nicer guys. Thanks, Izzy."

"No problem."

I called the paper and filed what I had just learned, plus

a bit more from my own experience. Mel wasn't there but the editor on the desk was very happy. I suggested a headline. It was out within the hour, added as a new top to my earlier story:

TIME RUNS OUT FOR NEW MINUTEMEN

82

Izzy and Phil were at our door bright and early and refused Jane's offer of coffee. We sat in the kitchen.

"Where were you last night?" Izzy demanded.

"When I spoke to you? Right here."

"No, earlier."

I gave them the sanitized version, saying I came home to Jane's after I left the animal hospital—leaving out little details, such as the coffee shop, the car service, the pier and the calling down of hellfire onto evildoers.

"Funny thing," Phil said, looking at his notebook. "Somebody anonymously posted online threats against the ship on behalf of the New Minutemen."

"Yeah, Izzy told me."

"It seemed valid—they had the authentication code."

"Okay, Izzy didn't mention that. So the New Minutemen made the threat, tried to carry it out and got wasted. Sounds like a happy ending to me."

"Yeah," Izzy agreed, "but here's the thing. Late last night, the 911 operator got a call from some guy who claims he picked up a man in shorts and sandals and took him to the same pier just before this shitstorm blew in. He says the young man acted weird, called the cops, threw away his

405

phone and ran—and that four guys with long beards and coats and hats showed up in a black van and ran after him."

"Sounds like my guys, alright. What happened to the other guy?"

They were silent.

"We don't know," Izzy admitted. "The caller didn't want to get involved. He said he left but called after he heard about the attack."

"Too bad. Maybe he'll call back? Who does the van's plate go back to?"

"The van was gone and the man who called said he didn't get a license plate. There may have been another guy in the van, a wheelman—who took off when the shit hit the fan."

"But what about the guy the New Minutemen were meeting? The guy in shorts and sandals? Was he killed with them?"

"Who said that man was meeting them?" Phil asked. "The anonymous caller said he thought his passenger was going to jump in the river but when he saw the other guys run in, he thought maybe they were chasing him. He didn't want any part of it. He may be shy because he's an illegal."

"So I should look for this car driver and maybe for the guy in shorts and sandals?"

"How do you walk with those nuts?" Phil asked. "Don't they pinch?"

"What?" I asked, in mock shock.

Phil asked me if anybody could verify that I was at home from about nine thirty until ten thirty. I told them Jane found me at home about eleven and I spoke to Izzy around then but they said that was too late and asked what I was doing when I was home alone.

"Nothing," I told them. "I spent most of the time on the phone, talking about the case with my boss, Amy."

"That's good," Phil said. "Very good."

"If anybody asks Amy, she'll back you up? If some agency

happens to look up the phone records and cell tower hits, will they show that?" Izzy asked.

"Absolutely. Why? Are you going to check?"

"Not us," Izzy said. "But it's comforting to know you've got a solid alibi."

"And comforting to know we won't go down with you," Phil smirked.

"For what?" I asked. "You think *I* blew away the New Minutemen?"

"Not directly, a harmless pacifist like you," Phil sneered. "But it is a serious crime to make terroristic threats. Also, I don't like destroyers spraying cannon fire around my city. It's a damn good thing innocent people didn't get hurt."

"Shepherd would never do that," Jane scolded them.

"I agree," I said. "It's a good thing innocent people didn't get hurt. And it's also not a bad thing that guilty people got hurt."

They didn't argue.

"I hope it's all over," said Jane. "I worry about Shepherd."

"Jane, trust me, don't ever worry about Shepherd," Izzy told her, with a smile. "*El Diablo se ocupa de su propia.*"

Jane laughed. "The Devil looks after his own."

I hoped to hell it was true.

"He's right, Jane," Phil added. "The Force is strong with this one."

"Okay, maybe I'll keep him," Jane giggled.

I suggested we all go out to dinner to celebrate.

"Later," said Izzy. "In a day or so. We still have a lot of work to do. I'll be thirsty when we're done."

I was worried that we still didn't have any evidence against the management of the New Minutemen corporation, so I asked if any of the hotel shooters they had arrested, along with Bryce, were saying anything—like who the possible criminal mastermind was?

"Zilch," Izzy said. "They denied everything and clammed

up. I'm not even sure they know enough to tell us much more. There may not be some Mr. Big," Izzy chuckled. "Most of them come from serious old WASP money but we can't find any links to your Aryan Purity Nation, your four attackers. So, we have four dead enforcers, six hotel shooters in the jug—except for a possible van driver in the breeze, that may be the whole gang. Close enough for government work."

After Izzy and Phil left, Jane asked me what that was all about.

"Guys I didn't like got killed, so that was professional routine," I explained.

"But those killers shot at the ship and the navy fired back," she said. "It's silly to think you had something to do with it."

"Exactly. They're just touching the bases."

"Okay. Are we finally done with this nightmare?"

"Looks that way."

She looked at me and sighed.

"Shepherd, I hate it when you lie to me—especially when you think it's for my own good. I'm going to ask you that question again. This is very important to me, to us. If you tell me the truth this time, I promise I won't be angry. But, if I ever find out you lied to me again, we're through—do you understand?"

Damn. For the past ten years, I had done little else except detect and eliminate threats and then keep my mouth shut about it. I took a deep breath and told her the truth, the whole truth and nothing but the truth. She listened and waited until I was done.

"I knew it!"

She began cursing and slapping me on the chest. I backed off.

"You promised you wouldn't be angry at me!"

"I lied! Of course I'm angry—who wouldn't be? Are you crazy? You go off on some insane secret mission for no reason and…"

"There was a reason."

"What possible reason would make you act as a live target for psychos with shotguns?"

I told her my reasons.

"Oh, so by sneaking out on this suicidal operation you're protecting me and Skippy and America and all the ships at sea?"

"Yes. It was a matter of time before they or someone else decided I was a problem and one way to get at me was through you or Skippy."

"You are no longer in the army."

"I know but I am a reporter and, now, I guess I'm a private detective. I'm pretty good at it but sometimes it comes with some risk."

"Only the way you do it. I think you're doing all this *because* you're not in the army anymore. You miss the rush, the charge, the danger."

I didn't disagree.

"Are you going to stop doing things like this and live a normal life?"

"I'm pretty sure I don't know what a normal life is."

"I'll teach you. If I ask, will you stop this risk-taking, Shepherd?"

"If I ask, Jane, will you stop being an animal doctor?"

"That's not the same. That's my chosen profession."

"Exactly."

"Oh, my God. It's not over, is it?"

"No. I don't think so."

"And you think we still might be in danger?"

"Yeah, maybe. Nothing is settled, but I'm trying to find whoever was behind the killings. I don't yet know what I might have to do." I hugged her. She hugged back.

"Shepherd, I don't like not knowing what's going to happen."

"I know. Me too. That's just life, isn't it?"

We were still together but up in the air.

83

My suit had been destroyed in the shotgun attack on me and Skippy so I put on my best chinos and walked out into a beautiful, blisteringly hot day. My parents were back on the picket line at 740 Park Avenue but now they had a lot of company—hundreds of demonstrators shouting against the Roehm brothers. Dozens of cops held them back behind barricades. Signs proclaimed them TRAITORS. One used the phrase from my column: GUTTERSNIPES OF PARK AVENUE. The attack on the naval vessel was worse than just bumping off a group of GOP politicos, apparently. Radical tea baggers were now considered to be evil and un-American. Everybody was mad at the right-wingers, even a lot of Republicans. Bizarrely, I got a hero's welcome from my parents and the others. They cheered my name out loud. Very odd. Even stranger, my mother hugged me and kissed me on the cheek, an event I had not experienced since my sixth birthday. My dad grabbed my hand and told me what a great job I was doing. Now I was in Alice in Wonderland territory.

"Just in time," Amy told me, pointing to the front door of the billionaires' building. Several pumped security guards in uniform appeared in a phalanx around two lanky gray men in suits, escorting the twins to a waiting black limousine at the curb. The mob went wild, surging against the barriers, roaring hatred. One brother sneered and said something snarky that was drowned out. His silent twin looked scared. I shouted questions but they vanished into the vehicle, which sped away, leaving two PR people handing out pieces of paper. It was a press release, denying any involvement in the deaths of Speaker Chesterfield and the others. It also detailed their open scorn for "libelous falsehoods published in the *Daily Press*," which implied the siblings had some kind of connection to illegal events. The release said they were considering legal action. I assumed that would be against my "Park Avenue Guttersnipe" column.

I had to get into the building. I went to the doorman and tried to get my toe in the door and asked to see the other tenant I knew, Walter Cantor. The doorman used his phone and told me Mr. Cantor was unavailable.

Amy pulled me aside to give me a surveillance report. She said it was virtually impossible to get into the vertical fortress of 740 Park Avenue, especially now—security had been increased, especially around the Roehm brothers.

"In a month or so, I can try my Fedex woman uniform or my city building inspector disguise. My dog-walker lady won't work because none of these guys have dogs," Amy told me. "So, I'm temporarily out of tricks—unless you have a Plan B?"

I did. I told her. She laughed. I started to explain but she stopped me.

"Pass. I'm not up for this one. I will assume what you just said was a joke. I'm going to tell the GOP that we are done with the case. Shepherd, you have to learn when to back off."

"Not something I want to learn, Amy. Do I still work for you?"

"Sure. But take a few days off. Chill out. Develop a relaxing hobby."

"Good advice. Thanks, Amy."

After she left, I had fun with my parents while it lasted—chanting slogans and singing songs. In between songs, I called Sparky and arranged to meet him later. The next song was my favorite—"We Shall Overcome." But what do you sing when, fifty years later, you have to overcome the same injustices all over again? For some reason, I remembered Sparky's joke about the silver bullets and werewolves—monsters who could only be killed with pure weaponry. The New Minutemen were certainly hairy but the whole scheme seemed more like the Lone Ranger—killing bad guys with silver bullets. The Lone Ranger was also a good guy who hid behind a mask—because the bad guys controlled the law and the government. Who was that masked man? I wanted to thank him. My mom interrupted my wandering thoughts to inform me they were flying back to Kansas in the morning. I could have my apartment back. Just in time for Jane to kick me out again?

"Have a nice flight," I told them.

That night, after dinner, I changed into long black pants and shirt and put on my backpack. Jane asked where I was going. I told her I was meeting Sparky and would try to interview somebody on the case.

"Who?"

"It's important that you don't know. Please trust me on this, Jane."

"Okay, Shepherd, I trust you. Will you be in danger?"

"I don't think so but there is a certain element of risk involved," I admitted. "Of course, I may not be able to get the interview, in which case I will be home sooner."

"And if you get the interview?"

"That would take a bit longer, not sure how long. Of course, this person may not talk to me at all. Succeed or fail, I hope to be back in an hour or two."

It was always much easier to get forgiveness than it was to receive advance permission.

"You hope?" Jane said. "Does he have a shotgun?"

"I didn't say this person was a 'he.' The person might have a shotgun but I assess the likelihood of the individual using it on me to be very small."

"Why can't you tell me where you're going?"

"Because it's possible I might do things that could be seen as not exactly legal. I don't want to harm you."

"But you're above the law, right?"

"No, but in some situations I'm used to *being* the law. Look, if you can't handle this, I won't go. Seriously. Your call."

"Really?"

"Yeah."

She thought a long time and then hugged me hard and kissed me.

"You're a strange man, F.X. Shepherd, but I love you. Okay, go. I think maybe I can stand this. I don't feel like being alone, so I'm going to get Skippy and bring him home. When you get home, we'll both be here, waiting for you."

84

The flight was exhilarating, passing over the Manhattan skyline lights at night, the City That Never Sleeps. The landing was surprisingly gentle. Top of the world. My destination was breathtaking, illuminated by Malibu mood lighting hidden in the Japanese landscaping. I took the plastic bag with the gray tube out of my backpack, removed the weapon and kept it ready. I walked past the burbling turquoise pool, the chaise lounges and built-in barbecue grill, and reached, with my gun-gloved hand, toward the brass handle of the closed glass patio door, the second hurdle. If you lived in a guarded, inaccessible luxury penthouse two hundred and fifty feet in the sky above Park Avenue, would you bother locking your patio door? I hoped it had never occurred to him. I hoped he was one of the few people living in Manhattan who didn't have to worry about that. Fortunately, it was unlocked and I stepped inside.

There it was.

In the huge, high-ceilinged living room, with cream-colored carpeting and furniture, on the white wall above a cream couch, was a huge, framed grass-green flag under glass. The "Don't Tread On Me" symbol of the American rebels. I turned on a few more lights to get a better view.

Looking closer, you could see that around the bottom edge it had faded to a yellowish green over the past two hundred and fifty years or so. When I had caught a glimpse of it on Sparky's drone footage of the penthouses at 740 Park Avenue, I had mistakenly thought it was one of those one-color paintings that sell for millions to gullible rich folk. It was actually one of the earliest versions of our flag, Old Glory. It was awe-inspiring. Brave men fought and died under that banner for the divine right not to pay taxes.

I was pretty confident that any scientific comparison tests would prove this was the flag from which the Tea Party Animal cut his musket ball wadding. The problem was the frame covered up the bottom of the flag.

I flipped the trigger assembly open on the octagonal tube. The red diode lit up. Weapon hot. I gently placed the live weapon on the glass coffee table in front of the couch, at the ready. I stood on the couch, no doubt leaving footprints. The black picture frame was custom brushed aluminum, the kind that fits together at the four corners with grooves and interlocking L-shaped metal strips. I looked around and spotted a pile of circular stone coasters on the table. I borrowed two, placed one flat on the glass in the lower left corner. I placed the second disc above it and started gently whacking the lower one with the upper. Nothing. I hit harder—which was a bit louder but did the trick. The bottom horizontal frame disconnected. I waited and listened, judging my distance to the weapon. I thought I faintly heard a television somewhere else inside the apartment. No alarm sounding, no dog barking, no shots. I carefully did the same thing to the right side, removed the bottom frame piece and quietly placed it, along with the coasters, on the couch.

Bingo.

The revealed bottom margin of the flag was badly yellowed and almost half of it had a longitudinal section missing, which was hidden by the framing. Siri was right.

The cut looked fresh. This was the guy. He owned the flag and the hotel, secretly. Mr. Big, mastermind of the vast right-wing conspiracy.

Now what?

I came here to perforate the bastard with his own techno-musket but that would mean pulling a trigger, or at least pushing a button. I really didn't want to do that. It would violate my oath. Clearly my imagination, or fate, was required.

He snuck up on me so silently, he was on the couch before I noticed. I jumped and almost yelled out in surprise. He was staring coolly at me.

A large, long-haired, fluffy white cat with yellow eyes.

"Goddamn, you scared the shit out of me," I whispered to him.

He cocked his curious head at me. I was not expecting a watch-cat. He fluttered down onto the cushions, hopped onto the glass coffee table and began sniffing the loaded weapon. I scooped it up and backed away gingerly, before the pussycat could do anything loud or fatal. I exhaled and realized I had been holding my breath.

"Anything I can help you with, Shepherd?"

This time, startled again, I almost fired the damn weapon. I turned and there he was, in checkered red and green golf pants and green polo shirt, smiling at me like a warlord who knew I could never touch him.

My new friend, my parent's hero—liberal billionaire Walter Cantor.

85

"Actually, yes you can help me," I told Walter, vaguely pointing the mini-musket at him.

"What's that?" he asked, pointing to the tube. "Isn't that one of the gun gadgets I saw in your paper?"

"Yeah," I chuckled. "You know it is. Mind if I sit down for a sec?" I nodded at one of the two facing white armchairs.

"Please," he said, sitting opposite me and confidently crossing his thin legs.

His white cat took a seat on the couch and glared at me.

"How the hell did you get in here?"

"Magic. I'll show you later. Right now I'd like to talk about your big green flag, Walter."

"Incredible, isn't it? Flown at the Battle of Long Island in Brooklyn Heights, a decoy action that allowed Washington and the Continental Army to escape capture by the British—and later win the war. Touched by men who gave their lives for this great country."

"And by the man who is trying to destroy it."

"You lost me there, Shepherd."

"You're going to play dumb? Really? Okay. You and your New Minutemen cut a strip off the edge of your nifty souvenir here to use as silk wadding for the silver musket balls that killed Percy Chesterfield and the others."

"I see. Your theory is that my flag was used by these killers but that's impossible, Shepherd. It's been hanging right there for years. Hermetically sealed in nitrogen—which you have let escape. I'm very angry about that, not to mention your mysterious break-in."

"You don't look angry at all, Walter."

"I don't?"

"No. You look… I don't know… pleased. You finally get to brag about how you engineered this whole plot. It must have taken years and millions of bucks but the downside was you could never take credit for it."

"What plot? The murders? Sorry to disappoint, but there is no proof I'm involved."

"When the police and feds use their expensive machines to compare your flag to the silk used in the shootings, they'll have a match, not to mention other evidence against you."

"Firstly, I assume you caused this damage yourself, this evening. You are aware, I hope, that there are several other flags like this in existence, including one or two that have gone missing? Tests of silk wadding, flags, silver musket balls or silver Flowing Hair dollars will prove nothing I have to worry about. Anything else? I'm flying to the Virgin Islands in the morning."

"You own the Knickerbocker Convention Center. You can deny it all you like, but the proof is there—buried under a mountain of paper and shell corporations."

"Did you bring a copy of this proof with you?"

"No. A witness. Several, actually. Some of whom were just arrested. We know about your access to the staff, the soundproof rooms, the smoke detectors, everything."

The crow's feet wrinkles around his blue eyes crinkled quizzically but his game face didn't crack.

"I know that's not possible, Shepherd. It's late. Please

don't waste my time with bluffing. I know I have done nothing wrong."

"Not doing anything wrong is sometimes not the same thing as not breaking the law."

"In terms of logic, yes, you could make that argument. Isn't that the position of these New Minutemen, that they didn't commit murder but executed traitors?"

"Yes, that is your thinking, I assume."

"You also seem to be familiar with that line of thought—the ends justify the means."

"I am. So are you."

"So you say. I *was* happy to hear that the police locked up that whole group of right-wing zealots. I wondered if you had a hand in the arrests?"

"I did. Sorry."

"Don't apologize, son—you've done the country a service."

"Like you?"

"I was also happy to see those New Minutemen gunmen brought to justice. Terrible way to die but they *were* traitors. You did that also?"

"Me? They threatened a U.S. Navy destroyer and then they attacked it. Didn't you see that story of mine? It was also on TV."

"I did, yes," he laughed. "But it struck me as incredibly foolhardy to warn a warship in advance that you were going to attack and then do so. Suicidal, in fact."

"That's the thing with zealots, Walter. They go too far."

"Sometimes with a little help, eh, Shepherd?"

"I don't think any of us here, including your cat, will be admitting any crimes this evening."

"Exactly," he concluded, with a palms-up, we're-done gesture. He shot a bored glance at his gold Rolex.

"Your problem, Walter, is you're a zealot, but you're a sentimental zealot."

"I'm a registered Democrat. But I am sentimental about my grandchildren."

"The zealot part is easy, Walter. You spent the last few years plotting to exploit the rift between Republicans and the Looney Tune Don't-Tread-On-Me Tea Baggers in a way that would ensure a Democratic victory, shatter their party for a generation and end any chance of a Republican president for decades."

"Sounds like a good thing to me."

"I'm sure it does sound like a good thing to you, Walter."

"My guess is you agree with me."

"It doesn't matter what I think."

"Of course it does, my boy. You might want to join the winning side."

"No thanks. I was on the winning side for the past decade," I told him. "The problem was we had to keep winning every day. So, what did it for you, Walter? Gerrymandering? Union-busting? Denying black people and others the vote? Candidates like Miranda Dodge coming too close to the Oval Office and the nuclear button?"

"Those are all terrible things," Walter agreed. "You know, Wall Street has been very good to me but capitalism is stronger than democracy and has actually defeated it. Greed has infected our country and is metastasizing. Our liberty has been bought and sold. They are currently reversing a generation of civil rights progress and rigging elections in advance to throw the result to someone with fewer votes. I can't pretend I'm not glad someone took them on. But it has nothing to do with me and it's past my bedtime."

86

It was not quite Walter's bedtime yet.

"The sentimental part, Walter, is that you allowed me to live," I told him. "Thank you, by the way."

"I allowed you to live?"

"Yeah, that's why you're so amused by me being here. You like me, admit it."

"Well, Shepherd, I did—until you burglarized my penthouse and damaged my priceless historical artifact."

"That's why you ordered the New Minutemen not to kill me—just to scare the shit out of me, to warn me off. I don't even think you told them to shoot my dog. That was only because he attacked one of them."

"You think I gave orders to those gunmen?" he asked, smiling broadly now.

"Sure," I smiled back. "Not directly, of course. Insulated. I'm sure the blue blood hotel shooters and the New Minutemen all thought they were being funded and directed by right-wing militia central and maybe they were—but it was just little old Liberal you, Walter, and your mountains of money."

"You know, Shepherd, listening to you spin your conspiracy theory, it occurs to me that you, and those around you, might still be in great danger."

Neither of us was still smiling.

"You make a good point," he continued. "If there is big money and other fanatics behind what you've uncovered, they might be coming after you very soon—especially if they hear that you have proof against them. You wouldn't want to lose your parents or your lovely girlfriend Jane. Please be very, very careful. Your opponent may not be the kind of man to make the same mistake twice."

It had been a while since I had been threatened with death so politely.

"Thanks, Walter. And thanks for making this easier. Did you say you were flying to the Virgin Islands in the morning?"

"Yes, I have a place there."

"Don't be so modest, Walter. I read you have your own island."

"Correct. As the license plates there say, it's 'The American Paradise.' It's very relaxing."

"Yes, I'm sure paradise is very relaxing."

"I'm afraid I should really call the police now," Walter announced, starting to rise.

I pointed the weapon at him and waved him back down into his seat.

"Are you threatening me, son?"

"Not if you sit down."

He sat down. I used my phone to send a text and to look up a GPS heading. I plugged it into a program that slaved to two nearby remotes. I had to cancel and override several error warnings before I could re-program the course, heading and altitude.

"Do you understand what I told you, about the danger you face?"

"Yeah, got it, Walter. Thanks, I'm taking care of that right now."

"On your phone?"

"Sort of."

"You kids and your gadgets. Meanwhile, the real world passes you by."

"I'm arranging to end any threat from my opponent first, because I don't like it when people play God and fuck with my country. Or tread on me or my family. Or my dog," I told him.

"So you're risking your life and those of your loved ones, for macho revenge?"

"No. Please understand me, Walter. I had a job, a responsibility. I promised my client, Percy Chesterfield, that I would keep him safe. I failed. My job then changed—find the fucks who did it and take them down. Even the rich fucks too powerful to get caught. It's not really about rich people, left or right, buying the government. It's about We The People. Not Me The People."

"So it's macho pride."

"No, professional ethics—and good business. If I let you bump off my customers and get away with it, how will I ever make a living as a private detective in this town? Tonight is about cutting off the head of the snake. That way, nobody else gets bitten."

"If you're going to scotch a snake, make sure you have the right snake," he warned.

"Oh, I have the right snake—you."

"Shepherd," Walter said, in a condescending tone, "what have we been talking about all this time? You have no proof, son."

"First, I don't always operate on a law enforcement model. I sometimes function in intelligence mode. If it looks like a snake, moves like a snake, hisses like a snake, bites like a snake—it's a snake. Second, I do have evidence."

"Other than the flag?"

"Yeah. You talk too much. You said I should be worried about the safety of my loved ones, including Jane. You've never met Jane and I never mentioned her. How did you know her name, Walter?"

"I... I'm not sure. Did I use her name? Maybe your parents told me. Yes, of course, that's it."

"Bullshit. You also said the cops wouldn't find anything if they tested the flag, the silver musket balls or the Flowing Hair dollars. I never mentioned silver dollars in print or to you, much less Flowing Hair dollars specifically. How did you know the balls were melted coins, Walter? Oh, snap!"

Walter seemed confused about the colloquial meaning of the word snap but he knew when he had fucked up.

"I never said that!" Walter tried. "Wait! You told me about the first silver coins being melted down—you told me, down in the lobby, remember?"

"No. Actually, I told you the musket balls were silver and were a police holdback—but I never told you that Flowing Hair dollars were melted down to make the musket balls. You just know that, Walter. It was your idea. See, that's the thing. These Tea Party nuts profess to revere our system but break all the rules. You really believe in America and democracy, Walter. That's why you used sacred coins, a historic flag and young people whose ancestors were Founding Fathers. These weren't mass murders or political assassinations to you. This was almost a religious sacrifice, a sacred purgation of evil for a higher cause."

He stared at me, stunned for a moment—like I had read his mind—before he snapped out of it.

"You can't prove that! Do you have that alleged statement on a recording device?"

"No. You got me there, old buddy. I can't prove in court that you spilled the beans—or, the coins. I guess you win again. I should be moving on. Do you still want to know how I arrived atop your skyscraper building this evening?"

"Yes, I do."

"Okay, Walter, I'll show you. Out on the patio. But then I really have to go."

87

It was still warm outside and a gentle breeze stirred the puffy sea grass clumps near the pool. I directed my host to the flat area near the barbecue, where the two large octo-copter drones sat silent, my twin stealth aircraft. A long, looped twelve-foot line from each was stretched out on the paving stones. I hit a key on my phone and both whirlybirds buzzed into life and lifted off. They stopped and hovered ten feet above us, lines dangling straight down.

"Presto!" I told Walter. "I used magic to get here."

"You have got to be joking," Walter said, shaking his head in disbelief. "Drones? You are suicidal."

"No, I'm not. Actually it was great, really cool. Airborne. I recommend it, Walter. Two thumbs up. Speaking of which, put your hands up, please," I ordered, pointing the tube gun at him again.

He raised his hands.

"You're going to rob me?" he sneered.

"In a way," I said, quickly grabbing the lines, looping them over his wrists and tightening them.

"Hold on, Walter," I told him, hitting another command on my phone. "Hold on tight!"

Walter, panic in his eyes, clutched the ropes above his

wrists, as the black drones buzzed furiously and pulled him ten feet vertically into the night air.

"Wait! What are you doing? You have no proof! You have no proof!"

"Walter, son, you only need proof if you're going to court. I'm settling out of court. You said you were flying to the Virgin Islands in the morning? I just got you a free ticket to your island tonight on the Red Eye. God Bless America. Have a nice flight!"

Of course the batteries in Sparky's drones would last less than an hour, so it was impossible for Walter to actually reach paradise. Hey, it's not about the destination. It's about the journey. At about thirty miles per hour, Walter would become Icarus and fall from the sky about twenty-five miles out to sea. Unless he got free of the ropes sooner and his weight brought him down in a controlled descent. It was a long shot but he could still come out of this alive if he didn't panic. It was better odds than he gave Chesterfield and the others.

I hit the last command and Walter rose high into the sky, toward two thousand feet, and began moving on his south-south-easterly course, which would take him over midtown, the East River, and the harbor. As he rose higher, Walter's cool cracked. I thought I heard yelling. The drones were swallowed by the background of night, leaving a surreal image of a thin man in loud golf pants, flying gently through the sky. In a few seconds I couldn't hear him anymore. Soon after, his checkered golf pants vanished behind the sparkling skyline.

Presto.

I walked back inside and made sure the cat had enough food and water until the cops arrived. I shut off the tube gun and left it on the coffee table. I found one of my host's baseball caps in the front closet and let myself out. I took the stairs because I didn't want to get caught in the elevator or by its video camera. It was a long descent but at least it was downhill. At the lobby, I peeked out. The same doorman from the other night was on duty, nodding off in a chair behind his podium. I waited until I saw his chin drop to his chest and I sneaked out, the cap's brim low over my face. I silently shut the stairwell door behind me. Walking quietly to the elevator door, to give the illusion I had just emerged from it, I then walked straight out, startling the drowsy doorman.

"Night, Eddie," I mumbled from under Walter's hat, hustling out the swinging door, hoping most guards didn't pay as much attention to people leaving as they did to those trying to get in.

"Can I get you a cab, sir?" I heard Eddie say halfheartedly inside, not bothering to rise, as I disappeared.

As I walked, I thought about what I had just done—framed a killer with planted evidence and executed him, without trial, in a state without the death penalty. All in a day's work. I felt bad but not nearly bad enough. It felt like justice to me.

Walking faster, I made a traceless digital web call through a free internet service in Amsterdam called ZeroTrace, which distorted voices and deleted all electronic signatures once the call ended.

"Hello?"

"Is this Detective Lieutenant Negron of the Major Case Squad?" my robot-like, altered voice asked.

"Yeah, who the fuck is this? Iron Man?"

"Not important," I told him. "What's important is that a secret source is tipping you off to who is behind your political murders but you need to move fast to get him."

I told Izzy Walter's name, address and penthouse number and suggested he get there before Cantor committed suicide or fled the jurisdiction. I mentioned a flag as evidence, a dangerous weapon on the coffee table and reminded him to feed the cat. That was probably enough for NYPD to get in the door without a warrant.

"Who the hell is this?"

I hung up.

Walter Cantor had ordered the deaths of five people to throw an election but I wanted my last memory of him to be a positive one. I tried to think of him as a winged bundle of consequence, speeding toward his fate. His view of the city he loved would be magical right about now. High over the harbor, on his way toward the Atlantic Ocean, he would have a once-in-a-lifetime view of the Statue of Liberty, lifting her light beside the Golden Door.

I tossed Walter's cap in a trashcan and headed home to Jane and Skippy, my real magic.

ABOUT THE AUTHOR

KIERAN CROWLEY was a *New York Times* bestselling author and award-winning investigative reporter, who received communication from an actual serial killer and deciphered his secret code. He covered hundreds of trials and thousands of murders and recovered evidence missed by police at numerous crime scenes, some of which helped bring killers to justice. He passed away in 2016.

HACK

AN F.X. SHEPHERD NOVEL

KIERAN CROWLEY

It's a dog-eat-dog world at the infamous tabloid the *New York Mail*, where brand new pet columnist F.X. Shepherd accidentally finds himself on the trail of The Hacker, a serial killer targeting unpleasant celebrities in inventive—and sometimes decorative—ways. And it's only his second day on the job. Luckily Shepherd has hidden talents, not to mention a hidden agenda. But as bodies and suspects accumulate, he finds himself running afoul of cutthroat office politics, the NYPD, and Ginny Mac, an attractive but ruthless reporter for a competing newspaper. And when Shepherd himself is contacted by The Hacker, he realizes he may be next on the killer's list...

"A witty and incisive mystery set in the raucous world of tabloid journalism. It's like Jack Reacher meets Jack Black."
Rebecca Cantrell, *New York Times* bestselling author

"Delivers high and frequent thrills. A rollicking, sharp-witted crime novel." *Kirkus Reviews*

"The man is a legend, a master of his craft. It's a joy to read and captures the imagination from the start."
Long Island Press